Deerfield

BRIAN FARR

Deerfield

© 2022 Brian Farr

ISBN 978-1-66783-704-8

eBook 978-1-66783-705-5

The characters, places, and events in this book are entirely fictional. Any resemblance to actual persons living or dead is completely coincidental.

This book is dedicated to all of the souls we've lost to substance abuse disorders and to the broken-hearted survivors who loved them through it all

PROLOGUE

"There were over 64,000 opioid overdoses last year in the United States. That means the casualties from the War on Drugs now exceeds the number of American soldiers killed in Vietnam over two decades of fighting.

Death from opioid overdose is not immediate. When a lethal dose of heroin (or any other opioid) is taken, the user has inadvertently set off a timer in the brain that systematically slows down and decreases basic life functions within the body until, at last, breathing and heartbeat stops completely. The average time frame for death by overdose is three to four hours after taking the opioid."

Excerpt from Travis Kent's term paper, "Opioid Addiction in America"

"9 11 – what is your emergency?"

"There's been a heroin overdose! We need help now! Narcan. And an ambulance. We're at 23 Maple Ridge Lane. It's in the Gables Development in Moheneck Falls. Please get someone out here!"

"Okay, sir, I'm going to contact an ambulance and get some help to you. Can you tell me…"

"The police are here already. I'm with Deputy Roscoe Montgomery. It's some kind of house party. We need Narcan."

"Sir, I'm going to get someone out there right away. They'll bring Narcan. I'm glad there's an officer already on the scene. Can you tell me your name?"

"Paul. Paul Durkin." His voice quavered.

"Okay, Paul, help is on the way. Can you tell me who overdosed?"

"Her name is Angela Baxter. She's 23. Jesus, she's only 23 years old!"

"Do you know how much heroin she took, Paul, or how long ago it was?"

"No. We just found her like this. She'd been off it for the last few weeks." He paused and then added, "Or at least that's what she said."

"Is she breathing, Paul?"

"I'll check," he said and leaned down close to her on the bed. His hand shook as he touched her cheek. It felt unnaturally cold. Her lips were tinged grey blueish. It brought back horrible memories, and Paul felt himself unraveling, losing what little control he had. He held his hand under her nose and watched her chest, willing it to rise and fall. Seconds seemed endless. There was nothing, no hint of a breath.

"Angela!" he wailed and dropped the phone to the floor as everything inside of him came crashing down. A mumbling voice continued talking from the phone, but it didn't really matter now. It could wait. Nothing really mattered, and everything could wait.

He shook her shoulder, repeating her name in a frenzied voice that was not his own.

"Angela! Angela, wake up! Wake up, God damn it! No! No! Not again! You can't have her! Not this one too! Fuck you! Fuck you!"

CHAPTER 1

"Recent research about alcoholic blackouts shows that many are caused when a person's B.A.C. exceeds .14%. Drinking quickly and on an empty stomach is also a factor. People continue to function during a blackout but will not remember the event due to the toxic effect of alcohol on the short and long-term memory centers of the brain. More research is being done on brownouts, where people will remember certain events when drinking, but forget others..."

Professor Dunleavey, *Substance Abuse 101* class lecture

THE STUMBLE INN BAR – 3 WEEKS EARLIER

"This is it for me," Paul Durkin said as he tipped the dirty glass to his lips and finished the dregs of cheap beer. "I should go home now."

"To what?" The man on the barstool next to him asked, already signaling the bartender for two more beers. "Besides, it's my round."

"Good points," Paul said, "but let the record show that I did consider stopping this madness before your kind offer."

"Sure," Wayne replied, "and that's the third time you announced that you were leaving since I found you here this afternoon. I'm starting to think you're a fucking liar."

It troubled Paul that he didn't remember saying he was going to leave earlier. Maybe Wayne was busting his balls about that. He knew that he should have stopped drinking a long time ago. But he was just not ready yet.

"This place used to draw in quite a crowd from the mill," Wayne said as he picked up one of the fresh beers the bartender had set down.

"Yes, it did," Paul agreed, noticing that his words were slurry, the tone of his voice oddly unfamiliar. He hadn't been this drunk—at least he hadn't felt this drunk—in a long time.

"I'd drive by here in the morning and see the parking lot filled with pick-up trucks," Paul said and directed his face slowly and carefully to the rim of the full beer before sipping.

"We called them first-shift drinkers," Wayne answered, and Paul was sure he'd said that already.

"Old Gary was smart," Wayne said, and Paul looked at him curiously, anticipating the pretzel and egg comment that was about to replay. He'd definitely heard that already. Or had he?

"When he opened the place back in the '80s," Wayne continued, "the rule was you could only serve booze before noon if you also served food. That's why it's the Stumble Inn Bar and Grill. Back then he had a breakfast menu, but we all knew that the only real food in here was stale pretzels and pickled eggs."

Paul knew Wayne had worked at the paper mill for many years, but he couldn't recall what his job was. He wondered if they'd already discussed why he left and if it was before the place shut down for good. The two men weren't friends, really, but occasionally landed on adjoining stools at the Stumble Inn.

"I was more of a second or third-shift drinker," Wayne continued. "Once they closed the mill, well, those guys with families and mortgages and truck payments headed out of here faster than shit through a mongoose."

He shook his head solemnly under the brim of his crisp N.R.A. baseball hat.

"Gary's smartest move was to dump it," Paul said. "This place is a real shit hole now. Only assholes and losers drink here."

"I'm amazed," Wayne said, looking at Paul with something akin to hurt in his eyes, "that anyone still likes you anymore. You used to be the salt of the earth—do anything for anyone. It was awful what happened to you, Paul, but telling everyone else to go to hell while you drink yourself to death don't seem like a great plan for getting over things."

Paul picked up his full beer and contemplated the amber liquid floating behind the soap-stained glass.

"He makes the sun rise on the evil and on the good, and sends rain on the just and unjust, isn't that right, Father Wayne?"

"Look, Paul," Wayne began, I ain't judging you, and I certainly ain't no priest or saint; I'm just saying that seeing you like this is hard. I mean, you had it all. You were living the dream, for fuck's sake…"

"Ha!" Paul laughed and waved his hand at Wayne.

"Enough! Enough of the righteous intervention. You've thrown the golden life preserver squarely at my head, and I choose—being of somewhat sound mind and diminishing body—to let it bounce off and be carried away by the tide. As for people not liking me anymore, well, that's really the point, isn't it? How fragile and temperamental the opinions of others can be!"

"Ha!" Paul laughed again and raised his glass.

"Let's drink to the power of alcoholism and asshole-ism to keep all decent folk at arm's length."

The screen in Paul's mind went blank then, as his brain receptors misfired, failing to accurately record any conscious thoughts or behaviors for a spell. In what seemed like the next instant, he knocked into a small table.

"Watch it, grandpa," a sharp voice warned. Paul focused his eyes on a young, thin girl sitting alone and scowling at him.

"I'm drunk," Paul said and fell into a sticky wooden chair across the table from her.

"No shit," she said.

"I should have left this place earlier. But sometimes you have a drink or two, and things change, you know? It's like the ship has pulled away from the dock, and it's too late to get off the damn thing. It's just full steam ahead farther and farther from the harbor..."

Paul looked at the girl, who stared evenly back at him from across the table. He knew he was rambling, as he often did with women. Still, he felt especially uncomfortable because this one looked so young and unhappy— too young and unhappy to be here. He thought about the drunken fool from the Andy Griffith Show and wondered how much he must look and sound like that idiot now, blathering away. *Was his name Otis or Opie? No, not Opie, that was the red-haired kid.*

The girl took her phone out and was busy pressing buttons with both thumbs.

"Otis," she said and held her phone outstretched so Paul could look at the screen.

"Sorry," Paul said. "What?"

"You just asked if you looked like the town drunk from that show. I looked it up. The guy's name was Otis Campbell, and he was played by Harold Smith. Anyway, you're old like him, but he looks fatter and kind of bald."

Paul leaned across the table and squinted his eyes, struggling to focus on the small screen that she held up for him to see.

"Huh," Paul said, unsure what else to add. "Well, that's interesting. Let me buy you a drink."

The girl pulled her phone back. "No thanks. Alcohol's not really my thing, and you might want to call it a night before you sink your ship for good."

"Not your thing," Paul repeated sarcastically. His chair seemed off-balance, wobbling continually beneath his weight. "Well, you picked a great goddamned place to spend the evening then!" He heard the words drive through the air and across the table, loud, defensive, and angry. *Why did he care if she drank or not? Wayne had it right – he was a first-rate asshole.*

But she surprised him and smiled slightly for the first time. Paul opened his mouth, meaning to apologize.

"Yea," she said. "My Prince Charming only takes me to the best places on our Saturday night dates."

He thought about asking more about her relationship but was afraid it would seem lecherous. A pathetic come-on from Otis, the drunk.

She looked to be in her early twenties, but he never really knew these days. She had that angry, angsty look he'd seen on so many of the screwed-up kids in his office over the years. There was an overall darkness about her, from the straight jet-black hair to the darkened eyes (hard to tell if that was make up or not) to the long-sleeved Harley Davidson shirt that hung loosely on her small body.

A burst of laughter erupted from behind them.

"It's been real," she said, and stood up, grabbed an old army jacket from the back of the chair, and walked toward a crowd of young people standing at the bar.

He turned, feeling the chair's wobble worsen, and looked around the place. Wayne was gone. Maybe it was something Paul had said, perhaps a conversation about politics or religion. He normally avoided these subjects, especially after drinking and particularly with Wayne or the host of under-educated but over-privileged rednecks around the bar. Their stated intent was usually to fight and die for the rights of all Americans while

7

simultaneously screaming about the infiltration of fags, wetbacks, and welfare moms that now made up the majority of their sacred country. But Paul had declared this a Fuck-It Day earlier – when he left the house to come to the Stumble Inn. Anything was allowed on a Fuck-It Day, so the chances that he had broached these subjects and unleashed the bees in Wayne's N.R.A. bonnet were roughly fifty-fifty.

The Stumble Inn never drew a large crowd anymore, which Paul liked. He came here when the depression and isolation of his empty house became unbearable. He usually left well before this point in his drinking, but today was different. It was a special day, after all, one that warranted both extra stimulation and deeper numbing of the pain.

"So, Fuck Wayne," Paul thought.

There were about thirty people in the place, most of them hovering around the bar. Paul saw the girl with the army jacket near the largest group, which consisted mostly of other young women. They were loud and brightly colored, all with phones out, trying to incite some online jealousy with selfies depicting the epic evening they were having. The word *bubbly* came to Paul's mind as he watched these girls bobbing up and down, fixing their hair and screeching loudly. They made him think of champagne, crystal glasses, and ball gowns. He doubted that any of this crew would ever live that life, and that their futures were far more likely to involve countless hours shopping or working in dollar stores and watching reality TV in the break room every night. He pictured them in ten years, thumbs and bodies expanding as they texted and posted away about the excellent lives that existed only in their minds, all of them waiting desperately to gulp cheap beer from Solo cups each weekend in a neighbor's garage while retelling old tales of glory days that never were.

Paul roused himself from these dark thoughts, realizing none of this was his concern, and who was he to judge anyone else so harshly? God was in His heaven, moving the chess pieces around and conducting the whole shit show without any input from Paul.

Or maybe He wasn't, but enough brooding. Tonight, he would view this young crew as he once was, an excellent example of living and drinking just for the day. They were fine, fizzy, cordial company. He lifted himself from the chair and shuffled slowly over.

The thought of ordering another drink crossed his mind as he neared the crowd. He reasoned that his body could process the stuff faster and more efficiently because of his regular consumption. It was only beer, which didn't have much alcohol in it to begin with. Perhaps he'd get one more before leaving. Just one more for Sean, if that's what he should even be calling him at this point. Or was it her? One more drink for the kid, for all these kids, and then he'd turn the ship around and head for the lights of the shore.

"Come on, just guess what it is!" Paul found the bar as one of the bubbly girls implored Teddy Monroe to play.

Teddy was the bartender at the Stumble Inn and had gotten into trouble in the past for dealing other drugs from the place. Paul knew the Monroes. Anyone who grew up in Moheneck Falls couldn't help but know at least some of them.

"Dumber than a bunch of monkeys trying to hump a football," his father had said after Teddy's father, and a few of his close cousins, lost fingers and their rowboat while fishing with dynamite in a nearby reservoir.

"But keep 'em close, Paulie. Keep 'em in your line of site. What they lack in brains they make up for in numbers, and with folks like that it's always good to stay on their good side if you're able." Paul's dad liked to remind him.

Teddy was the proverbial apple who hadn't fallen far from the family tree, and Paul watched him form from a young, angry punk diagnosed with conduct disorder issues to a thirty-year-old anti-social narcissist with several felonies on his record.

One girl was perched on a barstool, her leg stretched out from under a short skirt and resting on the corner of the bar. She'd peeled back a layer of cotton gauze, exposing what looked like a terrible infection or scar from a recent accident. Teddy was next to her, leaning in close and inspecting the thing.

"You really should keep that bandage on," Teddy said. Especially during the first few days. You don't want it to get infected. He emphasized his concern by blowing the smoke from his cigarette away from the open sore.

"Oh, stop! Who are you, my dad?" The girl's reproach triggered a chorus of laughs from her entourage.

"Well," she taunted him, "tell me what you think it is."

Paul stood next to the girl in the black tee shirt, near the edge of the crowd. She was staring down at her phone. Paul leaned toward Teddy and the girl on the stool, trying to get a better look at the disfiguration on her leg. It had puffed up around the edges, and the colors were smeared together, but there was no denying the first impression. It appeared to be a yellow-colored penis, thin and elongated, stretching away from a single black testicle that rested just above the girl's knee. The penis acted as a road sign, pointing up into the nether region of her skirt. What made the thing even weirder to Paul was that the testicle had a symbol on it.

Teddy peered closer, and Paul imagined his small brain spinning wildly, searching for a lie about the horrid marking that wouldn't scare off the girl and the other young ladies. Teddy took a few drags on his cigarette, seeming more desperate with each puff. Finally, one of the female friends, who looked even younger than the tattooed girl (Teddy never checked IDs, which attracted these young patrons), chirped:

"Oh my God! It's an eight ball, duh! And a pool stick. Haven't you ever played pool? You have a pool table right over there in the corner!"

The rest of the young crowd exploded in laughter, and the girl with the mutilated thigh announced proudly, "They call me eight ball."

"Yup! That's exactly what I was going to guess," Teddy said. "It's beautiful work."

Next to Paul, the dark-haired girl looked up from her phone and motioned to a young man standing nearby. The young man leaned closer to Teddy, said something, and the two of them walked off to a room behind the bar.

"That must be Prince Charming?" Paul asked the girl.

"That's him," the girl said. "And hopefully, he's done playing around with the Barbie Posse so we can get the fuck out of here."

A few of the girls closest to them turned and looked, rolling their eyes and glowering. She cocked her head and gave a wide smile in return.

"I wondered what brought you here," Paul said. "It doesn't seem like your type of scene."

"My scene? No, this is definitely not my type of scene," she answered and looked over to the room behind the bar where Teddy and Prince Charming had gone.

"I don't normally come here, either," Paul said. "And when I do, it's usually for a few beers. But tonight's my kid's birthday, so I guess I went overboard." He wondered why he was telling her any of this.

She turned and looked at him. "How old is your kid?"

"He would have been twenty-seven." Paul saw something in the girl's eyes soften.

"Oh, wow, I'm—" she started to say, but at the same time, a tall blonde girl from the Barbie Posse pitched herself forward and vomited violently. The warm liquid sprayed onto several other girls before reaching the floor and splattering everywhere. A strong smell like rancid cheese and hot vinegar began to rise around them.

Teddy ran out of the backroom and shouted, "What the fuck!" Paul caught one last look at the girl, who covered her face with her army coat.

He heard Prince Charming say, "We're good," before grabbing her by the arm and heading toward the exit.

Paul felt his own stomach start to pitch and walked as quickly as he could toward the bathroom.

He entered the restroom and stood at a small leaking sink that hung from the wall at an odd angle. He wondered if the damage was caused by two people in some sexual act involving the sink or if it had been an alcohol-induced assault on the thing. He turned the cold water on and held both hands underneath the stream. The feeling of the water and the sound of its flow soothed him. He breathed deeply, hoping his stomach would settle.

In the cracked, cloudy mirror above the sink, his father's eyes stared back, but the graying hair, unshaved face, and puffy visage around those eyes seemed foreign—the look of an old friend who had sickened since their last meeting.

"What the fuck were you thinking?" He asked the man in the glass. He leaned down, splashing water over his face and head and neck, feeling it run down his shirt and chest. He thought of churches and baptismal fonts, and of Sean. Beautiful, baptized baby Sean. And then the curtains closed again.

"Paul! Paul! Time to wake up, dude! It's closing time, time to go home!"

He was on a barstool, sprawled out on the bar with his head resting on his right forearm. He saw Teddy standing there, one hand on his shoulder, shaking him awake. Paul looked around slowly and noticed that nobody else was in the place. He sat up and moved his hands to a position that would better support him on the stool.

"You okay, Paul? You want me to call someone to come get you?" Teddy asked, having no real intention to do anything of the sort.

"Where is my drink?" Paul asked instinctively. "I wasn't done with it." He looked at the spot on the bar where he normally left his cash to keep the drinks coming. There was nothing there.

"Your drink was gone, man," Teddy assured him, in a tone that convinced Paul he was lying. Paul heard a faint humming noise followed by an odd but familiar mechanical melody. Teddy pulled his phone out from a back pocket and the tune blared.

"Is that playing 'Dirty White Boy'?" Paul asked.

Teddy grinned wolfishly. "Sweet, right? I don't like a lot of that old shit, but Foreigner knew how to party!"

Paul shook his head slowly and dismounted the barstool.

"Well, I guess you'll just owe me a drink. I guess you'll owe me a few," Paul said as he steadied himself and walked slowly and carefully toward the exit. He ran his fingers through his hair and felt the dampness, remembering his time in the bathroom. He tried to pull up anything before Teddy woke him up. There might have been a conversation with another man in between—something about immigration laws, green cards, and the fake news? He couldn't be sure it happened, but he hoped that his nap on the bar pushed most of the booze out and sobered him up for the ride home.

"Yeah," Teddy said, "Sounds good, Paul. I'll see you around." He focused on a text from the girl with the thigh tattoo urging him to join a house party currently in progress and to "bring booze and whatever else you've got that might make things fun."

The night was cold and still, and cloudless. Paul cinched his coat tightly around himself as he exited the bar and looked up at the brilliant constellations of stars and the bright, clear moon. He paused next to his car and took several long, slow breaths, thinking that a few minutes in the frigid air was just what he needed before driving. He stood beside the car while the silence and the cold embraced him. It hadn't snowed for the last few days, but temperatures stayed in the single digits, and everything outside was frozen firmly in place. The parking lot was covered with patches of ice that reflected the glow from the moon. February could be a very long month in the northeast.

Paul needed to piss. He wanted to use the restroom in the bar before he walked out but thought he'd look even more pitiful to Teddy, that crook of a bartender. He glanced back at the entrance to the bar, but the lights were already off, and Teddy was probably on his way out the back door.

Paul stepped near the trunk of the car and began unbuttoning his pants. The cold was beginning to penetrate him, slowing down all movements. His hands trembled while he unzipped himself, and there was a growing numbness in his fingertips. Trying to stay focused, and with some effort, he released a steady stream onto the icy surface near the car's back tire. He realized it would have been smart to start the car so that he could climb in after this and warm up more quickly.

Panic seized him. He wasn't sure where the keys were. Normally he took them out and set them next to his money on the bar. But the money wasn't there. Had Teddy run off with his cash and keys? He took the hand he had been using to steady himself from the car's trunk and dug around in his front pants pocket.

At the same moment Paul felt the metal bulk of a key ring, he also realized that moving his hand was a mistake. This slight change in his stance, along with a small movement of his left foot, had been enough to throw off his balance. If he hadn't been standing on a patch of ice slick with his own urine, the movements might not have sent him to the ground, but this wasn't the case. Paul's feet slipped away from the car, causing his head and upper body to fall backward. He tried desperately to remove his hand from his front pocket, but everything happened too quickly.

In an instant, he was on the ground, feeling the first signals of pain from his head, shoulder, and hip, all of which collided first with the car trunk and then with the frozen ground. He pulled his hand out of the pocket and rolled on to the front of his body, placing both hands on the wet ice beneath him. He pushed himself up slowly, bent his knees and became aware of the slushy puddle he was kneeling in. Paul used the side of the car to pull himself up to a standing position. He realized at that moment that he was exposed to the world and tucked his penis away but didn't attempt to button or zip his pants because his hands were numb and shaking badly. Taking a deep breath and holding it, Paul listened for sounds of life. A pine tree cracked loudly from far off, the bitter temperatures had frozen its core and confirmed that he was completely alone.

Convulsing more violently, Paul removed the keys from his pocket and fumbled with them before finding the hole for the door lock. He fell into the driver's seat and, after some effort, guided the key into the ignition. The engine hesitated then coughed a few low mechanical grunts before it came to life.

"Yes, yes! That's it old girl!" Paul encouraged the car and turned the heater on full blast. He hunched over the steering wheel and rubbed his hands together while cold air blasted through the vents. It was just a matter of time until things warmed up. Soon things would start to get better. He just needed to wait it out, to give time time. Paul chuckled sourly at this last thought. *Give time time.* Where the Hell had that come from?

The air slowly warmed as he leaned back in the seat and finished tucking himself into his pants, zipping and buttoning them up. His clothes were soaked through. Apparently, he had continued to urinate during his fall, and the stream had thoroughly soaked his underwear, pants, and shirt. But he was in the car now, and everything would be fine, just fine. Paul turned on the interior light and adjusted his rearview mirror to look at himself. While there was no blood on the side of his head, he could feel a dull thudding deep inside his skull, and he knew this wasn't good—best to get himself home and deal with the consequences later. He pulled on the seatbelt, straightened himself up, and turned on the car's headlights. He put the car in reverse and backed into the empty parking lot. The increasing warmth around him and his ability to regain control of this situation helped to improve his mood. He approached the exit to the parking lot and turned on the radio.

"This is 106.7 FM, Upstate New York's home for Classic Rock, and you're hanging out with the Falcon. At this time of night, I wonder if anyone out there is listening at all, or if the Falcon is flying all alone on this long, cold journey through the night. This next song goes out to anyone else out there traveling down a lonely road tonight."

The song "Road to Nowhere," by Talking Heads, started to play.

"We're on a road to nowhere. Come on inside. Takin' that ride to nowhere. We'll take that ride."

"Sounds about right to me," Paul said to the freezing pine trees.

He turned up the radio and drove down the road.

CHAPTER 2

"You'd think that with all the trouble you can get in, and with all the bad things that happen when people decide to drink and drive, that nobody would ever do it. But you'd think wrong."

Sheriff Roscoe Montgomery,
from a Deerfield Elementary School D.A.R.E. Graduation

Mm, I'm shattered, uh

Shadoobie, shattered, uh

Shadoobie, shattered…shattered…

When Paul opened his eyes, his first thought was that the bass on his car's radio must have been turned up to maximum volume. The Rolling Stones were in mid-chorus when he heard the Thump! Thump! Thump! of a large metal flashlight on the car window. He noticed the car was stopped and sitting at an odd angle. Instinctively, he turned off the radio and glanced briefly out the windshield. The car had left the road completely and run into a sign reading "DIP AHEAD," which was bent down over the hood and leaning towards the windshield like a talisman of bad fortune.

The flashlight banged on his window again, softer this time, and Paul became aware of red and blue strobes of light reflecting from his rearview mirror.

Panic siezed him. "Shit! Shit! Shit!"

He reached over and pressed the button to lower his window. The flashlight outside came to life and shone brightly over Paul's legs, torso, and face which caused Paul to squint and push his head back into the seat. He put a hand up to shield his eyes.

"Paul?" a familiar voice said.

"Yeah," Paul responded, not sure what else to say.

"Can you put the car in park and shut the engine off, please?"

"Sure. Yes, of course." His voice sounded higher than usual. Unnatural and nervous.

The flashlight turned off, and the face of Roscoe Montgomery appeared in the open window.

Roscoe looked around the car's interior, and Paul became acutely aware of the pungent stench of booze and piss. He thought briefly about Otis, the drunk, bumbling around Mayberry while the laugh track played in the background. *Hadn't he talked about Otis earlier? Yes, with someone at the bar, a young woman...*

"Paul," Roscoe said, "you went off the road. I found you here with the motor running. Are you hurt? Do you need an ambulance?"

Paul looked up into Roscoe's face, but his old friend quickly looked away. He couldn't blame him. Things had gotten bad since they last saw each other.

"Do you need me to call an ambulance, Paul? Are you hurt?"

Paul pulled himself up in the seat, ran a hand slowly through his hair, feeling the large bump and something warm and sticky on his fingers just above his left ear. He cleared his throat. *If only he could take a few breaths, step out of the car, and look around a bit, just slow all of this down a bit. Maybe some recall of how exactly he got here would come.*

"No. No, Roscoe, I'm fine. I'm really just fine." Paul looked out the windshield at the DIP AHEAD sign, leaning down and listening in to their private conversation. "I must have hit a patch of black ice in the road."

The cold and silence settled in for a few moments before Roscoe said, "It smells like you've been drinking tonight. I'm going to have to perform a field sobriety test, and then we'll work on getting your car out of here."

Paul stared out through the windshield and into the dark, freezing night. *He wished he could fly out of the car and far up into the darkness, never looking back.* He closed his eyes and bowed his head. "I don't think we need to bother with that sobriety test, Officer Montgomery. I'm well beyond the legal limit to be driving. Let's just get on with the next part."

Roscoe allowed him to sit in the backseat of the cruiser without handcuffs while the tow truck pulled his car from the small ditch. The officer asked for the car to be delivered to Paul's house rather than the impound yard. Paul knew that Roscoe was breaking protocol on this when he came over and asked Paul for a credit card to give to the tow truck driver. He saw Roscoe point toward the cruiser as he presented the credit card and assumed he was calling in a favor with the driver.

Paul remembered meeting Roscoe Montgomery in his role as the D.A.R.E. Officer for the Deerfield School District. Sean was in fourth or fifth grade, and his essay "Why I choose to stay away from drugs and alcohol" won the school wide D.A.R.E. Contest that year. Sean told Paul he felt guilty about winning, saying that growing up with parents who didn't drink or use drugs gave him an unfair advantage. In the end, Sean accepted the award and nervously read his essay in front of the large school crowd of students and parents assembled for the ceremony. Paul thanked Officer Montgomery for the great work he was doing with the kids. Roscoe said that Paul's work was a huge service to the community as well, and that they would have to get together to exchange notes sometime.

As they drove to the sheriff's office, Paul considered breaking the awkward silence that filled the cruiser but couldn't think of anything to say. He felt quite sober now but wondered how drunk he was by the standards of the law. There were sharp, pulsing aches from parts of his body he assumed were bumped, bruised, or bleeding. He held his hands up. They weren't trembling yet. That was good. Staring out the window, he tried to convince himself: *This would be it. This would be the bottom he needed.* The blowing of the cruiser's heater fans and the occasional chirp or metallic sounding voices from Roscoe's police scanner seemed vague and surreal as they drove toward the lights of town. *So much for this Fuck-It Day.*

At the station, Paul sat beside Roscoe's desk while the officer tapped away at the keys of his computer. Roscoe offered Paul a cup of coffee when they sat down, and Paul fidgeted in the squeaky vinyl chair next to the large metal desk, doing his best to steady the small Styrofoam cup.

Another officer gave Paul a breathalyzer test. She didn't reveal his blood alcohol level, and Paul was too ashamed and embarrassed to ask, but he sensed that she was both saddened and sickened by the results. While he was performing the test, Paul noticed that Roscoe went to his desk and made a phone call. Paul had no idea what Roscoe was doing but assumed the call pertained to him and that the outcome would be bad. The room's acoustics were poor, or maybe Paul was feeling the alcohol more than he realized because the sounds were all blending. The voices of officers talking on phones and to each other mixed with laughter and occasional shouts, loud and angry, from people who'd been arrested and sounded completely deranged. He heard one deep voice shout, "Fuck you and your mother, you pig ass commie," followed by another voice laughing loudly and merrily as if the funniest joke had just been told. Paul closed his eyes, hoping he might wake up at any moment safe and warm in bed. The thought of flying up and away into the cold night crossed his mind again.

"So," Roscoe said, "I think all of the paperwork is done for now. Normally we hold people overnight and have them go in front of the judge in the morning, but Judge O'Malley is on the bench this week. So, I called him and told him what was going—"

"Look, Roscoe," Paul interrupted. "You don't have to do all this. I mean, I really appreciate what you're trying to do, but you don't need to..."

Roscoe continued, "Well, I'd rather have O'Malley pissed off that we woke him up than keep you here tonight. The single cells are all filled, and I can't see you socializing with the crew we got screaming away down in the drunk tank. Saturday nights are busy in this county, and it's hard to get a good room sometimes." Roscoe smiled wryly, and Paul remembered this side of his friend, the countless jokes, and stories they'd shared about hysterically tragic people and situations over the years.

Paul smiled back. "I suppose I should have planned ahead and booked something."

"Anyway, the judge said we could release you on your own recognizance tonight as long as you have a ride home. He'll schedule a date for you to show up in court when he gets in on Monday. I'm imagining you'll want to give John a call?"

"Yeah," Paul said, "I'm planning on it." He hadn't yet considered that he needed a lawyer.

Roscoe gave a slight nod of his head.

"Good. Well, let's get you home then."

As Paul got up and followed Officer Montgomery toward the door, two thoughts were on his mind. One was how amazingly compassionate and understanding people can be—the overall goodness that drove the hearts of so many in this world. His second thought was that he didn't have enough booze in his house to get through what he knew was coming next.

CHAPTER 3

"Step One in the A.A. Program told me I was powerless over alcohol.
That was pretty plain to see. It also told me my life had gotten
unmanageable. That took longer for me to recognize."

Linda Fulmer (a.k.a. Medicaid Linda) sharing at her Homegroup

Paul rode home in the front seat of Roscoe's cruiser. The seriousness of his situation and the consequences it would have leaked into his consciousness, but mostly he just wanted to crawl into his bed and sleep. They pulled up to Paul's house and saw that his car had been towed and left on the street.

"Here's my card," Roscoe said as Paul opened the door to get out. "Give me a call. Maybe we can have a cup of coffee at our old meeting place."

"Sounds good," Paul said. "Roscoe, look, I really appreciate—"

"It's nothing," Roscoe interrupted. "Protect and serve, right? Just get some rest, Paul. You're one of the good guys, don't forget that."

Paul wasn't sure what to do next once he got inside the house. The silence of the place unnerved him. He took off his coat and boots, then walked instinctively toward the freezer. He opened it, removed the bottle of vodka, unscrewed the cap, and took a long drink, trying to ignore the fact that the bottle was nearly empty. There was not going to be enough—there never was these days. He put the bottle back in the freezer, hoping that keeping it out of sight might keep it out of mind.

He opened the refrigerator's door and peered around at the meager contents. Eating had become secondary to drinking – an optional activity that was often more trouble than it was worth. There was no real food in the fridge anymore, no fruits or vegetables or leftovers packed away in Tupperware containers. She loved using Tupperware.

He closed the refrigerator and explored a few cupboards. There was an open box of cereal but no milk. He chewed tentatively on a few of the corn flakes inside, which tasted like stale cardboard. Paul found a can of sliced pears in syrup. He picked it up, inspected the outside for dents, and checked the expiration date. To his surprise, it looked in good shape and wouldn't expire for another month. He dug around in the silverware drawer and found an ancient-looking can opener. Opening the can took some effort, and he wondered when he'd last used this awkward tool. Charlotte had purchased an electric opener at some point in the past, and Paul assumed she took it with her, along with her prized Tupperware and anything else of value that wasn't nailed down at the time.

He managed to make a rough cut around the edge of the can and peeled back the top. Paul grabbed a bowl from the cabinet and dumped in the contents of the can. He found a fork and speared the first pear. He placed it in his mouth and greedily chewed, then swallowed it. The taste was wonderfully sweet and filling, and he wondered why he didn't eat pears more often. He decided to go shopping first thing in the morning and stock up on these wonderful pears. Perhaps he would buy some milk and maybe a few other items that fell into one of the recognized food groups.

Paul sat down at the kitchen table with his bowl of pears. He looked toward the darkened window and noticed the ugly yellow curtains hanging there, pathetically dusty and threadbare. Had she consulted with him before hanging those wretched things? Like so much from that period in the past, it was likely that the curtains just appeared without his consent or awareness. It might have been weeks or months before he'd even acknowledged them. Perhaps Charlotte had asked his opinion, and maybe at the time, these yellow aberrations seemed just the thing to brighten up the family's kitchen table and dining pleasure—but he would never know for sure. He thought about standing suddenly and ripping them down, pulling and ripping until they were strewn in pieces around the room. It seemed that would be a great source of satisfaction. And after the curtains were gone, he might tear down some other remnants of the past in this cursed place as well. He stared past the curtains and into the dark, distorted reflection that the glass cast back.

The impulse to destroy the curtains passed, but the next pear he ate was nowhere near as rewarding as the first, and he felt the first signs of what he knew would become intense acid reflux in his gut. Paul placed the unfinished fruit, with the spoon in the bowl, into the fridge and walked down the hall to the bathroom. He turned on the faucet and let the water warm up while he looked at himself in the mirror. He gently touched the tender, discolored bump on his head. He grabbed a washcloth and held it under the hot water. The washcloth smelled like dirt and old cheese, a blunt reminder that he really needed to do a load of laundry soon. Paul held the cloth to his bruised head and then wiped his face with it, trying to ignore the pungent odor. He remembered pissing himself and stripped down completely, tossing his clothes in a pile near the corner of the room. He used the soiled washcloth for a quick body wipe before adding it to the growing pile.

He found the nightclothes he'd left on his bed that morning when he walked into his bedroom and settled himself under the blankets. As the minutes ticked by, he became aware of a dull throbbing from his left side. He also felt a sort of heat, a tight constriction from deep inside his chest. He closed his eyes, planning to rest for just a minute or two before going to get some aspirin for the pain.

Paul awoke suddenly and sat bolt upright in bed. He felt the bile rise quickly in his throat and grabbed the plastic trash can nearby just in time for the vomit to spill out. He felt a painful throbbing pressure in his head with each heaving convulsion. There wasn't much solid food coming up, but he noticed a thick, crimson fluid, and the awful smell that rose from the plastic can started his stomach twisting and heaving for a second time. He rode the second wave of sickness out and rested the can back on the floor, falling back into the pillows. Gritty acid stuck to his teeth and coated the inside of his mouth as sleep took over.

Light leaked past the drawn blinds in his room, and he guessed that it was around midday. Paul sat up straight against the bed board. He groped around on his nightstand, hoping to feel the bottle of vodka. It wasn't there, but he found a large glass of water. So, he picked it up and took a tentative sip. It tasted warm and dusty, but the wetness soothed his mouth and throat. He took another, longer gulp and swished the water back and forth before swallowing it. He put a hand on his nightstand and moved until his feet were on the floor. Slowly, tentatively, Paul stood up. He set the water down, picked up the trash can, and used his empty hand to steady himself on the bed and then the walls as he made his way toward the bathroom.

The house needed a good, deep cleaning. An unexpected visitor might imagine the occupant had aged significantly or had suffered a severe medical event, which had caused regular cleaning and housekeeping to fall off as a priority. Dust covered everything Paul did not use regularly. He left his room and passed through the hallway gallery of framed pictures of a young man's transition from kindergarten to high school. The worn rug, which hid the aging hardwood floor, was beyond any help a vacuum could provide. Something crunched under his foot, but he made no effort to stop and look down at what it might be.

Paul entered the bathroom, which had a distinct smell of Old Spice aftershave and moldy towels. Dampness in the room indicated a water leak somewhere, but time and procrastination had put the problem far down on a long list of things that Paul only occasionally acknowledged as needing attention. He set the trash can in the bathtub, planning to clean it out some-time later in the day, then went to the toilet and steadied himself with one hand while he urinated. It took some time until the stream began, along with a burning sensation that had gotten worse over the last few months—another pain to add to his list of ailments. *But age was like that, and there was certainly no reason to go running to the doctor over every little thing.*

He flushed the toilet and walked toward the door when he noticed his reflection in the large mirror over the vanity. His face looked pale and lifeless, with deeply set wrinkles. Paul's mustache needed a trim, along with his eyebrows, nose, ears, and receding hairline. He recalled looking at older men when he was a boy and wondering how and when hair began to grow so wildly and in so many of the wrong places. He stepped up to the mirror, placing his hands on the counter, and scrutinized his reflection. He took an inventory of the slumped shoulders, the growing stomach paunch, the overall deterioration of his body. He stared briefly into his own eyes, but what he saw there made him look away.

He picked up a toothbrush, ran some water over it, and scrubbed at the layer of grime and grit on his teeth. It felt like a healthy and progressive decision. Embracing it, he found the toothpaste, applied it to the brush, and continued the process. He tried to remember his last dentist appointment and decided to set one up soon. Perhaps he would call this afternoon. The toothpaste tasted minty and refreshing. He was inspired to take a shower, and pulled back the curtain on the tub, removed the vomit-filled trash can, and turned on the water. He took off his clothes and stepped in, facing the hot spray of water. It felt warm and soothing against his bare skin, and he stood there a long while before turning and looking for the soap. There was a small, fragile, yellowed bit of it sitting on the edge of the tub where the tile began. Next to the soap was a nearly empty bottle of shampoo. Paul picked up the bottle and shook it, verifying that he'd already added water to the mixture, trying to make it last. After his shower, he should check around for the spray bottle of tub cleaner. He knew that Charlotte used to keep it under the bathroom sink and assumed it hadn't moved in all these years.

She insisted they install the bathtub themselves and hang the tile, assuring him that it would save money and that it wouldn't be too difficult. It was difficult, of course, but she was right about saving money and, in the end, they were both quite proud of their work. They celebrated by taking the first shower together, both nervous the tiles would come popping out or the entire bath would crash through the floor.

"We're quite a team when we try to be," she'd said, smiling and leaning in to kiss him as the steam rose around them that morning.

"We certainly were," Paul thought, "when we tried to be."

The small bit of soap crumpled when he tried to lather it up, breaking into small pieces and collecting around the drain. He poured the watery remnants of shampoo into his hands and watched it flow through his fingertips as he tried to apply it. He tossed the empty bottle over the curtain and onto the bathroom floor.

Paul turned off the water, stepped out, and realized he hadn't thought to leave a clean towel out. He stepped toward the linen closet, aware that the floor was becoming more slippery with each step. There was a bathmat in here at one time, but Paul had thrown it out some time ago, believing that it was the source of the unpleasant smells which continued to linger long after its removal. He reached the closet, pulled open the door, and saw that there were no towels in the closet.

"Shit!"

He thought about walking to his bedroom or to the laundry room to find a discarded towel but wasn't sure where he would find one or how clean it would be. He looked down at the pile of clothes he'd deposited in the corner the night before. Just looking at the dirty washcloth triggered the awful smell and made him flinch. He moved the washcloth and picked up the shirt.

"Idiot," he muttered, attempting to carefully dab himself off, pretending that the shirt was somehow clean and fresh smelling while he wiped it over himself.

He held the shirt over his midsection and walked back to the bedroom. After dressing, he straightened the blankets and pillows on the bed and walked back toward the kitchen. As he did, he stopped at a closed doorway in the hallway, looking at the "Sean's Room" sign that hung from a tack there.

"Mommy, Daddy, look! It's my name; it says Sean!"

"Yes, honey, it does," Charlotte had agreed, picking up the sign and holding it down for him to see.

"Would you like to get it for your bedroom door?" Paul asked.

Sean's eyes widened. "Maybe," he said, "or maybe we could look at these!" He'd gone to the other side of the store's rack, where the girl's names were listed.

Paul closed his eyes and took a long breath. He reached up and ran his finger over each letter of the sign.

"Happy Birthday," he whispered, then walked down the hall, into the kitchen, and straight to the freezer door.

It took a moment to realize that the vodka tasted foul because of the toothpaste he'd just applied. Paul walked into the living room and glanced out the large bay window into his front yard. He never parked in the street, and seeing his car there was strange. It was a clear indication to all who passed that things were out of order, *"Out of control again at the Durkin house."* He also saw a bright orange paper of some kind tucked under the windshield wiper.

"Great," he muttered, "let's just let everyone know our business."

He pulled on the large boots near the front door and headed outside. The burst of cold air felt invigorating on his face. He stretched his neck and arched his head toward the sunshine as he stepped off the front stoop. He hadn't used a snow rake on the roof all winter, and large, sharp icicles hung from the edges of the house as a result. The icicles dripped water down onto the cold cement stoop and sidewalk, where it froze again and created a thick layer of ice. Paul used to spread salt on these surfaces to help with this problem but had neglected to buy any this winter. Instead, he applied the common North Country solution of simply using his garage to enter and exit the house most of the time.

With his gaze focused on the sky, Paul didn't see the slick surface until he lost his footing while stepping off the stoop. His right foot shot forward while his left foot went backward. He made a fleeting attempt to right himself by moving the position of his feet, but this only threw the core of his body more off balance. He knew he was going to fall, and years of downhill skiing instincts helped him to immediately seek out the softest landing. He pitched his body away from the house and tucked in his shoulder as he sunk into 20 inches of snow that edged the sidewalk. His upper body landed safely but pain shot up from his right knee as it impacted with a loud "*Crack!*" on the hard, icy walkway.

Laying in the snow, he recalled his fall from the previous night and wondered if he was beginning to lose his balance as he aged. He pushed himself into a kneeling position on the sidewalk, brushing off snow from his face and shirt. There was a flash of red from the nearby oak tree. He looked up and saw a large, male cardinal perched on a branch facing him, its head cocked in observation. Paul had never seen a cardinal in his yard before, even when he'd diligently kept the bird feeders in the back yard filled every day.

He attempted to stand, but his knee buckled and struck the ground again. He screamed out, "Ow! Fuck!" as bright shards of pain stabbed through his head, pressing out and against his skull.

He slid and crawled with his hands and legs back up the icy steps and glanced over at the oak tree, but the bird was gone. The phone was ringing as he pulled himself through the doorway. It sounded distant and off-key, and he had no intention of trying to answer it. His head was bursting with hot pressure and flashes of bright light. If he could just do something, take something, or call someone to help with the pain. Walking to the freezer seemed impossible, as did searching around for the phone. *Who would he call? 911? Oh, how the neighbors would love that. First, his car gets towed home, and then the ambulance comes to collect the corpse of the pathetic drunk out of his house. It wouldn't be the first time his curious neighbors saw a body removed from the house, though, would it?*

He tried to silence his mind, control his thoughts, slow down his breathing. He remembered the classes about mindful meditation, the power of staying calm, remaining in the moment. It seemed like bullshit now, but anything was better than focusing on the pain in his head or the image of the ambulance, the E.M.T.s, the body bag.

Paul took deep breaths and walked slowly to the couch. He grabbed the TV remote from the coffee table, pressed the red power button, and sat down, keeping his feet on the floor. He knew that laying down aggravated the acid reflux, and sitting like this, remote control in hand, somehow made him feel more normal and relaxed. Paul closed his eyes as the old TV set in the even older armoire buzzed slowly to life, and soon he heard the familiar voice of Lester Whiteside. Lester was a long-time weatherman for the local news station. Paul respected him. He had held up many drinks and toasted Lester's dedication to the job over the years. Paul slowly opened his eyes, grateful that he could see and that the blinding lights inside of his vision had passed. His head continued to throb, so he hit the mute button on the remote.

Lester looked animated and lively, in front of a digital map of the region that promised horrible impending weather. From what Paul saw on the screen, it certainly seemed that Lester had a good sense of the course this storm would take. The weatherman walked in front of the screen, pointing at the areas of blue and white that were approaching from the northwest. Paul didn't want to chance turning up the volume; instead, he imagined Lester's predictions based on the countless forecasts he'd heard in the past.

"It may seem clear now, folks, but in a few short hours, we're going to enter the blue zone. That's when a high-pressure system will continue to pick up power and intensity, pushing us into the white zone. Some places may lose power at that point because the freezing rain and wind will knock down electrical lines and trees. You should prepare by breaking out those candles, flashlights, and extra blankets, if you haven't done so already. Keep it tuned right here for the latest weather updates, and I will tell you the same thing again in ten minutes." Paul smiled at his summary and was pleased when a warning of bolded red font began scrolling across the bottom of the screen: "SEVERE STORM ALERT FOR ENTIRE VIEWING AREA. STRONG WINDS AND FREEZING RAIN MAY CAUSE POWER OUTAGES AND DAMAGE. VIEWERS ARE ADVISED TO TAKE COVER IN SAFE AREAS UNTIL THE STORM ALERT IS LIFTED."

He laid on his side on the couch and faced away from the TV and the light streaming in from the front window. He turned the volume up slightly so that he could hear the voice of Herb Fillmore, local Great Value Hardware store owner, reminding people that now was the time to invest in a generator – "and Great Value has them in stock with payment plans available!" Paul concentrated on his breathing again, allowing the drone of other voices and commercials to lull him away from thinking too much about the storm that was on the way.

CHAPTER 4

"I think great counselors are like great teachers. They're born, not made.
I mean, you've got to have more than just book smarts to really make a
difference. You need to have a helper's heart and be in this for the
outcome, not the income. They say anyone who keeps working in this
field after five years is a dinosaur, and I can't count the number of
people I've seen hang it up before then. Maybe we should get summers
off like all those teachers do. But what the hell do I know?"

Bill Hughes, Addiction Counselor, St. Michael's Substance Abuse Clinics

Travis Kent held his breath and gripped a pillow tightly to his chest while the school closures scrolled along the bottom of the TV screen.

"I don't know why you won't just check the website," C.J. said. They were lying in bed together under the grey duvet. The room was small and orderly, and the full-size bed with the black wooden frame (IKEA's NORDLING Model) took up most of the space. There was one window, which was cleaned so well and so often that several birds had thumped into it until C.J. had applied the rainbow light catcher to deter them. Light now danced off the rainbow and sent lines of red, blue, and orange onto the plain white walls of the room. There was a medium-sized flat screen TV attached to the wall. The bracket had been there upon moving in, which was the main reason C.J. put the TV in the bedroom and not the living room. Still, he complained every time they watched it that whoever had mounted the bracket had not centered it correctly on the wall. Normally the only channel they watched was HGTV, but Travis had insisted on the news this morning.

C.J. made a move to grab one of two cell phones on the bedside table, but Travis yelled "No!" and swatted the recently assembled glossy black nightstand (IKEA's BRIMSTED Model) with his pillow, sending the phones off the stand and onto the spotless grey area rug.

"You bastard!" C.J. yelled. "Not only are you going to break my phone, you're trashing my apartment in the process!"

"Two phones on the floor is not exactly trashing your apartment." Travis watched C.J. looking anxiously at the phones on the floor. He wrapped an arm around C.J.'s waist, creating a playful restraint.

"Leave them there. It's good therapy for you."

C.J. settled back into Travis's hold.

"God, this is taking so long!" C.J. said. "And the guy doing the weather is so old! This is not what people want to be looking at first thing in the morning!"

"You're horrible," Travis said, laughing. "That guy has been doing the weather since I was a kid, and he still seems to love his job. I hope we can say that someday."

"Right," C.J. said. "That's why we're both up at this ungodly hour on a Monday morning, hoping that school is closed, because we love our future jobs so much?"

"Just shut up now," Travis said and poked C.J. in the ribs.

"Oh, look, they're almost done with the G's."

They both sat up straighter in the bed, leaning forward as the list of closings changed to places starting with H.

"Come on, come, on," Travis said.

Hamilton Community College – Closed, appeared on the screen.

"There it is! Yes, we're closed," C.J. screamed, and the two of them fell into each other, laughing.

"Oh, we're going to have a proper snow day today, lover," C.J. said. "We're going to be like John and Yoko and not leave this bed unless it's absolutely necessary!"

Travis looked at him, not smiling.

"Oh no, you're not going to tell me you're thinking of going to your internship. Are you crazy? No way! I'm not going to mine. No freaking way!"

"The dental lab is on campus," Travis said, "and the campus is closed. I highly doubt that St. Michael's Substance Abuse Clinics are closed today. I have to go in."

C.J. pulled back and sat against the bed board with crossed arms and an exaggerated pout.

"But I don't have my class this morning," Travis said, inching closer. "And I don't have to be at my internship until noon. That gives us plenty of time to play Yoko and John this morning!"

"Humph," C.J. replied. "Well, that just sucks. You keep saying how they're not letting you do anything at this internship anyway! It's your second semester. Shouldn't you be running groups or working directly with clients by now?"

"Yup, I should. And I keep bringing that up with Professor Dunleavy, but he just tells me that each clinic operates differently and that it will happen in time. Some people in my class have been working with clients since last semester, and I'm really trying not to take it personally, but it's hard. I just hope they think I'm ready, that I could handle working with people and doing more of the clinical stuff."

C.J. moved closer. "Well, it sounds like some of those codgers in your class are close to retirement age themselves, and you're only twenty-one! I know it's not fair, but I see the older students get more responsibility and respect in the dental program too. It sucks, but you'll get your chance to show them how amazing you are."

Travis looked unconvinced, so C.J. took his hand and gripped it. "Hey, you're going to be a great counselor—a fucking life changer! And maybe your professor is right; maybe you shouldn't sweat it. I know I couldn't wait to start working on a patient's teeth, and now I spend half of my time at the internship trying not to gag out loud at some of the rank looking things that people have going on in their mouths. And forget about the smells!"

C.J. pulled the duvet up to their necks and curled into Travis' arm.

"I just don't want to graduate in May and feel like I'm nowhere near ready to step into a full-time position as a counselor. The state certification to be an addictions counselor is very specific about all we should be observing and doing during our internships, and it doesn't feel like I've done half of them! Every week in class, I hear other students talking about being overwhelmed or treated like unpaid employees because of all the responsibilities they have. I'm totally underwhelmed. Most of the time, I'm just watching the other counselors do things and trying not to bug them by asking if I can jump in. Professor Dunleavy says we all need to ask for what we want—to make ourselves uncomfortable by naming our needs— but it's just not that easy. Matt, who's supposed to be my Field Supervisor at the place, is locked up in his office half the time, and when he's not, he's frantically buzzing around the clinic trying to deal with some problem or another. It's always chaotic, and I just don't know what to expect from day to day. It seems like I'm the last person they think about, and I get that because I'm not one of the patients, and I'm not really an employee, but sometimes I get so jealous of the students complaining because they're doing so much. It seems like they'll have no problem getting a job."

They watched the list of closings scroll silently by on the TV screen for a few moments before C.J. spoke again.

"Maybe today will be your day. Manifest it to yourself."

Travis rolled his eyes.

"No, really," C.J. insisted, "come on, sit up and repeat after me."

C.J. turned the TV off, set the remote on the night table, and switched on a large salt lamp. He sat himself up on the side of the bed and stared at Travis expectantly.

Travis grudgingly pulled himself out from under the covers, copying C.J.'s movements and crossing his legs, sitting up fully.

"Good. Now rest your hands on your legs and gently touch the thumb on each hand to your index finger and breathe slowly in through your nose and out through your mouth."

Travis followed the instructions.

"Now repeat after me." C.J. took a long slow breath before speaking. "Today, I ask to be a helper to everyone I come in contact with."

Travis repeated the sentence.

"And today, I will ask for what I need in order to help others and to be of service."

Travis echoed the words, and C.J. took another breath before continuing.

"I open myself up to be a channel for goodness and light, and healing to all I encounter."

C.J.'s eyes were closed, but Travis had never felt completely comfortable doing that. Instead, he bowed his head and concentrated on the words, trying to give this a chance and not make a joke of it all as he normally would. He both admired and envied C.J.'s seeming comfort with this, and he knew that it was an area he needed to work on, especially because he'd heard from the professor that healing addictions required tapping into a broad spectrum of spiritual beliefs and practices. Some of it was just so hard to believe; it seemed so contrived…"

Travis looked up and saw that C.J. had opened one eye, squinting at him.

"Sorry," Travis said, "what was the last line?"

C.J. appeared unshaken. "Higher Power, please work through me today to show everyone what a fucking life-changing counselor I am."

Travis smiled, repeated the last line, and added a hearty "Amen."

"Great," C.J. said proudly and slid back down beneath the covers, grabbing the remote and scrolling through the channels. "That should do it! And since we've got a few hours before my boyfriend runs off to save some lives, I think he should be the coffee barista!"

"Sure thing, lover boy," Travis said and uncrossed his legs. "Coming right up, Yoko."

"Oh no," C.J. corrected him, "today I'm John, and you're Yoko!"

CHAPTER 5

"Every addiction to a substance or a behavior involves a stronger and stronger pathological relationship. This means that someone who is addicted will continue their use despite growing negative consequences. It also means that you can't reason with an active addict. We've got to do something to interrupt the cycle and the cravings that keep any addiction active."

Dr. Alexander Romanski, training for St. Michael's staff members about medication-assisted treatment

The noise seemed to come from far away, and Paul couldn't associate it with the safe, deep sleep he had fallen into on the couch. It came again—a loud, brash horn. It seemed very close. Too close. He opened his eyes slightly and was surprised that the room was filled with brilliant, white sunlight. This immediately caused his head to ache again, and he tried in vain to blink away the pain. The horn sounded again, followed by the loud whoosh of air brakes being applied to a large vehicle. Paul suddenly realized what it was: a snowplow truck.

Deerfield had a strict ordinance about parking on the streets during snowstorms because it blocked the plows.

There was a knock on his front door.

"Oh great, just great," Paul stammered as he rose from the couch.

He noticed that Lester was no longer on the television. Instead, a well-dressed man sat across from an attractive woman, both looking far too happy sipping from coffee cups and staring into the camera.

"So, Veronica tells me that darker colors are always more slimming, and I figure that's easy for her to say because she weighs about a hundred pounds soaking wet, am I right?" the man asked.

"Well, it doesn't matter what you wear when you're addicted to exercise and celery!" the woman responded cheerily. Laughter erupted from the small studio audience.

Someone knocked again, and Paul heard the low, deep thrumming of the plow truck's diesel engine idling outside. He threw open the door, startling the man on the other side.

"Oh, hey!" said the man. "Good morning Paul. Sorry to wake you up, bud, but you've got to move your car."

Garth Healy smiled cordially as he explained.

Garth was a stout man, the type for whom the terms "husky" or "chunky" were most often applied. Like many men of his stature, his strength and stamina were impressive, and he seemed destined from a young age to become welded to a career that involved regular lifting, moving, or destruction of things which were larger than himself. Garth was wearing his signature NY Giants wool cap, slightly askew on his head. His long mustache and beard sparkled with ice crystals, which along with his cheery demeanor, earned him the rank of Santa's Head Elf in the last five Annual Deerfield Christmas Parades.

"Okay, Garth, no problem. Sorry to hold you guys up this morning. I completely forgot to move the thing last night." Paul looked out at the large plow truck and saw another man he knew, Marty French, behind the wheel. Marty was a few leagues taller and a few pounds thinner than Garth, and many of the old-timers at the town garage referred to the pair as Laurel and Hardy. These men always rode in twos, one driver and one wingman. Besides being known for their physical differences, Garth and Marty also had a reputation for being the most prominent male gossips in Deerfield.

"That's alright, Paul," Garth replied. "We've been out most of the night, and we're probably gonna be out all day, too. Lots of overtime pay, you know?" Garth continued smiling as Paul realized he had no idea where he'd put the keys after the car was towed to his house.

"Sorry," Paul said, "I've just got to find my keys." He went into the kitchen and began to look around frantically. "So how bad was the damage last night," he asked, moving around in circles, and scanning the room as best he could. His head was tightening up, and it felt like his eyes were ready to explode out of their sockets.

"We got pretty lucky," Garth answered. "The whole storm was sleet and freezing rain. Nothing to really shovel or plow up, but quite a few power lines and trees came down. Some of the roads are slicker than cat shit, too! It's warming up now, so, lots of things are melting already. I seen some power trucks out already, and hopefully, they'll get things patched up quick."

"Good, that's good," Paul replied. He tried to keep the panic out of his voice. He stopped moving and stood perfectly still in the kitchen, placing his hands on his face.

"Are these your keys here, buddy, in this bowl?" Garth asked.

Paul slowly opened his eyes and felt his face flush. He straightened himself up and walked back toward the living room, putting on a broad smile. Garth held up a set of keys.

"Yup. That looks like them," Paul said, "I guess old age is setting in." Paul hoped the comment sounded light and amusing, but he saw something on Garth's face that disturbed him – pity, maybe?

"No problem, bud, no problem," Garth said good-naturedly.

The two men went outside, taking care not to slip on the new layer of ice formed on the stairs, the sidewalk, and the driveway.

"Do you have any salt or sand, bud?" Garth asked.

"No, not yet. I'll have to get some."

"Well, we can give you some to get started." The two men made their way down the driveway and walked toward the back of the large plow truck, loaded with a mixture of salt and sand. Several five-gallon plastic buckets were hanging off the side of the truck, and Garth unhooked one. He went to a small door at the side and unlocked a lever. Garth slid the door slightly sideways on its track, which took some effort and began filling the large bucket. When it was nearly full, Garth slid the door back into place and handed the bucket over to Paul.

"There you go, bud. That should set you up for a while."

"Wow," Paul replied, "thanks, Garth, that's nice of you. Let me give you a few bucks." Paul realized after he said this that his wallet was inside the house.

"No need, Paul. I appreciate all you did for my sister back in the day."

There was an awkward silence, and Paul thought to fill it, to ask about Garth's sister, even though he couldn't remember her name. He dreaded finding out if she'd remained sober or if she was even alive anymore. But Garth spoke first.

"And besides, this is just your tax dollars at work," he joked and patted Paul firmly on the shoulder.

"Hey Healy, we gonna do any more work today, or you want me to just shut down the engine, and we'll give the rest of the load away in buckets from here?" Marty yelled out the driver's side window.

Paul and Garth walked toward Marty, who was smiling broadly. He tapped his wristwatch.

"Sooner or later, they'll want to know where we are and when the hell we're coming back. Probably should get back to it."

"That's why they hired him," Garth said, "always the company man!"

"Good morning, Marty," Paul said. "Sorry about holding you two up. I'll pull the car in the driveway."

"Don't worry about it," Marty said, "I'm just busting chops. I could sit here all day as long as they're paying me." He pointed toward Paul's car, "You may want to get that bumper looked at though, Paul. She don't look too healthy!"

Paul glanced over and noticed that the front bumper was severely slanted toward the road and had a large indentation in the middle.

"Yes," Paul agreed, "that old thing must just be holding on by a thread at this point. I'll have to bring it down to the garage and see what Cookie can do to patch it up. Well, I'll let you boys get on your way."

Paul set down the bucket of salt Garth had given him in the driveway. He walked over to his car and pulled the orange slip out from under the windshield wiper before putting his key into the door lock. The cold and ice from the night before made it impossible to move the key at first, but after wiggling it for a few moments, the lock popped up. As he got in, Paul heard Marty's voice.

"Just be careful pulling in the driveway, Paul. Watch out for the dips!"

Paul looked over, but Garth and Marty were hunched down in the cab of the large truck and appeared to be chuckling to themselves.

He closed the door and put the key in the ignition. Thankfully, the engine turned over, and the car started idling. Ice was thick on his windshield, making it almost impossible to see, but the last thing Paul wanted to do was to get back out and scrape the glass off. He was unsure what Marty's comment had meant, but he just needed to pull the car in the driveway and get back into his house. Now that he was sitting down and away from the men, he felt a sharp pain starting in his head, and acid beginning to churn in his stomach, bringing with it the familiar pitching and rolling.

Paul put on the defroster at full power and felt a blast of cold air move up and around his head. He pulled the lever to spray windshield washer fluid, and the wipers began to move, but no liquid came out. Paul couldn't remember when he'd last filled the reservoir, and if it had been the type of fluid that wouldn't freeze up. He made a mental note to open the hood and check the fluid sometime soon. A small circle of clear glass formed near the bottom of the windshield, and Paul put the car into drive while he peered through this tiny porthole and maneuvered off the street. He pulled in at an odd angle and heard the bumper scrape angrily against the ground as he entered the driveway, but the car was off the street, and he would be left alone for now. Paul turned off the engine and stepped out onto the icy surface of the driveway. At the same time, he heard the engine of the snowplow grind into gear, and Garth waved a hand at him as the hulking truck started slowly up the street.

Paul went to the bucket of sand and salt. He reached down and grabbed a handful of the cold contents. He threw his hand out, pitching the mixture over the driveway. He reached down again and repeated this motion, throwing in a different direction this time. When he bent down a third time, Paul felt a surge of dizziness that nearly made him fall. Sweat beaded on his forehead. He stood up and walked to the trunk of his car, steadying himself with both hands. He felt vomit rise and then fall in his throat and became acutely aware of the strong smell and taste of diesel fumes the plow truck had left behind.

He stood there until his fingers went numb before slowly returning to the house. He sat back down on the couch and gently pulled off his boots, realizing that he had never taken them off last night and had answered the door wearing them. He wondered if Garth had noticed and if he and Marty would add it to their tale.

He focused on the television again.

"I'm telling you, there's nothing better than homemade muffins on a cold morning like this," the toothy male TV host from earlier said. Both he and the woman were standing behind an island in the studio kitchen. They wore crisp, matching aprons and stirred some type of batter around a large, clear bowl.

"Well," the woman replied, "I can think of a few things that are better, but they involve booze, money, and a weekend in Vegas!"

Laughter boomed again, and Paul realized that it might be a laugh track. The man pointed a finger at her. "Well, I can't argue there," he said.

Paul turned off the television and went to the kitchen. He found the vodka bottle in the freezer, waiting for him, and panic struck when he picked it up and realized how little was left. Had someone else been here? He knew the thought was ridiculous, insane really, but it was hard to believe that so much was gone. He stood for a moment, pondering if he should wait to finish the bottle, but knowing he wouldn't. He placed the vodka next to the sink, grabbed a tray of frozen ice cubes, and twisted it. The ice cracked and broke, frozen bits spilling over the tray and onto the counter. He filled his glass with ice, pouring in what was left of the vodka. It wasn't enough, he knew that, but he drank what was there and immediately refilled the glass with cold water from the tap. He took a tentative sip, and the strong taste of copper filled his mouth. Paul wondered just how long the ice cubes had been in the freezer and hovered the glass over the sink, about to pour the water out, but stopped in case some vodka residue remained. He drank again, longer this time, and emptied the ice cube tray into the sink. He filled it back up with fresh tap water, thinking about those newer refrigerators that had ice cube and water dispensers built into the door. That seemed very convenient, and somehow healthier than this method. He should look into buying one of those models soon. His hands trembled slightly, and water pitched over the sides as he placed the tray into the freezer. This small task felt very fulfilling, and Paul resolved to drink more water with freshly made ice cubes from now on.

He opened the fridge and removed the few pears left in the bowl. He forced himself to eat one before dumping the rest into the garbage. He had a sudden urge for a piece of toast and found a package of bread in the refrigerator that didn't appear to have any mold on it. He removed a slice, placed it in the toaster, and pressed the button down.

"Pop-Tarts, please," Sean insisted as Paul listed possible breakfast choices.

"I swear, you're going to become a Pop-Tart if you keep eating those things every morning," Paul teased him.

"Yum," Sean replied, "well, I hope I'm strawberry flavored because those are the best!"

He watched and waited at the toaster, knowing that his son liked it just right – not too raw and not burnt. When he saw the edges starting to brown, he quickly removed the pastries, draped a kitchen towel over his arm, and delivered the breakfast to the table.

"Pour Monsieur, bon appétit," Paul said, in a mock French accent.

"Merci, Papa," Sean replied, his young voice trying to imitate Paul's as he used the few words his father had taught him. "You're the best, Dad! Someday when I'm allowed to use the toaster, I'll make Pop-Tarts for you!"

The toaster popped up. Paul found the smell pleasant and felt an unfamiliar pang in his stomach that he hoped was hunger. He carefully buttered the toast, slicing it in half diagonally, and said, "Bon appétit." before taking a bite. It was good, very good. He drank some more water, finished the toast, and repeated the process with another piece before putting on his coat and shoes and heading out the door.

He walked to the driveway and examined the front bumper, which looked like it might fall off at the slightest knock or bump. Paul went into the garage and brought out a bucket filled with bungee cords and bits of rope. He bent down on one knee in front of the car and, using several of the bungees, attached the sagging bumper to parts of the vehicle that looked more secure. This quick fix would have to do for now because he could feel the tremors in his hands increasing. It was just a matter of time before serious withdrawal set in.

Paul stowed the extra bungee cords and rope, carefully moved the salt closer to the garage, and threw a few more handfuls of the mixture around the driveway and up the sidewalk. It seemed to be getting warmer, but he wondered if this was because he was moving around. Paul opened the driver's door to his car, leaned in, and started the engine, turning the defrost on full power. He opened the back door, grabbed the ice scraper, and removed the ice from all the windows. It wasn't too difficult, and by the time he got into the driver's seat, the heater was blowing warm air around the interior.

"Okay," Paul heard himself mutter to no one, "here we go." He turned on the radio and shifted the car into reverse.

"Happy Monday morning, campers. Mother Nature certainly did her best to make this a long weekend. We'll have a list of the school closings coming up soon, but first, let's start the week off right by thinking of a man who knows all about warm weather and easy living." The familiar voice of Jimi Buffett filled the car singing about Margaritas and wasted days as Paul backed out of the driveway and motored down the street.

The drive to the liquor store was not far, and Paul was impressed with the job that Marty and Garth had done clearing the local roads. As he pulled into the parking lot, he noticed one other car there, a white S.U.V. He came here enough to know that it was not the owner's. Paul looked at the clock on the dashboard and realized that it was 8:43 a.m. The store didn't open until 9:00. He parked and glanced at the driver of the other car. She was a woman with long brown hair and a small profile. Her head was down, and she appeared to be staring at a phone. He fidgeted with various buttons on his car's radio to appear busy and found a station reporting the school delays and closings for the day. There were many. Paul felt a growing sense of excitement as the list continued, methodically and in alphabetical order.

"Mohenick Falls," the announcer read – closed for the day.

"Yes," Paul said, "No school!"

"No school!" Sean's ecstatic young voice echoed from somewhere in his head. He recalled the dull thumping of small feet coming down the hallway just before the bedroom door burst open.

"Mommy! Daddy! No school! School's closed! I just heard it on the radio!"

He pictured their son covering the space between the door and the bed with a few swift bounds, almost floating, and then leaping up and landing squarely between them, quickly burrowing his small body under the covers, the untapped magic of the day bursting out in all directions.

"This is so great! No school, no school, can you believe it?"

"That's great, buddy," Paul said, *"and I don't have to go into work until this afternoon. Maybe we can make a snowman and a fort outside this morning!"*

"Yeah, maybe," the boy answered.

The room became quiet, warm, and safe for a few moments while the three of them watched the snow tumbling endlessly downward outside their bedroom window.

"Or," Sean said, turning to his mother with eyes growing wide, *"we could stay inside and make it a baking day!"*

Paul heard the slow crunching of tires over snow and ice and looked in his rearview mirror as the owner's car pulled into the lot.

The brown-haired woman got out of her car, but Paul waited, not wanting to rush the owner, and trying to deny his own desperation. Once he saw the interior lights go on, he slowly left his car.

Paul went directly to the vodka section and picked up two bottles of the brand he always bought. He paused, noticing other types of vodka that he'd never paid much attention to. They were flavored and had vibrantly colorful and cartoonish labels. They looked like candy wrappers. There was a watermelon flavor. And licorice. There was even one named Birthday Cake. Each looked sweeter and more enticing than the next. His eyes fell on a bottle with a large pear on the label. He thought of the refreshing taste of the pears and grabbed it. Holding the three large bottles while walking to the front wasn't easy, but Paul managed to do it. He waited behind the woman, who had selected some type of bourbon. He wondered if bourbon was sold in different flavors now as well.

"Can I please have that gift wrapped?" she asked.

The owner took the bottle and slid it into a tight-fitting decorative bag. He cut several pieces of ribbon and ran the sharp edge of the scissors over the thin material, which caused each one to curve and dance lightly in his grasp.

Gift wrapped, Paul thought. *What a great idea.* He could have used that excuse years ago. Nine o'clock a.m. on a Monday after a shit-show of a snowstorm, and I'm just casually stopping by to pick up a small token of appreciation for the hosts of the party to come. This is just one stop of many this morning, in case you were wondering, and my life is fine, just fine. He thought the woman was beautiful and tragic, and he wanted to share a drink or two with her. He could imagine telling her his story, at least some of it, the parts she might most relate to, because a long time ago, he would have bought only one bottle and paid in cash, leaving no trail or evidence of where he'd been. He would have taken his business to several stores, buying only the one bottle at each, and always paying in cash. But he never thought of having the bottles gift-wrapped, and as he looked at the brightly colored bag sitting on the counter, ribbons tied to the top, springing back and forth waiting for the happy celebration to begin, his heart ached for the brown-haired woman.

The owner hadn't said much during the transaction, only wrapped the bottle, taken the money, and given a slight nod of his head when the woman headed for the exit. He waited for Paul to put his items on the counter, keeping the same cool countenance and never making direct eye contact. His name was Victor Pierce, a Deerfield native. This store had been in his family for two previous generations, and Paul remembered many high school parties at the Pierce house where alcohol flowed freely. The police never came to question or bother the under-age drinkers or to quiet down the loud crowds that were there every weekend. Paul knew that was a different time and that nowadays such hosting and promoting of drinking would be viewed with more resistance and social outcry than back then. It seemed odd that Victor had become so somber and quiet because Paul remembered him as much more outgoing and friendly when they were young. He was the life of the party, always wearing a smile and up for some mischief. Paul recalled that Victor had owned a sports car with a convertible top and chrome rims, which his parents had bought him as a sixteenth birthday gift. A Ford Mustang, maybe? He knew there'd been an accident which crippled Victor's high school sweetheart. He couldn't recall too many of the details except that Victor had been the driver and that he never saw the Mustang, or the girl, at those parties again.

Paul removed his wallet and pulled out the credit card while Victor scanned the bottles and placed them in a bag. It took some time before the purchase slip printed out, each moment intensified as he imagined that the card would be declined, that he would be forced to go home with no alcohol. This thought made his heart race, and beads of sweat form on his forehead. Slight tremors began in his hands again. The receipt finally printed out, and Victor slid a pen across the counter. When he'd finished signing his name, Paul took the bag and gave a slight nod of his head to Victor.

"Be careful out there, my friend," Victor said.

Paul nodded again and headed for the door. It wasn't the warning that disturbed Paul. It was the "my friend" part of the sentence that bothered him. He didn't consider Victor a friend or even a peripheral acquaintance, but there was no denying Paul's role as a frequent and reliable customer.

It took restraint not to open a bottle before he got back to his house, but Paul was able to do it by reminding himself of his pending DWI charge.

He felt the anticipation growing as he pulled into his driveway and parked. Once inside the kitchen, he set the bag on the counter and put one of the two bottles in the freezer. He hesitated, looking at the flavored alcohol and wondering if he should open it first. He decided to start with his regular brand, not wanting to upset his stomach or body chemistry with something new.

Paul took a clean glass from the cupboard and filled it with vodka. He picked up the glass and turned toward the window behind the kitchen table, holding up his drink as if toasting the outside world. He noticed the empty, rotting bird feeders in the backyard. A bright red cardinal was sitting there, on the empty feeder, staring directly at him through the window. It looked like the same one from yesterday. Paul stood still and watched, and the bird made no efforts to move or redirect its gaze. There were four feeders in the yard, all clustered into one area to provide a focal point from the kitchen table or the outside deck. The whole family used to sit together and watch the birds and squirrels. He couldn't recall the last time he filled any of them, and he assumed the birds had accepted the closure of these feeders and moved on. Something unnerved him about this bold, red cardinal. It seemed to demand a further explanation of the situation.

"Alright then, here's to you," Paul said and slowly finished the vodka in the glass. When he looked at the feeder again, the cardinal was gone.

The phone rang, startling him. He walked into the living room and picked it up on the third ring.

"Hello," Paul said.

"Paul, it's John," the voice began, "where have you been? I tried to call yesterday and earlier today but couldn't get ahold of you. Are you alright?"

The tone of John's voice and his probing questions agitated Paul, but he decided not to become confrontational until more was revealed.

"I was here. In the shower." Paul said. "Why, what's going on?"

"What's going on? What's going on? That's a good one!" John replied. "I was calling to ask you what the hell is going on?"

Calls from John usually meant bad news, but Paul wasn't sure what direction the bad news was coming from.

"I guess you haven't read the paper yet," John continued. "You're in there today. Off the road over at Kellett Junction and driving under the influence. Why the hell haven't you called me about this yet? Or did you figure you wouldn't need your lawyer for this one, that you would just call some old friends, and this would all blow over? This is serious shit nowadays, Paul!"

"Listen, John, I was going to give you a call, but—" Paul began.

"I know, I know, you've been in the shower. I get it. Listen. That doesn't matter now. What does matter is that you get out ahead of this thing before your court date. You need to make an appointment at one of those clinics for an alcohol evaluation. Of all people, you should know how this works! If you don't get one of those done before we answer these charges, it really pisses off the judges, and they'll come down on you a lot harder. You need to call and make an appointment, Paul, today. You need to call, like, right after I get off this phone with you. Do you understand?"

Paul's head was swimming. He thought about Garth and Marty's comments and the way they had looked at him – the way they had laughed. The "dip" sign. It was in the paper. They knew. Everyone knew now, and he had to do something. He had to "get out ahead of this."

"Yo! Paul! Are you still there, buddy? Are you writing this all down?"

"Yes," Paul responded, "I've got it. I need to call and make an appointment. Anything else I should do at this point?"

"Yes," John said, "stop drinking."

There was a silence. It had been a long time since anyone close to him had suggested this. Since anyone had actually cared enough to say it.

John spoke again, "Seriously, though, are you okay? Is there anything I can do? You want me to come over?"

Paul felt his defenses crumble when he heard this, and he drew in a long slow breath. He rubbed his forehead with his palm and closed his eyes before speaking again.

"No," Paul said softly, "No, you don't need to come over. I'm okay. I'll be okay. Thanks, John, for everything…" He didn't know what else to say.

"We nitwits got to stay together, right, Paul? Some smart guy told me that a long time ago. As a matter of fact, I think it was you."

There was a short pause.

"Just make the call!" John repeated.

"I'll make the call," Paul said and hung up the phone.

He looked over at the answering machine and saw it blinking wildly. He should make the call. Pick up the phone and do it. But he wasn't picking up the phone. He was walking back into the kitchen, heading straight for the glass of vodka.

The phone was in his hand, and he told himself that he would get out the phone book and make the call as soon as he finished this drink. He picked up the glass and took a sip. He didn't drink it all in one swallow. He knew there was plenty in the house, and that was comforting. No need to rush. He set the glass down on the counter and took the bread and butter out of the refrigerator. Paul put two slices into the toaster and pressed down the lever. He took another drink. The glass was nearly empty. He finished it and decided to have just one more with his breakfast before making the call.

When the toast was ready, he buttered both pieces and ate them. They tasted good, and he reminded himself to add bread and butter to the shopping list for the store. He washed his plate, dried it with a dish towel and put it back into the cabinet. He finished his drink and stared at the phone on the counter. It was time. He considered going for the phone book, perhaps looking up another place to call. Any other option would be better. But going anywhere else would mean a long car ride and considering that his driver's license might soon be revoked, that didn't make sense. He took a deep breath, let it out slowly, picked up the phone, and punched in a number. It rang a few times and went to an automated system. He hoped that he could simply leave a message, one that might get lost deep in the answering machine world, never to be heard by human ears.

"To make an appointment or to speak to a receptionist, please press zero," the recorded voice instructed.

He pressed zero, and after two rings, someone answered. He didn't recognize the voice.

"Good morning, St. Michael's Outpatient Clinic. This is Carla. How can I help you today?" the cheery voice on the line asked.

Paul froze, unable to speak. He felt his pulse rising.

"Hello?" the voice said. "Is anybody there? Hello?"

"Yes," he began, "I'm here. I just spoke to my…I mean…I, uh, I was hoping to set up an appointment," Paul stammered. His words didn't sound like his own. They seemed lost and desperate. He wondered if she noticed.

"Yes, sir. I can certainly help you with that," she replied. Her voice was kind and friendly. He knew she heard similar confusion and worry in many of the calls she received.

"And were you looking for a drug and alcohol evaluation, sir?"

"Yes," Paul answered, starting to feel sure of himself. "Yes, I was hoping to set up an evaluation sometime in the next few weeks."

"Very good, sir. Let me look at our schedule and see what we have."

Paul heard her tapping on keys. After a few moments, she spoke again.

"Sir, it looks like the first available appointments we have would be near the end of March. Is there a certain day and time that works best for you?"

Paul thought waiting until the end of March would be just fine, but he remembered John's stern words about getting in as soon as he could, hopefully before the first court date.

Against his better judgment, he said: "That seems like a long time. Do you have anything any sooner or a list I could be put on for cancellations? I don't live far away."

"Well," Carla said, "we actually have some cancellations today because of the weather. Would you be able to come in? The first available time is at one o'clock. Would you like that appointment, sir?" she asked.

Paul's mind raced as he tried to come up with any reason for refusing the appointment and asking for another, but nothing surfaced to help him.

"Shall I book that appointment for you, sir?" Carla asked. Her voice was calm and cheery as if she was simply scheduling a haircut or a massage.

"I, uh, yes, I guess that would work," he heard himself say.

"Great. So, let me just get your name and some basic information down, and then we'll get you plugged in at one o'clock today."

Paul gave her the information and hung up the phone. Then he took another drink and looked at the clock. It was 10:43 a.m. He would need to leave in less than two hours. He wasn't sure what to do next, so he walked into the living room and watched the local forecast. The temperatures were supposed to stay just around freezing, and the sun would be out for most of the day with little cloud cover. The storm was over. The news station reported that hundreds of people lost power during the last twenty-four hours, but emergency crews were out today, and things would be back online soon.

Power outages had always excited Paul. He remembered learning in school that Thomas Edison had lived in Upstate New York and started one of his first electric companies not far away. Paul's immediate reaction was how much society owed to Mr. Edison and how much blame he deserved for making everyone so dependent on this convenience. One of the reasons

Paul remained in the northeast for most of his life was the excitement foul weather often brought. Edison and countless other inventors may have worked hard to make life just that much easier, but Mother Nature liked to remind everyone who was really in charge from time to time.

Paul remembered being young and going without electricity for days sometimes, huddled around the woodstove at his grandparents' house, with oil lamps burning and the smell of pipe tobacco in the air. His grandparents built and operated one of the first general stores in Moheneck Falls. It sat on the same plot of land as their home, what the Durkin family and many in town referred to as The Big House. At any time, someone might knock on the door of the house if the store was closed and ask for a bottle of milk or pack of cigarettes. Paul never heard his grandfather refuse a sale, and often he was paid by the barter system, exchanging items from the store for other goods or services.

During those outages, Paul's family moved from their own house, just a mile from his grandparents, into The Big House with the giant woodstove and the ornate pendulum clock in the corner. The clock kept time through it all, sounding on each half hour and hour. Paul's sister and cousins complained about the noise, saying it kept them awake and that it was creepy. Yet Paul found the rhythmic ticking comforting, like a strong slow heartbeat of The Big House.

He did think the root cellar was creepy, though. Paul's grandfather had grown up in The Big House, and he'd helped his father dig and build the cold storage room under the backyard. When they lost power in the warmer months, Paul and his family moved any food that needed to stay cold into this underground cavern. In the winter, they used it as a walk-in freezer. To access the room, he had to walk down several steps, which were actually cinder blocks dug into the ground. They sunk and tilted at varied angles over time. The room was constructed of these same cement blocks, which weren't properly cemented into place. Many had shifted and cracked, seeping dirt, and giving the impression that the walls could crash in at any moment, burying the occupants alive. There was a small wooden door that led into the room, which was locked from the outside with a padlock to prevent any theft. Paul and his cousins feared becoming locked inside of the root cellar, especially around Halloween, which seemed a particularly cursed night to become stuck inside such a room. The ceiling was made from a combination of plywood and metal sheeting, supported in several places by large, uncut timbers that Paul's grandfather tended to continually, wedging new beams into places where the roof sagged. Standing in the backyard, it took a discerning eye to notice that the grass level was lower over the room. Paul never liked running the push lawnmower over this section, fearing he would fall through at any minute.

Electricity was never installed. The only type of illumination used were oil lamps and flashlights, which cast long shadows of the support beams resembling ghouls in waiting. Occasionally a mouse or rat would chew his way through the wooden door, and Paul and his father were sent to kill the intruder with the large shovel kept on a high hook in the garage. Paul shivered remembering the dark damp feeling of the root cellar. He decided to take a hot shower and get cleaned up before his appointment.

He started down the hallway but went back and poured more booze in the glass—not to the top, though. He entered the bathroom, stared at the large pile of dirty clothes, and realized there were no clean towels for a shower. He set the drink down, collected the pile, and walked to the washing machine, sniffing each of the towels and choosing the least offensive to use for his shower.

By the time Paul needed to leave the house, he had cleaned himself up quite well and laundered most of the towels and linens. He finished the not-full drink during these chores. He wondered if his body would hold out until he made it home for the next drink. Probably not. He found a large plastic water bottle and filled it with vodka. It seemed a good sign and a show of great self-restraint that he didn't drink anymore while filling the plastic bottle. Knowing that the vodka would be in the car waiting for him would have to be enough to put his mind and body at ease.

He walked outside and realized the temperature had climbed. The sun shone brightly off the icy, crystalized world around him. Paul placed his vodka supply in the car's console and had a sudden strong feeling that things might get better now. He remembered someone telling him once that in every crisis, there was opportunity, and he hoped that these opportunities would reveal themselves soon. Perhaps he would go shopping after his appointment and pick up some groceries, maybe look at new curtains for the kitchen. It occurred to him that he never made a shopping list or measured the curtains. He thought briefly about going back in to do so but decided against it, thinking that it might somehow interrupt the good mojo that was starting to flow.

As Paul started the engine and backed out of the driveway, the radio came to life. The station was playing something by Pink Floyd, which seemed too somber for a day like this. He rummaged around in the pile of cassettes on the passenger seat and pushed in a tape he'd recorded himself. The first song was a live version of a song by The Who, in which the question, "Who are you?" echoed continuously.

Now, this is more like it! He thought as he put the car in drive and moved forward into the bright sunlight and down the street.

CHAPTER 6

"I just felt so alone. My addiction isolated me completely,
and I didn't think there was anyone that could understand what
I was going through, how I was feeling. Counselors and the women
I've met at A.A. keep telling me that I need to build supports and
that I have to stay connected to others in recovery. I'm starting to
understand why. Connection seems to be the key to staying sober..."

Diane S., checking in during the St. Michael's Relapse Prevention Group

Travis didn't realize how tightly he'd been gripping the steering wheel on the drive to St. Michael's until he saw the indentations in the padded cover. C.J. had given him the steering wheel cover as a gift after they first rode together in Travis's car. It was bright blue with hundreds of Superman emblems emblazoned on the fabric. It was mostly meant as a joke because the Hyundai compact was far from Super-Powered (though the leaking exhaust was impressive in volume). Still, after putting it on, the cover made Travis feel like the car was better, more invincible somehow. Travis suspected that C.J. liked the idea of covering the used steering wheel with something new and clean because C.J. was concerned about the spread of germs in all environments. Travis found this hysterically ironic for a person pursuing a career in dentistry. Travis suggested ordering the matching Superman seat covers, but C.J. thought that would be a waste of money, having already covered the interior seats with grey blankets that matched the interior, and which were removed and washed weekly.

Travis turned off the engine, took out his phone, and punched in a text, "I'm here. Alive."

He tilted the rearview mirror down and checked his face and hair. He noticed a few places where acne was forming, which was unbelievable and extremely frustrating. Travis had, in the words of many, a "babyface," which seemed to him to remain small, roundish, and unable to produce any type of hair. His acne issues were more irritating than overwhelming, and an occasional zit or spot seemed to show up whenever he was trying to convince himself that his transition from adolescent to young adult was finally complete. He frowned at the new spot on his face, knowing there was nothing to do about it, and ran his fingers through his short, dark hair. He didn't like the way his hair looked today (he never liked the way it looked) but knew that was a helpless battle as well.

His phone vibrated, and he saw the text from C.J.

"Hooray! I'll keep the bed warm. KKWWSS."

He typed back, "WWKKSSS," and put the phone away. Travis and C.J. didn't like texting and refused to use many of the abbreviations and text-speak that was popular for their generation. When they did text, they agreed to type their messages out. The use of K, W, and S had started early on in their relationship when neither had used the love word yet, and they were listening to a song by the Black Eyed Peas. The song was about using X's and O's to define how much a couple loves each other, and their discussion turned to why these two letters were chosen over all the others to express love between people.

"I don't think I would have picked X or O," C.J. said, "I think S is a much sexier letter."

"Yes," Travis agreed, "I like S too, or maybe W. Or K. K is very sexy!"

When C.J. laughed and asked for further explanation, Travis said,

"I don't know. Maybe it's because the lines remind me of two arms or legs extending from the vertical line of K. Or because of the sound of the letter makes when you say it."

Whatever the reason, ever since that conversation, the two had been including S, W, and K in their text messages and written notes to each other. It started as a laugh, a way to mock their peers, but it became just another part of them, of their relationship and communication together, and it always made Travis smile.

Travis looked at his reflection in the rearview mirror and said, "I am a fucking life-changing counselor!"

"Wow, look at this one!" Carla said when he entered the front door of the clinic and stepped into the waiting room.

There was a low table in the middle of the room stacked with magazines and surrounded by several chairs. One wall was filled almost entirely with plastic brochure holders stocked with information and resources about addiction. Beneath the brochures in one corner of the room, there was a bin full of old toys and well-worn children's books. A few bent and chipped Tonka trucks sat next to the container. There was a small table underneath the window with a radio that Travis assumed Carla put there because the reception was best. The radio was always tuned to one of C.J.'s favorite stations. In the morning, two sassy deejays sarcastically commented on the day's events before playing "America's Top Hits." The reception area was adjacent to the waiting room, separated by a counter with a sliding glass partition and a keypad door.

"You are a very dedicated young man, Travis! Your parents raised you right."

"Thanks. Good morning Carla. How was the ride in?"

"It was fine for me," Carla smiled, "I got a ride."

Carla was short and petite, with dark hair that Travis had seen worn only in a bun. He had also seen her in only conservative-looking slacks and long-sleeve blouses that she buttoned up nearly to her neck. Travis knew she was Hispanic, although they had never discussed it. He also noticed the snapshots she had pinned up of herself with two children, a very young boy, and a slightly older girl, standing on beaches or dressed formally together. Carla was in a few of these pictures, her hair down and arms embracing the kids. Travis noticed she wore no wedding ring, and there was no parent-figure in any of her photos. He never commented or asked about this, having been taught early on in his college classes to remain professional with all staff and to never consider himself a friend or colleague of the people working at the clinic. He was an intern and sharing too much about himself or asking too much of others could be seen as a lack of professional boundaries. So, he asked little about Carla or any of the staff at St. Michael's and told even less about himself unless someone asked him directly.

"Bill is on his way," Carla informed him, "and Matt called to say he'll be here in an hour or so. We've had a lot of cancellations, but Bill's group should have a few people this morning."

"Great," Travis said.

He punched in the code on the door lock and stepped into the file room. Travis grabbed his employee I.D., and a daily schedule from the small mailbox marked "INTERNS/VOLUNTEERS." He hung the lanyard around his neck and walked into the hallway, making sure the door closed and locked behind him. He walked to the kitchen, hung up his coat, and sat down to look over the schedule at a large table in the center of the room.

The Monday routine hadn't changed since he started interning there. The first group of the morning was listed on the schedule as "Weekly Goals." Bill had explained to Travis that the group's purpose was for each patient to write down and then read aloud a set of specific goals to achieve during the upcoming week. Bill collected the written goals each Monday and then brought the papers back into the Weekly Wrap Up Group every

Friday. In that group, patients discussed their progress toward reaching the goals. The papers were again collected on Friday, and each was filed into the patient's chart. Travis had been keeping track of these papers each week and filing them on Fridays.

At first, he enjoyed the group and thought it was an effective way of keeping the patients focused on identifying and reaching short-term goals. But he soon realized a problem with the format of the group was that the patients who attended were in the Day Rehab level of care. This was the most intensive form of treatment provided at an outpatient clinic and ran Monday through Friday for five hours each day, with the average overall length of treatment lasting about one year. Most patients in Day Rehab lived in a nearby halfway house or in a supportive living apartment program run by the halfway house. Because they spent so much time together, the Weekly Goals Group could become redundant if not downright boring, in Travis's opinion. Bill, the counselor who ran the group, seemed not to notice or to mind that the goals patients wrote down and discussed each Monday morning seldom changed. Most patients in attendance appeared to be going through the motions, displaying minimal investment in the group, or accomplishing nothing substantial each week.

Travis heard someone entering the front of the clinic and talking with Carla. He got up, taking the schedule with him, and left the room, closing and locking the door behind him.

"When you work with liars, cheats, and thieves," Matt Denton told him back in September during one of his first days in the internship, "you've got to expect that they're going to try to rip you off. That's why we lock up everything we can around here." Matt was the Clinical Director and Travis's Field Supervisor during his two semesters of internship at St. Michael's. Travis was initially shocked to hear Matt talk about patients this way, but in the six months since that conversation, he had come to understand that dishonest behaviors were a regular occurrence for people in treatment, especially during early recovery. St. Michael's served lunch to the patients in

Day Rehab, and staff members had to keep a close eye on the food because extra portions often went missing from the kitchen. The clinic also offered coffee, limiting it to mornings before groups began and during lunchtime. Matt threatened to stop this service because of the repeated problems with packets of coffee, sugar, and even sleeves of Styrofoam cups going missing. Patients often fought over the injustice of not being allowed to have coffee during groups or getting to the coffee urns just as the last cup was poured out by someone in front of them. Some patients filled two cups of coffee and then hid one on a shelf or in the bathroom and drank it in the break time between groups.

"They'll go to any lengths," Matt told Travis, "To get over on us and get that immediate gratification. I'm not sure what you're learning in school about these behaviors and how to deal with them, but my two cents: we're not helping people at all if we don't point this stuff out and call them on it."

This topic came up often in Travis's college class because the interns saw similar behaviors in their clinics. What Travis heard at college reinforced what Matt told him, that addiction feeds on dishonesty, secrecy, and breaking the rules. They often talked in his classes about "care-frontation," which the professor defined as different than confrontation because a clinician should always have the best interest of the patient in mind. The professor explained that breaking through denial or deceit was extremely common and a necessary tool for counselors, when using it would help a patient to change these behaviors.

"We always do what is in the best interest of the client," the professor repeated, "and remember that timing is everything. I don't recommend using care-frontation when a patient is newer to treatment and their defenses are extremely high. If we start the counselor relationship by telling our patients everything they're doing wrong, it doesn't set the stage for a healthy, trusting relationship moving forward."

He walked down the hall and saw Bill Hughes in his office staring at a computer monitor. Bill was the oldest clinician at the clinic, and Travis frequently heard him talk about retiring. He spent his weekends out of doors, camping, hiking, and kayaking, which contributed to his thin build, and weather-worn, rugged-looking face, much of which was covered by a thick but well-groomed mustache and beard. His office had several pictures on the wall of hikes and camping trips into the Adirondacks, and he dressed as if he'd ordered his wardrobe from L.L. Bean. Travis felt a kindness exuding from Bill, an authenticity and genuine concern for the patients, even when he was confronting or care-fronting someone, which happened frequently in the groups he ran. Bill was in recovery from alcoholism and talked about his sobriety regularly with the patients. This open disclosure surprised Travis, who heard in all his college classes never to talk about one's own recovery or other personal matters too quickly or too often as a counselor.

"Boundaries are the number one reason counselors get themselves into trouble," Professor Dunleavy warned, "and you must question if you're using self-disclosure to benefit the patient of yourself! This approach to counseling might be effective in the short-term, but it can be a real double-edged sword."

Travis never asked Bill why he discussed his own story of recovery so often, but he saw times when it worked – and when it didn't. Many patients seemed to immediately form a stronger bond with Bill because he told them about his own recovery, and a few of these people told Travis that they preferred Bill because he knew what they were going through and could relate to them more. But other patients would use Bill's sobriety against him. One patient recently replied to a story Bill told about his own recovery by saying, "Well, there you go! You don't think anyone should drink. So, of course you're gonna call me a fucking alcoholic."

Sometimes Bill's self-disclosure caused patients to ask more about his addiction, what he drank, for how long, and what exactly happened to make him stop. If Bill answered these questions, as he often did, these patients found a reason Bill's story, or his drinking, or his life situation was somehow different from their own and insisted that he couldn't truly understand how tough treatment and sobriety was for them.

In his internship class, the professor pointed out that patients might ask personal questions of counselors and then twist this information to prove they were utterly different or too sick for treatment and help. The professor asserted that the issue of whether a counselor was in recovery or not wasn't really the primary question for the patient in these situations. He insisted that the real issues were a lack of trust (maybe fear of trusting) or an unwillingness to change. Travis was learning that a good counselor could establish trust with their patients over time, regardless of the counselor's own background story, but that true desire to change eventually had to come from the patient.

"I've got an old school approach," Bill said frequently, and Travis saw through Bill's style how classroom concepts of self-disclosure, personal boundaries, and always being professional were important, but nothing really worked as well as the power of being sincere and authentic.

"Looks like we'll have some customers this morning," Bill said and looked up at Travis from the computer screen.

"Yeah," Travis replied, "the brave souls that made it here through the weather. How was your ride in?"

"Oh, it was great." Bill leaned back in his chair and smiled. "Days like today are why God created huge American four-wheel-drive trucks. I'll get you to convert to the religion of the gas guzzler one of these days."

"Maybe someday," Travis said, smiling back, "but I did beat you in today, so let's not forget that."

"Touché!" Bill said.

This car taunting started the first time Bill saw Travis exiting his old Hyundai in the parking lot as Bill stepped out of an immaculate Dodge 1500 King Cab pickup truck. He offered Travis a parking spot in the bed of his truck where he could drive the Hyundai home more safely.

"I'll go set up the room," Travis said.

"Sounds good. And tell them they can keep their coffees this morning. That should make them happy, or at least happier than usual!" Bill turned back toward the computer screen.

Travis walked down the hallway and into a large room in the center of the building. There were no windows, and although it held the most people, it was Travis's least favorite place to run groups. It seemed too confining and disorganized. A hodgepodge of chairs littered the space. New donations to the mismatched collection were occasionally dumped at the clinic by a large van sent up from St. Michael's Hospital. Some of the chairs were in decent shape, but most were worn and bent and, in Travis's opinion, hideously ugly. The colors of the chairs varied, but none matched the interior of the building, and although Travis had separated them several times, trying at least to keep the matching pieces together, patients and staff invariably mixed them up again. He was told these were the hand-me-downs from the hospital. Travis had seen a few chairs break under the weight of particularly obese patients, or when a younger person toppled over in one while leaning at just the wrong angle against a wall. Leaning chairs against the walls was against the rules, but like so many rules at the clinic it was only enforced by certain counselors. The broken chairs sat around for days or weeks until Travis would eventually ask permission to bring them out to the dumpster. Travis learned in class that choosing to sit in plastic chairs was always safer, as the potential for acquiring bedbugs, fleas, or lice was less in these seats. He heard patients at the clinic routinely complain about these issues, but he never mentioned the problems to C.J., knowing that the repercussions would be daily fumigations and inspection rituals, which might last for hours.

There were also two large dented and bent file cabinets in the room, which Travis assumed were also castoffs from the hospital. Both were stuffed and overflowing with seemingly random art supplies; construction paper, coloring books, crayons, markers, several types of glitter, cotton balls, cellophane tape, small, round-tipped scissors, Elmer's Glue (no other brand was allowed because it might be sniffed by the patients), and a vast assortment of old magazines that were mostly cut to shreds. These supplies were used in the weekly Art Therapy Group, where patients created pictures and projects which hung on the dull walls of the room. He looked around at the Vision Posters from last week's group adorning the far wall. Patients had drawn pictures or cut out magazine photos of things they wanted from their lives in recovery and glued them onto large sheets of construction paper. Several patients complained about the project at first, as they often did in the Art Therapy Group, saying they just wanted to live in the day, to not think about all the things they had lost, or that they thought the entire thing was just a bullshit waste of time. Travis noticed that once the group began, the negativity decreased. Pictures of houses, puppies, and kittens were common. So too were smiling families, far-off destinations, and new cars, motorcycles, or boats. Some newer patients designed their art around advertisements for booze, cigarettes, and sloppily drawn syringes, pot pipes, or money symbols. These clients were taken aside for a discussion about how their images might trigger other people to use and questioned about their own motivations for being sober and in treatment. The offensive art was either destroyed or kept on record, where it was eventually shared with parents, probation officers, or judges when the patient left treatment against medical advice to go get high again. The approved pictures hung at odd angles on the wall, some too heavy for the cellophane tape, which was applied liberally but inevitably failed and sent the artwork downward, until it folded into odd angles on the floor. Travis made a point of taping these fallen pictures back up on the wall, but it was an exercise in futility. He had asked about using tacks to hold the heavier pictures and was told it was forbidden by the landlord. This seemed odd to Travis because the residual goo left by the tape and the wall mosaic of places where the thin layer of paint had been ripped with the falling art seemed just as damaging, if not more than tack holes might be. Nevertheless, Travis grabbed the tape from the cabinet and reattached some fallen art to the walls.

There was a kitchenette with a sink, cabinets for storage, and a large countertop. Bagged lunches were placed here for the Day Rehab Patients. Several people gathered around the large coffee urn, which gurgled and churned loudly. Outside drinks were forbidden in the clinic because patients might mix alcohol into their coffee mugs, water bottles, and soda cans. There was a water fountain near the bathroom that patients were encouraged to use. People often complained about the warm, chlorine-tasting water that trickled weakly from the spout.

The crowd of patients gathered at the kitchenette was normally larger, and a few of the people took notice of Travis preparing the room.

"Look at him go," an older man with wild-growing facial hair and a multi-colored, worn wool hat on his head remarked.

"Good morning, Walter," Travis said.

"They ought to hire you," Walter said, sipping from the white cup. "You're the only one of them around here who seems to give a shit how the room looks, and you're not even getting paid for this!"

As Walter talked, the large orange pom-pom on top of his wool hat swayed back and forth, hanging precariously from a few frayed strands of yarn. He looked like a tired old clown who recently took off the rest of the costume. His clothes were oversized and mismatched. Travis guessed they were donations from the Salvation Army thrift store, which supplied all residents of the halfway house with clothing and other supplies free of charge. Travis heard that before entering treatment, Walter was homeless and spent most of his time pushing a shopping cart loaded with all his belongings around Deerfield. Until he began interning at the clinic, Travis never thought about the backstories and daily lives of the people shuffling around Broadway pushing these carts. In other towns, Travis had been approached and asked directly for money by people looking much like Walter. He'd seen people in bigger cities sitting on crushed cardboard boxes or standing feebly outside of businesses holding up signs describing dire situations while dangling coffee cans for donations.

But Deerfield was different. Great efforts were made to keep the struggles and suffering of the homeless out of mind and out of sight. The staff at the clinic told Travis that the City Council had passed several laws over the last year forbidding people from "Aggressive Panhandling" anywhere in Deerfield. Downtown Broadway during the summertime was specifically off-limits, as the Council and the retail businesses didn't want deep-pocketed tourists bullied and harassed by these street people. There were other places for the homeless to go, according to the Council, if appearances and profits were to be kept up. When questioned about where these other places might be, the Council gave no definitive answers, and no new resources were offered to assist with the growing homeless population.

There was a small homeless shelter and food kitchen in Deerfield, which many of the clients attending the clinic relied on. It was on the same street as the Thrift Store. The staff of the shelter attended weekly meetings at the clinic to discuss their shared clients, and Travis learned from them that the City Council was applying more and more pressure to shut down the shelter and the thrift store.

Travis also learned about Anthony "Tony" Pelligrino at these weekly meetings. He was an active member of the City Council and one of the biggest advocates for closing both places. Tony was a well-known contractor and developer in the area. Many people had suspicions that most of his money was funneled through drug sales, gambling, and prostitution.

The name Pelligrino was printed on the jerseys of many youth sports leagues around Deerfield, and Tony always greased the right palms to stay out of the public eye and to slide his latest projects through town hall and zoning board meetings without fuss. It was common knowledge that he liked to knock down or pave over old things to build new things, regardless of who happened to live there or the historical significance of a place. But his cronies on the City Council and the fine folks that Tony paid off shared a common axiom when it came to where and when to draw the lines concerning building and growth: Don't ever bite the hand that feeds you.

Tony's most recent Project Proposal involved building condomini-
ums on the site of the Deerfield Homeless Shelter. That section of town
was one of the few that had not yet been "revitalized," which meant that
the area offered real estate and rentals that were affordable to people below
a six-figure annual income. A local volunteer organization, Rehabs After
Rehab, had worked with surrounding churches, the Homeless Shelter, and
the clinic to raise funds and restore some of the beautiful, centuries-old
houses that fell into disrepair over time. Rehabs After Rehab transformed
these houses into shared living spaces, and it was common for patients
from the clinic to pool their limited money together and find their first
apartments in those old houses after completing treatment and returning
to work.

Tony originally ignored building in this area, but as the sprawl of his
projects grew, so did his greed. Demolishing the Shelter and the surrounding houses would also force the homeless to move away from the area, or
at least that was the Council's hope. Pelligrino had recently stated in an
interview for the local paper that he intended to "Revitalize much of the
area, keeping the history alive, while providing reasonably priced, deluxe
condominium living." At a town meeting after the newspaper interview,
Tony was asked by the Shelter's Director to elaborate on what he meant
by reasonably priced. The rates he gave for his new housing were three
to four times higher than the current average for rentals in the area. The
Director asked a follow-up question about whether or not Tony would be
willing to work with the Shelter on rebuilding elsewhere in the area, and he
floundered for a few moments before the Chairperson of the City Council
interrupted, saying they would table that discussion for now.

Bill walked into the group room, and the small assembly of patients
immediately started drinking their coffee faster, taking large gulps from
the cups.

"Well, it's certainly fun to watch the addict behavior at work," Bill said, shaking his head. "In case you didn't hear, coffee is allowed in the first group today, so, everyone just calm down."

Most of the patients smiled, knowing Bill's humor. A few hustled to the coffee urn to fill their cups.

Bill handed Travis a clipboard with a paper and pen attached before finding a seat in the circle. Some clinicians always sat in the same place in the room, but Bill switched it up, and today he picked the seat next to Walter.

"Okay," Bill said as the patients filled in the seats, "let's plan out some goals for the week."

Travis grabbed a plastic milk crate from near the art supplies cabinet. It was filled with clipboards, blank sheets of paper, and a small plastic cup with pencils. As the supplies circulated, a hand went up. It was Caitlin, one of the newest (and youngest) members of treatment. She had dyed her short hair blue at some point, but Travis noticed the roots were growing out blonde. Although she was short, she seemed too thin, too frail, and very pale. She always wore dark-colored sweatpants and matching tee shirts or sweatshirts, all of which hung from her frame and drooped downwards. She had a piercing in her nose, several in her ears, and a mark just above her left eyebrow that Travis guessed was a tattoo and not a scar.

"Yes, Caitlin?" Bill asked.

"I could use some group time," she said. "Something happened at the halfway house that I want to talk about."

"Oh, here we go," said Theresa, an older woman who sat directly across from Caitlin. Theresa was "heavyset," to use a term that Travis's mother employed often. She had dark hair that looked as if it had just come out of large rollers, and she rarely smiled. Theresa seemed to have an endless supply of Looney Tunes apparel, mostly of the Tweety Bird or Sylvester the Cat variety. Unlike Caitlin, Theresa's clothing stretched and pushed around her, often accentuating a part of Tweety's body in an odd way. Most of the time, she spoke only to complain or criticize others for something they had said or done, and when pressured by Bill or another counselor to share more about herself, she assured everyone that it wasn't worth getting into because she was leaving the house and treatment as soon as possible.

Theresa turned toward Caitlyn and locked an icy stare on her:

"Is this about your cookies? Because I think we pretty well covered it at the house attention meeting you called last night."

Travis counted ten patients in the room as he handed out the clipboards. All but three were living in the halfway house, and normally counselors tried to redirect any issues or drama that spilled over into the clinic from the house back to the house. But it didn't always work.

Everyone in the group had stopped writing on their clipboards, and they were looking at Bill to see what would happen next.

Bill crossed his legs and looked first at Theresa and then at Caitlin.

"Cookies?" he asked Caitlin.

"Yes. Oatmeal and raisin cookies. I asked permission to bake them at the house because I'm new there and can't go anywhere yet, so I'm like, stuck there every day."

"I really don't think anyone ate the cookies to intentionally upset you or to disrespect you," Theresa said softly. "I had one myself, and until you called the house meeting, I had no idea who made them or that they were not to be eaten. I can tell you that it was a gift just to come into the house and smell fresh baked cookies. It really made my night. And they tasted wonderful. I said it last night but thank you for making and for sharing them."

"I had about four of them, and they were awesome," Jason said. "Everyone told you that already. And we also told you that we all started off being stuck in that house!" Jason was tall and lean, with sleeves of tattoos on both arms. He was a bit older than Caitlin, and Travis heard that this was his second time in treatment but his first try at living in a halfway house. Travis also noticed that Jason seemed honest about wanting to give up drugs, and the things he said to other patients were often quite harsh but true.

"We talked this all through last night at the house meeting," Jason continued, leaning forward in his chair and talking to Caitlin rather than avoiding looking at her as many of the patients did. "If you follow the rules, you'll get off assessment in another week. Then you can go out on passes, and you get more privileges. Do we really need to rehash all this?"

Bill looked at Caitlin. "Do we?"

Caitlin blushed, looking down. "No. I guess not. It's not really about being on assessment, or that everyone ate the cookies without asking me. It's just that when I was making them, and after they were done, sitting in a pile on the plate, I felt so good, so normal. It's stupid, I know, and I don't know why it's still bothering me."

Travis looked around the group. Most of the people had picked up their clipboards and started writing. A few others looked visibly annoyed that Caitlin was being allowed to use up group time with this subject.

"I get the feeling," Bill said slowly, looking at Caitlin, "that this isn't really about being on assessment or people running off with the cookies." He continued to look at her, letting a few moments pass. Travis saw Jason look at Brianna, another younger woman living in the halfway house, and roll his eyes.

"I don't know," Caitlin said softly, her voice shaking. "It's my mom's cookie recipe. I never made them without her before. The last time I saw her, I mean before she was in the hospital, she showed up at my door with a plate of those cookies. She and my dad had kicked me out of the house after I stole some jewelry and the pain pills she was on. I had moved into this trailer. It was in Moheneck Falls, that run-down trailer park near the old mill. I don't even know the name of that place. I just remember realizing that it was bad, that my life was bad, out of control—"

"Peaceful Pines," Melanie said. "Sorry to interrupt, but yeah, I know that place." Melanie was a middle-aged woman who reminded Travis of a kind middle school teacher he had. She was tall and attractive and always wore conservative blouses and loose-fitting pants that concealed her beauty. She had been living at the halfway house since before his internship began, and Travis was shocked to hear that she almost died from a heroin overdose (which may have been a suicide attempt) before coming in. Travis looked through her chart and discovered she had a long history of domestic abuse from a boyfriend that was now in prison.

"I lived there for a while too," Melanie continued, "It's weird that you bring it up because I was thinking about that park just the other day. I was shacked up with a total prick in a trailer with no heat and rusty, brown tap water. Living the dream, you know?"

A few people laughed, and Caitlin smiled at Melanie before speaking again.

"Peaceful Pines," she repeated, "well, that's ironic because that place was anything but peaceful, and I didn't see a tree anywhere in the park."

More laughter, a few heads nodding in agreement.

"So that's where your mother found you?" Bill asked.

Caitlin folded her arms on her lap and leaned forward in the chair, becoming smaller.

"Yup, she found me there, and I have no idea how. I'd moved in with my dealer and some other people. I didn't even know most of them. I'm not sure who actually lived there and who was just crashing for a day or two. The inside of the trailer was packed with stuff—not, like, clutter. It was all like new stuff, things that people would bring by and trade for Oxy or heroin, or whatever they could get. Most of it was brand new, still in the packaging. My dealer was smart. She would have me list the stuff on eBay or Craigslist for less than people would pay at the store, and then we'd ship it off or drive to some fast-food parking lot and meet someone to buy it.

I guess it was my job to list the stuff, though I didn't really think of it like that back then."

"Not something you can really put on a resume, huh?" Walter said.

It caused several patients, including Caitlin, to burst out laughing.

"No," she said, "no, I don't think that will help me get my new career started when all this is over."

"And that's when your mom came to the place," Bill prompted again.

"She came to the door and asked for me. It was so weird to see her there, standing in the doorway all made up and her hair just right, holding that plate of cookies. I don't know how she found me. I thought she had…"

Caitlin's body started to shake, the tears flowing now, "I thought she had given up!"

Joanna stood up, grabbed a box of tissues, and handed them to Caitlin.

"People who love us never give up," Bill said softly.

Jason reached down and unzipped his backpack. He retrieved something from the pack, walked over to Caitlin, and placed a cookie in her hand.

"They were so good. I kept one for today," he said. "Your mom would be proud of you."

When the group ended, Travis walked with Bill back to his office.

"How did you know there was more to her story than having the cookies eaten?" Travis asked.

"I didn't," Bill replied.

Travis looked at him, expecting more. Bill sat down and powered up his computer, suggesting the conversation had ended. When he noticed that Travis was there, waiting, he said, "Sometimes you've just got to trust your gut. You'll find out that we're not really in charge in there. Something else is at work. In a good group, you can feel that higher energy, the higher power we keep encouraging our patients to find. Over time, you'll learn to look for it, listen to it, and follow it."

CHAPTER 7

*"Effective treatment begins with a good assessment
followed by an accurate diagnosis of what is wrong."*

Highlighted sentence in Travis Kent's Treatment Process class textbook

Carla had made more of a misjudgment than a mistake. There were several cancellations for appointments that morning, but as the day went on and the weather improved, people either called and rebooked themselves into those appointments, or they simply showed up.

"Mr. Durkin," she began, "I am so sorry about this. The Director was supposed to be here, but he got held up at a meeting, and I can't get in touch with him. This is all my fault but let me talk to the counselor in charge and see if we can find someone to do your evaluation. Either way, why don't you fill out this paperwork so that we have that part done. I am really, really sorry about this, sir."

Carla seemed to Paul to be sincerely distressed and apologetic about the mistake, and he found it difficult to be angry with her. He could see why she got the job.

"Thank you," Paul said. "I'll get to work on this. It looks like it will keep me busy for a while, anyway."

"Yes, it should," she replied. "If you have any questions about the forms, just ask me, and I'll try to explain." Carla gave him a pen and clipboard, which held a large stack of papers.

Paul walked over and sat near a small radio that was playing underneath the only window in the waiting room. A female voice was shrieking out lyrics that promised to slice her boyfriend's car tires and break his windshield for what Paul assumed was an act of infidelity, although the term "borderline bitch" seemed central to the chorus. He thought briefly about changing the station but didn't want to upset Carla, whom he assumed was in control of the station selection.

He glanced out at his car before sitting down, reassuring himself that the vodka was there – close by and waiting for him. There was one other person in the waiting room. His clothes were dirty and torn, and it looked like he might tumble from the chair at any minute. The man had deep lines in his face, and his hands twitched from time to time as if swatting away invisible insects.

Paul was surprised at the size of the packet Carla had given him. He could understand the need for basic information like his name, address, and insurance information. But some of the questions seemed irrelevant, and he fought the urge to answer them sarcastically.

Do you feel safe at home?

Only when watching Lester, the weatherman.

Are you feeling threatened or abused?

Only by myself. And the voices in my head.

Is there anything that makes you angry or uncomfortable?

The horrible music in your waiting room.

Paul scribbled "No," or "N/A" as he went through the pages. He wondered how many people read these responses and what weight the answers had on a final treatment recommendation these days. The other man in the waiting room was slumped over at an impossible angle, presumably asleep or dead. Bill walked around the corner and approached the sleeping man.

"Roger!" Bill said. "Roger, are you with us? Are you awake?"

There was some scrambling and a shuffling of feet as the man woke up.

"Yeah, yeah, I'm awake," Roger stammered, "I'm just really tired, man, you know, from working last night."

"Your probation officer told me you lost your job, Roger," Bill said. "Where were you working?"

"Oh, yeah," Roger responded. "I did lose that job. But I was working, you know, just around my house. Getting some things in order."

"Oh," Bill said, "Well, why don't you come on back to my office? And we're going to need to do a urine test today. Can you pee now, or do you want to wait?"

"No!" Roger said quickly. And then, with his voice a bit more controlled, "I, I just went a while ago. Why do we need to do a test today? Didn't I do one last week?"

"Well, your P.O. would like another one," Bill answered.

Paul felt Bill's eyes on him, but he kept his head down, looking intently at the paperwork. Bill walked Roger down the hall, and the two men stopped at the drinking fountain to fill up a plastic cup with water for Roger to drink, Bill stating that it might help him with the impending urine screen. Paul flipped through the pages in front of him and saw that he, too, might be asked for a urine screen today during the assessment. That shouldn't be an issue unless he had smoked some pot or taken something else during a recent blackout. He was more concerned about blowing into a Breathalyzer machine. If he did, it could complicate his chances of getting back into his car and driving home. The thought made his heart beat faster and sweat form in his armpits.

Carla returned, and behind her was a younger man whom Paul knew right away was not a staff member. He was considerably younger than Bill and dressed more formally and in modern, stylish clothes. Around his neck was a lanyard and employee identification badge, and as he and Carla came closer, Paul read the small, black font on the badge: Travis Kent, Student.

"Mr. Durkin," Carla began, "All of our other counselors are busy right now, but this is Travis Kent, our student intern, and if you don't mind, he can complete the initial evaluation with you."

Travis stepped forward and put out his hand. "Hello, Mr. Durkin. It's nice to meet you, and I'm sorry about the mix-up. I'm certainly able to do the assessment with you if you're willing."

Paul reached out and shook his hand. It was a firm handshake, but the young man's palm was damp with sweat. Paul guessed this kid had never done an assessment by himself before and that he would be as happy as Paul to let the whole thing drop. The thought of rescheduling was attractive. On the other hand, meeting with someone so new and naïve could give Paul a huge advantage.

Carla and Travis were staring down, waiting for a response.

"So would that be okay?" Carla said finally.

"Sure," Paul said and gave a broad smile that he hoped didn't seem too insincere. "Yes, that would be just fine."

"Great," Carla said, smiling back. "Thank you, Mr. Durkin. Why don't you two get started then? You can use the Director's Office, Travis, since he's not here."

Travis led Paul to a corner office and opened the door. The office was large, with windows on two walls, but the shades were pulled down, which cast most of the room in shadow. Travis hesitated, feeling around for the light switch.

"Try the wall on your left, just above the desk," Paul said.

"Oh," Travis responded, "yes, there it is. Thank you."

He turned on the fluorescent overhead lights which slowly buzzed and flickered to life. An L-shaped desk was positioned in the corner, away from the windows. Papers were piled everywhere on the desk in no discernable order. There were two chairs against the wall, identical to the ones in the waiting room. Travis positioned the chairs so that they were facing each other, and he invited Paul to sit down.

"Do you mind if we just sit here?" Travis asked. "I'd rather not disturb the Director's paperwork."

"Sure," Paul said. "Here is fine."

They sat down, and Travis placed a large manila folder on his lap.

"Did you have any questions or problems with the paperwork that Carla gave you?" Travis asked.

"No, here they are," Paul said and handed over the clipboard and forms.

As Travis reviewed each page, Paul took stock of the office. The current Director hadn't done much to personalize the space. The walls were painted the same color as the hallways, and the only pictures hung up were two framed documents that Paul assumed were diplomas or counseling certifications. There was one small, framed picture propped on the desk, and that was of a tall, dark-haired man on the deck of what looked like a chartered fishing boat somewhere on the ocean. The man was holding a large fish, grinning broadly for the camera.

Paul hated the gloomy, cave-like feeling of this place. The fluorescent lights' buzzing seemed to be getting louder as they sat there, and he wanted to walk over and open up the blinds to let some light in. Maybe he should replace the kitchen curtains with blinds...

The door in the office next door slammed loudly.

Paul heard a mumbled voice through the wall but couldn't make out the words.

A louder, higher-pitched voice shouted: "Yes! Yes, I'm angry! God damned right I'm angry!"

The first voice murmured a reply.

The second voice yelled, "That's bullshit! He's a God-damned liar!"

Paul looked over at Travis, who had been meticulously reviewing the paperwork, seemingly unfazed by the voices next door. Paul was unsure if that was a good sign or not. He glanced around the office again and noticed a small, round plastic device near a very unhealthy-looking plant. The electrical cord was neatly wrapped around the thing, and it sat in a thick cocoon of dust.

"Do they ever use that machine?" Paul said.

Travis looked up.

"What machine is that?"

"Over there in the corner," Paul said, pointing. "Do you ever use those anymore?"

Travis looked over briefly. "Um," he said. "I don't know if they use those. That's the first one I've seen here. What is it?"

As if on cue, the voices through the wall rose again.

"Well this is bullshit!" someone yelled. This was followed by some low muttering and then the loud slam of a door.

Paul looked at the wall, which had fallen silent now, and then back at Travis. "It's a noise machine," he said. "It's used so that people won't hear your conversations through the walls."

"Oh," said Travis, "Would you like me to plug it in?"

"No need now," Paul said and smiled. "I guess we'll see if she gets another screamer over there, and then maybe fire it up."

"Oh. Okay. Yes. I guess we could do that. If it would make you more comfortable, though, I could try it now."

"It's fine, kid." Paul said. "It's just fine. Can we get started, though?"

"Yes," replied Travis, "Certainly. Yes, we can get started. I just wanted to be sure your paperwork was correct."

He placed the clipboard and the papers on the floor and flipped open the large manila folder, splaying it across his lap. He took the cap off a pen and held it over the first page of questions. The sight amused Paul. This kid had no idea what he was in for.

"I'm going to ask you a series of questions and then write down your answers," Travis said. "The purpose of our meeting today is to get some information about you that I will present to the entire clinical team. Once I do that, you will be contacted and told of our recommendation for your treatment. Do you have any questions about the process before we begin?"

"How old are you, kid?"

Paul knew it was an unfair thing to do, a stupid power play, but he couldn't take it back.

"Is my age important to you?" asked Travis.

The answer surprised Paul.

He knew he should back down and let it go, just move forward with all this, but he kept pushing.

"Have you ever had an addiction?"

There was a hesitation. Travis set his pen down.

"Whether I'm in recovery or not is really not relevant to our meeting today, and I'm also going to ask you to call me Travis and not "kid" during our time together. If you would prefer to wait for someone else, who is a full-time staff member that is older and in recovery, I'm sure we can reschedule your assessment."

Travis picked up his pen. It shook slightly in his hand.

Not bad, kid. Not bad at all, Paul thought.

He said, "Okay, fair enough, Travis. Sorry to be so nosy. I guess I'm just nervous."

Travis gave him a tight smile.

"So, the first question asks why you're here today."

"Well," replied Paul, "I'm here for an evaluation."

Paul noticed Travis's body stiffen a bit, and he decided to back off and not make the kid work too hard for a longer answer.

"I made a bad decision and decided to drive after having a few drinks. I got caught. So, my lawyer suggested I come in."

"I see," said Travis and began writing.

"And have you had any other legal charges for drinking and driving or for anything related to alcohol and drug use in the past?"

Paul hesitated, contemplating choosing luck or honesty before he answered. His luck hadn't been too good lately, so he went with honesty

"I had one other charge for drinking and driving. But it was a long time ago."

"How long?"

"Twenty-five or twenty-six years ago."

Travis didn't show any noticeable reaction to the answer. He just wrote something down and continued.

"So, now I'm going to ask you some questions about your use of alcohol and drugs. Please try to give me the most specific information you can."

Paul nodded his head.

"At what age did you first start to use alcohol?"

"It was around age 14," Paul replied.

Travis continued looking at Paul, so he added, "I had stolen some beers on the first day of summer from my grandfather's store, and me and Debbie Robinson took them down by the boat launch. My first beer and my first kiss, both on the same night."

This was a story he had told many, many times over the years, and it was somehow comforting to hear it again.

Travis gave a slight nod of his head and then looked down at the paper. "And can you tell me when your drinking became more regular?"

"Well," Paul started again, "after that night with Debbie, I saw the power that I could have with a little alcohol on my side. Over the course of that summer, I took several young ladies to the same spot. It worked like a charm each time. Except for Linda Williams. She threw up after her second beer, and that sort of ruined the make-out session I had planned."

This brought a smile to the kid's face.

"So, your drinking became regular fairly quickly, then?" Travis asked, pen hovering above the paper.

"Yes. I would say that over the next few years and throughout high school, I was out drinking almost every weekend. By senior year, I may have added a few days onto the schedule, but I was definitely a week-end warrior."

Travis was busy writing as he asked, "And did drinking cause any problems in your life back then?"

"Back then?" Paul weighed the question. "No, I wouldn't say it caused me too much trouble in those days. Just a lot of fun and a few broken hearts."

"And how about later on?" Travis continued. "You mentioned the D.U.I., but have there been any other problems associated with your drinking?"

Paul smirked and turned his head toward the window, really wishing those fucking shades were open. He wondered how to accurately describe the list of "problems associated with his drinking." In time, Paul knew the kid wouldn't need to ask most of these questions to his patients because the familiar and predictable pain, sorrow, and "problems associated with their drinking" would become horrifyingly transparent. But maybe the kid would wise up and find another profession before that time came.

"Yes," Paul answered, "yes, there have been other problems. Many problems."

It was getting darker in the room, and Paul smelled a trace of his grandparent's root cellar, a mixture of mold and rot. His hand shook slightly, and he hoped the kid didn't notice. If those blinds were up, he could just see his parked car through the window. The vodka was there...

"And when was your last drink?" Travis asked.

Paul closed his eyes, tried to will the shaking and the fear away. "Put down 'last Friday night,' when I got the D.W.I. That should be close enough for them."

Travis looked at him for a long moment before speaking again. Paul kept his eyes closed and realized he was holding his breath.

"The next question is about other drugs." Travis finally said. "Have you used any other drugs?"

"Yes, sure," Paul replied curtly.

He didn't want to recount the glory days of his use anymore but knew that more of an explanation would be required.

"Can you tell me which drugs you've used?"

"Which ones are on your list?"

Travis began to name off various drugs, and Paul shook his head for a "yes" or a "no" to each one. When they had gotten through all of them, Travis said,

"So, for each drug you've used, I need to find out your age of first use, when you last used, and if you had any negative consequences from any of them."

"Let's keep it simple," Paul responded. "You can put down age fourteen or fifteen for the start date on everything. I haven't used anything but alcohol for twenty-seven years. I relapsed about five years ago and started drinking again. All of the drugs I used caused me some trouble, but none as much as the booze."

He looked at Travis again.

"It's the booze that's going to kill me."

"And have you received any treatment in the past or attended mutual aid or twelve step programs to assist in your sobriety?"

"I went to treatment after that D.U.I," Paul answered. "And I completed treatment successfully. I was also involved in A.A. meetings during and after treatment. So, yes. I've been to both. But before you ask the next question on your list, my last A.A. meeting was about four or five years ago. Make sure to put that down. They are going to want to know that at your Treatment Team meeting. If you get that far when you tell them about me."

Travis gave Paul a questioning look, hesitating for a moment before speaking again.

"The next section is about your family," Travis went on. "Can you tell me the names of your parents and siblings?"

"My father's name is William, but he always went by Bill. He died twenty-four years ago from a heart attack. He never had any problems with booze or drugs. Mom's name was Laurie. She passed fourteen years ago after living for a long time with Dementia. No drug problems for her either."

"Do you have any brothers or sisters?" Travis asked.

"I have one sister, Molly. We don't talk much. But no, before you ask, she's not a druggie or drinker either. It's just me. I'm the black sheep, I suppose, the faulty gene floating in the gene pool."

Travis hesitated for a minute before asking, "So you don't know of anyone else in your family that struggled with an addiction?"

"Only workaholism. But I'm pretty sure you folks don't provide treatment for that one yet."

Paul felt the tremor in his hand again. It was getting stronger now, demanding attention. He sat back, stretching in the chair, and took a long deep breath. He thought talking his way through it might help.

"My grandfather built and ran a business for most of his life. The whole family was involved in keeping that place going. Most of our summers and holidays were spent making sure other people had what they needed to enjoy themselves. The business never turned a profit, but it kept my grandfather busy, so we all played along. My own father worked two other jobs and then went to help his dad at the store. So, my dad and I did not have a real close connection outside of working together. It wasn't so long ago when they would have described this as a strong work ethic, but nowadays people don't like to work so much, or too hard, so now it's become an addiction."

Travis asked, "Do you work now?"

"I'm retired," Paul answered.

"And what type of work did you do?"

Paul smiled and looked at Travis again. "Well, you can just put down that I worked for a hospital for many years, but I took a forced retirement about the time my relapse happened. Everyone seemed to think it was best. Now I do nothing. My workaholism has been put into remission. I'm completely abstinent from the stuff."

"Okay," Travis said. "Now, a few more questions about family. Are you married?"

"Divorced," said Paul quickly, "separated officially, but on our way to divorce."

"And how long were you married?"

"Well, I suppose we're still married officially. So that would be 24 years. But we met ten years before that in college."

"And do you have any contact with your spouse now? Was the separation a mutual decision?"

"We haven't talked in a long time," Paul said, looking toward the window. "A very long time. And I guess your question about the separation being a mutual decision depends on which of us you talk to. I don't think she had many options but to leave me. I may not have wanted her to go, but I certainly didn't make it easy to stay."

"And do you have any children?"

"We had a child. One child. Together."

Paul heard his own voice crack slightly, and he looked down at his hands. The trembling was becoming worse. He tried gripping them together to control the shaking. He knew he needed to say more before the kid asked.

"There was a suicide."

Paul looked up and into Travis's face.

"Five years ago."

The room became completely silent. The earthy smell of the root cellar returned, stronger this time, and Paul felt his entire body constricting, tightening, preparing for the pain of his next words.

"I found the body at home, in the bedroom. We both knew something was wrong. My wife and I noticed that there were problems, depression, but we had no idea. I mean, no parent wants to think that their kid could…"

Just then, two people entered the office next door and began talking.

There was a loud laugh followed by, "Oh my God! He did NOT tell you that!"

"I am so sorry," Travis said to Paul and moved a hand slightly toward him but then stopped awkwardly, not knowing how to proceed.

"That is awful, and I'm very sorry for you and your family," Travis added quietly.

Paul noticed the air was more rancid, the room tightening. He'd always propped something at the root cellar's door and checked the lantern or flashlight several times before walking further into the darkness down there. Why didn't Matt keep those God-damned blinds in his office open?

There was a sharp throbbing in his head, becoming more painful every minute. The voices continued next door, exploding into occasional fits of laughter.

"How much more have we got here?" Paul asked.

This seemed to awaken the kid, who said, "Yes, sorry, right. Well, there are just a few more pages of medical information, and I need you to sign some releases in case we have to call collateral contacts."

They continued the interview, Paul reporting that he hadn't been to a doctor in "quite some time," and Travis informing him that he could meet with the staff physician if he did enter treatment. Paul couldn't think of a single person to put down as a contact in case Travis needed more information about making a treatment determination.

"What could you learn from those contacts that I haven't told you?" Paul asked.

"Collateral contacts are usually used if we are unsure about recommending treatment," Travis said. "This helps us to know what level of care, if any, is going to be determined."

"Well," Paul responded, "I don't think it will be a question of if treatment is recommended. I think the real issue will be what the hell to do with me. Your treatment meeting should be very interesting this week."

Paul saw confusion in the kid's face, but Travis only said, "Alright, I'll be sure to call with our recommendation after we discuss your information."

"I look forward to it."

Paul hoped that the kid didn't notice the sweat forming on his forehead or how badly his hand was shaking as he reached out to shake Travis's hand before leaving.

CHAPTER 8

"'Normal' is a fucked-up word, and you probably shouldn't say it to your clients. Who gets to decide what normal is? And if that's someone's goal, to live a 'normal,' ordinary life, I'm probably not interested in anything else they have to say. I want to live an extraordinary life."

C.J. to Travis at the H.C.C. Dining Hall

On Tuesday, Travis sat in a large lecture hall at Hamilton Community College. He was one of twenty-six students studying to be addiction counselors and interning in nearby agencies. The H.C.C. campus was in what Travis' mother considered to be the only safe section of the city of Smithtown. She disliked his decision to attend H.C.C. and prodded him to go back to the four-year business school he'd quit after sophomore year

"I don't understand it," she said, "you did so well there. Your grades were always so good. You're an adult now and free to do whatever you want. It just doesn't make sense to me that you would go and sell yourself short after all that work."

"By selling myself short, you mean I won't make enough money, right?" Travis asked. *"Because if the money you and dad are making is the main reason you're both so happy and fulfilled with your lives, I'm alright with trying another way."*

His mother missed the barbs in his comment completely, as she often did when he tried to communicate in a way his professor would say was passive aggressive.

"Well, of course, money is not the only reason we're happy, honey. We also spend plenty of time by ourselves doing the things each of us enjoys with that money. Spending too much time together can choke a relationship, and I don't care if it's friendship or, you know, something more than that. Everyone needs time to themselves."

His mother hated C.J., though she'd never come right out and said it. There was very little that she or Travis' father would ever come out and say directly. Most of his upbringing involved guessing what to do based on an endless diet of subtle disappointment and unmet expectations from both of his parents.

Travis enjoyed college life and his business classes at first, but soon rejected the greed he saw in most of his classmates enrolled in the program. The idea that he would be a wealthy, successful businessman was an assumption both parents seemed to have agreed on without mentioning it to him. He had heard them gloat to their friends about the remarkable success and accolades Travis received for starting the Project Humanity Club in his elementary school, but neither recognized that his incentive was never financial. After a classmate lost her home and most of her family's belongings in a fire, Travis took it upon himself to make flyers and to set up an online website asking for donations. When the school's principal found out about the project, she awarded Travis with his first (and only) trophy and a framed Certificate of Outstanding Citizenship. The school continued to support and expand their Project Humanity Club, though few current members would have any idea about who Travis was or his role in starting the club.

During his sophomore year at the business college, Travis was pushing himself to be more social. He thought this might cure, or at least lessen, the growing emotional void and loss of desire to complete the program.

His moment of clarity came while on a date with another business major. They went to an exclusive restaurant in town, ordered the most expensive entrees, and proceeded to drink several bottles of wine, all paid for by Travis' date who was a senior at the college and insisted on picking up the tab.

"It's really funny, isn't it?" the older student asked Travis in a slurred voice.

"What's that?" Travis asked. He felt drunk, something he rarely allowed because it made him feel out of control and too vulnerable.

"Well, just look at this place. Look at these people. Every one of them thinks they're so fucking special, so successful, and rich, and unique. With all that money and all that power, you'd think we'd all be getting the best of everything, right?"

Travis leaned across the table, unsure where the conversation was going and concerned that his date was getting louder with each word.

"But then you think about the food we just ate. I mean, that salad was probably picked by the same illegal wetbacks who ship the shit to every fast-food chain in the country! And did you check out our waitress? I mean, that cheap-ass nail polish and that Gap blouse might be fine for her overnight cashier job but come on, sweetie! Big money means big girl clothes and make-up! Well, she's going to have to pick up an extra shift or two after tonight because I'm not leaving shit for a tip."

Travis left all the cash in his wallet for the waitress that night. A month later, when the spring semester ended, he knew he wouldn't be returning in the fall. It was another two months until he informed his parents of this decision.

He didn't mention that awful date at the restaurant to his parents, and he didn't bring it up when he first met with Professor Dunleavy to discuss why he was signing up for H.C.C.'s Credentialed Alcoholism and Substance Abuse Counseling Associate Degree Program. Dunleavy required an individual meeting with every prospective student before deciding if they were a good candidate for the program.

Travis had investigated H.C.C. after meeting C.J., and both were surprised at the strict admission criteria for the Addictions Program.

"God," C.J. said after learning that Travis had to do the individual meeting, "I mean, it's only a community college. You'd think they needed everyone they could get! Maybe you should just sign up for the dental program I'm doing. They don't do any kind of screening or background check. You could be Jeffrey Dahmer or some other crazy psychopath and still get a degree in dentistry!"

It wasn't the background check, or the fingerprinting, or even questions about Travis' own addictions or mental health treatment history that most worried him when he met with the professor. It was explaining why he wanted to become a substance abuse counselor.

"I've seen people I know die from drug and alcohol use," he told the professor and immediately wished he could take the words back.

"That's too bad," Dunleavy said evenly. He had kind, brown eyes, and a deep calming voice. Travis had researched him before their meeting and found out that he was sixty-two and had spent the last fifteen years teaching at H.C.C., plus had been a graduate of the program twenty-five or thirty years ago. Dunleavy also had a lengthy career as a mental health and addiction counselor, and he continued to run a small private practice outside of his work at the college. The lines in his face and gray hair attested to his age, but he had kept himself in relatively good shape, and around the college he had a reputation for youthful energy and a passion for his job.

"So did you go to therapy or any self-help meetings after those losses?" he asked Travis.

"Well, not really. I mean, I talked to some close friends and family about it. They helped me process some of it." In truth, he hadn't spoken to anyone about the deaths, not even C.J.

"Say more about the people you lost," the professor said.

"The first girl died from drinking too much. Her name was Caitlin, and she went to this sleepover in middle school and drank too much. The girls had snuck out and gone to a house party, and they were afraid to wake the parents when Caitlin was getting so sick. I guess she choked on her own vomit in the night. I remember going to her house for a birthday party when we were really young. Most kids had parties at the bowling alley or at this cheesy, cheap pizza place that had video games and laser tag, but that was the first birthday I went to in someone's house. My parents told me it was in the rich section of town. I wore a tie for the first time."

Cody died during my senior year in high school. He was known as a burnout. We were in a few classes together and started hanging out in tenth grade. I figured he smoked pot and drank, but I thought most kids were doing that. It's weird to me that people think peer pressure is the reason kids start using drugs because Cody never offered me anything. We didn't even talk about it. He used to come to my house after school because neither of us had joined sports or clubs. I wondered a little why he never suggested going to his place. We'd play video games or watch television. I thought, maybe, people had labeled him wrong. He wasn't what I considered to be the stereotypical *druggie*. And then they found him dead, in his room, alone. Hardly any kids went to his funeral, but news cameras did show up at the high school, and plenty of students were talking about it. There actually were counselors in the school for about a week after that, but I didn't go to talk to them..." Travis trailed off, not having any words or explanations left.

"So, you're getting into this field to process some of these losses? To understand addiction a bit more?" The professor asked.

"Honestly," Travis said, "I'm really not sure. It just feels like I have something to give, that I can help people somehow, and this is the direction I need to go in."

"I see," Dunleavy said, "well, in my experience, this is a career that often chooses you. Welcome to H.C.C."

Travis heard the professor calling his name from the front of the classroom.

"Travis," the professor said, "I read in this week's log that you had an exciting event. Tell us about your first solo evaluation."

Each week before the Tuesday class, interns submitted an online summary of what had happened during the past week in their agencies. This was the first time Travis had been asked to share about something he wrote.

"Uh, yes, sir, there was a mix-up in scheduling, and I was asked to meet with someone." Travis was not one of the regular speakers in the class, primarily because he felt like everyone else was doing more at their placements and that he had nothing of value to contribute.

"Good for you!" The professor said. We have talked about how crazy things can get at your placements, and I'm glad that you stepped up and helped. What can you tell us about the person that you interviewed?" Dunleavy asked.

"Well, he is a 55-year-old, separated white male who came in for assessment after an incident involving drinking and driving. He hadn't been to court yet for the charge, and he reported one prior treatment followed by a long period of sobriety after a D.W.I. charge he got about twenty-five years ago."

"That is good basic information. Very succinct, and I like the clinical language. Now try to go deeper. What do you think is his primary motivation for being there? Why is he reaching out for help now? Do you think it's all about the D.W.I. charge?"

"Well, yes, I think the D.W.I. forced him to come in, but I don't think it's the only motivating factor. He talked openly about many problems that drinking caused; so, I don't think he's in denial. He also knew a lot about how treatment works. He's been in long-term recovery, and he knows what that's all about. He definitely has the knowledge and knows what he needs to do. It just seems like he..." Travis trailed off, looking for the right words.

"He wants to stay sick?" the professor asked.

Travis shook his head slowly in agreement. "Maybe that's it. Or it might be that he's just accepted his sickness if that makes any sense. I got the feeling that he's punishing himself. Like he believes he deserves to be miserable."

"That is his right," the professor added. "We've talked in class about the importance of remembering that all of our patients have the freedom to make choices about their lives. We can't make anyone do anything. That sounds simple, but I think you're all finding out how hard, how emotionally draining it is when you try to help someone who is clearly sick and dying, and their answer is, "No, thank you.""

"Or fuck off!" a voice near the back of the classroom said. Some nervous laughter went up in the room, and Monica, a tall red head who was leaving her fifteen-year career in insurance to become a counselor, blushed.

"Or that," the professor said, smiling. "Because it's really the same message, I suppose."

"Sorry," Monica said. "I actually had a patient say that to me yesterday after I asked him if being around his friends who continue to smoke pot was part of the reason he can't stay sober."

"You asked a good question," the professor said, "and I think all of you future helpers know the answer."

More laughter in the room.

"It sounds like he knows it, too. He just doesn't want to hear it!" Darnell said, turning around in his chair and smiling at Monica. Darnell was a thin, young Black student whose tight-cropped hair and meticulously maintained goatee made him look much older. He and Monica had formed a tight friendship of the kind that often happened in Professor Dunleavy's classes – despite the variety of students and their apparent differences.

"I've said this before," the professor continued, "we can lead all of these horses to the water, but we can't make them drink…"

"Or not drink!" a chorus of voices in the classroom sang out.

"So let's circle back to Travis. Is what you hear helpful?"

"Yes," Travis said. "It all makes sense. But I think he wants help, or at least part of him does. He was sober for over twenty years, and then his only child committed suicide. When he told me, my mind just blanked. All I was thinking was that I have no idea how painful that must be or how he gets up and functions each day. It's horrible to admit, but I thought that I'd probably fall apart in that situation too."

The professor went to his stool at the front of the class and sat down, taking a deep breath, and looking around at the silent, solemn faces in the room.

A soft voice behind Travis Spoke. "I'm really glad you shared that," the middle-aged woman added.

"Say more, Heather," the professor prompted. "Why are you glad?"

Heather adjusted her glasses before speaking.

"I just get really freaked out when I hear things like this, and sometimes I think I'm the only one."

The professor asked, "Does anyone else get freaked out by these things?" Hands went up around the room.

"Well, Heather, it looks like you're in good company. Honestly, I would be surprised if you folks weren't a bit freaked out at this point!"

Nervous laughter skittered through the tension.

"I guess I never thought that I would be working in these life and death situations," Heather continued.

Travis realized for the first time that she always wore her auburn hair in a bun, and he wondered what it would look like if she let it down. Heather had shared with the class that she was a mother of two children, but she hadn't said anything else about her personal life. He wondered why she joined the program, why she wasn't happy and content raising her kids and living her life.

"I knew that helping people to stop using drugs would be hard, really hard," Heather continued, "but I didn't realize how unwilling or unable some people would be to stop using. The other day at my internship, a guy who has been there for about a year showed up drunk. It was the first time anyone knew he'd been drinking, and he was scheduled to complete treatment and get his driver's license back in two weeks. This is a guy who has three charges for drunk driving! It worries me to know that we are the people deciding if a guy like this gets his license back, or if someone else will see their kids again, or if they can go back to a job or a home or a relationship after almost dying or killing someone else because of their drug abuse. You see stories all the time of people who successfully complete treatment and then go right back out and do something dangerous or deadly. I get really scared, scared that I'm going to be that clinician who misses something or says a patient has finished treatment and then find out that the person killed themselves or someone else because they used again."

The class fell silent, and Travis felt a tight ball of tension in his throat.

"The scenario that Heather just described sounds awful, doesn't it?" Heads started to come up in the room, and Travis was surprised to see that some of the students had tears in their eyes or were sniffing softly.

"And unfortunately, that may happen to some of you in here. It's happened to me over the years in this field, and at those times, I questioned if I should go on or if I could be an effective helper for my patients."

Dunleavy leaned back on the stool and rubbed his forehead contemplatively. "But then someone reminded me of something. It was an old friend of mine, a guy who didn't know much about addiction, or treatment, or counseling. He was just a really astute guy, and he said that as far as he could see, most people who live through the worst parts of addiction are survivors, just like people living through any other disease. He wondered, and got me wondering, if people who get sober might see themselves as living on borrowed time, like anyone who survives something deadly, and, because of that, they can make some foolish impulsive decisions. I found this interesting because it sounds like the theory of protracted withdrawal you've all learned about here at H.C.C. So, for our grand prize of a year's supply of car wax, who can tell me what protracted withdrawal is?"

The professor often queried the class in this game show fashion, and Travis could see that he was attempting to redirect the students and lift the mood. The term was familiar and he thought he had learned it in the pharmacology class last year. A hand went up near the front, and the professor pointed to Jason, a white man who looked to be in his forties and fit the criteria for being clinically obese.

"I believe that is when someone has been sober for a long time. Years, even, and then they…use again?"

"Don't ask me. Tell me, Jason." The professor smiled widely. A few more hands started to go up. "You're on the right track, but can you tell me why this phenomenon happens? And here's a hint – I'm asking a bit of a trick question here." More hands went up, but the professor kept his focus on Jason, giving him a chance at it. He eventually asked,

"Would you like to 'phone a friend,' or poll the audience, maybe?"

Jason laughed.

"Sure," he answered. "I'll 'phone a friend.'" He turned in his chair, scanned the raised hands, and then said, "I'll phone Darnell."

Hands went down, and Darnell began to speak, trying his best to play the part of the phoned friend in the audience.

"Well, thank you, Jason." Darnell began. "Now, I believe that protracted withdrawal is the type when someone's senses trigger them to use a drug or even an addictive behavior after they've been sober a long time. The person might see, smell, taste, hear or touch something which triggers memory deep in the brain of something fun or pleasurable that happened in the past while using the drug or doing the addictive activity."

The professor smiled, continuing to sit on his stool. He turned to Jason.

"What do you think? Do you want to go with Darnell's answer?"

"Yes," Jason quickly answered. "Yeah, that is what it is. And before you ask, I will make this 'my final answer.'"

There were some chuckles in the classroom as the professor made a display of getting off his stool.

"That was a wise choice, Jason, because Darnell is absolutely correct! Hopefully, you will share some of that car wax with him! Protracted withdrawal gives us an explanation for why someone who has maintained sobriety for years might go back to using a substance or participating in an addictive behavior. Darnell told you about the way our five senses trigger memories, and that is true. People used to think that this was the psychological part of addiction, but in truth, there is science behind it—an actual chemical process. Remember when we learned that memories, especially those that are out of the ordinary, are actually bits of protein stored in our brain's long-term memory? Memories are real, tangible things that can be seen on brain scans. Think of them as memory cards, if you prefer, and the thing that causes them to boot up and start running is often something that we encounter through one of our five senses. Therefore, the logic of staying sober by willpower alone is false. There is a biological and scientific explanation for triggers and craving, and why people might have a strong desire to go back to the harmful addictive thing even long after stopping." He paused and looked around.

"Is this all making sense?"

Travis saw a few heads nodding ascension, and without really realizing it he began speaking before being called on.

"But what about the bad things? Does protracted withdrawal explain a relapse after tragedy, or loss, or a really bad time in sobriety, even if they were sober for years?"

"Another great question, Travis. And the answer is—" The professor gave a dramatic pause.

"Maybe."

A few more laughs arose from around the room.

"I want everyone to think about this: The science we're talking about with protracted withdrawal indicates that even after a long time being in recovery—years, decades even—a person might trigger that microscopic memory stored deep in long term memory and that event could be enough to make them relapse. But what Travis is asking is a bit different. Someone in long-term sobriety goes through a devastating loss or a very stressful, intense, difficult time in their lives. Why might they turn back to an addiction at that point? Has a memory been triggered? What do you think?"

It took longer this time for a hand to go up. Eventually, a liberally pierced Black woman who occupied the desk closest to the doorway raised her hand.

"Yes, Shanice," Dunleavy prompted, "please tell us what you think."

"Well, maybe they just want to numb out—to not feel. Or they want to forget about things. Or they wonder if staying sober is really worth it. I mean, if the bad shit is going to happen anyway, well, why bother, right?"

The professor let her words sink in.

"Why bother, indeed?" the professor asked. "Why did I do all of this work to survive in a world that could care less? Why should I keep doing this? Who cares? What is it all worth?" These thoughts bring us back to my friend's explanation about why people might go back to using and doing irrational things. They give up. They aren't buying into the wonderful lives in recovery that we counselors told them exists. They lose hope. The terms aren't really that important, I suppose. You can call it protracted withdrawal, or relapse, or giving up. But I want all of you to recognize when your patients are slipping and do your best to intervene. Alcoholics Anonymous talked about alcoholism as "cunning, baffling, and powerful" back in the 1930s, and I think that was a great summary of what we are saying now." The professor surveyed the class one more time and then rested his gaze on Travis.

"It sounds like your patient went through a horrible loss, Travis, and I'll bet he has some insight into the causes of his own relapse. I don't know that he will ever share the true pain with you or with anyone, but it certainly would help him to start healing. I think there's a high risk he will continue drinking, and it sounds like he might need a detox and then a twenty-eight-day rehab. So, you might not be working with him for long. What is the next step for you with the case?'

"We have our treatment team meeting tomorrow, where I'll review his assessment with the other counselors."

"Well, I look forward to hearing about how that goes," the professor replied, "and we'll end class here for today. Thank you all for playing, and we'll see you soon – same time, same place."

As Travis was packing up his notebook and supplies, a few students mumbled, "Good luck, man," and, "You can do it, Travis." He felt a pat on his shoulder and a voice said, "It's a hell of a first patient, that's for sure." The professor passed by him and exited the room.

Travis pulled his phone out and turned it on. The phone immediately vibrated and pinged, indicating a recent text from C.J.

Meet me in the Blue Room KWS

He punched in "OK on my way," and sent it. It was sunnier than he expected outside, and he regretted not taking his sunglasses out of the car when he parked this morning. Travis found those students who wore sunglasses too often around campus were self-absorbed, and for this reason, limited wearing them to those times when they were truly necessary.

He cruised across the small quad toward the campus center and its dining hall, bookstore, and large, informal study room— "The Blue Room" (known by students for its overstuffed blue lounge furniture). Travis wondered if Paul would end up dead from drinking before he saw him again and, if so, how guilty he should and would feel about it. Dark thoughts came easily and habitually, which caused Travis to worry that he would never radiate the positive, constructive energy that seemed natural and effortless to so many other students, counselors, and especially to Professor Dunleavy. He saw how patients coming into treatment desperately needed good energy and hope that life gets better through sobriety. Travis often viewed life as dark, difficult, and filled with rotten assholes who don't care about anybody but themselves. There had been so many times in his own life when the best he could do was to drag himself through the countless minutes of each day and not think too much about what pain tomorrow would hold.

The professor often talked about counselors needing to "have their own houses clean" and the importance of outside therapy for people in this field. Travis remembered sitting in the cramped room of a high school guidance counselor's office with his mother and first hearing the word depression to describe his unwillingness to attend school, his chronic medical complaints, and the feelings of loneliness and isolation Travis reported to the counselor.

"Well, we all get depressed in this life, right?" His mother said while straightening herself up in the chair. "Travis has always been kind of mopey. This is really nothing new. Maybe if he would find a few more friends or a girlfriend, he'd cheer up. I've told him over and over to ask that nice girl Donna out to the movies. Depressed? He certainly has nothing to be sad about with the life we've given him."

The meeting was never mentioned again, and Travis wasn't sure his father knew it had ever happened.

He entered the campus center and climbed the stairs leading to the Blue Room. Perhaps he was just a realist, a person who approached things from the cause and effect perspective. He understood that if a person did unhealthy things, like using drugs, that eventually the person would become unhealthy. He also believed that if you went around being rude and unkind then people were more likely to be rude and unkind to you: the cause, and the effect. Of course, sometimes people seemed to be rude and unkind for no apparent reason. And these behaviors affected Travis personally. He was not brought up with any strict religious guidelines, and when he encountered people who appeared to bask in their religious and spiritual convictions, it activated a wave of bile in him that he only recently discovered might be jealousy.

He reached the top of the stairs, entered the Blue Room, and looked toward their favorite couch. Under the large windows at the front of the building, C.J. was stretched out in the sunshine like a satisfied cat. Travis placed a gentle hand on his shoulder and said:

"Hey, you, is this couch taken?"

C.J.'s eyes slowly opened before the reply came, "Only by you, mister tall, dark, and handsome."

They embraced for a moment. C.J. tried to respect Travis' discomfort with public displays of affection. Instead, he grabbed Travis' backpack, rummaged around in it, and retrieved a package of Pop-Tarts. He opened the package and handed one of the pastries to Travis, who took a bite and looked around the room.

"Not too busy in here today," he said.

"No," C.J. replied, "I suppose everyone is outside getting their Vitamin D and pretending that it's not so freaking cold out. How did your class go?"

"Class? It was good. Fine. You know, about the usual. How about you? Did you see any interesting mouths today?"

C.J. made a game of trying to disgust Travis by telling him stories about the worst-looking mouths and rotting teeth that came through the college's dental clinic each day. Students in the dental program were mostly involved in examinations and cleanings. Since the clinic was so inexpensive (in many cases, they work for free), it attracted people who hadn't had dental care in many years, many of whom were living on the street.

"Well," C.J. began, "Today there was this woman with only four teeth, two on the bottom and two on the top."

"It's good that they were balanced like that," Travis interjected.

C.J. gave him a playful slap on the arm. "She came in for a cleaning and examination. Normally I have the patient in the room for fifteen or twenty minutes to do that, but when there are only four teeth to clean, it really doesn't take too long, you know? I mean, I had already put the fluoride, toothpaste and floss out in the tray before I saw what she had going on – "

"Or not going on," Travis interrupted, smiling broadly.

"Stop!" C.J. said. "So, I'm trying to make the cleaning last, to kind of spread out the time, but we are taught not to ask too many questions of the patients because they normally can't answer anyway, with your hands all up in their mouths. I can't really floss anything on this lady because the teeth are so spaced out, and the fluoride and toothpaste are only doing so much because the teeth she does have are either brown or turning black, and I'm starting to feel myself sweat because it's only been like four or five minutes since we started…"

Travis laughed and said, "Oh my God, I can just picture it."

"I knew there was no way we were getting to twenty minutes; so, I told her that I needed to let the fluoride dry and set on her teeth, and I offered her a magazine to read while she sat there."

Travis laughed again. "What magazine did you give her?"

"The only things I had brought into the room were *Teen Beat* and *Cosmopolitan*." C.J. paused to make eye contact with Travis

They laughed as they fell into each other's arms on the couch.

C.J. wiped away his tears. "Tell me about your new guy. What's going on with him?"

Travis looked down, wringing his hands together and becoming more serious. "You know I'm not supposed to talk about clients. It's all confidential stuff, and you know that."

"Oh, bullshit!" C.J. said. "You haven't told me his name or anything specific about him, just that he's this really pathetic guy whose kid died. That could be, like, anyone!" C.J. elbowed Travis in the side, trying to get him to smile. "And I really don't care about his specific life situation. I'm more interested in how my boyfriend is coping with landing such a sad and depressing client."

Travis looked into C.J.'s face, trying to decide what to say next. "I'm worried that I won't be able to help this guy, that somehow I'll make things worse for him because I'm so new, and I can't understand why he's so fucked up, and I really don't know what I'm doing or how to convince him that his life will get any better. I'm not a great salesman about how wonderful and fulfilling life can be for anyone."

C.J.'s face became softer, and he looked back at Travis, taking one of his hands. "Maybe all you need to do is be there for him. Just be present, you know? I think that sometimes all people really want is to have someone that will listen to them. They're not looking for someone to tell them what to do, or even that things will get better. Most of us already realize that life can suck and be wonderful, too. Sometimes we just need someone to hear our whole story, to share the sorrow, and the pain, and the tragic beauty of our little lives. We all seem to answer our own questions about what to do next once we find out what we're really looking for."

There was a silence before C.J. looked at Travis again and said, "What? Why are you looking at me like that?"

"Nothing," Travis said, a warm smile on his face, "it just sounds exactly like what I would hear in my class. Are you sure you're studying dental hygiene?"

"It's not just hygiene, you ass!" C.J. said, leaning into him. "It's dentistry—all of it! I'm just stuck cleaning quad-toothed patients' mouths for now!"

Travis smiled and laughed again. "Hey, you want to get out of here?"

"And go where?"

"I wanted to stop by the library and see if they have any books about helping people get through a suicide. It's not something that we've studied a lot, and maybe it will help this guy and me."

C.J. frowned. "And here I thought you were going to take me someplace romantic."

"Sorry, babe. Work before pleasure."

"Fine," C.J. said, "but you are definitely buying me a hot chocolate after the library!"

"Deal."

CHAPTER 9

"When I was drinking, I thought everything was a sign to keep drinking.
A bad day, a good day, a sale on my favorite booze, whatever!
But when my Higher Power kept putting people in my life to help me
stop drinking, I was completely clueless to the signs.
My sponsor says that's the definition of denial!"

Jack P., celebrating six months of sobriety for the fifth time at the
Fight for Your Life A.A. meeting

Paul was wandering through the grocery store, doing his best to remember the items that seemed most important to stockpile. His cart contained a few cans of pears, a loaf of bread, and a large bottle of aspirin. He was looking at the alcohol content in various brands of mouthwash when someone slapped his shoulder brusquely.

"Why it's Paul Durkin," the deep voice boomed.

Paul looked up into the warm, crooked smile of James "Jimmy" Curtis. He looked just as polished and substantial as Paul had remembered him. There were many mysteries surrounding the man, like how old he was, how he had wound up in Deerfield, and if he was Black, Hawaiian, Hispanic, or some combination of them all. It was undeniable that he was big in all senses of the word. Paul guessed that he was somewhere close to seven-feet tall and somewhere near four hundred pounds of well-maintained muscle, though he was never seen in the local gyms, nor did he join in on conversations with other recovering muscle-heads around town. Paul guessed he was around fifty years old, but he appeared ageless, and Jimmy was always well dressed, often in bright colors that seemed more appropriate in some Caribbean setting than in the cold, drab Northeastern climate. Today he wore his signature vest, coral-colored, over a crisp white shirt that bulged over his upper body and thick biceps. He had dark dress pants and two-toned shoes, which appeared recently shined. The outfit was topped by a turquoise-colored Trilby hat pulled down over Jimmy's closely cropped hair.

"And here I heard you had run off and joined the circus!" Jimmy said cordially as he put his hand out. "How are you, Paul? It's good to see you."

Paul returned the mouthwash bottle he was holding to the shelf before reaching over and receiving Jimmy's hand.

"Hey, hello, Jimmy. It's good to see you again. I'm fine, doing just fine. How about you?"

Jimmy laughed and gave Paul's hand a firm shake. "Fine," he said. "Yes, fine about covers it for me too. I forget who it was that told me what FINE really stands for—fucked up, insecure, neurotic, and emotional. So, yes, I'm just fine as well!"

Paul laughed, trying to remember the last time he saw Jimmy. It might have been that night when a group of guys showed up at Paul's house, to coax him back into A.A. meetings. Jimmy was there that night, and Paul had promised he would see them all soon in the meetings.

Jimmy continued smiling—no judgment or reproach that Paul could sense. "So, if you're not traveling the country under the Big Top, what have you been up to?"

Paul wondered if Jimmy knew about the D.U.I. and was being coy, but that seemed contrary to Jimmy's straight-forward nature. It seemed self-centered to Paul that he would think everyone was talking about him, and he wasn't sure if he chose to believe that because he didn't want to imagine that he may have been forgotten completely by folks he considered friends.

"Well," Paul said, "I've been around, you know."

"Yeah, me too. I'm around a lot of the same old rooms that we used to run in together. There's always extra seats in there, too, if you're looking."

"I know," Paul said. He thought about how often the two of them had gone on Twelve Step Calls, informal interventions for people who had called the A.A. hotline asking for help. Paul always followed Jimmy's expansive frame into those houses or hospital rooms, knowing his friend shone with strong, healing energy Paul feared he would never tap into.

He fought back an urge to throw his arms around Jimmy and let the dam finally break, to surrender completely, to cry out about how it's all turned to shit and that if he could just get a foothold somewhere, get some traction and start himself moving forward things might level off. He wanted to believe that it really wasn't too late. He could leave the mouthwash on the shelf and the cart in the aisle and go directly to St. Michael's Detox Unit with Jimmy. Jimmy would drive him there if he asked. Right to the detox. Right now. No more waiting. No more resisting. No more hurting.

The moment passed.

"Well, maybe I'll take you up on that. I'm in the process of getting myself back on track."

Jimmy hesitated, "My number hasn't changed." He looked over to the counter where Paul had placed the bottle. "You know they make alcohol-free mouthwashes now." He squeezed Paul's shoulder tightly before moving on down the aisle.

Paul watched him go, considered the mouthwash for a moment, and walked toward the check-out lines. He passed an eye-catching display of birdseed and put a bag in his cart. When he reached the registers, Paul picked up two packs of spearmint gum and put them on top of the bird-seed bag.

By the time he reached his car, his hands had started shaking, and the familiar wrenching of muscles in his stomach kicked in. He opened the trunk and put the groceries in, grabbing one of the packs of gum and putting it in his pocket. In the car, he instinctively grabbed the bottle from the console. He removed the cap and took what he considered a small sip, telling himself that this controlled drinking was a sign of great progress. He capped the bottle and returned it to the console but kept his trembling hand on it, reassuring his body that the toxic medicine it craved was there, well within reach.

Paul looked around and noticed how many stores had been built in the last few years. Deerfield was about twenty miles to the east of Moheneck Falls. The town had embraced a large-scale exodus of people from New York City and other metropolitan areas after the September 11 attacks. Deerfield had always drawn "city folks" in the summer because of the horse racing track and the promise of escape from the urban hustle and bustle. Tourist attractions in the area drew massive seasonal crowds, but after 9/11, people came for different reasons, and they didn't just pack up and leave after Labor Day.

According to local businesspeople, especially those in real estate sales, this migration was not a bad thing. The economy of Deerfield shot up, as did the population and need for more housing. Land prices soared, along with average monthly rental costs. Suddenly the area, which had traditionally been described as "quaint" and "rustic," was now termed "desirable" and "suburban." Paul remembered an interview on the local news with Tony Pelligrino and a few other members of the Deerfield City Council. The terms "growth and prosperity" were used repeatedly to describe the demolition and adjustments being made for the wealthy tenderfeet. One of the biggest areas of change Paul noticed was that the newer residents demanded more purchase options, and they also had more money to spend. Soon new stores, restaurants, and businesses opened everywhere to accommodate affluent tastes.

Several large chain retail stores were built just East of Deerfield's historic downtown, closer to the four-lane highway that took people from Albany to Canada. Paul found it ironic that the stores, which promised diversity and new, upscale products, all offered the same things. There were two giant box hardware stores directly across the street from each other. There were two well-known book retailers on opposite sides of the road. He normally avoided the mega-retail store nearby, on account of the large crowds and the people he might see there. The trove of restaurants in the area offered similar selections and were mostly fast-food joints. In the very recent past, a trendy national health store had opened in the nearby mall, and a competing trendy national health store was being built close to the plaza Paul sat in. He remembered the limited inventory of his grandfather's small store and how certain people were seen as "fussy" or "spoiled" if they complained about the brand of flour or coffee or toilet paper that the store carried. Most customers were grateful and satisfied to use what was there.

Some nearby communities rallied against this expansion and tried to protect their farmland and forests from being exploited for profit. They promoted privately run, family businesses and went to town meetings, wrote letters, and protested on local sidewalks about the importance of supporting Main Street stores and preserving large tracts of land as open spaces and hiking trails. Some towns were successful in keeping the large retailers away, at least for a while. But as Paul looked around at the growing commercial sprawl, he couldn't help but think it was only a matter of time until it metastasized outwards. Tony P. and his associates on the City Council would keep pushing relentlessly and powerfully for any idea that involved making money, even if it meant shutting down private shops, polluting the environment, and filling only the pockets of those whose pockets were already overflowing.

Paul realized as he looked around that most of these businesses and newer plazas were built upon the large farms, fields, and woodlands which once encompassed this area. He remembered going to a friend's dairy farm as a child and seeing his first black bear with two cubs following close behind her in a field near the tree line. He tried to guess where that farm was and thought it might have been close to the Mega-Wash, a giant car-wash and lube/oil store nearby. It was hard to place any old landmarks without the trees. The rapid expansion of this land had caused much of the wildlife to move on. The animals who had stayed and tried to adapt to the changes could often be seen dead on the side of the road or termed "nuisances" by business owners plagued by animals that had found dumpsters could make for good feeding spots. Paul liked to think that if he was one of the animals, he would raid the dumpsters as well and maybe piss on a few of the buildings while he was at it.

He saw a police cruiser pull into the parking lot and park a few spots away. Roscoe Montgomery stepped out. Paul thought about starting his car and pulling away, but Roscoe was already looking at him, waving a friendly hand. He was trapped. Paul pulled out the pack of gum and put a piece in his mouth, chewing rapidly. He turned the key in the ignition enough to power his window down as Roscoe approached.

"Well, good day, Officer Montgomery," Paul said, trying to keep his voice calm and friendly.

"Yes," Roscoe responded, "it is a good day. The sun is shining, and I think we've finally got most of the county back on the power grid after that storm. How did you make out?"

"Oh, I was fine," Paul said, "I never lost power at the house. The driveway was a bit slippery, but Garth and Mark donated some salt and that melted things off pretty quickly."

"I heard about that," Roscoe said. "I ran into those boys down at Dalby's, and they told me they had checked in on you." Roscoe looked down at Paul and then continued in the same, conversational tone, "If you ask me, they milked that storm for every last cent they could, but the roads do look good now, so who am I to argue?"

Paul wasn't surprised to hear that Roscoe had gotten a report on him from the two men at Dalby's. It was one of those family-run businesses in Moheneck Falls that had survived the changes of the last decade. Most of the customers were locals, and it was a hive of blue-collar activity and rumors about anything happening around town. Some of the counters and shelving units in the store had been sold by Paul's grandmother to Curtis Dalby when he bought the former saloon and transformed it into a general store and eat in diner early in the mid-1960's.

Paul could picture Garth and Mark sitting in a booth at Dalby's, while their plow truck sat idling outside. He imagined they had quite a laugh talking about rousing Paul from his house to move his car. Paul could almost hear some of the words that were used: "drunk," "lush," "rummy." These thoughts didn't make him angry. He rarely got angry; instead, he preferred to remember something he was told many years ago: "What others say about you really is none of your business." He had not understood the saying at the time, but like most of the wise things he learned back then, it proved true over time.

Roscoe had one hand on the open window of Paul's car, looking down at him. Paul chewed on the gum and wondered if this was truly a chance encounter. He knew that Roscoe had a clever and subtle way of mixing business and pleasure, which had made him particularly effective at the job.

Roscoe spoke, "I'm on my way home from my shift. Thought I'd stop by the store first and bring home some dinner for Stephanie." Stephanie was Roscoe's girlfriend, and it was common knowledge that the two had frequent fights and arguments that usually ended up with Stephanie moving back in with her mother for a few weeks or longer. Eventually, the couple always seemed to reunite, though they had avoided marriage for many years.

"Well," Paul said, "I'm sure she'll like that. The deli is having a sale on submarine sandwiches today. We always loved the roast beef subs from here." The word "we" stung him unexpectedly.

"Thanks," Roscoe began, "but she's not eating meat now. All of a sudden, she's a vegetarian, or a vegan, or some kind of bullshit. I'm not sure what any of it means. I just know that it has made dining together a lot more challenging."

Paul looked at Roscoe with a smile but said nothing.

Roscoe shook his head slightly and said, "So, are you alright? Is everything working out?"

"Yeah," Paul said, feeling more confident that Roscoe was not here to arrest him. "I called St. Michael's and went in for an evaluation. I know it's time to pull myself together. Thanks again for, well, you know, looking out..." he trailed off.

"We go back a long way, Paul. Let's get that cup of coffee soon."

"I'd like that," Paul said.

Roscoe patted his hand on the open car door and said, "Well, off to find some non-animal product to shove down the throat. Be good!"

"You too," Paul said and watched the officer walk toward the store entrance. He reached down to start the car and felt immense and sudden sadness at not having three roast beef subs to bring home and share.

CHAPTER 10

"It often surprises people that someone in recovery can relapse after years of sobriety and having what appears to be a great life. But this only supports the fact that addiction is a chronic, progressive, incurable disease that can come out of remission without continued treatment and vigilance to signs and symptoms of the illness. This is especially true during times of great stress, loss, or life-changing events."

Jennifer Bishop, Nursing Program Term Paper,
"Addiction: A Misunderstood Disease"

Wednesday afternoons were always less hectic in the clinic, and normally Travis looked forward to the long staff meetings because they gave him a chance to relax and listen to the employees talk about patients and issues that needed to be addressed. Today he was presenting a patient for the first time. He had awakened several times during the night, his heart pounding and his belly churning with dread. He wondered if these moments of intense, uncontrollable fear would ever leave him. They started during the awful years in high school when he stayed up night after night, dreading the thought of going into school to face the inevitable taunts, jeers, and bullying.

So far, his day at St. Michael's had gone smoothly. One patient, Deborah, showed up to the clinic drunk. Travis knew her well and had been in many groups where she talked convincingly about the benefits of being sober. All the clinicians agreed that Deborah was progressing in her sobriety, and she was scheduled to finish treatment in a week or two. Travis was shocked that she had relapsed and shown up to the clinic in such a state. He did his best not to show a reaction.

After Carla reported smelling alcohol, Travis and Bill gave Deborah a breathalyzer and recommended she go directly to the St. Michael's Detoxification Unit. Although she denied drinking and put-up resistance at first, it became clear to Deborah that the truth was coming out one way or another. Unlike other patients who came to the clinic after drinking, Deborah wasn't hostile or resentful. She shed no tears while Bill and Travis talked to her. In fact, she appeared relieved. Travis sat with Deborah while she waited for a taxi to bring her to the detox. She made only one phone call to a neighbor, whom she asked to feed her cat. When Travis walked outside with her, she took his hand in both of hers and softly shook it.

"Bless your heart," she said before climbing quietly into the back seat of the taxi.

Travis had reviewed Paul's chart several times, rehearsing how he would present the information at the meeting. His biggest fear was that the other staff members would start to ask questions about the case that he was not able to answer. He had seen this happen before during these meetings when a counselor would present a case and make a recommendation that seemed logical, but one question about past treatment attempts, or legal problems, or insurance coverage could derail the clinician's entire plan. Travis had seen other counselors from the clinic with far more experience than he become flustered and unsure of themselves when this occurred. Dr. Romanski was particularly skilled at grilling counselors and seemed to enjoy watching them struggle to find answers.

Alexander Romanski was the son of Russian immigrants. He was younger, thinner and more fashionable than any of the other doctors Travis had met. He had long brown hair, tight sideburns, and an oval face with piercing blue-grey eyes above his thin nose and lips. Travis rarely saw him smile but did pick up on "the gay look" he sometimes got from Romanski. Travis had heard about this look from C.J., who insisted that many gay men have a look they will give to other men to determine their sexuality. Travis doubted this at first, knowing that C.J. had some questionable theories about people, not the least of which was that most men were gay and in denial of the fact. But once C.J. had described the look and planted the seed in his mind, Travis couldn't deny the truth in it, at least as Romanski was concerned. He had also heard several of the St. Michael's staff describe the doctor as gay, which reinforced his suspicions.

Romanski was a new hire at St. Michael's and the youngest Medical Director of Outpatient Substance Abuse Clinics they had ever hired. His job required meeting with patients and prescribing medications for mental health issues or to help ease cravings during early recovery. He traveled to all eight of the St. Michael's outpatient clinics each week and wrote hundreds of prescriptions along the way. Travis knew from his classes and from listening to conversations at St. Michael's that this protocol of prescribing medications directly from the outpatient clinics was a new practice. According to Bill, this change in procedure caused the former medical director to quit abruptly after twenty-five years of loyal service to the hospital. St. Michael's was not the only substance abuse clinic to change their prescribing regulations, and it made sense to Travis that treating all issues in one place was more logical and convenient than referring a patient to several places. But he did wonder if the countless patients Romanski met with received a reasonable amount of time or care. The question and its ethical implications bothered him, as did the fact that Travis had avoided writing about these concerns in his weekly log and never brought them up during class.

The majority of Travis' interactions with the doctor left him feeling uncomfortable and intimidated. It was unclear if Romanski's arrogance and unhappiness with his new position were forced or truly genuine, but he certainly enjoyed putting other clinicians on the spot and subjecting them to constant condescension and sarcasm. Travis had also heard patients talking about either hatred or fear of the doctor, and he could understand why.

But Alexander Romanski knew about addiction. Despite his superior attitude and lack of bedside manner, he always knew what questions to ask, and his diagnosis, medical advice, and prescriptions were always clinically accurate. Travis supposed that was enough for St. Michael's to continue employing him.

The doctor sat in his regular position at the head of a large conference table in the staff room. He was looking over a medical chart from the large stack that sat on the table awaiting his signature. He didn't raise his head when Travis entered and made no attempt to acknowledge his presence in the room. Travis said a cheery "Hello!" to everyone who was present but did not expect to hear anything in return. The three other clinicians that were at the table also had their heads down, looking at the charts they had brought in for review.

Bill said, "Hello, Travis," and looked back down at his charts. Travis sat down next to him, putting as much distance as he could between himself and the doctor.

Mandy Summers was the older of the two women at the table. She took great pains to maintain her manicured nails, always wore a full face of makeup, and made sure her eyebrows were plucked in thin, crisp lines. Travis noticed that her outfits were all name brand and that she rarely repeated an outfit. Mandy preferred heels to flats, which accentuated her height and elevated her above most of the patients she encountered at St. Michael's. She transferred to the clinic after working in the hospital's administrative offices for fourteen years. She was a Patient Care Advocate who worked exclusively with health insurance companies. Mandy had a social work background, and the rumor was that she never worked directly with patients until coming to the clinic. Travis also heard she was currently dating a married man and that she'd been divorced at some point in the past. He guessed that Mandy was in her late forties or early fifties, and she kept herself in good shape by going to a private gym in Deerfield regularly. He wondered if the makeup melted from her face when she exercised or if she kept the workouts easy enough so as not to break a sweat.

Mandy constantly questioned the length of treatment patients were receiving. The other staff members, including Dr. Romanski, generally agreed that longer treatment resulted in better outcomes. Yet, Mandy constantly argued against these lengthy time periods, and Travis heard her frequently ask people in her groups, "Don't you think you've been here long enough?"

A mantra from Travis' H.C.C. class was to "Avoid office politics and staff drama at all times!" Travis frequently heard Carla and other clinicians complaining about Mandy, predicting that she had shopped her resume out to the health insurance companies and that she was just doing her time until she could land a desk job again. Travis sat in on Mandy's Relapse Prevention Group every Thursday night, and Carla repeatedly tried to get him to complain about how horrible the experience was, but Travis refused, choosing instead to redirect the conversation as he'd been taught.

A few weeks ago, Travis had walked into Mandy's office and found her in a discussion with Jennifer Bishop, the newest counselor at the clinic, about Andre, a patient who was scheduled to complete treatment.

"He just moved out of the halfway house, and he's living in an apartment near the shelter with a few other guys who completed our program," Jennifer explained, her voice beginning to rise. "They got him a part-time job washing dishes, and at this point, I want to put Andre in your group for another month or so until he finds a balance between work, living at the apartment, and getting himself to N.A. Meetings."

"Look," Mandy answered, "this guy has you wrapped around his little finger. He's been in treatment for over a year now. Just because he has Medicaid and you want to keep the government handouts coming to him, isn't enough of an explanation for continuing his care. If he was on any other insurance plan, one that we're not all paying for, he would have been out of here and back to work months ago." Mandy inspected chips in her nail polish as she explained this.

"No," Jennifer countered, her face flushing, "Andre would have been dead or in jail if he'd left treatment a few months ago! Yes, he's been here for thirteen months, but he used marijuana and drank at about six-months into his sobriety. Don't you remember that?"

From the expression on her face, Travis guessed that Mandy didn't.

"I thought his drug of choice was heroin?" Mandy asked.

"Yes, opioids," Jennifer said, "but he knew enough not to go back to using them. He came to us and was completely honest about the pot and booze. Don't you remember the meeting with the halfway house staff about this? That was when we put him on a contract, and he started going to more outpatient groups here. The halfway house also insisted he step up outside meeting attendance and work with a sponsor. That was when I really saw a change in Andre's motivation and attitude toward treatment and being sober. He really started to do some work. And I know he's afraid of slipping backward now, of losing everything he's worked for. I'm just asking for another few weeks while he adjusts because I really believe that he's sincere about getting better."

"Hmmm," Mandy responded, "well, that makes one of us. I guess it just upsets me, as a citizen and a taxpayer, when I see these people hanging around and hiding out here for months and years rather than reintegrating themselves into the real world."

"How about as a counselor?" Jennifer asked.

"What? What do you mean?" Mandy asked.

"I'm trying to understand your feelings as a citizen and taxpayer but, personally, I try to make all work-related decisions clinical, based on what's best for the patient. I'm pretty sure we both took an oath to do that when we began this job."

Mandy opened her mouth to speak, but Jennifer spoke first: "So I'm going to recommend that Andre begin attending your group on Thursday nights. If you have any questions or issues with that, you can bring them up with Matt."

Jennifer stormed past Travis and out of the office. Later that day, Carla asked Travis to dish out the blow-by-blow details of the encounter but, once again, he dodged the question.

Jennifer was hired at St. Michael's because of her nursing certification. She said at lunch one day that after dating a man in college who was addicted to heroin, she gravitated to substance abuse counseling. She had long, black hair that she often wore down, and Travis guessed that she was in her late twenties. Unlike Mandy, she rarely wore make-up to work, he'd never seen her in heels, and her outfits were professional but loose-fitting and entirely unrevealing.

She appeared skillful as a nurse, but other clinicians, especially Mandy, criticized her for being too soft on the patients and not enforcing the rules of the clinic enough. Patients often used Jennifer's office phone or asked for her permission to leave treatment early and go back to the half-way house or homeless shelter, claiming some vague ailment. She was usually kind and cordial but also seemed constantly overwhelmed, and Travis noticed she was often the last counselor left in her office each night. Her outburst with Mandy surprised Travis, and he noticed that the two women hadn't spoken since.

The meeting normally started at 3:00 p.m. At 3:14, Matthew "Matt" Denton, the Clinical Program Director, walked into the room with Adolfo Rojas behind him. Matt reminded Travis of the stereotypes of frazzled newsroom editors he had seen in movies growing up. He was slightly shorter and slimmer than Bill, but his weight management system hinged on the thirty cigarettes he smoked each day rather than on regular physical activity. Matt always wore wrinkled button-down shirts, with mismatched wrinkled ties and semi-creased pants that hung off his frame. His black hair was a tangled mop upon his head. It changed so regularly, Travis could not identify the style Matt preferred. To complete his look, he had large, outdated glasses that he frequently removed and tried unsuccessfully to clean with his tie.

"I don't care if she calls the governor, or the president, or anyone else!" Matt said to Adolfo. "If that kid doesn't meet the criteria for inpatient treatment, we are not going to recommend inpatient treatment for him! The kid has been to rehab three times already and always leaves after the first two days. Jesus! Maybe the mom should go to rehab. She might have a better chance of staying!"

Matt sat in one of the two remaining seats nearest to Romanski. He said, "Hi, Doc," and turned to the rest of the table. "Sorry we're late. We had a bit of a crisis."

The doctor glanced up from his charting and gave Matt a nod. There was a cup sitting next to the doctor, which Travis assumed was filled with the green tea that Romanski made a production of preparing before these meetings.

Adolfo Rojas walked around the table and took the last remaining seat, directly across from Matt. Travis thought that Adolfo was Latino because of his dark skin and his accent. It was hard to guess how old Adolfo was. He was not a tall man, and he appeared to be in good shape. He kept his hair cut short and wore long sleeve shirts. Travis assumed this was to cover the ornate tattoos on his hands and neck that bordered his cuffs and collars. It was common knowledge among the staff that Adolfo had an ugly past with his own addiction, but Travis never asked for the details. All he knew for sure was that Adolfo had gone through this program some years earlier and that he was employed as an Associate Counselor, a position which paid the least and required minimal training.

"Alright," Matt said. "What do we have on the agenda today? Please tell me we have some easy recommendations! No new headaches right now, please!" Matt smiled as he said this, but Travis clearly saw the clinicians shuffling their charts around, looking for the patients they felt would be the simplest to diagnose and recommend for treatment.

"I see that Travis brought us a case today," Mandy remarked, smiling. "Why don't we hear from the intern to get things started?"

"Yes, yes," Bill said, "I'm sure the intern would love to get it over with!"

Travis didn't mind being called "the intern," and he knew that this teasing would help to lighten the mood a bit. He really wanted to get it over with, so he smiled back at everyone and said, "Sure, I can start if you would like me to."

"Yeah," replied Matt. "I forgot that you picked up the slack after the storm the other day and did the evaluation on that last-minute guy who came in. Good job stepping up like that. I'm sure you're learning how important flexibility is around here, Travis!"

Travis had certainly learned how to be flexible since he started at St. Michael's, starting with Matt, his assigned Clinical Supervisor. Matt was supposed to be Travis' "go to," the counselor who could help with any of his questions at least once a week. In fact, Matt was barely available aside from a wave and a passing, "You doing okay?" Professor Dunleavy and his classmates assured Travis it was common to have busy and distracted supervisors. During this second semester, Travis had learned to seek out other clinicians for mentorship.

"Alright," Matt said, "Tell us what you've got."

"Well," Travis started, his voice quavering and his heart beating faster. "The patient is a sixty-year-old male who is currently separated from his wife. He states he was a self-referral for evaluation after he was pulled over for D.U.I. He has not yet been charged but has a court case pending."

"Don't you just love when they consider that a self-referral?" Mandy commented.

"More like saving your ass or looking good for the lawyer," said Bill.

"Did he sign a release for his lawyer?" Matt asked.

Travis flipped through the chart to the section that held releases of confidentiality.

"Yes," Travis answered. "His lawyer is John Lawrence. I haven't contacted him yet, but I thought we would do that once we made the recommendation."

"Absolutely right," said Matt. "Look at how much you're learning here! Well, if John Lawrence took him on, there must be some hope. John doesn't usually mess around with the real knuckleheads. What else can you tell us about this guy?"

"This was the patient's second charge for a D.U.I. He stated that the first occurred over twenty years ago. He also reported going through treatment at that time and maintaining his sobriety up until five years ago, when he lost his only child. He reported that the death was a suicide."

Travis paused briefly, waiting for a question, but the room was silent. It seemed too quiet. Dr. Romanski was swirling the teabag slowly around in his cup. Bill and Matt seemed particularly interested in Travis' description, and he started to wonder if he had done something horribly wrong. The lightness and levity that had been there moments before were completely gone.

Travis looked down and continued, "So after the death or the suicide…"

"Was the kid a boy or girl?" asked Matt.

Travis became flustered. "Well, that part was a bit strange. He never made it clear, and honestly, I was afraid to ask. I mean, he was getting pretty upset talking about it all, and he was guarded about many other things as well. I didn't push it. I know that we will be recommending treatment, so, I figured I could find out more later. Does it matter? I mean, it seems clear that the suicide was what caused him to…"

"How old was the kid?" Matt interrupted.

"Nineteen," Travis answered and decided to keep talking until he either finished or someone jumped in again with another question. "After the suicide, the patient stated, he retired from his job, but I got the feeling that he may have been let go. As I said, he was guarded about some information. He reported his last contact with the A.A. community and his sober supports was back then, and he said that it was at that point when everything really went…"

"Oh, Jesus," Matt said, putting both hands to his head.

"What is this patient's name?" asked Bill.

"Give us the name. What's the name?" Matt looked up from the desk with his hands cradling his chin.

"His name is Paul, Paul Durkin. Why? What's going on here?"

Matt took a long, deep breath and said, "Beautiful. Just beautiful." He stood up. "Can you give me that chart, please? I need to make a call. Keep going with the meeting and let me know if you have any new patients that you need me for." He took the chart from Travis and left the room.

Travis looked around. Everyone but Jennifer looked shocked. Even Dr. Romanski stopped stirring his tea.

"Can somebody tell me what just happened?" Jennifer asked.

"Yes, please," added Travis. "Do you all know Paul or something? Has he been here before?"

Bill laughed at this and looked at Travis. "Know him? Yes, we all know him. He hired most of us, and Matt took over his job as director of this place when he left five years ago."

"Holy shit!" Travis said without thinking.

CHAPTER 11

"Rarely have we seen a person fail who has thoroughly followed our path.
Those who do not recover are people who cannot or will not completely
give themselves to this simple program, usually men and women who are
constitutionally incapable of being honest with themselves."

Alcoholics Anonymous (The Big Book), Chapter Five

It was 3:52 p.m. when Paul's phone rang. Paul set down his glass of vodka with the fresh ice cubes in it and picked up the receiver.

"Hello, Matt. I thought I might be hearing from you today."

"Jesus, Paul!" Matt said. "Why didn't you call me about this? If I had known it was you, I would have made a point to see you myself."

"I'm not sure it would have been okay for you to meet with me."

"Good point, but I'm sorry I wasn't there. Alright, we need to figure out what to do with you."

"I don't suppose not recommending treatment is an option?" Paul asked.

"Is that what you would do—Look, before we get into that, let's back up. How are you doing? I thought about calling you a few times. Checking in, you know, but—Damn, Paul! This is awkward for me, but I hope you know that…" his voice faltered, "I hope you know that I'm here if you need me. And I will help you in any way I can."

Paul looked at the large glass of vodka on the counter with the melting ice cubes and thought about his next words carefully.

"I'm hanging in there," he said. "You know, this was a good wake-up call, and I'm kind of relieved that it happened. It was time to make some changes. I'm planning on getting back in touch with some of my sober guys from the program. Honestly, I don't know what I would recommend for me if I was you, Matt. I suppose I'd check on what my insurance benefits will cover first, though."

"Yeah, well, that's always a consideration, huh? And if you're still on the benefits they gave you from this place, I'm guessing your coverage stinks!"

There was a long pause before either man spoke.

"Well," Matt finally said, "the only outpatient group we have that fits your situation is the Relapse Prevention Group. It meets tomorrow night, and Mandy is running it now. Travis, the intern you met, has also been sitting in there. The format hasn't changed much since you were here. Most of the group has been sober before, so, this is considered a "tune-up." It's really all I got unless we go for a higher level of care and get you in here three to five days each week for the day rehab program."

"Pretend you are talking to my insurance company right now," Paul said, "and tell me how you're going to justify that recommendation given the information from my assessment."

"Well," Matt responded, "you're not the insurance company. And for all I know, you're sitting there right now with a fresh glass of booze in front of you. I'm willing to recommend coming to only one group a week as long as you also meet with a counselor over here every week as well. If we see any indication that you haven't stopped drinking, we recommend a restart and it's straight to detox. I'm okay with helping you out here, Paul, but I'm not going to get jerked around on this."

Paul looked at the drink on the counter and then lowered his head toward the floor before responding. "Relapse Prevention Group it is. I thought Mandy worked with health insurance. When did she join the front lines with you?"

"Trust me," Matt replied, "it wasn't my idea. The higher-ups needed to move her out of there, and we were the lucky recipients. I gotta say, though, her charts and paperwork are the best in the clinic!"

"Well," Paul laughed, "there's always that, then."

"Yup," Matt agreed. "There is always that. I've only got one counselor here who doesn't know you from the old days. Her name is Jennifer. She's younger, but she's good. I'm thinking of putting you with her. I'll have to check, though, because I think she may have a full caseload of patients as it is."

"What about the kid? The intern?" Paul asked. "Shouldn't he be working with someone at this point? Why not give him a shot with me?"

Matt laughed. When Paul stayed silent, Matt asked. "Really? You want to work with the intern?"

"It makes sense, Matt. He already built a therapeutic alliance with me during the assessment, and he doesn't know me from my former role within the organization. No conflicts of interest there."

"You really are full of shit," Matt said and laughed again. "But okay, fine. The kid should have been assigned to a patient by now anyway, so… what the hell. But I'm going to be the official counselor following your treatment. And I'm going to be checking every note and every group attendance sheet to make sure you're not just dope-fiending your way through this. Deal?"

"Deal," said Paul and turned to look out the window into the backyard. The cardinal had landed on the old feeder, waiting expectantly.

"Are you really doing alright?" Matt asked, a softer tone in his voice.

Paul gazed out at the bird, who appeared to be staring back at him, it's head slightly cocked to one side, perhaps wondering something about the man in the house. In that moment, the light from the sun became brilliantly bright, perhaps coming out from behind a cloud, and the reflection from the snow created a scene that looked perfectly staged somehow and far too radiant and inviting to be real. It reminded Paul of a movie scene in which the location of some buried treasure is finally revealed.

"I'm okay, Matt," Paul said. And then, "I'm just fine. I'll be there tomorrow night. Let Trevor know he's doing a fine job, and I look forward to working with him."

"It's Travis," Matt corrected him.

After hanging up the phone, Paul looked around the kitchen and found the bag of birdseed he bought. He was relieved that the call with Matt was over and that a referral to detox was mentioned. That was just the threat he needed to stop drinking completely. His plan was simple. He needed to taper his body from the alcohol slowly, decreasing his drinking over the next few days. Paul knew that withdrawal from alcohol could be serious, even deadly if not done correctly, but if he started reducing the booze today, he could be sober by the weekend—Monday at the latest. He picked up the glass from the counter and took a sip, careful not to drink too much or too fast. Everything was under control.

He retrieved the large boots from near the front door and brought them into the kitchen. The phone rang again, and he hesitated before picking it up.

"No fucking way!" John said, not waiting for Paul to say hello. "Look who's answering the phone now!" Paul stiffened and started to talk.

"Hi, John. I was going to call you. I went—"

"Let me talk, Paul. You're paying me, remember?" Paul wasn't sure they had worked out the details of payment yet, but he was happy to stay quiet for now.

"So, this morning I get a call from Judge O'Malley. And he doesn't usually call me, Paul. You should send Sheriff Montgomery a nice arrangement of flowers, or at least a meat platter, old friend, because if he hadn't called O'Malley the night you got picked up, I think you'd be neck high in Shit's Creek right now, with the fucking gators circling everywhere, capiche?"

Paul thought about telling John that Roscoe's girlfriend didn't eat meat and opened his mouth to speak, but John began again.

"Anyway, I think he's trying to give you a break because of what you did for his niece when she went to your place after the drug arrest. Of course, he would never say that; he never could say that. So, don't bring it up. As a matter of fact, forget I ever said it. O'Malley wants you to complete whatever treatment St. Michael's recommends for you. Did you call and set that up yet?"

"Yes," Paul said. "I went yesterday and just heard from them. They want me to go to a group tomorrow night, and I'll be meeting with a counselor for one-on-one sessions."

"That's it?" He asked, "That's all they want you to do?"

"Well, yes, I mean as long as I show up and they don't think I'm drinking..."

"Oh, that's beautiful," John interrupted, "you're hitting the jackpot, Paul. I can't believe you're getting off this easy. You're a lucky guy."

Paul bristled at this and considered correcting John about just how lucky he'd been. He could feel the vodka bottle staring at him.

"You will need to get a breathalyzer installed in your car if you want to keep driving," he continued "O'Malley was clear on that. It's a newer D.W.I. law that's required by the state. You've got to bring your car to a garage that's on a list of certified installers. They've got a few places in Deerfield that can do it. Carl Cook's place is on the list. You know Cookie, don't you?"

"Oh, I'm sure Cookie would love to do the job!" Paul interjected. "Half the town will know I've got the thing in my car. He loves to talk as much as the snowplow boys do!"

"No offense here, Paul, but I think more than half the town already knows you've been living in the land of the fucked for a while, my friend. They'll probably feel safer knowing you've got the goddamned thing in your car. What I'm trying to tell you is that you're not holding any good cards here, buddy, and I'm pulling some aces out of my ass for you. This is as good as it's going to get."

"So, I'll have to blow in this breathalyzer every time I go some-where?" Paul asked.

"Jesus!" John yelled. "Yes, Paul! Every time you get behind the wheel to drive your car, you'll need to be sober. Is that really your big-gest concern?"

Paul walked over to the glass of vodka. The ice had melted com-pletely, and the drink looked clear and pure and wet.

"Well, it sounds like an offer I can't refuse. How much am I paying you, anyway?"

"Not enough!" John answered. "Just get your ass to treatment, have the machine installed in your car, and for fuck's sake, stop drinking."

When Paul put the phone in the receiver, he took a slow, measured sip from the glass. He then put on his boots, grabbed the bag of birdseed he'd bought, and walked out into his backyard toward the feeders.

The sun glared off the snow and was at once intense and blinding. He shielded his eyes until everything came back into focus. He didn't come back here much anymore. During the past few summers, he would mow the grass when it became too tall to ignore, often so drunk that he was unable to cut straight rows. To call his yard a "lawn" would have been gen-erous. Lawn indicated an area that was tended to and cared for.

One of Paul's first jobs growing up had been mowing lawns for neighbors, and lawnmowing had provided a time when his mind could relax and stay present, a suburban meditation and centering exercise, though he wouldn't learn about those terms until much later. These days he probably would have been labeled with attention deficit disorder and been put on medication. But the disorder did not exist back then, and he was simply dubbed "hyper" or "fidgety." The adults who had to deal with his excess energy and hard time focusing sent him outside or gave him chores to complete. "Get out of my hair," his mother often said as she swept him outdoors, the expectation being that he would not return until dusk fell.

Paul would wander around, stopping in at his grandparents' store where there was always some type of work to be done. If his grandmother was there, she might ask him to mind things while she used the bathroom or checked the laundry at the big house next door. He remembered that many of the customers who came in would ask to be "written down," which meant that Paul had to grab the notebook under the counter with the names of people receiving a line of credit. There were many. Others brought vegetables from their gardens or fresh eggs to barter, and his grandparents always complied. "It's amazing we keep the lights on," his grandmother often said, "with the amount of money we don't make." When his grandfather was there, he would respond, "Maybe, but we'll never go hungry, my love!" Theirs was a true, committed love. Or at least Paul remembered it that way.

He noticed the top bar and decaying net of an old soccer goal sticking up through the snow near the shed in the yard.

"That's it, Sean, just kick it past me into the goal!"

"I haven't gotten one in yet. Can we go inside soon?"

"Just a few more, buddy. Come on, give it a good kick."

"Why are you forcing him? He doesn't enjoy it, and he didn't ask for any of those gifts. It's his birthday, Paul. I mean, Jesus!" Charlotte's eyes could be both pleading and fiery at once.

"Sean needs to try to fit in. Do you have any idea how cruel kids can be?"

"That's just it, Paul. Sean doesn't fit in anywhere, and I think he spends most of his time pretending he's someone that he's not. I don't want him to have to pretend in his own home. But we need to be together on this. I just don't know how else to tell you this. It seems like we keep coming back to it again and again. I'm surprised you don't see it. With all your education and experience…you counsel people who don't fit in every day. Why are you in denial about your own son?"

Paul didn't remember his response, only that it erupted from a place deep within him that he thought had gone permanently dormant once the drinking stopped. Yet the cruel molten magma had returned—never really left at all. It was hidden under the thinnest crust of sober functioning, waiting for the right amount of pain and rage and thirst. The unquenchable thirst.

At the birdfeeders now, he wanted only to turn around, to go back into the house, and drink. He should have brought the vodka out here. He went to the largest feeder first, which was made mostly of wood and was mounted on a long pole. He tried to lift the roof where the seed could be poured in, but it remained stubbornly stuck in place. He set the bag of seed down by his feet and used both hands to release it. Using his full weight as leverage, he stretched and strained to free it. One more jerk and the roof snapped in half, splintering out and across the yard.

"Shit!" he heard himself yell at no one. The roof was beyond repair, so, he moved on to the next feeder, which hung from a metal pole nearby. It was cylindrical and made entirely of plastic. The top was meant to screw off, and seed poured down the tube. He took the feeder down, removed the top, and steadied it between his legs while he ripped a small hole in the bag of birdseed and began slowly pouring. The seed slid down the tube and drained out the bottom thanks to three jagged holes gnawed by industrious squirrels. Nearly all the fresh birdseed spilled into the snow.

"Great," Paul said. "That's just great."

He attempted to pour the remaining seed from the broken feeder back into the birdseed bag, but the hole he had made in the bag was too small. In frustration, he shook the feeder violently, liberating its remaining contents onto a patch of ice.

Paul hurled the broken plastic cylinder toward the buried soccer net in the back of the yard and yelled, "FUCK! JUST FUCK IT! FUCK!"

He stopped himself, took a few deep breaths, and picked up the bag of birdseed. He made his way to three other feeders, all deteriorated and broken. He left them hanging there, empty and useless, before returning to the roofless wooden feeder. He raised the birdseed bag high into the air and filled the feeder until the seed was spilling out and over the top of the walls. He headed back toward the door. The birdseed bag slung over his shoulder. It was time for that drink.

CHAPTER 12

"No, ma'am, I'm not saying you have to go to this specific rehab facility.
I'm saying that this is the only rehab that ValTec will cover. You're free to
pursue treatment wherever you like. You'll just have to pay for it..."

Mandy Summers, ValTec Insurance Customer Care Specialist

"I hate this group," Mandy told Travis.

Travis knew that already because she said it every week. She also regularly reminded Travis that she didn't enjoy running any groups or meeting with patients for individual sessions. It didn't take long for Travis to realize why he frequently heard the nickname "Mandy the Monster," whispered under the breath of patients and a few staff members at the clinic to describe her overall attitude and demeanor. It fit nicely.

Mandy frequently and lovingly described her former work as a case manager for ValTec, the managed care company that contracted with St. Michael's. She told Travis that ValTec executives loved her work, and they insisted it was nothing personal when the company discontinued their contract with St. Michael's a few years ago. It was purely an economic decision, she said, the business of doing business.

"Say no first, then let them fight for it" was the mantra ValTec caseworkers followed when it came to approving any treatment for addiction.

Mandy was very good at that. She earned her monstrous reputation by denying requests for treatment from the counselors she now worked with, regardless of the situation or severity. She may not have helped clinicians to effectively treat patients, but she saved the insurance company plenty of money. Unfortunately, new company policies were implemented at ValTec at the same time they parted ways with St. Michael's, which required all case managers to have a master's degree. Mandy no longer met the company's minimum requirements for her job.

She was left behind as others in her office advanced on the profitable ladder of ValTec's growing hierarchy. St. Michael's had promised everyone in Mandy's office that if the hospital lost the insurance contract, they would do their best to relocate employees somewhere within the hospital's system. Nobody thought she would accept a position as a counselor, but it was the only offer she got. Thus, "Mandy the Monster" joined the same counselors and patients she had once worked so vigorously against.

Travis would never say she was incompetent. Her bachelor's degree in social welfare, earned from a prestigious and respected college, prepped her for a first job with single mothers at a domestic violence center, Bill had told Travis. It sounded like an extremely challenging position with a high-risk population, but he hesitated to ask her about it directly, in the same way he hesitated to ask her about anything from her past. Travis was also impressed that Mandy was the only counselor who never complained about the paperwork and documentation required of the counselors. Unlike all the other clinicians, she never appeared to struggle with writing or signing documents within the required timeframe. "Great paperwork skills," Travis remembered Carla saying once during his first few weeks of internship. "You should definitely review her charts to see how things are supposed to be done." As she handed Travis several of Mandy's charts to review, she added, "But you might want to pay attention to how the other counselors actually talk to people."

Every counselor in the clinic was contracted to run two nine-ty-minute groups each week. For Mandy, the groups were on Monday and Thursday nights. The week started with the Woman's Group, which Travis sat in on occasionally. The group essentially ran itself, though Mandy sometimes offered a question or topic. Most of the patients had been in treatment for several months and had formed a bond with each other. They needed little guidance or prompting to talk, and Mandy spent much of the group time filling out her paperwork and writing notes on each group member, so that when the group ended, she could leave as soon as possible.

Thursday nights were more challenging. The Relapse Prevention Group, in theory, included patients who had been doing well in treat-ment, had attained a good deal of knowledge about staying sober and were invested in keeping themselves that way. But this wasn't currently the case. Most of the members of Relapse Prevention had been put there simply because the number of patients in the group had dropped. The treatment team made referrals to the group just to keep it running, not because indi-viduals qualified for the intended purpose. Several other groups at the clinic had waiting lists of patients who hoped to work with their favorite counselor. Nobody requested to be in Mandy's groups.

Mandy had run the Relapse Prevention group since she was hired at the clinic and initially attempted to let the group just run itself like the Women's Group did. But this technique didn't work. Many of the patients had no desire to share anything about themselves or their lives and pre-ferred sitting in silence. Mandy resorted to the use of thick, photocopied workbooks for the group, some of which would take three or four weeks to complete. The subjects of these weekly worksheets varied from "Better Communication Skills" to "Healthier Eating." Mandy also incorporated videos and movies about addiction into the group. She found she could divide each movie screening into two weeks, and with the exception of the movie title, the notes she wrote for these groups were nearly identical.

Today she had announced her hatred for the group when Travis walked into the copy room, and he was unsure how to respond, so he said nothing.

"I'm photocopying a new workbook that we'll start tonight," she said. "It's about how to save money and balance a checkbook. We haven't done this one before, but I saved it from a training I did many years ago and thought we could give it a try."

"Cool," Travis said. He wanted to say, "Are you kidding me?" The last thing most of these patients were worried about was balancing a checkbook. Many of them didn't have enough money for their next meal.

"I found an activity that I thought you might be interested in for a group in the future," Travis said, holding up a packet of papers.

"Oh yeah?" she asked. "About what?"

"Well," Travis began, "it explains how we all make assumptions about people without really knowing them. So, at the beginning of the group, each person writes down something they have achieved that they do not think anyone would guess about them. This can be something as simple as winning the Third Grade Spelling Bee at your school, or getting an award for community service, or anything else as long as it's something positive, you know, an accomplishment of some kind."

Mandy laughed sarcastically and said, "Well, that would be impossible for most of these losers. Some of them haven't accomplished a damn thing besides becoming addicts!"

Travis felt the heat rising up through his body and coming into his face, but he continued, "Well, that's why you let them know it can be something small, anything at all that they are proud of. The activity is centered on acknowledging that we all have strengths and on boosting a person's self-esteem."

Mandy continued to stand silently at the copier as it churned out packets on responsible finances.

"So, once they have thought of something, everyone writes the thing down, but they don't put their names on it. It's completely anonymous. The group facilitator collects all the papers and reads each one out loud. The patients try to guess who wrote down each clue. I found the activity in a great book about group skills at the college bookstore yesterday. A few students in my class have mentioned doing similar things at their internship settings. They said it's really amazing what you find out about people, and it also helps with cohesion and bringing group members closer together by getting to know each other as more than just sick people with substance abuse problems."

"Yes," Mandy said, "because we want them to be one big, happy family, right? When they go out after group, they'll have more to bond over at the bar."

Travis pressed on.

"Well," he continued, "it's just an idea. Some other students in my class have been more involved in running groups, and some have even done it alone, so I want you to know that I'll do whatever you want me to do."

Travis lowered the papers to his side and waited a minute for a reply. When none came, he said:

"I'll go make sure the room is set up. See you in there."

The group was held in one of the smaller rooms at the clinic. Travis liked the intimacy of the space and the wall of windows that looked out onto the street. Travis always felt uneasy in dark places or in spaces lit only by light bulbs. Fluorescents were the worst. He hated the incessant buzzing that the long, industrial bulbs made. The sound reminded him of the disgusting machine that hung above the deck in his grandparent's backyard. They called it a "bug zapper," and it operated by luring insects in with the eerie glow from a fluorescent light and then killing them—electric chair style. A constant buzz came from the contraption at night, broken only by the percussive "zap" of a frying bug that had been drawn toward the fatal light.

Travis would have avoided the noise of the machine and stayed out of the backyard completely had it not been for his grandparents' pool. Growing up, his parents talked about putting in a pool at their house, but it never happened. Instead, Travis and his mother spent endless hours at his grandparents' pool, a decrepit above-ground model that threatened to fall inward or outward every summer. An ancient pump that Travis' grandfather constantly battled kept the water relatively clear. Many times, he and his mother would show up for a swim on a blazing hot summer day only to find his grandfather by the pool, toolbox in hand, swearing to God and the saints about why his wife made him keep the "blasted, damned eyesore" in the backyard to begin with.

On those days, Travis and his mother stayed inside the house, which was not a bad alternative to the pool because it had central air conditioning (another promised convenience which never quite materialized). Travis, his mother, and his grandmother reclined in the cool house and laughed about his grandfather's refusal to ask for assistance with the pool pump. The idea of buying a new pump was never mentioned. Travis' grandmother insisted she had married a jack of all trades and master of none. She told stories of the projects and repairs he took on around the house over the years, some nearly ending their marriage and others nearly ending his life.

Travis never knew for sure what his grandfather's full-time job had been. He had the impression it related to blueprints or engineering work for a local contracting company. This seemed a waste of time and talent for the man who Travis considered capable of fixing anything. On some days, if the weather was not too hot, and his grandfather was not spewing too many expletives, Travis worked with him.

"Come on out and get a lesson at the school of hard knocks," his grandfather beckoned.

Unlike Travis' father, who seemed to detest any kind of domestic project, his grandfather enjoyed the process of learning how a thing worked, understanding why it had broken, and devising a plan for repairs. He explained each step in this process to Travis, who felt tremendous pride in cooperating to restore old, broken things to working order.

"Nowadays, everybody wants to throw things out and get a new one!" His grandfather often complained. "That will only get us bigger piles of trash and a bunch of dummies who don't know which end of the screwdriver to use! When we used to build things in America, they were built with pride, and they were built to last. Now we import it all to save ourselves a nickel in the short term just to lose jobs, skills, and quality in the long run. Greedy, greedy bastards, all of them..."

Travis heard this speech, or something similar about the sad state of the world, many times when working with his grandfather. It only bothered Travis when these grievances were voiced in front of others at the local hardware store. Almost every repair they made involved a trip to search out a bolt or clamp or a small piece of tubing. And each time the elusive bit was found, Travis saw the look of disappointment and despair when his grandfather discovered the thing was not made in the U.S.A. Travis did his best to avoid eye contact with the pimple-faced kids working at the hardware store's register, who took an ear full from his grandfather about changes they should make in the store's inventory and suppliers.

The bug zapper had been made in Milwaukee. Although Travis secretly wished the horrid thing would break, it held strong for many years. His grandfather eventually replaced it with a newer device that promised to be more efficient at attracting and terminating insects and backyard invaders. This newer technology involved a propane tank, fire, and some type of chemical gas. Shortly after the instrument was placed on the back deck, the pool finally caved in, and this time his grandfather made no effort to repair it. By then, his grandmother was insisting that they sell the house and move south.

"It's time for us to slow the hell down and finally enjoy our retired lives," she said.

Within six months of the move to a luxurious condo adjacent to a world-class golf course, his grandfather suffered a massive heart attack while sitting in a lawn chair near the complex's pristine inground pool. Travis was told he died instantly.

Before they moved, his grandfather had given Travis an ancient toolbox, handed down for at least two generations. Sometimes he opened the box and removed the forged iron hammer just to feel the weight of the thing in his hand.

Travis shut off the fluorescent lights in the group room and raised the shades on the windows. Night groups ran from 5:30 p.m. to 7:00 p.m. Even though the February days were getting longer, he knew the lights would have to come back on at some point, or the group would be sitting in the dark. At college, Professor Dunleavy advised students to create an environment in group rooms and counseling offices that helped people to feel at ease. The students recently spent almost an entire class discussing the importance of the therapeutic environment. Travis noticed that many counselors at St. Michael's didn't seem to care at all about how the clinic's appearance lent itself to effective treatment.

Bill's office seemed especially bland and sterile to Travis.

"Is there a reason you don't bring more stuff in here?" He once asked Bill.

"Why?" Bill asked. "Do you want to decorate it for me?"

"No," Travis had replied, "but why don't you bring some things in to make it feel more like your space, you know?"

"It is my space," Bill said, "my name is on that little plate beside the door. That means it's my office."

They hadn't spoken about it since.

Jennifer's office seemed to be the most personalized, so Travis asked her why she went to the trouble when it seemed like nobody else had.

"I want to feel at home and safe in here," she said. "So, I brought in items and pictures that soothe me. Hopefully, the patients can relax in here, too." She pointed to a framed picture of the beach with the poem *Footprints* printed below the image.

"I love the beach, and the ocean, so I really like that picture. The poem is kind of corny, but I think it's good for our patients to notice. Many of them may not realize that they are being carried right now."

"Why don't you have any pictures of yourself or your family?" Travis asked.

"That's where I draw the line," she declared. "I really don't want some of these patients to know anything more about me than they have to. I need to be a part of some decisions they don't like, talking to probation, or parole, or making Child Protective Services reports, so, it doesn't feel safe to have them know too much personal information about me."

He wanted to ask Jennifer and all the counselors more about their private lives and how they managed to keep the boundaries between work and home strong but feared it would seem too invasive. He already felt embarrassed for snooping around each counselor online. Travis was not surprised to find that Jennifer had a presence on most of the sites, though she had appropriate blocks set up for most of her information. Matt had a Facebook page, but he last posted two years ago, and no pictures were available. Bill had no presence in the online world, and Travis could find nothing about him in any of the search engines. Travis was too embarrassed to mention this snooping to the professor or his classmates, but he did ask C.J. if he should stop.

"People are fucking psychos," C.J. explained, "and I have a right to know if that guy pouring my coffee chopped up some people a few years ago or is posting some weird shit about putting anthrax in everyone's food."

"But don't you feel like you're peeping into their private lives sometimes?" Travis asked.

"The internet is not private!" C.J. insisted. "And this is not peeping. It's investigating."

After meeting with Paul, Travis had punched his name into the search bar and found several stories in the local paper. The most recent was about his D.W.I.—no new information there. A series of older stories referencing his ideas about the problem of addiction in America. There were four separate articles, each highlighting a drug of abuse, an interview with someone local who suffered from abusing the drug, and information about where and how to get help. Paul was mentioned or quoted in all four articles, always as the Director of St. Michael's Rehab.

There was an older article about an award issued to Paul from the Town Council for "selfless and humanitarian efforts around Deerfield." The article highlighted Paul's success in setting up monthly meetings and improved communication between St. Michael's, the newly renovated homeless shelter, the food bank, the mental health clinic, and several other agencies in the area.

"Paul Durkin has been pushing for these agencies to work collectively to improve access to treatment services in the area. He believes the best path to progress is for area providers to sit around a table, face to face, and talk about how their services can help, as well as to identify the challenges and roadblocks that stop sick people from receiving the care they need. Durkin, who is a native to the area, said Deerfield has more than enough financial resources to effectively treat mental health issues and a growing addiction problem, but often people remain in denial about these things, preferring to ignore the problems in their backyard."

In the picture that accompanied the article, there was a small, thin man in an expensive suit shaking a much younger-looking Paul's hand while he presented a wooden plaque. Travis also noticed an attractive, dark-haired woman standing just behind Paul, her hands in mid-clap.

There were no traces of Paul on any of the social media sites, but Travis found a Facebook site for Shawna Durkin that intrigued him. The profile picture showed only the back of a young woman's head as she stared into an unfinished painting on an easel. The woman, presumably Shawna, had thick, chestnut hair, and Travis thought the unfinished scene on the canvas looked like a town square, with people gathered around a juggler. The only other pictures Travis could access without friending Shawna were of dresses, ball gowns, and an array of negligees. He could not determine for sure the date of the last activity on the page. Instead, he clicked down the rabbit holes of a few of Shawna's listed friends, all of them were women who appeared to be in their mid to late twenties now. He spent some time scrolling through the conversations of these friends where he could and saw no trace of comments left by or about Shawna. He tried his luck at plugging the name into a few search engines but found nothing there either. He knew this poking around was in direct violation of the boundaries and ethical behaviors Professor Dunleavy repeated so often, but he justified the behavior by convincing himself that his intentions were only to better understand his new patient.

As he rearranged the chairs into a circle, Travis wondered how Matt's office had looked when Paul was the director. He wondered how different the clinic might have been back then. Travis picked up two coffee-stained Styrofoam cups from the floor and recalled asking Bill why the clinic's group rooms were left so messy and disorganized each day, why the patients weren't required to clean up the place before they left.

"They used to have to clean up after their damn selves," Bill told him. "Back in those days, if they left this place in half the God-damn mess that they leave it in now, we would have spent the next day busting asses and sitting in one large group talking about the importance of respecting yourself and others. Those things were just as important to maintaining sobriety as not using. And no one would have gotten out of that group for any reason until we thought they really got the message. I remember spending the whole day in that room a few times, having what we called a "come to

Jesus" meeting, where people got confronted on all types of dope fiending behavior. And after those marathon groups, if one thing was out of place in a group room the next day, we'd do it all over again. I suppose if you used those tactics nowadays, you'd have everyone from little Johnny's mom to the rotten insurance companies screaming bloody murder about how abusive it is. *Not fucking evidence-based practice enough.* But I'll tell you this, we changed some lives and started some good recovery out of here back then. Because those things matter."

"What about now?" Travis asked. "Do you think more people are relapsing now because treatment has gotten softer?"

"It hasn't gotten any softer," Bill smirked, "at least not in my groups."

Every day Travis picked up cups, pencils, and pieces of paper left behind on the floor or scattered in chairs. On Thursdays, after the Art Therapy Group, he might find glue bottles, sequins, or piles of glitter in the corners or under chairs that had not been moved. On any given day, patients took magazines from the waiting room and brought them into group rooms during lunchtime. Travis gathered those too and discovered glamour shots of prominent TV stars embellished with cartoonish sex organs, crayoned glasses, mustaches, or swastika tattoos. He asked permission to discard the more offensive works, at first. Over time, though, Travis decided what was acceptable.

The white boards in each of the group rooms also fell victim to acts of vandalism or unsolicited pictures and messages from patients. Travis erased the words "I don't know much, but a fifty-pound groundhog is a fucking big groundhog" from the board tonight. He found it interesting that Jennifer and Bill were the only two counselors who ever used the boards. Bill was more likely to write a single word, like "denial," and then ask the patients to give him words that described it. Jennifer went deeper, and sometimes ran out of room from writing so much about codependency, enabling behaviors, or the process of grief. Travis couldn't remember

Mandy ever writing anything on the white board, but each Thursday he dutifully wiped it clean anyway.

After cleaning the board, he made sure the room's clock matched the time on his phone. It was common for patients to set the time on the clocks ahead five or ten minutes so that the group facilitator would let them out early. Travis didn't notice this in his first month at the clinic; he thought that counselors were simply releasing the patients at different times. One day when patients were wandering the halls of the clinic twenty minutes before the group should have ended Matt walked out of his office and grumbled, "What the hell is this? Are you all here to wander the halls or to get sober?" As the patients scattered, finding places to hide from him, Matt came to Travis and told him he would be the "official timekeeper" for the clinic. Since then, Travis kept a vigilant eye on every wall clock.

He set up a seat for himself directly across from the white board, putting down his clipboard and a sign-in sheet for the patients on the chair to designate his spot. Normally, counselors sat near the board and Travis followed a strategy suggested by Professor Dunleavy, which was to sit directly across from the counselor.

"*Remember that we are vastly outnumbered in these group rooms. If you sit right next to the counselor, it tends to make the imbalance more noticeable. Try to sit about halfway around the circle to balance things out.*"

Although the suggestion seemed sound to Travis, he doubted that any group involving Mandy would ever feel balanced. Travis looked up at the clock and wondered if his first official patient would show up tonight.

CHAPTER 13

"There is something indescribable but deeply therapeutic
about the group process. You're going to experience groups that
are run very well and others that go completely off the rails.
But never underestimate the power of the group dynamic."

Professor Dunleavey, lecture to first semester interns

Paul was in the parking lot. He blew breath into his hand and took a quick sniff. He couldn't smell the vodka, but he knew this meant little because his sense of smell for the stuff was probably gone by now. He unwrapped a stick of gum and chewed purposefully. The trusted water bottle was there in the car console, waiting. Just ninety minutes away. By his estimation, Paul was making some progress in tapering himself off the booze. His last drink was about an hour ago, and the one before that had been two or three hours earlier. Slow and steady. He already noticed feeling slightly better, not at constant war with his guts. Before coming to the clinic, he ate some scrambled eggs, toast, and bacon. Just a week ago, that amount of food would never have stayed in his system. Paul checked his face in the mirror, unsure of what he might do to make the image that stared back any better. He stepped out of the car and into the crisp, bracing evening air.

It was comforting to see Carla behind the receptionist's desk.

"Don't they ever let you go home?" He asked, smiling.

"And miss seeing you come here for your first group? No way, sweetie! Glad you made it tonight. Now we need to set you up with an individual appointment to meet with Travis, so let's see what works for you."

They scheduled his appointment, and Carla directed Paul toward the Relapse Prevention Group room. He liked her and wished she had been around when he was on the other side of the desk.

Paul hadn't paid much attention to what the clinic looked like when he came for the assessment, but he noticed now that the linoleum floor was badly in need of a good waxing and buffing. He also noted scuff marks on the walls; floor moldings peeled from the wall trapped ugly webs of lint, dirt, and accumulated debris. He wondered when the last state inspection of the place was done and how many citations Matt was issued because of these issues.

"And who the fuck am I to judge," he thought, "Mr. Detail-oriented, right? Well, there were certainly a few important details in my own life that I missed."

Paul walked into the group room, bathed in the late afternoon glow of twilight. He saw the young intern sitting in a chair near the old whiteboard on a wall adjacent to the windows. What the hell was his name? Trevor? Tim? Something with a T in it for sure. There was another young man sitting near the intern. He was dark-skinned with long dreadlocks that curled out from under a wool cap and nearly reached his shoulders. He appeared stocky and possibly overweight, but that might have been an illusion created by the double "XL" grey hoodie and loose jeans stuffed into untied work boots. It looked to Paul like everything about him just needed to be tightened up. A thin, young woman in much smaller, badly ripped jeans and black high-top canvas sneakers sat underneath one of the windows. She had a tattered-looking army jacket pulled tightly around her.

She looked familiar. Maybe she'd been in treatment before or was friends with Sean?

The woman was staring at her phone, and her legs were pulled up onto the chair. She looked very young and very raw. Paul assumed she was barely sober and most likely nervous, although she just looked pissed off at the moment. The fading light streamed around her silhouette, giving a foggy and ghostlike impression. She looked at him briefly but gave no indication of recognition or emotion before going back to whatever she had been doing on the phone. Paul heard the intern's voice then.

"Hi, Paul. It's good to see you again. I'm glad you made it tonight." Travis smiled as he walked over to shake Paul's hand.

Paul was going to call him Trevor but decided at the last minute to play it safe.

"Well, you didn't think you were going to get rid of me that easy, did you? I just made an appointment to meet with you next Tuesday at one o'clock." Paul smiled but checked his breathing and his distance from the young man. He hoped the kid didn't have the sensitivity for smelling alcohol that other counselors acquired over time and practice with people showing up half in the bag. Paul used to be able to spot someone who had been drinking or using drugs almost immediately. He wondered if he could have fooled himself now.

"Well," Travis said. "I'll look forward to seeing you on Tuesday, then! This is Andre," Travis said, turning to include the young man in on their conversation. "Andre just started the group last week."

"Hey," Andre said and waved a hand in Paul's direction. "Nice to meet you."

"You too," Paul replied.

"And this is Angela," Travis continued, motioning to the girl near the windows. "It's her first night in our group as well, so you two are the newbies, I suppose!"

Paul gave a tentative nod and wave of his hand to Angela, who looked up briefly again and said, "Hey Otis," before diving back into her phone.

Paul felt the heat rise through his body and up through his neck as his mind flashed back to the Stumble Inn. Sitting at a beer-soaked table, a cell phone, standing in a crowd of young people and staring at that wretched tattoo.

He opened his mouth briefly but couldn't think of a response. He sat across from Angela where he could look out the windows and, hopefully, distance himself from everyone in the room as much as possible. Just as he sat down, two men entered the room, laughing loudly.

"So, then she tells me that her boyfriend is this guy that I went to school with—a real douchebag, right? And I ask her if everyone still calls him "Shit Stain" like we did in high school. Oh, the people in line get a kick out of that one, and she just stares back at me from the cash register all dumb bitch-like!"

The two men laughed again, then took notice of Angela and Paul.

"Hey, look at this," the man continued, "we got some fresh meat!" Paul looked at them both flatly. Angela concentrated on her screen.

"Wow," he said, elbowing his friend, "they must have already heard what a picnic it is in here!"

"Hey," the man pressed on, pointing toward Andre, "and you came back for more? That is shocking!"

Andre gave a small smile and nodded toward the men.

Travis said, "Angela and Paul, this is Larry and Peter."

The man who was talking at first, Peter, winked at Angela and then walked toward Paul, extending his hand.

"Nice to meet you. Call me Pete. And don't worry, it ain't as bad as it looks in here."

He had a firm grip and a rough, calloused palm. Paul noticed the black, steel-toed boots they wore. They looked like blue-collar bookends, both wearing faded jeans and thick, industrial work jackets. The only difference Paul saw was that Larry's boots were caked in drywall dust, and he was wearing a t-shirt, while Pete wore a dark blue button-down shirt. Although he couldn't see it, Paul imagined a name patch stamped on one side of the shirt and a pocket on the other for Pete's cigarettes or his chewing tobacco.

"No," the man named Larry added, "it's fucking worse!"

Both men laughed and sat down on the same side of the room as Paul, continuing their discussion and laughter. Paul noticed Angela had twisted her body sideways in the chair and had disappeared further into the army coat.

A woman walked quietly into the room and toward the windows. She took off her coat and draped it over a chair, then sat next to Angela. She set down what looked like a cup of coffee on the floor near her seat. She leaned over and addressed Angela in a low tone while placing a gentle hand on the girl's thin wrist. Paul thought Angela might smack it off or lash out and bite the hand, but to his surprise, she slowly put her legs down on the floor and her phone away in some unseen inner pocket of the army jacket. The older woman then looked around the room and gave a slight wave to Travis.

"Hello, Diane. Good to see you." Travis said. "This is Paul. He's new to the group." Diane looked up at Paul, appeared to do a quick inventory of him from head to foot, and nodded.

"Hi," Paul said and tried to give his best-disarming smile.

He felt his face flush and his heart start to race. It seemed suddenly surreal that he was sitting in this room, in this place again. It was all too familiar and too strange at the same time. What had he gotten himself into?

"I see you've met Angela," Travis continued, "And I think you've met Andre, Larry and Pete."

Andre and Diane exchanged greetings, and Diane looked at the other two men, who were now talking about "fucking income taxes." They made no effort to acknowledge her, so she picked up her coffee cup and took a sip.

Outside beverages had never been allowed in the clinic in the past. Paul guessed that there was vodka in it, and he planned to bring in his own clever cocktail to the next group. He looked up at the clock in the room. 5:34. Another indication that things had changed since he was working here. Groups were expected to start on time back then. It seemed to matter somehow.

Mandy entered the room, switching on the fluorescent lights that flickered and buzzed to life. They cast a weird, institutional glow around the space and over everyone's faces. She was carrying a stack of papers and a cup filled with pencils.

"Why are we sitting in the dark?" she asked, giving a quick, disapproving glance at Travis.

"Oh, here we go!" Larry said.

"Better behave," Pete added, "the teacher is here. And it looks like she brought another pop quiz!"

Mandy sat in a chair near the whiteboard and placed the papers and pencils on the floor next to her. She looked around the room, taking in everyone, and then seemed a bit shaken when she saw Paul. He wondered if Matt told her he would be starting. Or maybe he told her, but she just forgot.

She gave him a tight smile and said, "Good evening, everyone."

Diane, Paul, and Travis mumbled, "Good evening," back to her. Paul was squinting in this bright glow of the room.

"So," she began, "I thought we would talk about the importance of finances tonight. Once you are sober and trying to get back things in your life, it's important to handle your money in a responsible way, right? So, I brought in these packets, and..."

Paul was shocked at how weathered Mandy seemed. In Paul's memory, this was "The Monster," the woman feared by so many counselors. The indestructible one. He assumed Mandy treasured and protected her status as the person responsible for holding others' feet to the fire. He remembered a few of their heated conversations about treatment denials for patients whom Paul felt clearly needed the help. He never feared or resented her, though. In truth, he respected the ferocity and commitment with which she did her job. He wondered if she felt as ashamed as he did about the position they now found themselves in.

"Let me just remind you," she said, "to shut off your phones and other devices during the group. Only one person should talk at a time so that we can give that person our entire attention. Please, raise your hand if you have something you would like to contribute, but we're not here to tell each other what to do. If you want to give someone feedback, concentrate on talking about yourself and your experiences, not on giving advice or criticizing others."

"Yeah, you'll take care of that part, right?" said Larry.

Mandy ignored him as the door opened again. Two men entered the room. One looked quite young, engulfed in a strong odor of marijuana and cigarette smoke. The other man was older and Paul knew him, but like Angela, he couldn't immediately remember from where. The room clock read 5:49, well beyond the time when patients should have been allowed to enter a group. This was a rule that was strictly enforced in the past not only because these disruptions halted the group's dynamics and flow but also because such lateness was contagious among the patients.

"Well," Mandy said, "welcome to those of you just getting here. Why don't you both find a seat, and we'll get started with our check-ins for the week."

Paul guessed that this new leniency around tardiness came from a lack of consistent enforcement of the rules by counselors or the need to generate as much revenue as possible from the patients. He decided it was probably both.

Pete fanned his hand in front of his face dramatically as the younger man walked past him. "Dude," he said, "there's some smog in your wake! Couldn't you wait until after group this week to smoke up?"

No one else commented on the smell or the glassy-eyed condition of the young man. He found a seat in the farthest corner away from Mandy and disappeared almost entirely into the bright green oversized ski jacket he wore once he sat down. He was also wearing a black wool ski cap pulled down tight and over his eyes. Yet another old rule about not hiding under hats and taking your coat off before you entered groups seemed irrelevant now. Paul wondered how long it would be until the young man fell asleep or left to use the restroom (after signing in on the attendance sheet) and never returned. Paul guessed he was on probation and that his P.O. was one of those types with all bark and no bite.

The older man sat one chair away from Paul and muttered in Mandy's direction, "Sorry about being late. The bus line was all screwed up tonight."

Paul recalled pressuring the city and the bus company to incorporate St. Michael's as a regular stop on their Deerfield route. He regularly attended city council meetings and brought the issue up for two years until they finally agreed, under duress, to include a stop at the clinic. He could hear the high pitch of the attorney's voice, the one the bus company had hired back then, complaining to the city council, "These drunks, junkies, and crackheads Mr. Durkin so vehemently defends will cause nothing but trouble for the upstanding bus patrons and for the town as a whole!"

For the first time, Paul witnessed John Lawrence, only a few months sober at the time and barely holding onto his law degree, unleash a torrent of legal holy hell. He smote the squeaky attorney from the bus line.

Afterward, John told Paul, "I don't think they're used to hearing from a junkie as loud and well-spoken as me."

"Mostly just loud," Paul told him.

"Okay," Mandy said, "Since we have some new faces in here, why don't we go around and introduce ourselves? I want you to include your first name, what your drug or drugs of choice were, and how long you've been sober. You can also tell us a bit about what brought you to St. Michael's. Would one of our group members who's been here for a while like to start?"

There was an awkward silence, then Pete spoke up.

"Yeah, what the hell, I'll start it off. I'm Pete, and I'm here because I really fucking like to smoke pot."

Larry and the young man who had come in late burst out in laughter.

"Yeah," Pete continued, "I don't really see anything wrong with that, you know, but my fucking job does. So, after I got all this training to drive the forklift, they decided to give me a piss test, and presto! Here I am in treatment. Is that enough, or do you want more? Cause I can just talk all group long if you want me to!"

Mandy asked, "How long has it been since you've used drugs or alcohol, Peter?"

"You know," Pete said, "you ask me that every week. And I ain't even here for drinking! But I guess I haven't smoked pot in, oh, I don't know, three weeks, maybe?"

"Okay," Mandy responded, "Three weeks it is." A few more chuckles circulated around the room, but Pete didn't look at anyone or say anything more.

"Who would like to go next?"

Diane jumped in.

"Sure. I'll go next. I'm Diane and it turns out I'm an alcoholic. I haven't had a drink now in 146 days. I came here after receiving my first D.U.I. last summer. Most of you know this, but I had fallen asleep on the beach.

On the beach, of all places! Anyway, when the lifeguards woke me up, they asked how I planned to get home, and when I told them that I was fine to drive, they called the police. As soon as I left the parking lot, the police were there to meet me."

"That is such bullshit!" Pete yelled.

"It's got to be entrapment or some shit like that," added Larry.

"Well, whatever it is, or whatever it was, it got me sober. It hasn't been easy, but I'm glad that I'm not drinking now. I'm also glad that my counselor here, Jennifer, convinced me to go to some Alcoholics Anonymous meetings. Attending those meetings was really helpful. I don't think I would have made it this far without the support I found at A.A. and my treatment here."

"Hey," Pete blurted out, looking at Mandy, "Bill is my counselor, and he's up my ass to go to those meetings too. Can they make us go to those places?"

"I would hope that anyone who wound up here would be willing to go to places where you might meet other alcoholics and addicts," Mandy responded.

"But I'm not a fucking alcoholic or an addict!" Pete spat back.

"Me neither!" Larry yelled, "but you guys just love to throw those labels around. That's how they get paid, you know, by labeling us as these sick, hopeless drug addicts!"

Larry was looking around the room for someone new to join his rant. Pete was the only one shaking his head in agreement, so the two of them settled back in their chairs.

"Way to light off that powder keg, Monster," Paul thought. He glanced at the kid, the intern, and wondered if Mandy would let him into the discussion at any point or if she told him to sit there looking helpless and mute the whole time.

"Let me bring us back on topic," Mandy said. "Thank you, Diane, and good job on your current sobriety. Would you like to share anything else?"

"Only that I am a "fucking alcoholic," as it was so pleasantly stated, and that I, for one, am glad that I realized it when I did. I remember detesting the phrase alcoholic and not wanting to be labeled, but I'm grateful that I recognized my issues for what they were. I'm just thankful not to be at that level of ignorant denial anymore." With this, Diane cast a glance at Pete and Larry, who seemed to have lost interest.

"Thank you, Diane. Very good points." Mandy said. "Now, who would like to go next?"

Andre put his hand up, and Mandy motioned for him to start.

"I'm Andre," he began. "Addict, alcoholic, and basically a trash can for anything that will get me high. I only started this group last week, but I've been coming around St. Michaels for the last year or so."

"That's classic!" Pete said! "Keeping you around for as long as the money train will hold out, right? I'd have my fucking lawyer down here if they made me come to this place that long!"

"Yeah, well, I'm trying to avoid lawyers at this point," Andre said. And even though I've been coming here for a year, I've only been totally clean for the last five months. I started living at the halfway house right after going through detox and rehab last year. I wanted to kick the dope, but for some reason, my dumb ass thought it could keep using other stuff. All the counselors at the house and over here kept telling me I had 'reservations' to keep using and come to find out they were right! So after putting myself in places I shouldn't have been and not doing nearly half of what they were telling me I should do around here, I ended up relapsing on booze and pot. I never went back to the heroin, though. After a few days drunk and feeling sorry for myself, I got up the courage to go back to the director of the house and ask them if I could have my stuff. I couldn't believe she actually offered to take me back in! After all the shit I pulled and the grief I gave her, the other staff and residents, and she's sitting there asking me if I'm ready to get to work now! It was unbelievable."

"Sounds like Amazing Grace," Diane said. "Isn't it wonderful how kind people can be when you need it the most? My sponsor keeps telling me that's part of the program, to give grace, acceptance, and love away in order to keep it for ourselves. It's just such a foreign concept to me."

"Not to me," Larry chimed in, elbowing Pete, "I've tried to give my love away to lots of bitches, but they just don't seem to want it!"

Pete and Larry howled together, and Diane mumbled, "I guess they don't know what they're missing."

"Yes, Ma'am," Andre replied, ignoring the two buffoons, "I'm not used to people giving me a second chance or believing in me at all. After they let me come back into treatment, I really started to get my act together. My sponsor told me I was only doing 'half measures' up until then, but I guess knowing people cared about me and that they really wanted to see me get clean helped somehow."

"So, are you living back at the halfway house now, or did they send you to the homeless shelter?" the man next to Paul asked.

"Well, they took me back into the house for a while after that, but a few weeks ago, I moved into an apartment program where I'm living with some other guys who went through the house and are working pretty strong programs. That's when I switched from coming to treatment every day to doing these night groups."

"Well, good for you," Mandy said. "It is nice that we live in a society that gives people so many chances, isn't it? Now, who should we hear from next?"

"Larry," Larry said quickly. "I'm here because of a D.U.I. Well, it's my second one, really, but the first one was plead down to a driving while ability impaired, not driving while intoxicated, so I'm really not sure how that will count against me in court."

"How long ago was the first one?" said the older man sitting next to Paul.

"It was almost five years ago. I had to do some kind of six-week class back then, and I had a conditional license, but this time they pulled my license completely. It really sucked."

"It's all just a way to make money," Pete added, "a huge fucking money maker, that's all it is."

He pointed toward Andre, "They'd love to keep us here as long as that poor son of a bitch! No offense, pal, but I bet they're thrilled you started using again! Now they can keep on collecting!"

"Who exactly is 'they,'" Andre asked, but Pete had settled back in his chair and seemed not to hear the question.

There was a short, awkward silence.

"So that's why I'm here. To make things look good for the court, and to get my license back."

"And when was the last time you drank or used drugs?" Mandy asked.

"Um, right. I don't really keep track, but I got my last charge about five months ago, so I guess five months. Yeah, five months."

"Okay," Mandy said, a smirk on her face. "Who's next?"

The man next to Paul put his hand up, and Mandy said, "Sure, Jack, go on."

"Yup," he began, "I'm Jack, and I'm an alcoholic. Been drinking and smoking and doing just about anything else that they'll put in front of me for too many years to count. I'm back again this time because I broke into my house, which I'm told is the ex-wife's house now, to get back a television that I bought. I shouldn't have done it, but it's a damn nice TV!"

Paul looked at Jack, waiting for further explanation, wanting to prompt him forward in the story. Paul expected to hear Mandy's voice at any minute, questioning how this led to treatment, but Jack turned to Paul, a grin on his face, and said:

"Of course, it was three in the morning when I decided to go get the TV and I was in a drunken blackout at the time." Jack let the impact of the statement settle in before he continued.

Paul couldn't remember when it was, but he knew that he met this man before and possibly even counseled him. He wondered if Jack's memory about their history was any better than his own.

"One minute I remember doing shots with my buddies down at the Stumble Inn, and when I came to, I was standing in the living room of my house trying to unscrew the television from the wall. I suppose I should have just left at that point once I figured out where I was and what the hell I was doing, but like I said, this was a really nice TV."

A smile formed on Paul's face as he remembered how often he had heard similar stories over the years. Stories that he took for granted, thinking that everyone had experienced similar problems and situations in their lifetimes. Maybe he knew Jack from the Stumble Inn. Did it really matter? He and Jack were the same person, with the same illness, heading down the same road. Counselor Paul was gone, if he'd ever really existed, and now he and Jack were equals. Neighbors in the nut ward, bozos on the drunk bus, trying once again to let someone else drive.

"So, I'm trying to take the thing down," Jack continued, "thinking I'm being super quiet, right? But then I turned around just in time to see my ex. She had picked up one of the wrenches I left on the floor and hit me right in the nuts with it. Even with all the booze in me, I felt that, and I went right down like a bag of potatoes!"

"Oh shit!" Pete winced and put his own hands to his genitals "you never told us that part before. Oh, she is a bitch for sure!"

"Yup," Jack went on, "and then when I'm down on the floor, she starts whacking me in the head with the wrench. Luckily, she called the cops before she found me in the living room, and they came busting in while she had me down. Good thing, too, because she would have killed me! So, she tells them that she thought I was an 'unknown burglar,' come to rob and rape her and whatnot, but I got the distinct feeling she knew exactly what she was doing."

Jack took another break from the story, surveying his audience to make sure they were sufficiently interested before he continued. Everyone was looking at him except Mandy, who was writing something in an official-looking chart on her lap.

"I didn't get the TV, but I did catch a breaking and entering charge and violating an order of protection that she had put out against me. And here I am. Before you ask, I haven't drank or used anything else since that night, which was December twelfth. Oh yeah, did I mention that she tried to strangle me with a strand of Christmas lights from the tree?"

The insanity and honesty, the pathetic tone caused Paul to burst out in a loud laugh.

Jack looked at him as if they were two soldiers who had survived the same battle only to learn it was a useless war.

"No shit," Jack smiled, "a fucking string of Christmas lights. They were still plugged in when she done it. And she didn't get charged with a thing."

Diane asked, "Is this the same woman you said you had dinner with last week?"

"Well, yup. But I can explain that," Jack replied. "She's Italian, you know? She gets pissed real easy but then cools down easy too. She said she'd try to make things work as long as I stay off the booze. So, that's what I'm doing, just not drinking one day at a time."

"And what about the order of protection?" asked Larry.

"Yeah, well, she dropped that, too. Like I said, she's Italian."

Nothing more was said, and eventually, the eyes of everyone in the group returned to Mandy, who continued to fill out her paperwork. After some time, she looked up.

"Alright, thanks, Jack. Diane, would you like to go?"

"I already went," Diane replied.

Larry and Pete laughed loud and raucously.

"Hey, maybe we should ask you the last time you did any drugs, Mandy?" Pete said and elbowed Larry.

"Oh, yes, of course you did," Mandy said, "Who would like to go next?"

No one spoke. "Jeremy," Mandy prompted, "how about you?"

The young man in the corner seat did not move. It looked to Paul like his clothing had been propped into the chair with no human form underneath. The black wool hat had receded down into the large coat, and no hands were visible from the coat sleeves. Everyone stared at this odd spectacle, a human laundry pile, and then back at Mandy when no response came from the chair. Even Pete and Larry were silent.

"Jeremy," Mandy said again, louder this time.

Slowly the hat started to rise from the coat, a turtle's head peering out from its shell. Gloved hands stretched from each sleeve. Long, dark hair draped down from the front of the hat, shadowing the boy's eyes and nose from view. One gloved hand brushed the curtain of hair aside and revealed two small, reddened eyes beneath.

"How about what?" Jeremy asked.

"How about you go back to sleep?" offered Larry, who nudged Pete.

"How about you go burn another one?" Pete added.

Jeremy turned toward the men, and it was unclear to Paul if he was attempting to intimidate them or to figure out who they were, but they both stared back at him and laughed.

"Let's hear about what got you here and how your sobriety is going, Jeremy," Mandy said.

"Not much to tell," Jeremy began. "I'm here because I pissed dirty at probation." He went quiet and stared at Mandy.

"And remind us of what you were placed on probation for," Mandy requested.

"Nothing to do with drinking or drugs. I don't even drink. I just smoke pot. And that shit's legal in some states, you know?"

Pete stopped sneering and said, "Damn straight! And it's gonna be legal here too, pretty soon. Then you guys will all be out of a job." He gave a foreboding look to Travis and Mandy.

Mandy ignored Pete's comment and asked Jeremy, "So what were you put on probation for?"

"Some bullshit," Jeremy began. "They said I was selling stuff, right, but I didn't even have any shit on me. The bitch I was with set me up. I can relate to what that guy was just saying." He motioned toward Jack, "Those bitches will set you up and knock you down."

"Wow, he was awake under there," Larry said.

"And what were you charged with selling?" Mandy continued.

"You know all this shit already! Why do I gotta come in here and repeat this same dumb shit week after week?"

"Well," Mandy answered, we do have some new people in here, so why not tell them?"

Jeremy hesitated, seeming to notice Angela for the first time, and then continued: "Well, we had some heroin in the car, but I didn't know it, see, and the bitch I was with did know about it, but she never told me, because she was a useless dope whore."

"Whoa! Tell us how you really feel, fella!" Jack said.

Paul looked at the two women across from him. Angela slowly pulled her legs back up into the chair, and Diane kept her eyes fixed straight ahead and away from the young man who was speaking. Paul realized he was flexing his hands into fists. He could feel the blood rising into his face.

Jeremy looked at Jack before he continued.

"Yeah, and this useless whore couldn't go an hour without her pills and powder and all that shit…"

"I don't think we should judge others." A new voice tentatively said. It was Travis, and everyone looked over at him, startled. Jeremy stopped talking and waited for Travis to say more.

His face was flushing, and he looked at Mandy for some support or validation. She looked shocked at his interruption but said nothing.

"I just mean," Travis went on, his face beaming red now, "I mean, we're not here to judge or criticize others, right? We're here to help. We talked about sharing our experiences but keeping the focus on ourselves. So, I don't think we should focus or blame other people for being here. I also think we need to watch out for language. Some profanity can hurt people and make the group unsafe. I think it's even a rule not to use certain words—" Travis looked over at Mandy again.

Paul was looking at her too and thinking the kid was goddamned right about it being a rule! Paul knew that Mandy should have shut that talk down the first time this punk used the word "whore."

"Well, that's true, Travis," Mandy began, "we shouldn't judge others, and I think we need to watch the language that we use. But we also shouldn't interrupt people when they are speaking because that is quite rude. By the way, for those of you who haven't met Travis yet, he is interning here and studying to become a counselor."

A few of the newer faces looked at Travis, smiled, and waved.

"His role in the group is really to observe and learn, so that's what he'll be working on."

She turned back to Jeremy and said, "So why don't you go ahead and tell us about the drug charges. Is that why you're here in treatment?"

Jeremy seemed unsure, looking first at Mandy and then at Travis.

"So, yeah, I ended up taking the charge for the drugs, even though that shit wasn't mine, and then they put me on probation. But I only started coming here after I pissed dirty, like I said before."

"Your urine screen came back positive for marijuana, and that's why you're here?" Mandy inquired.

"It came up dirty for weed and cocaine, but I hadn't used coke in, like, mad long, so I think they tampered with my piss, you know?"

Jack and Paul laughed.

Pete said, "They might have, you know! There's a whole website about how they can set you up like that."

Mandy let the comment and the laughter sit in the room for a few moments before she said, "And when was the last time you used?"

Larry said, "It's 6:05 now, if that helps," and elbowed Pete again.

Jeremy looked in the direction of the men for a long moment before speaking.

"I'm not keeping track of that shit, you know, but it's been a while. It's been like, a long while, you know, like since I started here, I guess..."

"Well," she said, "for your sake, and the sake of all those who love you, I hope that is the truth. Now, who else haven't we heard from yet? How about one of our new members?"

Paul looked over at Angela and said, "Ladies first?"

Angela put her legs on the floor and sat up a bit straighter in the chair. She pulled the army coat around her tighter.

"I'm Angela," she said, "and I'm here because of my drug use."

"Heroin, right?" Jeremy asked. "I'll bet a million dollars you like heroin."

"Yeah, like you got a million bucks, pothead," Pete joked.

Angela didn't look in Jeremy's direction but said, "And I'll bet you a million bucks that you'll be crying yourself to sleep in your cell bed next week when your P.O. violates your dumb ass."

"Word!" Andre said.

Laughter from the other group members filled the room, and Jeremy's head descended slowly back into his coat.

"I'm here for the same reason as everyone else," Angela continued, "because I have to be."

She didn't look directly at anyone and said nothing more. Paul had expected a sarcastic comment from Larry or Pete, but something about this girl made the men nervous about speaking. She had a feral cat quality. Paul found it interesting that Diane had approached the girl so quickly without sensing the same degree of danger that the men felt.

Mandy tried prompting her for more information.

"Would you like to tell us why you have to be here?"

"Not really."

"Did you get into trouble with the law?" Mandy asked.

"No. Not recently."

"So is someone requesting that you be here? A family member or friend who wanted you to come?"

"Something like that," Angela said, "but it's not family or friends. It's the people that hand out food and welfare checks to lowlifes like me. To us 'useless dope whores' that don't want to use dope anymore."

"I feel that," Andre said.

"Very nice!" Jack agreed and clapped his hands together, apparently delighted by this remark.

Angela leveled a gaze at Jeremy's seat, but he made no noise, and there was no further movement from the shell of clothing.

"Well," Diane said and grabbed one of Angela's hands in her own, "I think it's wonderful that you're here, and I give you credit for trying to turn your life around. I also don't think you should refer to yourself in those terms because it's clear to me that you are a brilliant, beautiful person."

"Is there anything else you would like to tell us about yourself?" Mandy asked.

"No. I'm good," Angela responded and pulled her hand back from Diane's while curling her legs back up and into the chair.

"I'm glad you're here," Travis said, looking at Angela, "and I really hope you will keep coming to groups."

"I guess that leaves us with my old friend Paul," Mandy said and turned in her seat to acknowledge him with a broad smile.

The comment took Paul off balance, and for a moment, he just stared at her. She continued smiling back at him but said nothing further.

"Oh. Okay, right. I'm Paul. I, uh, I'm here for my drinking."

He was surprised at how disjointed his current thoughts and words were. He took a deep breath before continuing.

"You can get better, Angela." he said. "There are people who can help you, and you are so young. I wish I had wised up at your age."

She looked up and over at him briefly. Paul thought he saw the faintest trace of a smile.

"Why don't you tell the group more about yourself, Paul?" Mandy asked. "My job is to give feedback to other patients, so why don't you just focus on telling us why you are here?"

Paul looked at Mandy again. Her wide smile seemed completely insincere, almost jeering. He realized "The Monster" was very much alive and well. She may have gotten bruised up over the years, but there was plenty of fight left in her. Paul considered taking off the gloves and starting the first round of this unexpected reunion between them by getting in a few cheap shots at her. Why not hit below the belt and make Mandy work for her paycheck tonight?

But almost as quickly as these thoughts came, he was reminded that Mandy had not gotten him here. And that reacting to her in anger would solve nothing.

"I'm here to stop drinking—again," he said. "I definitely consider myself an alcoholic, and I can identify with everyone in here in some way. I was sober for a long time, and then I drank again. And once I started, I just couldn't stop. Most recently, I got a D.U.I., and now I'm trying to get back on my feet. I have to get one of those breathalyzer devices in my car, and I'm not sure what else all of this will cost me. That's basically why I'm here."

"Oh, man," Larry chimed in, those breathalyzers in the car suck. I had one before, and they are horrible. They'll screw you on the price to get it installed, too!"

"Don't they charge you every month for those things?" Pete asked. "It's a fucking rip-off, another way for the government to get rich off us."

Paul looked at the two men but didn't contribute to the bluster. The group members slowly turned their attention to Mandy, satisfied that the check-in portion of group was over. Mandy was sitting quietly, the smirk of a smile remaining on her face. Her head tilted just a bit to the side. She stared at Paul. He noticed her gaze but remained quiet. He expected the next question to be when he drank last. Paul had no idea what he would say to that.

"Oh," said Pete, "she's coming for you, man! She's giving you the stink eye!"

Andre whispered, "Here comes 'The Monster Mash,'" under his breath.

The room was silent as the clock on the wall clicked another minute forward.

Mandy finally spoke, "I'm just wondering if Paul would like to share anything else about himself with the group? Are you working, Paul? Do you have any family? And you also left out when you last used alcohol. Would you like to tell us more?"

Paul felt sweat forming on his brow and under his armpits. He shouldn't have been surprised by this grilling. What balls on her, he thought to himself. Who did she think she was? But even as these thoughts came, another part of Paul respected her questions and that she was not letting him get off too easily. He certainly could have said more than he did, and perhaps he should have. He might have asked for more information if he was in the counselor's seat, although he wanted to believe that he would not come across as such a pompous bully in the process.

He felt all the eyes in the room upon him.

"What time did you say it was?" Paul asked Larry.

Larry looked back questioningly but decided to play along.

"It's 6:19; why?"

"Okay, then," Paul said and turned back toward Mandy. "My last drink, or drinks, to be more accurate, were a few hours ago. And the ones before that were a few hours earlier." Paul held out his right hand, which had a barely perceptible shake, to the people in the room. "I would estimate that I'll need a few more in the next two hours unless I want my whole body to turn itself inside out."

He looked around the room and then directly into Mandy's face.

"It's my own outpatient detoxification protocol, see?"

She looked shocked. Dumbfounded. No longer wearing the smile.

"Good." Paul thought. And then he continued.

"But if you like, I could stay after group, and you can test my blood alcohol content. We can also talk about how I got here tonight, and you can follow whatever protocol to make sure all your paperwork is completed. I've got nowhere to go, and I can stay for as long as you want. So, that answers your other question. I don't work anymore. I lost my career over the booze. But I'm pretty sure you already knew that. And you probably know that I lost my family, too, but I'll mention that as a means of introduction if you'd like. The people closest to me either ran away or died trying to get away. So that's me, Mandy, and my evening is pretty well open to suggestions from here on out."

The room fell silent again, except for Jeremy who emerged from his coat and said, "Holy shit!" to no one in particular.

Paul looked over at the turtle boy, a blank stare on his face, before bringing his full attention back to Mandy.

"Anything else you'd like to know, or should we get on with your activity? It would be a real shame to waste all that paper."

Mandy looked less certain, almost contrite.

"No," she responded quickly, "no, that will be enough for tonight, Paul."

"It can't be easy," Travis muttered.

"Being here can't be easy for you, Paul," Travis continued. "It can't be easy for any of you. This is probably not where you would choose to spend your Thursday nights."

Some nervous murmurs and chuckles came from around the room.

"But I'm glad you're here, Paul. And I hope you realize that you don't need to be alone anymore."

The room went silent. Paul's stomach started to churn and ache, the old, familiar bells tolling for alcohol. He could feel the tremors coming and wished he'd kept his cool and simply answered her questions. What did his rant prove? And what would happen if she or the kid did breathalyze him? Another ride with Roscoe to jail or to detox? He was the same old stupid, prideful, impulsive Irish drunk he'd always been.

"Well," Mandy said, sounding less confidant than usual, "that concludes our check in for tonight."

She sat up in her chair, squaring her shoulders, and organized the worksheet packets on her lap. The pencils rattled around in the cup when she picked them up.

"Tonight we're going to talk about money." Her voice and tone soon returned to the normal, monotonous inflection that the group knew so well. A robot with lipstick and manicured nails. The packets and pencils were handed out to each patient.

Diane said, "Well, thank you," as Mandy handed her the required materials.

Angela had tucked her hands deep into the pockets of the jacket. Mandy paused at her chair, waiting for Angela to take the items from her. Mandy then placed the packet and pencil on Angela's lap, and the pencil rolled off and onto the floor, followed by the papers. Angela made no effort to retrieve them. Jeremy stood up before Mandy gave him the materials and exited the room. Paul saw that Pete seemed eager to receive the supplies and immediately drew a large dancing penis on the cover page of his pamphlet. He leaned over and showed Larry his artwork.

"You could make some money with those pictures!" Larry said, but nobody in the group inquired about what they were doing.

Mandy's was the only voice they heard for the remainder of the time, and she ended the group promptly at 6:58 p.m. They were less than halfway through the packet. Mandy collected the assignments and told the group they would complete them at the next meeting. Jack was asleep, and Paul elbowed him slightly, nudging him awake. Jeremy never returned to the group. Mandy picked up the blank papers and pencil from his seat. Angela was the first one to get up and leave the room, leaving the pencil and papers where they had fallen on the floor next to her chair.

Larry asked Mandy if he could get an extra copy of the exercise to bring home.

"I want to share it with my church group and with our book club," Larry said. Mandy ignored the comment.

Paul was the last patient to leave, and he walked behind Jack toward the hallway. He handed his papers and pencil to Mandy, feeling the urge to apologize for his sharpness, and afraid she might retaliate by calling the police as soon as he left. But he doubted she would care enough to do so.

Travis approached Paul in the hallway and asked, "Are you going to be okay?"

Something about Travis was starting to unnerve Paul. Maybe Matt was right to question Paul's motives with working with the intern. Perhaps Paul had thought he could skate through this whole process untouched by this naïve kid.

"Me?" He asked Travis, "I'm great, never been better."

"Well," Travis continued, "it's just that you said you had been drinking today, and I know that you drove here, so legally, we really need to address that."

Paul's immediate reaction was to get this kid off his back so that he could get out to his car and to the water bottle. A strong sense of unease was growing inside of him. That need to hide and protect the insatiable thirst was strong, but he saw something in the kid's look that was familiar, sincere, and frightening. The kid cared. And that was dangerous.

"Look," Paul said, trying to control himself, "she just pissed me off, that's all. She knows my story, but for some reason, she wanted me to spill my guts out all over the place in there tonight, and I'm just not ready to do that."

Paul almost said "kid," but caught himself and took a long breath before he continued.

"I'm a mess. I get it. But I know what I've got to do. Hell, I could've run that group!"

Paul surprised himself with this statement. He had worked with many substance abuse counselors who relapsed, and the sickest of them would talk about their own competence to run the groups they were assigned to.

Any statement so arrogant and irrational just begged to be confronted, beat up, and brought down because it was a huge lie. Paul could not have run the group or anything else. Paul could barely run his own life, if it was even considered a life at this point.

"As an intern," Travis said, "It's not really my place to give you a breathalyzer without being told to do so by Mandy or another counselor. But I don't want you killing yourself or someone else when you leave here tonight."

Paul stepped toward Travis and put a hand on his shoulder.

"Hey, I get it. And you're doing the right thing. Really, you are. But look at me. Do I look drunk to you?"

Paul stared directly at Travis, leaning in a bit, and hoping that the old drunkard's myth about vodka being hard to smell held just a bit of truth.

"Take a look into my eyes. Do they look dilated? If someone is drunk, the pupils are going to fill up that eyeball. I'll take a breathalyzer test if you want me to. If it will make you feel better. But I also want you to remember that with an old rummy like me, you can't rely on the reading. Those machines will tell you someone's blood alcohol content, but they can't tell you what kind of tolerance someone has for the stuff. I don't think I've gone the last four or five years without some amount of alcohol in my bloodstream. I don't say that to brag, just to make a point. For someone like me, drinking so regularly, the B.A.C. will tell you if I'm legal to drive, but it won't tell you if I'm able. I'm detoxing myself, tapering off the booze. If it doesn't work, and hell, it might not, well, then I guess you and the team will have to send me to the hospital, but not right now. Besides, you don't want to lose your first patient that quickly, do you?"

Travis was looking at Paul, trying to assess his pupils and posture, speech and functioning. He certainly didn't appear intoxicated. Still, Travis had noticed the shaking hands, which shook more by the end of the session. He didn't know what to say or do. He was only the intern, after all, and he was glad that Paul was being honest, opening up to him. Professor

Dunleavy always stressed the role of honesty and the therapeutic relationship above all else.

Even so, Travis feared that Paul might be manipulating his way out of a tough spot. He wondered how Bill would handle this. He looked past Paul, hoping that Mandy might appear and take over this situation. The hall was empty. He was just an intern. His job was to observe and learn.

"The people who are still using," Paul went on, "are the ones who come in late for a group. That's a dead giveaway. Just look at our young friend, Jeremy. Or if someone's behavior seems different somehow. The quiet girl suddenly gets really chatty, or the guy who never shuts up, like our two friends in there that seem to love the sound of their own voices, have nothing to say. When someone falls asleep, like Jack, that could be another sign, though I think Mandy's topic was the cause tonight. Also, if they get up and go to the bathroom, especially if it's more than once, watch out for that. Many of the pill poppers and dope shooters will go that route. Watch them when they get back, see if they act differently. This stuff isn't rocket science. You'll see it all, and you'll get used to the signs, too."

"So, when someone tells you they drank before a group, just ignore it?" Travis asked.

"No. Nope. Not at all. Do exactly what you did. And then look for the signs."

Travis shook his head slowly, not sure what else to say or do. Paul gripped him on the shoulder firmly and asked, "So I'll see you Tuesday?"

"Yes," Travis answered, "Tuesday. Try not to drink."

"Good," Paul responded. "See? That's good advice. Simple, but good." He smiled at Travis and walked away down the hall toward the red illuminated EXIT sign.

"Fuck," Travis whispered to nobody.

CHAPTER 14

"I knew things were getting out of control when I looked around me and realized that the people I was hanging out with weren't friends. They were just sick, sad, addicts like me. If it wasn't for the drugs, we wouldn't have a damn thing in common..."

Mickey R., a brief qualification at the Deerfield Down and Out N.A. Meeting

The receptionist area was quiet and dark when Paul walked by it. He thought of all the nights he had walked by that desk, often the last one to leave the building, wondering what types of sick people and chaos the next day would bring. He pondered the manipulative bullshit he'd just spewed to the kid in the hallway. The lies came so easily and convincingly. Had he been one of the sickest people? The most manipulative? Completely incurable even back then? Even when he thought he was faking things so well? Just a ticking time bomb waiting to explode and blow up everything and everyone that dared to trust him. He'd blown everything to shit in the end, but here he was, trying the same old lies, the same old song and dance.

The night had turned cloudy, and a slow, frigid wind blew over the parking lot. Paul zipped his coat and pulled it tighter around himself. The moonglow cast light and shadows around the parking lot as the clouds rolled overhead.

As he walked toward his car, he heard the unmistakable guffawing of Larry and Pete. They were standing between mammoth pickup trucks near the end of the parking lot, away from the glow of any lights.

"Hey," he heard Larry's voice shout, "there's the new guy! Come on over here, buddy! This is the best part of group nights!" Pete cackled again, sounding like the court idiot in a poorly acted Shakespearean play.

Paul hesitated, but didn't want to seem unsociable, stuck up, or at worst, afraid of these two buffoons. He had dealt with enough narcissistic rednecks and dimwitted bullies in the past to know that walking away might have implied weakness, and these types fed on that. He was not completely surprised to smell bourbon mixed with cigarette smoke as he got closer. The two men were positioned between their trucks, Pete leaning against the open door of what Paul assumed was his vehicle. On the floorboard of the truck, he had a large Thermos that he picked up, drank from, and offered to Paul.

"You really told that bitch off," Pete said, inserting a cigarette in his mouth and taking a large draw. "That was beautiful."

Without thinking, Paul grabbed the Thermos and put it to his mouth. He took a long, slow pull and felt the tide of liquid flow warmly to the back of his mouth and ebb down his throat. He closed his eyes as he swallowed and immediately regretted what he'd done.

"Whoa, slow down, there, boss!" Pete said, snatching the Thermos away from him and taking another sip for himself. "We got to share that stuff. I'll tell you, I really prefer pot to booze, but this stuff won't stay in your piss half as long!"

Larry blew out a large plume of cigarette smoke, "Yeah, you got to watch out, man. Some nights they make us all take a breathalyzer or a piss test before the group starts. It hasn't happened yet in this group because she doesn't care enough to do all that, but I know other guys who come here, and they say the counselors are busting down on that shit all the time." Larry handed back the Thermos, and Pete raised it to his mouth.

"No, no, stop!" Larry signaled, waving his hands. Pete quickly placed the Thermos back into the truck. The three men saw the door of the building open, and Mandy walked out. She pushed a button on a remote she was holding, and a small, red, expensive-looking coupe parked directly under a light near the building started up and began idling. She had her phone to her ear, and they could hear low mumbles as she talked. Paul instinctively stepped toward the back of the truck, deeper into the shadows. Mandy walked quickly toward the car, not seeming to take any interest in the men.

"She's something else, all right," Larry said. "A real ice queen. I wonder what her story is, man." His cigarette was cupped in his hand, the red ember hidden from view.

Paul could feel the bourbon pulsing through his veins, steadying his nerves. The cigarette smelled good, familiar—an old friend come to visit.

"Yeah, she was definitely up your ass tonight," Pete agreed, "but you taught her a lesson, boy! I drank four hours ago, you said! That was fucking classic!"

Mandy's car reversed from the parking spot and sped out of the lot. Paul felt a pang of remorse again, especially hearing the two men retell the story of his outburst with such joy. But maybe they were right. Fuck The Monster. He thought about asking one of his new friends for a cigarette.

Pete raised the Thermos, but another car alarm chirped in the parking lot, and he quickly put it back down.

"Oh, wait, here comes the princess of the group," Pete said.

Travis came out the door and looked around the lot. He saw the men gathered at the trucks and instinctively raised a hand to wave. Before his hand got above his head, he realized it was a bad decision and pulled the hand down, making the movement seem awkward and jerky.

Paul raised his hand in response and waved. Travis' car was closer to the two trucks, forcing him to walk almost up to the men. Travis felt his pulse quicken, as it had hundreds of times before in his life. He tried to break the uncomfortable silence of the moment by looking up at them, these men who reminded him so much of the assholes and the bullies from his past, always traveling in groups and packs, like jackals on the hunt.

He turned to them and said, "Good night," in a voice that sounded too high and too panicked to be his own before opening the door on his small car.

"Good night," said Paul.

"To de loo!!" taunted Pete, in his most effeminate voice.

Larry attempted to say Bon Voyage, but it came out "Beon Vouyega," and he and Pete broke into laughter.

When Travis started his car, the loud, rhythmic, "Brap! Brap! Brap!" startled them. The rattling from the car's muffler peaked as he drove out of the parking lot.

Pete elbowed Larry.

"I guess they didn't teach him how to fix a car in beauty school!" Pete put his hand up to his head and ran it theatrically through his hair to emphasize his point. He picked up the Thermos and took a drink.

"No," replied Larry, "I bet they don't cover car repair where he goes, but I'm sure they learn a lot about loose tailpipes!"

Pete almost spit his drink out then doubled over in laughter.

Paul started to walk away, and the two men stood up, trying to compose themselves.

"Hey, hey, wait up, boss," Pete said, "it's your turn to drink, take one more for the road!"

Paul didn't turn around but replied, "No thanks, boys, I've had more than enough for tonight."

CHAPTER 15

"All certified clinicians have a legal and ethical responsibility to report any impairment of a client or staff member that might put others in an unsafe or compromised position within a treatment facility."

Canon of Ethics for Substance Abuse Counselors

"Well, write something, lover boy! Our show is coming on in ten minutes, and I made the popcorn already," C.J. said as he walked past Travis and sat on the sofa in the living room.

"I've been staring at this screen for the last five minutes!" Travis replied. "I'm just not sure how much I want to say. We're supposed to be honest in these weekly logs, but I think I really messed up tonight!"

"Well, I don't get the big deal about just saying that the guy showed up drunk. It's not like it's your fault or anything."

"Well, that's the thing. He wasn't drunk. At least, he didn't seem drunk to me. He just told us all that he drank. And I think he did that because he knew Mandy wouldn't do anything about it! He was so honest about it, and that's what makes it weird. It's like he knows what we're expecting because he's done the counseling work himself. But I also think he's telling the truth. He seems sincere and honest. But he was standing around with those idiots in the parking lot, and I'm pretty sure they were drinking out there! It's so hard to know if I should believe anything the patients tell me at this job!"

C.J. set down his bowl of popcorn, came over to Travis, and started rubbing his shoulders.

"And now," Travis continued, "I'm in this place where I don't know if I handled the whole thing right or not, but I don't want to write about it in the log. I really don't want to become the lesson in this week's class on what not to do, you know? I can just hear Dunleavy's voice calling on me, that all-fucking-knowing smile on his face. And then the students, looking at me, listening, shaking their heads! But I also don't want to lie about it. The professor tells us all the time to open up in these weekly reports, that there's no judgment and that this is a safe space to share our thoughts, feelings, and mistakes. But of course, there's judgment. There's always judgment—ugh!" Travis put his head down on the keyboard.

"Well," C.J. began, "I wouldn't blame you either way. I know you feel like everyone's judging you, but you're way too fucking hard on yourself. Of course, you're going to make mistakes, but you didn't do anything wrong. I think it was ballsy of you to even talk to the guy after group. I probably would have just let him go – fuck it. You're just the intern, you know? I think you did the right thing. It seems weird and kind of shady to me that they have you working with this guy to begin with. Not because of you, but because of him. He seems incurable. It would make more sense to me if they had you work with some young kid who got caught smoking pot or drinking before the high school dance. This guy is way too complicated for someone new. It would be like having me do a root canal by myself when I've barely learned how to do a good cleaning! This guy needs some serious help from someone who's been counseling for a really long time. Or maybe he just needs to kill himself and get it over with."

Travis looked up into C.J.'s face.

"Really?"

"Too much?" C.J. asked. "I know, I'm just a heartless bitch. Or maybe I'm enlightened. I know what I can and can't control. Serenity and wisdom personified."

"Or you just want to watch the show," Travis suggested.

"Well, that's true. And I want to watch it with my boyfriend, so hurry up and just write something."

"Okay, I can do it," Travis said, placing his hands over the keyboard, "I need to do it." He grabbed one of C.J.'s hands and squeezed it. "I'll be done in a minute."

C.J. leaned down and kissed Travis' head lightly then walked into the living room.

Travis looked at the blank screen, held his hands over the keyboard, and began typing.

"Not too much to report this week. I helped to co-facilitate a group that my new client is in. He opened up and introduced himself to the group. He said he would meet with me for an individual session on Tuesday.

And earlier, I sat in on a treatment team meeting…"

CHAPTER 16

*"He'll be back. These drunks and addicts always come back.
They're just too fucked up to do it any other way!"*

Teddy Monroe, Bartender, Stumble Inn Bar & Grill

Paul's car radio was blasting out a live version of The Grateful Dead's "Touch of Grey" when he pulled into the rutted dirt parking lot of Cook's Garage just after ten on Friday morning. He had countless Dead albums at the house but couldn't remember the last time he'd played one. Their music always put him in a better mood, especially when played loudly in a car on a sunny day with all the windows down.

He bounced along and stopped near several other parked cars in the lot, some at odd angles and one that looked as if it had not been moved in many months. The garage was a giant, ugly monstrosity of crumbling bricks that looked badly in need of mortar. The two large wooden bay doors stared like eyeballs above a nose and mouth that had already been swallowed by the dirt. Cyrus Cook built the place around the same time that Paul's grandfather opened his own store in town. Cyrus intended to sell cars from the lot and thought that repairing the vehicles would serve as a secondary income. But he soon found that the economic climate was not conducive to selling cars to the locals with any regularity. Cyrus earned the reputation as an adept mechanic straight away, having learned about fixing cars, engines, and most anything else that had wheels on it while growing up on the large dairy farm next door to the garage.

As Paul got out of his car, he noticed several dilapidated R.V.s and one sagging mobile home that Tank had deposited behind the garage, where acres and acres of crops used to grow. The space looked much smaller now, the fields shrunken. Paul knew, as most townsfolk knew, that this was the only section of the old Cook Dairy Farm that Cyrus' son, Frank "Tank" Cook, didn't sell off to Tony Pelligrino. Tony razed the trees, leveled and paved over the cornfields, and buried sprawling septic lines in the rich soil. He called his new development *The Gables*, and it was touted as "Moheneck Fall's first Upscale Community" on the Pelligrino website.

The sun was shining brightly off the small snow-covered field between the garage and the countless pristine rooftops and shuttered windows of *The Gables* in the distance. Paul smelled an unnatural, acrid burning odor in the cold air and saw dark black smoke rising from the lopsided chimney of the garage as he walked toward the crooked entrance door.

He opened the door and saw Frank's son, Frankie, Jr., or "Li'l Tank," stoking the large woodstove in the middle of the garage. Smoke was billowing out from the open door and filling the interior of the shop. A voice boomed from behind a colossal, industrial plow truck in the far bay.

"Jesus Christmas, Frankie. You think you can smoke us out anymore in here?" It was the voice of the elder Frank, loud but good-natured.

"Sorry, Dad. This damn oil is smoking up as soon as I get a log close to the fire," Frankie responded.

"Well, I'm not paying for anything if my car gets burned up in here," Paul shouted over to Frank and gave Li'l Tank a wink.

"Hoooolllllyyyyy shhhheeeeerrrberttt," said Tank, elongating each word while striding toward Paul with an exaggerated dramatic flair. "Look who rose from the dead!"

Tank's hands were already dirty from the morning's work, but Paul reached out and gave him a firm, tight handshake.

"How are you Tank?"

"If I was any better, it wouldn't be legal."

He looked at Paul a long while, the corners of his mouth rising into a wolfish grin.

"A better question," he said, his smile turning into something more like concern, "is how the hell are you doing, old bud? And what am I putting this silly contraption in your car for?"

"I guess you didn't read about it in the paper," Paul said. He looked at Tank, trying to determine if he really knew about the situation and was simply being respectful.

"I haven't read that rag in years—nothing in there but rumors, gossip, and bad news. I heard Pelligrino and his rich snob friends rallied those newspaper folks to come out here and take pictures of my property. They did some story about how the town council should force me to clean the place up. That's when I dumped that old trailer out there and added a few other eyesores for my fancy new neighbors to complain about. I also decided to start burning some of the old oil we got lying around out here. Those fine folks living on my blood land can fill their lungs with all they want of the stuff!"

An impish smile filled his face.

"So, no, I don't really know why I'm putting this thing on your car, Paul, except that someone's probably making you do it, cause people don't usually ask to have these things installed just for fun!"

Paul smiled back.

"Good point," he said. "I had too much to drink at the Stumble Inn one night and fell asleep behind the wheel. Luckily, I just rolled off the road and over a sign pole before Roscoe came out and found me there. Which reminds me, can you take a look at my bumper? I'm hoping not to replace it, but it needs some bending and realignment."

"Sure," Tank said, "we'll look at it." He thought for a moment before adding, "So, Roscoe busted you for that?"

"Yup. Roscoe busted me for that."

The two men stood silent for a moment.

"Huh," Tank said, shaking his head. "Well, I suppose they don't play around with that stuff anymore. You don't seem like the kind of guy that the law needs to spend their time and money on, though. I've mounted a bunch of these things over the last year or so, and I've got a feeling there's plenty more installs coming. Did they tell you anything about what you need to do with the breathalyzer or how long it'll be on your car?"

"John Lawrence set it all up. Judge O'Malley is calling the shots, and John knows he wants me to get this thing on as soon as possible, but I'm waiting for a court date."

Frank shook his head, his eyes warm and kind.

"Well, O'Malley's fair. And he certainly knows you well enough. Maybe that's not a bad thing."

Tank wiped his brow with the back of his wrist.

"I got to tell you that the stupid thing is not cheap. It's $250 just to install it, and then they want you to pay $75 each month for what they call maintenance. There's a sensor and a computer chip inside these breathalyzers that records the results every time you blow into it. Then the machine needs to be plugged in and downloaded every month by me. The report gets sent to the judge. It's a real violation of our freedom if you ask me, but nobody seems to care about what I think. Anyway, if the machine does pick up any booze on your breath, even the smallest amount, the system won't allow the car to start until the thing gets reset. Then I have to come out with the cops or whoever they want to send to your house and fix the damn thing there." His eyes met Paul's again. "It really sucks, Paul. This is some serious stuff."

Paul took a slow, deep breath and looked past Tank out a small, dirty window near the back of the garage. There was a giant stream of dark smoke floating on the clear breeze toward the upscale homes across the field. He imagined hearing Tank and Roscoe at his front door, knocking softly, waiting for him to come out.

"Look," Tank said, "I get $100 of the $250 for installing these things, but I won't charge you that. I also get a $30 cut each month when you bring it in to be calibrated, and I'm not worried about that either."

Tank took a step closer and lowered his voice, "I haven't forgotten what you did for me, Paul, and now it's my turn to help you out. So, take the favor. No questions or arguing."

"Thanks," was all Paul could think to say.

"I'm gonna try to get your car in today, but I've got a contract with the town to keep their pieces of junk moving, and as you can see, they need some work."

He gestured to the large, orange plow truck in the far bay that Frank, Jr. was working on, and then to a similar truck sitting in the parking lot.

"If I don't get to yours today, it'll be my first one tomorrow. So why don't you take my truck for now? It's the blue Ford out there, and the keys are in it."

"Thanks," Paul said again.

He thought of saying more, of sharing his gratitude with Tank for always remaining a friend and for never judging him. He also thought about letting him know that having the breathalyzer might just provide the motivation and accountability he needed to stop drinking entirely. But instead of this, he simply patted his friend firmly on the shoulder and walked out of the smoky garage and back into the bright, cold day without saying another word.

The heating system in Tank's pickup truck didn't work, reminding Paul of the adage his father told him about the best carpenter's houses always having leaky roofs. As he steered the old truck back toward town, the sudden, gripping urge to drive directly to a liquor store or bar gripped him. The vodka was almost gone at home. He'd only taken one drink so far today, and he intentionally left his trusty water bottle at home because he planned to be completely abstinent by tomorrow. This was especially important now with that fucking breathalyzer coming soon. He took a few deep breaths and tried to relax, telling himself that he didn't need the booze at this point.

"Yes, but you want it, don't you?" Something whispered from deep inside his head.

He turned on the radio to drown out the voice. The first station played newer music, the type that Paul considered bubble gum country or tight pants music. He listened to a great deal of country music during his childhood, all of which he considered quality and most of which had morphed into something cheap and indistinguishable over the years. He punched one of the pre-programmed buttons on the radio and let the unmistakable voice of Mr. Johnny Cash fill the cab of the truck:

"I fell in to a burning ring of fire..."

Paul sang along, loudly and without reservation, as the truck bounced down the lonely road. He saw a convenience store in the distance and looked down at the time, almost 11:00 a.m. He hadn't been in the store in a few years, but he distinctly remembered a large beer cooler near the back of the place. Beer didn't have the high alcohol content of vodka, nowhere near the same strength, and if he only had one or two, it would be out of his system by the time his car was repaired today or tomorrow. And beer sure did go well with Johnny Cash. The truck seemed to steer itself into the nearly empty parking lot.

Paul was relieved that he didn't know the cashier. She was a young girl, maybe too young to be working during school hours instead of sitting in a classroom somewhere. He found it harder and harder to determine the ages of people these days. It seemed like most of the girls looked older than they truly were, gobbing makeup on their faces and dressing in clothes that were too provocative and revealing for them. The irony was that many of the boys looked younger than they were, in their ridiculously baggy clothes with baseball hats turned around or wearing sandals and shorts in the middle of winter—real life Peter Pans, perpetually caught in pre-pubescent childhood and desperate never to grow up.

The girl was entranced in a magazine and didn't glance up when Paul entered. Paul remembered his grandparents teaching him to always greet each customer that entered their store with a smile and a friendly, "Hello, nice to see you."

He'd learned the art of easy, superficial conversation from those early years behind the store's counter, and it had also forced him to be more confident and cordial to folks. But conversation seemed to be a habit lost to the newer generations. He considered saying hello now, of testing this young woman's social skills but realized that the results might depress him, or worse yet, it could call more attention than necessary to the sad old man who just wanted (maybe needed) something to drink.

The beer coolers were exactly where he remembered them. There were so many brands and varieties to choose from, and each one promised something different. He walked slowly past each cooler, taking inventory of the malt beverages, wine spritzers, hard apple cider products, and, of course, beer. But even the beer selection had exploded and multiplied into all kinds of sub-categories. There was lite beer and ice beer and craft beer. There were also large single cans and bottles, six-packs, twelve packs, eighteen packs, and cases of the stuff. The sheer selection was overwhelming, and for a moment, Paul considered abandoning the whole idea and simply driving to the liquor store instead. But for some reason, he thought that taking Tank's truck to his regular store or to any liquor store was a bad idea. It seemed beyond disrespectful and could also be dangerous for him.

He noticed that some of the drinks were not really beer at all but were made from a mystery alcohol base and marketed as "chillers" or "mixed beverages." They ranged in flavors from watermelon to pomegranate and reminded him of the flavored sodas he used to get from the pharmacy in town when he was a kid.

Paul was concerned that he was taking too long at choosing, which could look suspicious to the young woman behind the counter. He heard the distinct pinging of a cell phone and looked up an aisle toward the register. She was peering down at the small screen on her phone and rapidly tapping away at the buttons with her thumbs.

He opened the cooler and grabbed a six-pack of what claimed to be plain old beer bottles. He walked along the back wall, following the cooler doors past cheese products and hot dogs and chocolate milk until he saw bottled water. Once again, he found a vast selection of beverages that promised to "quench thirst, hydrate completely, and fortify all vitamin and mineral needs." He grabbed a small, plain bottle from the lower shelf. On the way to cash out, he picked up a box of mints and set them in front of the young woman, who was off her phone and looking at the magazine again.

She folded the magazine on the counter, careful not to lose her place. The article was titled "How to Be the Slut He Wants in Bed!" Paul waited for her to say something, to acknowledge him, or at least to make eye contact and smile, but the silence continued. She picked up the water bottle, moved it around under the store's scanner until it beeped, and placed it in a small plastic bag. She repeated the process with the beer. He was fighting the urge to say something, to instruct her on how to have face-to-face dialogue. If she would just smile at him or do something somewhat human…

The mints were giving her a fair amount of trouble because they could not be scanned. Instead of attempting to punch in the numbers from the SKU code manually, she continued to run the red light of the scanner over the bar code. Paul couldn't contain himself any longer.

"They're $1.25," he said, trying to keep his tone friendly.

She looked up as if awakening from a dream. She hadn't seemed to realize that something, that someone, was attached to the products which appeared on the counter. She studied Paul's face—no signs of irritation or anger—genuinely surprised that this thing before her could talk.

"It won't take the code," she said. And then, "Sometimes if you get it at just the right distance..."

She held the scanner at various distances from the tin of mints, waving both hands through the air and waiting for the beep.

"They cost $1.25," Paul said again but realized the information was useless. She was taught to scan the code, and that was what she did. Her programming required it.

The girl's phone vibrated and rang. She instinctively set down the mints and scanner, reached for the phone, then realized the thing across from her, the man, was not gone yet.

She looked at him, her face a blank screen, and asked, "Did you see how much these were?"

"Seventy-five cents," Paul responded.

He waited to see her smile, to acknowledge the joke, but she didn't. Instead, she focused her attention on the cash register and started punching numbers in. It took a very long time, and Paul had the uncomfortable feeling that he was meant to walk away from the girl and the store. There were no good excuses for staying and seeing this through. But he was out of mints. And the water would help him to stay hydrated, which was healthy...

The girl finally finished punching buttons and told Paul the total. The amount she quoted seemed close to his estimation, so he didn't question the math. She snatched up her phone while Paul retrieved the money from his wallet. It was clear that any verbal interactions between them were over. She took his money and gave him the change. He left, and the familiar, comfortable misery was with him again as he drove down the snowy two-lane road inside the freezing cab of the truck.

Paul's plan had been to wait until he got home to drink the first beer. He would dump out all the liquor at the house and only drink the beer today. By tomorrow, he'd be completely abstinent. He opened the water and took a drink, then put one of the mints in his mouth, hoping the strong taste and sting of it would quell the growing cravings for the six-pack sitting next to him on the seat. The bottles clinked together like small chimes as the truck rumbled down the road. He shouldn't have bought it. He knew that now. The best thing to do would be to pull over and throw them all away in the first dumpster he could find. Or at least to throw away some of them, three maybe, and to keep the others so that he could stave off the withdrawal and taper himself down. Maybe keep just one. He opened the water bottle again and drank.

He decided it would make sense to drink that one beer right away. This would give his body time to start processing it, and it might also take away the compulsion that seemed to be growing each minute. He could just douse the fire a bit and then decide if the other five beers were necessary. One beer. Just the one.

He hoped that the aftertaste of the mint mixed with beer would be repulsive. It wasn't. The term "Euphoric Recall" came to mind as he took another swig of beer and thought of all the times he'd talked about the phenomena to patients at the clinic.

"You've got to stay away from people, places, and things. They all touch off your five senses and get those cravings to drink or use fired up. Once that happens, it's going to be hard to remember any of the bad times, the negative consequences. Our brains seem to have a built-in "forgetter" once you take that first one, and you'll go right back to remembering only the fun stuff, the good ole days of your use, the euphoria of it all..."

Paul took another drink. And it tasted good. Crisp, cold, and biting. Nothing like the burn that liquor gave him.

"What a sick fuck I am," he thought.

He was too smart for this, too strong to be beaten in this way. Years ago, an A.A. sponsor had called Paul out on a trait the sponsor called "terminal uniqueness." As much as Paul hated the term and protested at the time, he knew it was true. His sponsor repeatedly tried to remind Paul that every alcoholic was just as unique as him, another sick Bozo on the bus.

The first beer went quickly. So did the second. Halfway through the third bottle, a memory began to play from a projector deep back in his brain. It was about this time of year, the first time he went skiing. Paul's parents had considered skiing a rich person's sport and never asked or offered him the opportunity to try it. But during his freshman year of high school, Paul became friends with the Colton brothers. The Coltons were born almost ten months apart "Irish Twins," as Paul's father would say, and they both had blazing red heads of hair which fed the flames of trouble and destruction they constantly found themselves in. The Colton boys had attended several private and Catholic Schools during their elementary education, but by the time they reached high school, their parents had realized the family's money could be better spent elsewhere, and the two boys entered Moheneck Falls High School. Some of the Coltons' money came from an uncle who owned a large share of a small, local skiing area. The boys had acquired a good deal of used equipment from the place. Paul assumed people had lost or left behind the assortment of boots, skis, poles, and other things the boys sold at low prices. The possibility that these items had been stolen never occurred to Paul. If you were a close enough friend, they might simply give you the equipment. Paul found it hard to refuse his first invitation to ski with the Coltons when they offered to outfit him and give him a free lift ticket for the day.

Although he spent the majority of that first day on the small rope tow section of the hill, the experience inspired him to improve and to ascend the hill the next time. And he probably would have done a fair bit better on his second outing if the Colton boys hadn't taken Paul to a small storage shed on the grounds of the ski center and revealed a cooler full of beer. Paul didn't know that this scheme had been laid out by his companions sometime before their second trip to the hill and that the pair had done this same thing to a few other classmates. The plan was to get a skiing rookie drunk and then take him on some of the hardest trails the hill had to offer. They got a day of entertainment watching their guests struggle, flounder, and fall every few feet.

Unfortunately, they hadn't expected Paul's tolerance to alcohol to be higher than their own, and in the end, that was their undoing. From the very start of his drinking career, Paul had been able to drink more alcohol than many of his friends without showing any effects. He would learn later, much later, that this early tolerance put him at risk of becoming a drunk right from the start. Paul eventually learned that the ability to drink more as a teenager usually leads to just that – drinking more. Over time the increasing amount of alcohol a teenager drinks negatively impacts the natural growth and development of their bodies and brains. The more alcohol they ingest, the more severe this interruption in normal growth can be.

Of course, Paul didn't know any of that on the day his two friends pulled him into the shed and challenged him to a drinking contest. He only knew that he could drink quite a bit without really feeling drunk. So, he happily complied with the taunts and encouragement of the Coltons to "Drink just one more!" He simply said, "after you" and handed each of the boys fresh beers before taking one for himself, time and time again, until the cooler was empty. He remembered falling quite a bit that day, but there had been a recent snowstorm, and the deep powder on the trails kept him from getting seriously hurt. One of the Colton boys, the younger one, suffered a sprained ankle, and the older boy was found on the side of a trail vomiting ferociously. Both brothers were taken off the hill by Ski Patrol and questioned about a case of beer recently stolen from the ski lodge bar. It was also noted that they were wearing skis that belonged to the rental shop at the mountain, but neither could provide proof that they had rented anything before hitting the slopes.

That was the last time Paul was invited to ski with the Coltons. He smiled now, remembering that day. He'd heard some time ago that one of them was in prison and that the other one had a distinguished career as a New York State Trooper.

Paul felt a warm glow, despite the broken heater. He rolled down the window on the truck and let the frozen air rush over him and into the cab. He could see his breath on the exhales. As he drove through a thick grove of trees, he flung an empty beer bottle deep into the woods. He heard it sing and whistle as it spun through the air. Without hesitating, he grabbed the fourth beer.

The thing he remembered most about that day with the Coltons was the feeling of skis gliding over the snow. It was like nothing else, especially after the beers. Gravity and friction disappeared when he skied, and he could float and fly and be free from any cares while on the trails. The only reality was crisp, cold air over his face and the smooth, constant floating of the skis. He became unstoppable.

The piney air and whistle of the wind washed over him, and he imagined standing on top of his favorite ski trail, poised, confident, and ready to descend. He took another drink, surprised that the bottle was almost empty. He looked at his lap and the seat to see if any had spilled. It hadn't. Paul felt pressure and fullness in his bladder, which he knew would intensify soon.

"It's hell getting old," he thought. "You can't drink a thing without having to run to the bathroom every five minutes." But a bathroom would be hard to find out here. He rolled up the truck's window to freeze the urge and finished the beer in his hand. He placed the empty bottle in the cup holder of the truck's console to discourage himself from grabbing another beer. As he rounded a bend in the road, a small steeple came into sight ahead on the right. It was the old St. Thomas Catholic Church. The place had been closed for years, but Paul thought that the town plow trucks used the parking lot to turn themselves around. He hoped that was the case because his need to relieve himself was growing stronger every second.

As he neared the church, Paul saw that the lot was clear and empty. He meant to press lightly on the brake pedal to slow down, but Tank's brakes worked far better than the heater, and the wheels locked up suddenly on some ice in the road. The truck's back end slid out into the opposite lane as the front jerked violently toward a large snowbank and mailbox at the entrance to the plowed lot.

"Shit!" he yelled instinctively and took his foot off the brake while turning the steering wheel quickly to correct his direction. The effort brought the front of the truck away from the mailbox but not far enough to clear the snowbank, and the truck plowed up and over the large mound of snow. Paul's body was thrown upwards from the seat, and his head cracked into the roof of the cab. He heard a great cacophony of sounds as everything loose in the truck was launched up and then crashed down in a new location. He never let go of the wheel, and once over the snowbank, he pushed down hard on the brakes, which caused the truck to first slide over the icy parking lot and then jerk violently to an abrupt stop when it reached a section of the lot that had been exposed to the sun and was clean and dry. The sudden stop threw Paul's body forward, and his head would have crashed into the windshield if his body hadn't connected solidly with the steering wheel. He heard the sharp blare of a horn going off and soon realized it was because he was lying on the wheel. He pushed himself back, quickly put the truck in park, and with shaky hands turned the ignition off while sitting back in the seat and waiting for the wild beating in his heart to subside.

Just breathe, he thought and closed his eyes. The strong pounding in his chest filled his ears, drowning out all other sounds. This was the heart attack for sure, and he would certainly be dead by the time someone found him out here. It wouldn't be the worst way to go. People might talk, as they always do, but the ride to this point had been pleasant, and if it was his last,

Paul thought he could live and die, going out this way. To Paul, dying here would certainly be better than wasting away in some hospital, or nursing home, or worse. His mind flashed to a scene from a few nights ago, where he was stumbling around in the darkness, drunk and alone and retching into the toilet. Yes, it certainly was better than that. He thought of Roscoe patiently interviewing the young girl at the store who sold him the beer. That would be worth sticking around for. Soon the thumping in his chest found a normal rhythm, and his breathing slowed. He was going to live through this, after all.

"Great," Paul said out loud to no one and opened his eyes.

As he did, he noticed that the truck's interior looked completely different, everything asunder, some things broken and leaking. Work gloves, a bottle of motor oil, spare change, screws and nails of various lengths, bungee cords, rope, vise grips, several screwdrivers, and what seemed to be receipts but may have just been bits of paper –all littered the interior around him. He looked at the middle console and saw that the empty bottle he'd placed there was gone. At the same time, he noticed a large hammer laying in a growing wet stain on the passenger seat. It appeared that the hammer had broken the remaining bottles of beer. Jagged pieces of glass sat in the wet cardboard holder and were scattered everywhere. He leaned toward the mess, and as he did a great pain seized his upper neck and head. Paul touched the painful spot and felt a bump forming. But not blood. Blood would have been worse.

"Oh, that's just great. Just fucking great."

Paul could feel a throbbing from his bumped head and a tight, straining pain in his neck. He leaned back, closed his eyes, and tried to return to the idyllic scene he'd created moments before on the mountain, but it was no good. He fucked it all up, as usual.

Paul heard a car on the road, and pain shot up through his neck as he turned to look. The car didn't slow down as it went by, but he felt conspicuous being parked so haphazardly in the deserted lot in Tank's truck. The

smell of beer became stronger, and if someone did stop, it would be immediately clear to them that he'd been drinking. And what if the truck had a
flat tire or was damaged by the impact? How would he fix it without help?

He saw a small graveyard near the back of the lot. He reached up
to turn the key and start the truck. His hands were shaking badly. These
tremors felt different than those he experienced after going on a binge. His
body was filled with too much energy, and he wished he had another beer
or at least another sip to take the edge off. He glanced briefly at the damp
pile of broken glass on the seat before turning the key and driving slowly
back toward the cemetery.

After stopping, Paul opened the door to the truck and stepped out,
leaving the door open behind him to air it out. He walked to the front
bumper of the truck and looked around. It was perfectly quiet, and he
saw that all the lights were off within the church. He unzipped his pants,
exposed himself to the cold, sunny day, and relieved himself. He thought
how things in his life wouldn't be so complicated if he'd just been more
careful in the Stumble Inn parking lot. Life was funny like that. One little
mistake, one wrong step, and the avalanche of shit starts pouring down
around you.

Once he was done, he stepped back and inspected the front of the
truck. Nothing looked broken or dented from the impact. There was snow
crushed and packed around the bumper and the front passenger tire, but
it was beginning to melt and fall away. Paul walked back to the bed of
the truck and looked in. There were many discarded cans of soda strewn
about and plastic bottles of standard automotive fluids: oil, transmission,
and windshield washer. It was hard to know how much had been jostled
and rearranged by his collision, but to his eye, nothing of consequence
seemed broken. There were two empty cardboard boxes mixed in the mess,
and Paul picked up the smaller of them. He walked over to the passenger
door, opened it, and began putting bits of glass and random wet papers into
the box. It was difficult to determine if any of the papers were important

because they were soaked through, stuck together, and unreadable now. Paul did his best to collect everything into the box. He used an old red rag to wipe down the seat and the trails of liquid that had spread to the floor. He left both doors of the truck open and returned the cardboard box with the new contents to the back of the truck. He wished he had bought room spray from the small market or that he was the type who kept cologne on him at all times. That would be a good practice in the future.

Once the box was tucked away, Paul walked back to the driver's side of the truck and leaned inside. He found the tin of mints and his bottle of water. He popped three mints into his mouth and left the opened tin on the bench seat, hoping that it might work as a small diffuser, covering up the smell of alcohol. After only a minute or two of having the mints in his mouth, he felt his eyes begin to tear and reached for the water bottle.

As Paul took a long drink, he let his eyes settle for the first time upon the cemetery. The church and the land around it were quite small, and he guessed there were fewer than a hundred headstones in the graveyard.

Someone had shoveled a small, rough pathway into the place. Only some gravestones had been cleared of snow, and there were items on the ground and adorning these cleared headstones. He set the water down on the hood of the truck and entered the cemetery, noticing one set of small footprints on the path.

He walked over to the first cleared headstone, which read:

PETER WESLEY OWENS

BORN 1921 – DIED 1923

"Beloved Son and Child of God"

Stuck into the snow near the grave was a solar-powered marker with a small angel on the top meant to light up once nighttime fell. There was also a blue plastic rosary draped over the headstone.

There was another cleared headstone close by, and Paul walked over. This one had the same angel light in the ground and a pink plastic rosary hanging from the headstone. The stone read:

MARGARET HAZEL OWENS

BORN 1920 – DIED 1923

"Our Beautiful Angel"

The nearest cleared headstone was in the next row, but Paul could see that each cleared plot had the same angel light and either a blue or pink rosary adorning the gravesite. There looked to be over twenty plots decorated in this way.

The only exception to the pattern of cleared memorials was in the middle of the cemetery. This wasn't a headstone but an old statue. Paul walked over to it. Weather and time had worn many of the intricate features away, but it looked to Paul like a man sitting on a box, his arms opened wide to any approaching visitors. At the base of the stone was a faint inscription that Paul had to lean in close and squint his eyes to read:

PETER MICHAEL GAFFNEY

BORN 1885 – DIED 1961

"A Life Spent in Loving Service"

A car's motor slowed down on the main road. Paul walked quickly back to the truck, closed the passenger door, and went around to the driver's side. The car was turning into the parking lot and driving directly toward him. The small, tan, unassuming sedan could have belonged to anyone. But he knew who it was before he saw the driver, and as suspicious and awkward as it would have been to jump in and flee, he had to fight the urge to do so.

The car pulled up and stopped.

It was Jennifer "Jenny" Farone. How perfect. Besides Garth and Marty, Paul couldn't think of a more perfect busy body to find him out here. She was a few years younger than Paul, and the two never really knew much about each other growing up, except that each had families who were somewhat respected around Moheneck Falls for their solid work ethic. Jenny became more prominent in Paul's life after he and Charlotte were engaged. As a stipulation of joining the Catholic Church family as a married couple, they began attending services regularly at St. Vincent's Parish. Paul was against the whole thing from the start and tried to convince his fiancé to get married at the local Justice of the Peace or outside in a local picnic site with a beautiful view of the river. But Charlotte wouldn't budge on the issue. Paul knew that her family was pushing all of this. He followed the path of least resistance, and they began attending Sunday masses together.

It seemed Jenny was always there, always involved in everything related to St. Vincent's, and seeking out any opportunity to be of service to the church. There were rumors around town that her family had been offered a full scholarship for Jenny to attend a prestigious Catholic college, but that the money was not earned by Jenny's academic performance alone, or by her service to St. Vincent's. Paul heard something about a real estate deal, or a stock sale involved in the funding, but he never got the whole story.

He found out enough about Jenny to form his own opinion. To Paul, she became the uptight, hypocritical bitch from the awful fucking church where he went to please his fiancé and her family all those years ago. And that hypocritical bitch from that fucking church had refused to hold a funeral service for his dead child, even though he and his wife had submitted the same weekly tithe as all the other good Christian Soldiers in the pews every Sunday. He had seen that car outside his house many times since Sean's death but had managed to avoid her and her pitiful, insincere acts of charity until now.

He could hear the engine of Jenny's small car click and tink and hiss as melting snow hit the engine and exhaust. Chunks of ice and slush that had clung to the wheel wells and edges of the car calved to the ground around the car. Jenny seemed to be taking a very long time to exit, and he wondered if she was stalling for time if she felt as uncomfortable as him at this moment, and if she desperately wanted to start her car and escape the situation as badly as he did. He picked up the water bottle from the hood of the truck and took a sip. For a moment, he thought about reaching and grabbing another mint from the open tin on the seat but decided against it.

Eventually, her car door opened, and the warning bell dinged, alerting her to the keys in the ignition. She ignored the sound, closed the door, and walked slowly around the car toward Paul.

"Well, hello, Paul, I certainly didn't expect to find you out here. How are you?"

"Hi there, Jenny. I hadn't planned on being here myself. I needed to have some work done out at Cook's Garage, and he loaned me his truck until my car is ready."

Paul's heart was pumping faster. He felt his face reddening, getting warmer and warmer, starting to boil like a lobster in the pot. He knew he should stop talking, that he really did not owe this woman any explanation of what he was doing out here. But for some reason, he continued to prattle on.

"On my way back to town, the truck was making some noises. It just didn't sound right. Which makes sense, right? The last car to get fixed is always the mechanic's. So, I pulled in here to check it out. Then I saw the headstones cleared off in the cemetery, and I decided to take a look. I had always known this place was out here, but in all these years, I had never stopped by. It hasn't been a working church in quite a while, right? But it certainly is a nice piece of property!"

He felt nervous, electrified, and trapped. He hoped she wasn't close enough to smell his breath. Tank may not have read the newspaper, but

Paul was sure that Jenny did. She probably read every word of the thing and wrote regular letters to the editor.

After what seemed a long pause, she began speaking.

"It certainly is a nice piece of land. I suppose that's why I haven't sold it off to the church or the town in all these years."

"I had no idea you owned this. I always thought it belonged to the Catholic Church, and they just didn't have enough people to fill the seats. So, they closed it down."

"Yes, well, that's quite an interesting story. Father Gaffney was a priest assigned to St. Vincent's a long time ago. My great grandfather and grandmother convinced Father Gaffney to start holding services out here. It was their land, but they asked other local farmers who were attending Father Gaffney's weekly visits to build the church. Once the church was finished, my great grandparents had a local lawyer write up an agreement to lend the land for church services under a very specific set of rules. I suppose it was a type of lease agreement, but they never accepted any money for themselves and only took enough to pay the taxes and for upkeep of the place when the church was able to provide enough money. The Catholic Church tried to buy the land outright from my family several times, but we always refused. Eventually, they forbid Father Gaffney from holding services here, but he continued and ex-communicated from the faith. He lived out the rest of his days in this place."

She looked over at the building and then toward the cemetery.

"It was a real labor of love."

"Wow," Paul said, "I always assumed this was another branch of St. Vincent's. I'm guessing that's Father Gaffney's statue in the middle of the graveyard?"

Jenny looked over and smiled again.

"Yes, that's him. And even if it may not look like it anymore, that is a hay bale he is sitting on, that was his original pulpit until the church was built."

She stopped and rubbed her gloved hands together. The sun was directly overhead, causing their shadows to almost touch each other on the frozen ground.

"That's the only adult headstone I clear off and tend to during the winter. The rest of these things are for the children in there. I don't know. It may be silly, I guess, but since the church is closed and I'm really the only able-bodied landlord to tend to the place, it seems like the least I can do."

Paul heard a car's engine from the road. It was straining, working too hard, nearing its breaking point. He saw a rusted, shaky sedan with vibrating plastic taped over the driver's side window rattle past the church.

"Well, I probably should get to work. I carry a box of lights and rosaries around in my car to replace the broken ones as needed. And I'm sure you don't want to stand out here in the cold any longer listening to me go on and on."

Their eyes connected, and Paul saw something warm, fragile, and desperate in her face.

"No, Jenny, I'm glad that we ran into each other. It's really a nice thing that you're doing out here. And I need to—I mean, I want to thank you. It's been very nice of you to drop those baskets off at the house,"

Paul heard his voice quake.

"I really appreciate the effort. And the thoughts. After Charlotte left, things got tough. I mean, I really became…"

He looked down, away from her face, and noticed that their shadows were completely intertwined and outstretched on the ground.

She put her gloved hand on the forearm of his coat.

"It's okay, Paul."

His voice quavered as he continued.

"When she left, I became very…unwell. I went off the tracks, really, and I don't blame Charlotte at all for getting away from all of it. I had nothing to help her, nothing to give her. I just gave up and fell apart."

He took a deep breath, hoping to get himself under control. "But I'm trying now. I'm sure you've heard about my recent troubles with the car and my license, but that may have been just what I needed. I'm getting some help, coming back to life, you know."

"Yes, that's good. It's really good to hear, Paul. We all need help sometimes."

A million thoughts were racing through his head, but he couldn't think of any way to express them. The anger he'd felt toward her, and her church and the whole awful thing had been so much easier. Much simpler to express. Much more comfortable to feel.

"I'm sorry," she said in a small, quiet voice. "I'm sorry for you, and for Charlotte, and for all that you went through after Sean passed on. And I'm very sorry for the things that happened with the church back then. For all the careless, ignorant, remarks, the lack of sympathy and compassion. I should have said something. I'm so sorry that I didn't do and say more to shut them up and to be there for you and Charlotte and Sean."

It was the first time in a long time someone else had spoken Sean's name. He glanced up at her and recognized a familiar ache, the deep scars of guilt and pain.

"Jenny, it's fine. You don't need to, I mean, it wasn't your call about the services or the burial. The whole thing was just so—"

"No," she said sharply, "No, Paul, it's not fine! It's really not. I can't imagine what it must have been like for you two. It must have been horrible. And to know that people were saying such cruel things, such awful things. I can't forgive myself. I won't forgive myself. I'm so very sorry, Paul. And I'm sorry that you lost your son, your only child…" She began sobbing harder and said, "I'm just so sorry for you and your family."

He reached out and held her gloved hand tightly. She moved closer to him, and they wrapped their arms around each other. Paul felt a million little fissures start to crack a frozen and hardened place deep inside himself. He couldn't remember the last time he'd hugged someone.

Moments passed and turned into minutes. Their breath formed into clouds and rose upwards, vanishing in the clear, cold sky. He heard another car pass by on the road, and Jenny released her arms.

"Well," he said and was relieved that the tremble was gone from his voice, "I'm glad that we ran into each other. It was good to talk to you."

She shook her head in agreement and rubbed her wet face with a glove.

After a moment, she said, "Yes, yes, Paul it was. And I hope we speak again soon."

She smiled.

"I suppose I should get back to the house. At this rate, my car will be fixed before I even make it home."

"Sure," she replied. "And I should get to work here." Her head turned in the direction of the cemetery.

"Oh, my, would you look at that! There's a cardinal sitting on Father Gaffney's statue. Why I haven't seen one of those birds out here for as long as I can remember."

CHAPTER 17

"I believe that Jesus' most challenging lessons were those about forgiveness.
And as difficult as it may be right now to choose forgiveness over righteous
anger and resentments, I implore you all to turn the whole matter over to
the God we all serve. In my experience and in my understanding of the
scripture, I believe that the weight of such anger and despair has kept many
people from making true spiritual progress. In order to move forward and
closer to God, we must choose to embrace love and forgiveness."

Excerpted from Father Gaffney's first sermon in Farone's Field following
his ex-communication with the Catholic Church

It was obvious birds had been coming to the roofless feeder in the backyard, or something had because the thing was nearly empty. The process
of filling the feeder went more smoothly this time, and when he finished,
he leaned down and picked up some of the broken pieces from the small
wooden roof.

It was Saturday. Weekends were known as the hardest times not to
drink in early sobriety, especially for people who lived alone and were close
to physical withdrawal from their drug. Paul hadn't drunk since yesterday,
since his talk with Jenny. His head ached, his guts went from feeling too
tight and strained to feeling uncontrollable and nauseous, and the tremors

he'd been avoiding at all costs came in waves but eventually subsided. He found two bottles of old but unopened ginger ale in the house and forced himself to keep drinking it, as well as water to settle his stomach and avoid the dehydration that alcohol caused. His plan was to keep busy by puttering with chores around the house, and to take a nap if the cravings to drink got too bad.

But the cravings left miraculously. Something had happened. Some powerful change had taken place yesterday. Maybe it was knowing the breathalyzer was coming, or that he had nearly gotten into another accident with Tank's truck and now had to figure out how to get the beer smell out of the thing. (More secrets he needed to hide.) Most likely, it was the pain he saw in Jenny's eyes. It was familiar and palpable and sincere. Whatever the cause, Paul could feel a difference, and in some ways, it was more uncomfortable than cravings for booze.

Jenny and all those people had been horrible, unkind, cruel—"unChristlike"—in every conceivable way.

"Fuck them," he mumbled as he picked up the bag of birdseed and walked toward the back door of the house.

What would Jesus do? Paul pictured the bearded man in sandals and pondered the situation for a moment while tightening the robe he was always wearing and stroking his wizened, stubbled face. Paul could hear the man's reply.

"Fuck them, Paul, that's what I'd do."

He walked into the house and over to a large pile of baskets and bags thrown haphazardly in front of his stereo system in the living room. He grabbed the garbage can from the kitchen and began sorting through all that Jenny had left at his front door. Many of the items were non-perishable: tissues, shaving cream, soaps. There were canned soups, vegetables, and jellies as well. He found some boxes of crackers and cookies that had gone stale. Small holes were nibbled in the side, and crumbs spilled out. There was a mouse nest centered under the pile.

Paul was impressed that the clever little rodent settled in under such a mountain of treasures. He felt a tinge of guilt as he looked under the kitchen sink for the supply of mouse traps he'd used over the years. He found an old, stained, and rumpled card down there, which must have fallen out of the trash a long time ago. He threw the card onto the counter and grabbed two traps. They were the older kind, simple designs with strong springs and an inclined bar to hold the bait. He retrieved a jar of peanut butter from the gifts Jenny had left, bringing everything into the living room and setting up the traps on either side of the nest. Paul nearly caught his own fingers several times while trying to set them, delivering a litany of expletives each time the spring released prematurely, and the animated little wooden base jumped into the air, then landed peanut butter side down in the carpet.

With the pile of donations removed, Paul could access his stereo system again. It felt like forever since he had listened to music at home. He considered the large collection of vinyl albums but worried that every song might hold a memory of Charlotte, or Sean, or the life that was over. That would be too much right now, a "total buzz-kill" (to quote a young patient he saw years ago reacting to the news that the amount of hallucinogens he had been taking may have fried and altered his brain circuitry forever).

He pushed the power button and brought the old system humming and cracking to life. It was tuned to 106.7 FM, and the familiar sound of Jimmy Page and the lads from Led Zeppelin boomed through the large speakers.

"It's been a long time since I rock and rolled. It's been a long time since I did the stroll. Let me get back, let me get back, let me get back, baby where I come from..."

Paul moved some donated supplies into the bathroom linen closet and filled nearly three kitchen cupboards with the food. His stomach ached dully, and it was hard to know if the feeling was hunger, withdrawal, or an ulcer acting up. Jenny had provided bottles of ibuprofen and acetaminophen, so he took a dose of each with the ginger ale, remembering some research he'd heard that this combination of pills was just as effective for pain and the treatment of withdrawal as many opioids were. There was one half-full bottle of vodka in the freezer. It was risky to have it there, a bad idea that he would never have recommended to anyone else. But there it was, and so far, the bottle had not beckoned him to its icy lair. He pulled out the old vacuum and ran it over the area where the pile had been, careful not to disturb the mouse nest or traps. It felt good to be productive, and he continued cleaning and straightening up the house well into the early evening. He'd always taken satisfaction from doing housework, especially tasks that offered quick results and immediate gratification like cleaning up a room, dusting, or vacuuming. His work as a counselor seldom led to such quick and tidy outcomes.

The house was darkening, and his headache and stomach pains were becoming more assertive and harder to ignore. He unplugged the vacuum but left it out in the living room, planning to use the thing more often from now on. He shut off the stereo. The sudden silence was no good, so he picked up the remote and turned on the television. Images of familiar newscasters popped up on the screen. They reported on a drug bust that happened nearby, Deerfield, perhaps, and it must have been a sizable arrest because the names and pictures, some young and some older, filled the screen. Paul didn't recognize any of them. Having the news on felt wrong to him, like calling that friend or family member after you've had a great day only to have them reply with details of their problems with explosive diarrhea.

He switched the channels several times until the screen filled with Rodney Dangerfield's smiling face. He was decked out in tacky golfing attire and upsetting a haughty rich man at the country club, the guy who used to play Ted Baxter on "The Mary Tyler Moore Show." Now, this was more like it. It was just the medicine he needed from Dr. Boob Tube tonight. Paul turned up the volume and walked into the kitchen to find something to eat.

He settled on a can of stew, the picture promising more than the product could ever deliver. He poured the contents into a pan to heat on the stove. Paul avoided microwaving soup or stew because it just never tasted as good that way. And now that he could eat, he might as well enjoy it.

He filled his water glass again, purposely avoiding adding ice cubes so that he wouldn't need to stare down the bottle in the freezer. Out of sight, out of mind. Paul noticed the old card he'd removed earlier lying on the countertop. He picked it up and read the front. It was a biblical quote:

"Ask, and it will be given to you. Seek, and you will find. Knock, and it will be opened for you.

For everyone who asks receives. He who seeks finds. To him who knocks, it will be opened."

Paul opened the card up and read another quote:

"Blessed are those who mourn, for they shall be comforted."

Paul squinted and concentrated on the faint, smudged words written in flowing cursive near the bottom of the card:

There are no words to express the pain I feel for your family at this time. I've always believed that God's love for his Son and for all his children is unconditional, all-encompassing, and forever. There is nothing I can say or do to ease the suffering and pain you must be feeling, but please know that I'm here for anything you might need.

In Deepest Sympathy,

Jenny Farone

Paul gripped the card tightly, preparing to rip the thing in half and throw it in the trash can. Instead, he read the front again. He closed his eyes, took a long, deep breath.

"Okay, I get it. Maybe not fuck her. Maybe not fuck all of them."

He walked over to the refrigerator and picked up one of several magnets placed haphazardly on the door. Paul thought of all the crayon drawings, "A+" papers, and photos that had been here over the years. Now, only the magnets remained. He placed the card in the middle of the door, affixing four magnets to the sides, then opened the freezer and grabbed the bottle of vodka.

Paul twisted off the cap, tipped it over the sink, and poured the last booze in the house down the drain.

CHAPTER 18

*"The treatment of addiction has traditionally focused on the
bio-psycho-social aspects of the disease. That means that we look at the
biological, psychological, and social changes which happen during
addiction, and we try to assist a patient in getting these areas healed and
functioning. But St. Michael's believes there's a spiritual ailment involved as
well, and to be effective, we mustn't ignore that aspect of the disease."*

Excerpted from the St. Michael's new employee training video

Quiet times and spaces in conversations were always uncomfortable for Travis. So, the silence that engulfed the classroom felt tortuous. But Professor Dunleavy seemed perfectly happy with it. He had asked the class a question and now sat on his stool behind the podium and smiled. The concept of "therapeutic silence" had come up more than once in the past, and Dunleavy insisted that counselors risked doing more work than patients if they interrupted reflection and quiet time during sessions. It was one of many things Travis learned at H.C.C. that sounded great in the classroom but was extremely difficult to practice in his daily life.

It didn't help that the professor's question felt more like an accusation. Travis didn't dare to speak up, but he hoped someone would say something soon and move the conversation away from the topic.

Finally, a hand went up, and the professor called out.

"Yes, Amber, what do you think?"

"Well, I'm not sure, you know? Because it's like, if you allow the person into a group, then you might, like, make the other people angry because he's drunk. But if you don't let him in, well then, he might just go back out and drink some more. So, it's, like, a really tough decision."

She looked over at the girl sitting next to her, who Travis knew was her best friend.

"It's really tough, right?"

The friend shook her head vehemently in affirmation but said nothing.

The professor also nodded, staying neutral and noncommittal. Another hand went up.

"Yes, Lamont, your thoughts?"

Lamont was the oldest student in the class. He told them that he was becoming a counselor after retiring from a twenty-eight-year career at the phone company.

"We shouldn't throw them out. That won't help the patient at all, and it will give them a great excuse to keep drinking. They'll end up at the bar and drink at us all night long after that."

The professor interrupted, "But is their choice to drink our responsibility?"

"Yes," Lamont quickly answered and then hesitated.

"Well, partly. Maybe. I mean, you've been telling us that the first ethical responsibility we have is '*Do no harm*' with all patients, and it seems to me that sending someone away from treatment is going to do them more harm than good."

That's true, Lamont. We are ethically bound to do no harm to patients. The difficulty here is that we have a situation where a person has been using one of the substances that we are trying to keep our patients away from. If we don't allow them into the treatment group, they might leave and drink more. But if we let them in, are we putting other patients at risk? Are we doing *them* harm?"

Several hands were up in the classroom, but before the professor called on someone else, Lamont responded.

"Yeah, well, it's a problem, I can see that. Honestly, I'm not sure what I would do. What should we do?"

The professor smiled, and another student shouted out.

"You know he won't just tell us – that would be way too easy!"

Laughter rose in the room.

"I need to make sure you get your tuition's worth by thinking about these things, folks. This is a situation that everyone in here will face. It's not a question of if a patient will show up to your group after drinking or using another drug. It's a matter of when. So, let's keep talking about it. Maria, what are your thoughts?"

Maria was another older student who spent most of her career as a nurse's aide in a hospital. She told the class she enrolled in this program to become more skilled at working with addictions because her training so far had not included much. She was currently interning in a detoxification unit.

"I think a counselor needs to assess how much the person has been drinking," she said, "and then determine if they might need to go directly to detox. The patient might have other health problems, and if we just send them away, that could be very bad. Not just for the patient, but for us. I have seen people come into the detox unit who have a blood alcohol content of .30, and if it wasn't for the reek of alcohol coming off them, you wouldn't even know they'd been drinking because they're acting so normal. Each drink is supposed to raise a person's blood-alcohol level by .02%, and if the level of alcohol gets to .40 most people are in a life-threatening situation and are almost comatose because the alcohol has slowed down their functions so much. People who don't normally abuse alcohol are acting drunk at around .10. So, the people we see at detox who have these high levels of alcohol in their blood and are acting sober have really developed a tolerance for it. They need help, but because they act pretty normal, most people don't realize just how much alcohol they have in their system. If there is another medical problem, it should be listed in the patient's chart. So I think every counselor needs to, at least, look in the chart before sending them away."

"All good points, Maria," the professor responded. "And a good reminder to everyone about why we use things like breathalyzers and urine screens in this field. We are dealing with an illness here whose symptoms involve lying, deceit and denial. If we only depend on the self-report of a sick person to determine if they are really getting well, that's a setup for failure. Despite what some of your patients might think, we counselors are not on power trips, and we are not trying to intentionally catch people lying and get them thrown out of treatment. We're trying to make people accountable. Accountability is essential with any behavioral change. Think for a minute about what good it would do you if you decided to lose some weight but never stepped on a scale. You could research the best forms of weight loss online and go to groups and meetings with other people, all trying to get thin each week in a group. You might binge-watch reality shows about the most obese people taking control of their lives. But if you never stepped on a scale, you really wouldn't have any means of measuring your progress, and you're not making yourself accountable for the weight loss. In the same way, we need to use breathalyzers and urine screens as tools for accountability. Does this all make sense? It really is a great topic, and I'm glad it came up."

"So it's a gray area." Travis wasn't aware he'd said it aloud until Dunleavy and several other students turned to look at him.

"Are you asking me or telling me?" The professor asked, smiling.

"I, uh, I'm not sure," Travis felt his entire body heating up, "I guess I'm just trying to work it out, you know…"

The silence came then. The deafening Dunleavy silence that screamed at Travis to say more.

"I mean, it's like you teach us all about the patient's personal account-ability and their freedom to make choices, but at my internship it seems like we're just glorified hall monitors, or even prison guards most of the time waiting to punish people when they break the rules. We tell patients about all the choices they have in getting sober, but in the same breath we threaten to discharge them or report them to probation, or parole, or who-ever said they had to be there if they don't do what we say. It just seems like a very mixed message to me. A lie, really."

"Sounds like the myth of choice." Monica said from behind Travis.

"Say more about that Monica." Dunleavy prompted.

"Well, I actually saw that term in the old book you recommended about ethics in addiction counseling. The language was outdated, but the book made a great point about how so many behaviors around substance abuse are illegal. So the sicker someone gets, the more trouble they get into with the law. So by the time we meet with them, the choices they have left are not really choices at all."

"Like do what we say or go to jail?" Jason said, laughing.

"Yes," the professor agreed, "like that. Or do what we say or lose your driver's license forever. Or permission to see your kids. Or a hundred other freedoms that the person's substance abuse is slowly taking away from them. And that's the point here. We are hall monitors or prison guards in a way, I suppose, but it's important to remember that the rules we're enforc-ing are always in the patient's best interest. We're trying to let them out of the prison cells they put themselves in – we're not trying to keep them there. And if someone is showing up for treatment after drinking or using a substance, they need us to call them out on it. If we don't, their freedom and choices will soon be completely gone."

Travis could hear the footsteps of other students out in the hallway. He looked at the old clock in the room and saw that class had officially ended two minutes earlier.

"I hope this makes sense to everyone." The professor said, looking over the students and resting his gaze on Travis, who thought he saw a spark of recognition in Dunleavy's eyes.

"I'm surprised you didn't bring up this topic of someone showing up intoxicated at treatment, Travis, because I would think that your patient is at high risk for that. When are you meeting with him again?"

The classroom door opened, and students started streaming in, finding seats for the next class. Travis felt his heart beating and the lump in his throat swell as he stood up and started to leave.

"I'm meeting with him again tomorrow."

"Well," the professor replied, picking up his own bag from the table at the front of the room, "it might be a good time for a random breathalyzer."

CHAPTER 19

"The most important aspect of the counselor-client relationship is establishing a strong and trusting therapeutic alliance. This involves being viewed as competent by the client, but more importantly, it comes from a sense of unconditional positive regard for all those people you serve."

H.C.C. Required Textbook: Becoming an Effective Helper

On Tuesday, Travis was surprised to see Matt near the reception desk when he went into the clinic. Matt was normally blustering around the building or parked in his office barking into the phone. But this morning, he was positioned behind Carla, pulling out what looked like a video game remote from a cardboard box. He reached into the box and retrieved a long string of small clear packaging with individually wrapped tiny plastic straws. Matt ripped one of the packages open and stuck the straw into the device he was holding. He pressed a button, and Travis heard the machine beep loudly three times.

"Okay," Matt said by way of greeting. "Come over here and blow in this thing."

Travis looked around the reception area. Nobody else was there.

"Just take a deep breath and then blow a nice, slow, steady stream through that tube," Matt said. "When the machine registers, you'll hear three beeps and then a clicking noise."

Travis held his backpack, which contained some schoolwork, lunch, and a biography of Kurt Cobain. He set the pack on the floor and walked over to where Matt was standing.

"You haven't been drinking today, have you?" Matt's voice was flat and deadpan, but when Travis looked up at him, he could see he was smiling.

"This isn't really for you," Matt said. "It's for your favorite patient who is coming in today. Let's check to see if he's staying sober, and I want to make sure this damn breathalyzer still works! I've been meaning to remind everyone to use it more often."

Travis nodded his head in understanding but didn't reply because he was holding his breath, preparing to exhale through the tube. He put his mouth to the machine and blew. As he did, he heard a high-pitched beeping noise for what seemed like a very long time. Finally, when he was almost entirely out of breath, the machine sounded off three beeps and a click. He stopped blowing.

"Huh," Matt said, "It looks like it works. What do you know?" He smiled again at Travis and then said, "So, how's it going with Paul?"

Travis glanced around again to make sure that no other patients were nearby. One of the topics that came up frequently in class was counselors' tendency to discuss patients in open settings like this even though it went against privacy laws. Travis thought these breaches of protocol happened primarily because clinicians were so busy and overloaded with patients and running groups that they didn't have extra time to go behind closed doors and discuss patients in more detail.

"That may be true," he remembered the professor saying in one class about the issue, *"but the more that you break this rule of confidentiality, the stronger a habit it becomes, and as we all know, bad habits are hard to break!"*

Travis looked at Matt.

"Actually, I was wondering if I could talk to you about him in your office. Do you have a minute?"

By the look on Matt's face, it seemed clear that Matt didn't.

He looked down at his wristwatch.

"Yeah, sure."

He handed Travis the box with the breathalyzer and straws.

"Here, take this thing and play around with it before Paul comes in today. Why don't you put it with your stuff and then meet me in my office in a few minutes? Sound good?"

"Sure, thanks," Travis replied.

By the time Travis put down his things in the small, spare office at the clinic and got to Matt's office, he found him on the phone, looking tense and rubbing his forehead. Matt motioned for Travis to come in and to close the door behind him. He held up a finger indicating for Travis to wait a minute while he finished up this call. Travis sat down in the same chair he'd used when completing Paul's assessment.

"Yes," Matt said into the phone, "Yes, I know that."

There was a pause, and Travis heard louder mumbling from the other end of the phone.

"Yes, we did that, yes, of course. Look…"

A louder rumble came from the phone receiver, and Matt held it further from his face as he looked over at Travis and shook his head slowly back and forth. When the rumbling subsided, Matt brought the phone closer.

"Look," Matt began again, "I've only got so many clinicians and limited time up here for them to do assessments on new patients."

The volume and intensity of Matt's voice grew as he spoke. He seemed to be trying to talk over the voice on the other end.

"We've had this discussion before, Vincent! I don't like having people wait to get in here any more than you do! If we're going to get these wait times down for assessments, the answer is to find me the money for another full-time counselor. You know that as well as I do! I've been down at least one staff person for over a year now, Vinny, and my other counselors are completely maxed out! More staff, Vinny! If you need more assessments, shorter wait times for new patients, and more money pumping out from up here, you've got to tell your boss to let me hire more staff! Do the math! It's not so hard to figure out. The addicts are dying in record numbers out there, buddy, and the only way we do more is if we have more counselors on the front line!"

Matt made eye contact with Travis, and Travis pointed toward the door, feeling more uncomfortable now and hoping Matt would allow him to leave and come back later, maybe much later. But Matt waved Travis off and rolled his eyes at the phone, seeming nonplussed by the argument.

The voice from the other end of the phone had quieted and become more subdued.

"Okay, yeah. I know. I get it. Yup. Look, Vin, I gotta go. Yeah. No, talk to Carla and see if there's any place we can get this woman in for an emergency assessment in the next week. Maybe I can do the assessment with her, or I can find a counselor up here that won't want to kill me if I give them one more thing to do. Yeah, okay, Vinny. Yes, you're welcome. But I need more staff, Vin. Tell her we need another full-time person up here! Yeah, you too, goodbye."

Matt placed the phone down and leaned way back in his large office chair, stretching his arms behind his head.

"So, do you want to do another evaluation?"

Travis was not sure if he was kidding or not.

"Sure, yes. I mean, if you need me to do it, I'd be glad to help out."

"Well, that's good," Matt said.

He brought his hands down and leaned over the desk toward Travis.

"Apparently, my bosses think we have an endless supply of free time to do assessments each week. I don't think the woman they want us to meet with will be appropriate for treatment here anyway. She's drinking way too much and probably has some psych issues, but no one can keep her sober long enough to find out what the real issues are. Her brother is a friend of someone higher up the food chain at St. Michaels, so, the pressure is on us to get her an assessment somewhere. She was in detox about six months ago and stormed out after the first day. The family is pressuring her to go back to detox, but she won't. There's no legal mandate, and she doesn't seem particularly motivated to get better. So, I figure she's got a fifty/fifty chance of even showing up here for the evaluation."

Matt leaned back in his chair again.

"If you're willing to meet with her, maybe we'll set up the appointment and see what happens. Is that okay with you? Is your professor gonna be pissed if we give you a couple of patients to follow at this point?"

"No," Travis said, "I mean, no, my professor won't mind. There are other students working with more than one patient, and he is alright with it. That would be just fine with me. Anything I can do to help, Matt."

"Well, careful, now. Don't say that around here, or we'll have you doing all kinds of stuff!"

A pinging sound came from Matt's computer. He looked at his screen, then picked up a pencil and wrote something down on the tattered legal pad on his desk. Travis heard some of the staff (especially Mandy) regularly complaining about Matt being clueless and apathetic to what was happening around the clinic, but Travis got the impression that Matt always knew more than he let on and that the shabby-looking notepad probably held more information, details, and plans than most people realized.

Travis had worked at a horrible coffee shop a few years ago where the manager constantly berated the staff, reminding them that they could be replaced at any time. He also micro-managed everything, from how much butter they were applying to bagels to how full they let the garbage cans get before emptying the trash.

"Those bags aren't free, you know," the manager would remind them, *"so you need to wait until they're overflowing before you take them to the dumpster. I know you're only going out there to talk on your phones and smoke your cigarettes! That's not what I'm paying you for!"*

Although it was a long way off for him, Travis occasionally thought about what it would be like to be in a management position in one of these substance abuse clinics. From what he'd seen at St. Michael's and heard the professor share in class, it sounded like most people who wound up in management started as counselors. This seemed like a double-edged sword to Travis. Promoting from within any organization was respectable, but the skill sets required for the positions varied greatly. It appeared Matt had the right stuff for the job, regardless of what Travis heard whispered around the break room.

"So," Matt said, "something was on you mind?"

"Yes," Travis started, "it's about Paul. I'm just a little bit overwhelmed by him, or maybe intimidated, if that makes sense at all. Not that he has acted intimidating, but just because of his age, and the fact that he worked here, and, well, he was sober for so long before he relapsed. It seems like it was all because of the suicide, and, well, he just seems like a lot to handle as my first patient."

Travis noticed that Matt was giving his full attention to the conversation rather than his usual habit of taking in information while multi-tasking with other things. This unnerved Travis more than being asked to work with another patient.

"Not that I don't want to work with him," Travis added, "because I do. I guess I'm just wondering if I'm the best person for this. I'm not sure that I can really help him."

Matt nodded his head slowly and took in a deep breath. He began lightly bouncing the eraser end of a pencil up and down on the desk.

Travis wasn't sure how to respond, so he said, "Does that make any sen…"

"I remember the first client I had," Matt interrupted. "I had only been out of rehab for about six months myself and probably had no business working in this field, but things were a lot looser back then. I came here as a patient, and Paul was my counselor. Did you know that?"

"No," Travis said.

In their former interactions, Travis had learned very little from Matt about his personal life except that his wife shopped too much and that his twin boys, both in their late teens or early twenties, did not seem in any rush to move out of his house, to pursue any kind of higher education, or to get jobs.

"I went to the same school you're at right now," Matt continued. "I got my counseling credentials there when I was about three years clean."

Matt motioned at the framed certificate on his wall.

"It was so much easier to get through the program back then. We knew so much less about treating addiction. Most of the people getting into the field were in recovery themselves, and we basically taught our patients what had worked for us. Anyway, that first job was as the overnight staff at a halfway house, where there were guys and girls living together. They hired me after firing the last overnight guy for sleeping on the job. When he wasn't asleep, they were pretty sure he was banging some of the women who were living there!"

Matt gave an exasperated laugh at the memory.

"It was a really healthy place to walk into, right? Like I said, I was in treatment here at the time and just getting my shit together, so the fact they hired me at all was a small miracle. Well, after telling Paul that I might want to be a counselor, he suggested that I ask if I could work with one of the residents at the halfway house—to see if I was going to like it, I guess, or to see if I was any good at it. I asked the woman that was the director of the house at the time, and she thought it was a great idea. In fact, she set me up with a guy that had just come into the house and that she had been working with."

Matt leaned forward, laughed loudly again, and slapped his hands on the desk.

"This guy," he said before laughing again and then taking a breath, trying to contain himself, "this fucking guy looked like a pirate. No shit, he really had the patch over one eye, and wore a bandanna over his head, and had scars and pockmarks all over his face! He was one ugly son of a bitch, right?"

"Sounds crazy," Travis said.

"Yeah, the staff even called him 'The Cap'n,' but we never said it to his face. I don't even remember what his whole story was, what drugs he had used, the trouble he got into, or how he wound up at the halfway house. I just remember that first time I saw him, I was scared shitless. He was ugly as hell and all kinds of pissed off that I was his new counselor."

"Why would he be angry about that?" Travis asked. "I mean, was he upset because you weren't an official counselor yet?"

"Oh no," Matt said, "I don't think anyone told him that. And I don't know if he would have given a shit. He was angry because he'd been meeting with the director, and she was a lot better looking than I was! I had to chase him around every time we had a meeting scheduled. Then he would sit there silent as a stone for our entire session while I tried everything to get him to talk!"

Matt flipped the pencil around in his fingers like a small baton.

"How did you handle him?" Travis asked. "I mean, what *could* you do?"

"Nothing," he said. "There wasn't a god-damned thing I could do to make this guy listen to a word I said. But I never skipped a meeting with him. We were supposed to meet once a week for an hour, which is exactly what I did. Most of the time, he would sit there silently, so, I started doing the same thing. We didn't have the internet back then, or I probably would have played around on the computer while he kept up the silent treatment. Everyone figured he would leave once the weather got nice. That may have been why he came into the house, just to get out of the cold. Anyway, I would see him playing card games with the other residents. We let them play cards back then, but no betting—no money allowed. I started bringing a pack of cards to our sessions. I asked him to play with me, which of course he wouldn't, so I began playing solitaire in front of him. Just him and I sitting there in the silence while I played solitaire. Jesus, nowadays the managed care companies and billing department would never allow that shit during an individual session! But I played badly, and I did it on purpose. I would hesitate and seem confused on purpose. I knew it would piss him off. Finally, he couldn't take it anymore. He had to take over the game and tell me what to do. After that, he would talk a little but not really say too much. If I remember right, he left the house in the spring, and they found him dead a month or two later from a heroin overdose."

The two sat in silence for a minute, letting the story settle.

"Nobody is a good first client," Matt said. "We don't have any control over who is sent in here to sit in front of us. All we can do is try to help those that are willing and hope the others become willing before this disease kills them."

Matt leaned in toward Travis.

"Did you know Paul requested to work with you?" Matt asked.

"Well," Travis corrected, "he was just kind of given to me by Carla. I mean, I was the only one available at the time."

"No, I mean after the evaluation. After our treatment team meeting when I talked to him on the phone. I suggested switching him to another counselor. But he wanted to stay with you."

"Why?" Travis asked and then answered his own question, "He probably thinks I'm the new guy, just a kid, and that he'll be able to manipulate me and get out of here easier."

"Yeah," Matt said, "that's what I thought, too. And I told him that I would be working with you and following him, that you would be reporting everything to me."

Matt rubbed his chin with one hand, slowly twirling the pencil in the other.

"He's one the best counselors in this business, or he was. I'm not sure who he is now, or how much of his brain has pickled since his kid died, but the fact that he relapsed after all those years clean, that this disease was strong enough to suck him back down, well, that scares me. And it scares everyone else who knew him back in the day. I think anyone who knew him then and sees him now would have a real hard time not feeling bad and giving him a break. They might be too soft on him. I think you might be the only person that can be objective here, Travis. And if he has even half the smarts he used to have, he knows that."

Travis sat for a moment, letting Matt's words sink in. He might not have believed it from anyone else, but Matt told things like they were.

"Okay," Travis said, "that could be true. It makes some sense, but I'm still not sure I can help him, besides being objective."

"Like I said before," Matt answered, "most of what we do is nothing at all, really. Maybe you just have to wait him out like I did with The Cap'n. Or maybe you need to bring the right deck of cards to the table for him to play with."

CHAPTER 20

"I've just never been comfortable with confronting people, and apparently that's a huge part of this job. I'm not sure I'll ever be very good at it."

Travis Kent, to C.J.

Paul's car wasn't fixed by the time of his appointment on Tuesday, and he wasn't in any rush to get it back. Cookie had called yesterday, saying that the process had been held up because Paul's car required a particular part to modify the installation. Cookie hoped to have the thing in by Wednesday or Thursday at the latest. When he first got the call, Paul had a strong desire to celebrate with a drink or two, but he resisted the urge. Instead, he loaded himself into the truck, drove past two liquor stores, and ended up in front of a church where he knew an A.A. meeting was being held. He didn't go in, didn't even leave the truck, but the hour or so spent sitting there was enough to get him past the craving.

It didn't surprise Paul when Travis asked him to perform a breathalyzer test before their session started. He was curious to see if any alcohol would register. It was obvious that Travis was new at the process, but Paul restrained himself from instructing the kid on the proper way to hold and operate the machine. He was amused that the breathalyzer was the same one St. Michael's had owned for years, and he wondered if it even worked anymore. He followed Travis' instructions, blew for what seemed to be a very long time into the tube, and eventually heard the loud beeps and a clicking noise that signaled him to stop. Travis held the machine, staring at the results.

"It says you haven't been drinking?" It sounded like a question.

"Then I guess I haven't," Paul said dryly. And then, "Do you want a urine screen as well?"

"No," Travis answered, "we don't need a urine screen today."

"Great. Do you mind if I use the bathroom because I've been holding it just in case?"

"Sure, no problem. Just meet me in the back, near the janitor's closet, when you're done."

Paul went to the bathroom, noticing several compliance violations along the way. He then found Travis standing in the storage closet, hoisting two chairs that had been stacked on a pile in the corner. The room was small, and there were cardboard boxes stacked up against one wall. Two large, bent, and rusting file cabinets leaned against each other for support against another wall. One small window faced the street. Travis had raised the blinds as high as they would go.

"I remember this room," Paul said, "and these old chairs, too."

"Yes, sorry about having to meet in here," Travis explained, "but everywhere else is taken. We recently cleared out a bunch of stuff and moved some things around, but it's still pretty cramped. I think Matt's hoping to get someone else hired and to use this as another office."

"It's a great idea." Paul said, "You can turn it into your own place until then, an intern den. And maybe I'll apply for the new position on the way out. Or maybe you should apply. I'm too old for this racket."

"Yeah," Travis replied, "I think I'll wait until I finish school, though."

The two sat down, facing each other. Travis was holding a medical chart and began flipping through the pages.

"So, I was hoping we could come up with some treatment plan goals today. I wanted to get your input and write some ideas down."

As Travis flipped through the chart, several papers that were not secured fell to the floor.

Paul resisted the urge to help the kid pick them up.

"How about this for a goal: don't drink and go to meetings?" Paul joked.

"Okay," Travis replied, "we can make that part of the plan. Let me just find the treatment plan section of the chart."

He had retrieved the fallen papers and was searching for the treatment plan section.

"And how many of these meetings do you think you should go to each week?"

Travis found the correct form. He balanced the folder on both knees, trying to write something while he spoke.

"How about ninety meetings in ninety days?" Paul suggested, amused that the kid was taking it all so seriously.

"Wow," Travis replied, "well, that sounds ambitious, but we can put it in here."

"And maybe I should get a girlfriend," Paul added. "I met an old friend last week that might be up for the challenge."

Travis looked up, narrowing his eyes slightly.

"Right, a girlfriend." He closed the file and set it on the floor. "Why don't we just talk for a while and not worry about the treatment plan right now?"

"Sounds good," Paul said. "Anything in particular, or are we just going to let the conversation go where it may?"

"Are you still drinking?" Travis asked.

"Didn't we already cover this?" Paul asked. "You just gave me the test."

"I know," Travis said, "but now I'm asking you. Just because you passed the breathalyzer doesn't mean you're not drinking."

"That's a good point," Paul agreed, "but no, I haven't been drinking. My last drink was on Friday after I ran into that woman I mentioned. I'm just bullshitting about dating her, but our conversation was long overdue, and for some reason, it gave me the kick in the ass I needed to get through a day or two without booze."

"Four days, actually," Travis said. "You've been sober four days."

"Has it been four days?" Paul asked, squinting and concentrating. "Yes. Wow, Friday until now. No booze. How about that!"

Paul looked at Travis and then raised his hands up in a "What do you know?" gesture.

"So, you're done drinking now?" Travis asked.

"Well, I'm done for right now. Done for today, probably. Isn't that the right answer?" Paul said.

"I don't know," Travis answered, "do you feel like drinking at all? Do you have any cravings?"

"Right now?" Paul asked. "No. At this moment, I feel great. But moments pass. Haven't they taught you about all this in school? The whole one-day-at-a-time philosophy of addiction? Or is that stuff just in the Twelve Step meetings? I'm not trying to criticize or bust your balls about it, but it sounds like you're asking me if I found a cure here, and I don't think there is a cure to what I got."

"I'm not asking if you're cured. I don't think addiction is curable, either. But I do think it's treatable. And it seems like we've learned how difficult early recovery can be for people, especially when they have strong cravings. A lot of what we learn in school is about recognizing substance abuse and then how to treat it. The goal is to treat and manage the symptoms of addiction so that someone's life will get better."

"What about abstinence?" Paul asked. "I mean, when I was counseling full time, that was always the goal, getting someone to quit using everything. Is that part of what they call managing and treating symptoms now?"

"Sometimes," Travis said. "The newer philosophies and strategies around treatment emphasize harm reduction—meeting someone where they're at, finding out what motivates them to stay sober, and trying to help them deal with the biggest problems and consequences in their lives at the moment. The abstinence-based approach was the norm, but we're learning that throwing someone out of treatment because they weren't able to stay sober isn't really helping them or their families in the long run. That's why we use more medications to control cravings when someone is first getting sober. We want to help them have a better chance of getting to complete abstinence."

"Hmm," Paul said, nodding his head, "Yeah, I get that. I mean, I get it to a point. People have been chewing nicotine gum and using patches to taper down and quit smoking for a long time. Hell, when I first started at St. Michael's, most of the counselors would go right out the front door and smoke with the clients between groups. We always saw it as the lesser of two evils and didn't offer any kind of help. So I get the concept of using medications to taper off a drug. What I wonder about, though, is the whole idea of using one addictive substance to get off another one. I mean, sure, nicotine is addictive, but tapering off the stuff is fairly straightforward. Even if someone relapses and smokes a cigarette again, they're not going to wind up dead from an overdose or anything. Some of the people we used to see were on methadone for years, and I used to wonder just when the tapering was supposed to start or if they would ever get off the stuff."

"Yeah," Travis said, "I understand what you're saying. What we learn and talk about all the time now is the difference between being dependent on something and being addicted to it."

"Aren't they the same thing?"

"Well, no," Travis answered. "I mean, they used to be, but now we distinguish between a person being dependent on something, like needing to take a medication for a health issue or to function, or to avoid withdrawal, and being addicted to a substance. I know it's a little confusing, and honestly, I'm not sure if I really understand or agree with it completely. The key point is that when someone is addicted, a tolerance always develops to the substance. You know, needing more to get the same result. Addiction also involves a person continuing to use the drug—"

"—despite negative consequences," Paul completed Travis' thought. "Yes, that's one of the things that hasn't changed in all the years we've been treating this monster. Alright, I think I get it. I don't exactly agree with all of it. I mean, I still think that not using at all is better than using some. Even before this whole shit show with heroin exploded, we had people who just couldn't seem to live a life of complete sobriety. Maybe this harm reduction stuff would have been a better way to go."

"I think the opioid crisis made us do things differently," Travis agreed, "but I also think that trying to support and encourage patients to live a completely sober life makes sense. Sometimes it's just not realistic like you said. Some people have more severe mental health issues or traumatic experiences, or—"

"Or they just don't want to stay fucking sober for the rest of their lives!" Paul interrupted again.

"Yeah," Travis agreed, "or that. The motivation for sobriety is never strong enough, or the desire to stay sober weakens over time. And according to Professor Dunleavy, that is every person's choice, and we can't deny each person the right to do what they want to do."

"I always liked Dunleavy," Paul said. "I remember when he first started sending interns over here. A lot of them got hired. Some others ran screaming from the building, decided they wanted to do anything but this for a career. He was always good, always level-headed about things."

"Let's get back to you and my original question." Travis said, "Do you think you're done with drinking now?"

"I fucking hope so," Paul said. "Why? Do you think I'm a candidate for harm reduction treatment? Are you going to recommend that I start methadone?"

"Not methadone, but there are some medicines more specific for alcohol cravings that you might benefit from. Are you open to meeting with the doctor here and discussing that option?"

Paul laughed. "I was just shitting you! Do you really think I need that?"

"I don't know. Only you know that. But I don't think it can hurt."

"Well," Paul said and put a hand up to wave off the suggestion, "I've done this before, and I didn't need any of that back then."

Travis opened his mouth to speak.

"I know, I know," Paul said, "you're going to tell me that it wasn't around back then. Or that if my way of staying sober had worked, I wouldn't be here, or that all the research shows that this stuff works. I'm just not sure if I need to do that."

"Or if you want to do it," Travis said. "And actually, all I was going to say was that it's up to you. Just let me know if you want to make an appointment with the doctor, and I'll set it up."

"Is Romanski still here?"

"Yes. And he seems good. He's well educated about addiction."

"Sure," Paul agreed, "he always knew his stuff. He was preaching about these taper medications years ago—way ahead of his time, I guess. He certainly is an odd duck, though. Not the warm and fuzzy type of duck either."

Travis chuckled, and the two men shared a smile.

"More of a tea-drinking type of duck," Travis added.

Exactly!" Paul laughed. "That's a great description."

There was a knock at the door.

"Come in," Travis said.

The door slowly opened, and Carla poked her head in.

"Sorry," she said, "I just need a box of tissues."

She went to the pile of cardboard boxes and rummaged through one until she found the tissues.

"Sorry," she said again and walked toward the door.

"No problem," Paul and Travis said simultaneously.

Paul added, "Don't you love what he's done with the place in here?"

"Yes, it's a perfect place to meet with our toughest clients," Carla said and winked at Travis before walking out.

"I like her," Paul said. "She's got a good way with people. They probably won't tell you this in school, but the people behind the front desk are really the ones who run everything in these places. You always want to be nice to them, get along with whoever is up there. I used to always ask them what they thought of job candidates before we hired people, and their opinions were right on the money every time."

"Good to know," Travis said.

"It's too bad we can't just zap this thing and have it be gone for good," Paul said.

"Say more. What do you mean by zapping it?"

"You know, like treating cancer or going to the dentist. You find out where the problem is, you drill down or cut the person open, and you remove the infected area. Problem solved!"

Travis nodded.

"Problem usually solved." He added.

"Right," Paul agreed, "and trust me, I would never want cancer. I wouldn't trade up being a drunk for it. Hell, I'm not even sure I'd choose some of the dental procedures over what I got, but what I'm saying is that I wish this wasn't such a crapshoot of a disease. I know way too many people that seemed like they had it beat, sober for years, and living great lives. And then – BOOM – relapse. I guess that can happen with cancer, too, coming out of remission and mucking everything up, but the idea that someone picks up that drink, or whatever the goddamn drug is after seeing all the shit it caused in their lives. I don't know. It just seems insane."

"Well," Travis said, "that's kind of your story, right? I mean, you knew all of the trouble it had caused in the past, but it wasn't enough to keep you away."

Paul felt himself tighten up.

Travis saw the change in Paul's face and posture.

"I don't mean to say your relapse was that simple." He leaned toward Paul in his chair. "I know we don't know each other yet, but me working here is kind of weird because I'm surrounded by people who only knew the sober you, and they all really liked that guy. I can tell that they looked up to you back then. You're something of a legend in the field if that makes any sense—"

"Or a cautionary tale," Paul said.

He rubbed his hand with his face and closed his eyes.

"I'm not so sure that picking up again had everything to do with Sean's death."

Paul opened his eyes briefly and looked at the kid. When Travis didn't respond, he closed his eyes again and slowly tilted his head toward the ceiling.

"It certainly put me over the edge. But for years while I was working here, listening to countless people talk about devastating, life-altering tragedies that happened in their lives, I remember thinking that I'd probably get fucked-up if I was in their shoes. Who wouldn't want to anesthetize themselves in the face of that much pain? I never talked about those thoughts with anyone, though. Maybe I should have. I had a sponsor and some other old-timers in A.A. that also worked as counselors. I could have unloaded that stuff on them, but I didn't. The longer I was sober, the more I just stuffed it down and kept silent. I think those last few years before I picked up a drink, my recovery was shakier than I wanted to admit."

Paul opened his eyes and glanced toward the window.

"Being a drunk who doesn't drink anymore is a funny thing. In the self-help meetings and in this place, in treatment, we just keep babbling on about how wonderful the sober life is, how lucky we all are having been saved from addiction, and how grateful we need to stay for our new and improved lives."

"So, you didn't feel that way?" Travis asked.

"Sometimes I felt that way. But things at home were hard. They needed to be dealt with, but I didn't do it. I wasn't there. I was saving the world at this place, listening to all these sad stories from hopeless cases, but I wasn't that guy at home. Sean had things he needed to talk about, things he wanted me to understand, to accept, and I just wasn't hearing it. The same with Charlotte. I let them drift further and further away from me while I pretended to everyone else that my life of recovery was wonderful and fulfilling—a dream come true. I guess I was like a person who declares himself 'born again' into deep religious faith after they've lived a life of doing terrible shit. You hear these people praise Jesus, or God, or Allah in voices full of sincerity and enthusiasm for the new lives they've gained, but part of you (or at least part of me) always thinks there will always be a part of them that's full of shit. The longer I stayed sober, the stronger those dark feelings grew but I was afraid, or maybe just too lazy, to tell anyone what was going on. The healer who couldn't heal himself."

"Or maybe you're just human," Travis said. "It sounds like you don't cut yourself much slack. I know I have a lot to learn about recovery, but to me it seems like staying sober is based on the same kind of spiritual awakening and continual growth and self-awareness that you talked about. Every spiritual icon I can think of constantly struggled with their faith and trying to hold onto a type of enlightenment long after their conversions or moments of clarity. A friend of mine, a devoted Christian, talks about how much Jesus questioned himself and struggled to practice what he preached. My friend believes that anyone trying to become more spiritual is going to have to spend their time in the 'Garden of Gethsemane.' My mom always quoted Mother Teresa and as I got older, I started to research her background story. I was shocked to find out that she spent a lot of her life trying to reconnect with God, to find the faith she felt like she had lost early on in her conversion. We might find the same issues with Buddha, or Gandhi, or Martin Luther King. Regardless of how you see yourself, it's clear to me that people liked and respected you not just because you were the sober guy but because you were trying to live an upright life, not to mention all of the people you helped along the way."

"Yeah," Paul said after a few moments of silence, "the great and powerful Oz of recovery really had nothing behind the curtain to help himself."

"I don't believe that. And if we're going to bring Oz references into this, remember that each of those characters had everything they needed inside of themselves, but they would never have known it if they hadn't worked together."

"It's like those great philosophers in the band America told us, right?" Paul asked and saw the look of confusion on Travis' face. "Never mind, it was before your time."

There was another knock at the door.

"Come in," Travis said.

Matt opened the door and stuck his head in.

"Oh," he said, "no wonder you're going overtime in this session, Travis. This guy will keep you here all afternoon!"

"I want to make sure I get my money's worth," Paul said. "My copay is way too high."

"How are you doing?" Matt asked, stepping into the room. "Is Travis using some of the newest techniques on you?"

"Well," Paul replied, "I passed the breathalyzer today, so, whatever he's doing must be working."

"Yeah, maybe," Matt patted Paul on the shoulder, "or maybe I need to get that thing recalibrated. You know how old the equipment is around here!"

He looked at Paul.

"Really, are you hanging in there?"

Paul shook his head, "Yeah, I think I'm ready to get out of the poppy fields and start walking down the yellow brick road again."

"Good," Matt said, "just like Dan Peek and the boys in America used to sing about, right? The Tin Man? Just make sure you get yourself here and let me know if you need anything, okay?"

"You got it," Paul smiled.

"And you," he said, pointing at Travis. "Can you run the next group? We've got an emergency assessment coming in, and we could use you in there."

"Is it okay for me to run it alone?" Travis asked. "I mean, is that something interns are allowed to do?"

Matt smirked. "Absolutely. And you'll do a better job than most of these other counselors would in there, but don't let them know I said that! Maybe you could have this guy be your guest speaker," he offered, nodding his head toward Paul.

Paul chuckled, "Yeah? I don't think so. Unless you're getting me back on the payroll. I don't work for free like these interns you've got around here!"

"Oh well," Matt said, "it was worth a shot. But you," he looked at Travis again, "we do need you if you think you're up to it."

"Sure," Travis said, hoping his smile looked sincere, "no problem."

"Alright, then, it's settled." Matt turned to leave. "Thanks, Travis. And good seeing you, Paul. You know where to find me if you need me."

"At the driving range?" Paul said.

"Not yet," Matt countered, "too cold." He turned and walked out.

"Well," Paul said, "that's my cue to leave."

He looked over at Travis, who was standing up as well. Paul moved toward him, checking to see that Matt wasn't nearby in the hallway.

"Look," Paul said, "remember that whether or not this group goes well is really not up to you. I suggest that you go in there and talk about something straightforward, but something that won't cause a lot of negative feelings or controversy. Keep it simple, and keep it positive. Ask each person to name one thing or one person they are grateful for and to talk about all the things that are going right in their sobriety. Pick some patients who seem to be positive to start it off. That will set the right tone for the group. And then try not to talk or interrupt anyone. And, above all else, don't try to be something you're not." He grabbed Travis' shoulder and said, "you've got this. You're a fucking great counselor, just remember that!"

Travis was pleasantly shocked by this quick tutorial.

"Thanks" was all he could think of to say in response, and then, "See you in the group."

"Thank you. This was good today." Paul said in return, and then, "Yes, I'll be there."

CHAPTER 21

"The therapist's biggest tools are the words and language we use. Choose your words wisely and with intention."

Paul Durkin, St. Michael's Outpatient Clinic Director,
speaking with a new intern.

"It happens all the time, and it's so annoying!"

Chuckles and noises of agreement permeated the classroom.

"No, seriously," the young woman continued, "it's like, am I just free labor here or what? I mean, my first semester I was doing more observing, more supervision. Now, it seems like they just throw me into everything all by myself. I know exactly how Travis feels!"

"Careful with saying something like that about his feelings," the professor reminded her.

"How might Grace express that in a different way?"

A moment passed before a hand went up. "Yes, Drew?"

"She could say, 'Why don't you tell me how that feels?'"

"That might work," the professor said, "But I think Grace is trying to show empathy and a connection with Travis' feelings. How else might she do that? Yes, Alisha?"

"She could say something like, 'Wow, that would make me anxious, or that might make me frustrated, or that would be scary to me.' Then she could ask Travis specifically about the feelings he had at the time."

"That's not a bad approach," Dunleavy said, "it might get him talking about his feelings and normalize his experience with being put on the spot to run the group. There's only one fault I see with that method. Can anyone say what it is?"

"Something about leading the witness?" A low voice said.

"What was that?" the professor asked, looking around the room.

A young man, sitting near the back, sat up straighter in his chair and said, "I'm not sure what it's called in counseling terms, but in a court, they might call it 'leading the witness.' I mean, if the counselor says that they would feel angry or upset or some other kind of way about being asked to do the group at the last minute, well that might plant the seed for the witness, or I guess in this case for the patient to agree with the counselor. But that might be different from the feeling the patient would have said at first. I don't know, I heard the term recently on some show or movie, and it seems kind of like what we're talking about here."

"Leading the witness. Or, in this case, the patient, or the student!" Dunleavy said and stood up. He began walking back and forth in front of the room.

"I like it, Connor, and I think it will be a good way for you all to remember the concept. Because he's exactly right, try not to say that you know how someone feels because you don't. The way you feel sadness or hurt or joy may be vastly different from how your patient feels these things. Part of our job is trying to understand what these words and emotions mean to the people we work with. But we must never assume to know exactly what someone else is feeling. As Connor pointed out, we also don't want to put words in our patient's mouths. It is better to ask someone how something felt than to name the feeling for them. If you are trying to show empathy or create a connection, use vague terms to prompt them to tell you about the emotion behind it. It's much better to say, 'That must have been difficult,' than it is to put a particular feeling on a situation for your patients. Remember that many of our patients may be experiencing feelings and emotions that they blocked out by using drugs for years. Having them identify and name feelings is an important and therapeutic part of this process. Don't deprive them of that."

The professor stopped pacing and looked around.

"Is everyone following this? There are some important topics here."

Heads nodded around the room.

"Okay," the professor continued, "so why don't we ask Travis how he felt since he brought the subject up. And I'm also curious how you thought the group went, Travis?"

"Well," Travis began, "it was very last minute. I was just finishing with the patient I've been assigned to, and I was feeling really good because our individual session went well. After yesterday's session, I might have convinced him to do some real work around the reasons he relapsed. I was shocked about how honest he was and how much he shared with me."

"Before we get to you being so rudely thrown into a group you were unprepared for, tell us about that," the professor said. "What do you think the deeper issues are for him?"

Travis thought for a moment.

"Well, he definitely is carrying around shame and guilt over the loss of his kid. And that makes sense to me. As you said, I have no idea how it feels to lose a child, especially to suicide, but it seems clear that intense guilt fed his relapse. At first, I thought that he might just want to die, to get the pain over with. Maybe he did. Maybe he was committing slow suicide with the drinking and self-destruction. Now it seems something is changing with him, not that his life has improved that much. In fact, things have gotten worse because of the D.W.I. But he told me that he stopped drinking last Friday, and I believe him. It's hard to describe why I think he's moving forward. It really is more of a feeling, something I sense, but it is hard to describe in words."

"Isn't it amazing how quickly the body starts to rebound from the effects of drugs?" The professor asked.

"Since we are talking about it, who can tell me what that is called, when our bodies work to get everything running in balance? A more clinical term would be what?"

"Homeostasis!" a few voices shouted out.

"Excellent. Although I'm not sure who nailed it first, so, no prizes can be issued at this time. Let's go back to our main contestant, Travis. It sounds to me like your patient is in a critical stage of his process toward change. It seems he is right on the border between contemplating making these changes and taking the actions to do so. In fact, he already took that vital step of not drinking. Keeping him moving forward and helping to motivate him sounds like the key to all of this, especially if he is dragging around unresolved grief. He needs some hope."

The professor let that sink in before speaking again. "So how do we supply this man with hope? What is our role as helpers in this? Anyone?"

A voice shouted out, "Show empathy!"

"Alright," the professor nodded contemplatively, "we can show empathy. But I'm not sure that will give someone hope for a better life. It may just help to strengthen our relationship, that all-important therapeutic alliance between our patients and us."

"How about staying positive? Just acknowledging the work and progress that the patient is making?" Connor offered.

"Good suggestion," the professor replied. "We really can't over-emphasize the role of a good cheerleader in all of this helping we do. Try to remember that many of our patients may never have received positive messages from their family and friends. Unlike other diseases, people are not wearing ribbons, or holding fundraisers, or praising the brave fighting that these sick patients are doing against their addiction. Typically, people outside of treatment, well-meaning family and friends, ask when this person will get back to work, start paying child support or stop going to those stupid Twelve Step meetings each night so they can help out more at home. Try to imagine saying to someone in the first year of cancer treatment, 'Aren't you done with that yet? Isn't chemotherapy over? When are you going back to work?'"

The professor's voice reverberated in the back row, and he had become more animated while talking. He stopped, scanned the classroom briefly, and moved back behind the podium. He rested his forearms on it and looked pensively out at the class.

"There I go, getting all worked up again," Dunleavy quipped. "My point in all of this is that it's important for you to remember how far we need to go to motivate our patients toward change. How do we expect any sick person to work toward getting better if we don't give them some hope or a goal worth working toward? We need to sell recovery as something worth fighting toward, something worth living for. Many patients show resistance and denial at first, but we need to focus and build on the healthy changes they are making, as small as those changes may seem. Those are the places where we can build motivation."

Dunleavy looked up at the clock.

"With the little time we have left today, let's go back to running groups. How many of you, besides Travis, have been thrown in to run a group at the last minute?"

Most of the hands in the classroom went up.

"Excellent!" the professor said.

He turned to Travis.

"And you all lived to tell your tale! For those of you that have not yet had the pleasure, I warn you to be ready. Your time is coming. This is a field with many moving parts and even more things that are outside of your control. We need always to be flexible and prepared to jump into anything at any time. It's also essential to remember that the quality of any group you run is not entirely your responsibility. You need to keep people on track, but the patients determine the outcome far more than we do. You will not always have the luxury of making a lesson plan as teachers do for every group you run. I suggest you all have some fundamental tools ready for use with any group already printed out and ready to go. That way, if you get called in at the last minute, you'll have a plan and some structure. You should watch and learn from seasoned counselors, those who have been around a long time, on how they run these 'off the cuff' groups. Over time these skills will become second nature, but as we've said so often in here, it's important to…"

The professor trailed off, and a chorus of voices completed the thought, "Give time time!"

"Excellent," Dunleavy said and looked up again at the clock. Speaking of time, we're out of it. Good job today, everyone. I'm sure we'll be discussing these things again."

Travis walked to the front of the room as his classmates packed up their supplies and walked past him and out the door.

"Hey Travis," Dunleavy said. "Good stuff today! It sounds like you're getting quite an education outside of the classroom at your clinic! You're also doing a great job with a challenging patient."

"Thanks. It feels like I've gone from doing almost nothing last semester to doing almost everything a real counselor does. It's weird how quickly that happened, but I definitely feel more like a working part of the team now."

"You should take it as a compliment! I've been placing interns at St. Michael's for a long time, and I know they wouldn't allow you to do these things if Matt and the staff didn't think you could handle it."

As they spoke, students arrived to find seats for the next class. Immediately after sitting down, every person produced a phone and started staring into the small screen. Dunleavy looked at this phenomenon, shaking his head. He was strict about cell phone use in his classes. Travis had sat through several passionate speeches, similar to the one today in class, about the importance of staying off phones at the internship sites. In his opinion, using the cell phone at work was unprofessional and immature. He also shared cautionary stories about interns that had lost their placements and dropped from the program entirely because they could not leave their phones alone.

"It's like the Zombie Apocalypse," Travis said, knowing that Dunleavy would appreciate the comment.

A girl nearby looked up and made a snarky face but quickly turned her full attention back to the phone.

"It won't be long," the professor said, "before we are offering treatment for that type of addiction as well. Anyway, we'd better get out of here. I'm heading to my office hours. Did you want to talk about something down there?"

"Oh, um, no, I mean, that's alright, I don't need to take any of your office time," Travis said, though he would have liked to sit down and process all that was going on. "But I'm heading that way, so I'll walk with you if you don't mind."

The two walked out of the classroom and down a crowded hallway.

"So, what's on your mind?" the professor asked.

Travis hesitated for a minute, trying to gather his thoughts.

"I'm not sure. It's just that this guy, my patient, sometimes gives me advice. Like yesterday, at the end of our session, he heard I would be running a group. So, he…well, he basically said some of the same things you just said in class. They were really helpful tips, but I just don't know if that was; I mean, I'm wondering if that was okay if it was …"

"A boundary issue?" The professor asked.

"Yes, exactly. It doesn't seem like he should be telling me how to do things. It seems weird for him to be giving me advice, to be teaching me about counseling!"

"But wasn't he a counselor?"

"Well, yes, but he's not now."

"So, do you think that counselors who have relapsed, or retired, or stopped working in the field immediately forget all that they knew over the years?"

They had walked to a part of the building that intersected with a pedestrian bridge leading to the parking garage.

"I'm parked in the garage," Travis said.

The professor pushed open the door to the stairway. Nearby was an elevator. No fewer than six young students stood there, waiting for the elevator while silently thumbing their phones and slurping neon-colored beverages purchased from the nearby convenience store.

"You'd never know this building had only three floors by the elevator traffic," the professor noted. "At least everyone's staying hydrated with sugar or caffeine-laden goo!"

Travis said, "I think I see your point—about my patient, I mean. I just wanted to make sure I'm not being manipulated, or crossing any boundaries. I've heard you talk about counter-transference, and I'm afraid I might get too involved with my patient."

"You will," the professor answered. "And you might be now. Keep your guard up. You're feeling this way because you care. You want to help, to make a difference. And that's something that can't be faked, and it can't be taught. As for you learning from this guy, I can tell you that my patients have taught me more than I could ever dream. I learn from you students each semester as well. Is that wrong? Unethical? I hope not. Travis, look, you will be a great counselor, and the fact that you're coming to me with these concerns proves how conscientious you are. I wouldn't say this to all students, but I think you need to hear it: so much of what you are going to do in this field will involve judgment calls, trusting your instinct, going with your gut, and asking people you trust when you need help. I don't think there are many coincidences in this life, and I have to believe your time with this man is part of a plan, a higher design. You are meant to learn from him, and he from you. Trust yourself and trust the process. You'll do fine."

With that, he smiled at Travis, gave a quick wave of his hand, and was gone.

"Fine," Travis said softly. "I'll be fine."

CHAPTER 22

"Many of you may be telling yourselves you don't belong here, but that might just be because you would never have come for treatment on your own. Most people need a nudge from the judge or someone else who sees things you can't about your drug use."

Adolfo Rojas, running a group at St. Michael's about early recovery.

Paul slowed down as he passed the old church and cemetery on the way to Cook's Garage, but Jenny's car wasn't in the lot. The day was cloudy and overcast. Lester Whiteside was predicting heavy snow by nightfall. It was days like these, cold and grey with more hours of darkness than of light, that reminded Paul of time spent in his grandparents' big house reading Jack London stories by the fireplace. He remembered the fear among kids his age, those also reading Jack London stories, of freezing to death out of doors while trying to light their last match or catching the dreaded "cabin fever" by never stepping outside during these long months. The latter fear may have been provoked by parents who strived to get their kids out of the house. If cabin fever did exist, Paul reckoned it must be an epidemic now, with young people staying mostly inside even during the best weather.

Once those youngsters grew up, most would undoubtedly follow the rituals of their parents and grandparents. Everyone migrating south for the winter, like masses of fragile butterflies. This strange ritual never seemed to have entered his grandfather's mind.

"Yup, it's cold out there," Paul's grandfather used to say from behind the cash register at the store on the coldest days of the year. "At least it gets dark real early so folks can complain about something else besides the cold."

The thought of his grandfather's quick wit and dry humor made him smile, and he wondered what advice the old man would have for him now. That generation seemed made of stronger stuff than their offspring. They didn't migrate when things got tough. He knew the man had suffered countless losses during his lifetime and that most of his time and energy had been spent working, fixing, and tending to problems rarely of his own making. Yet every thought and memory of his grandfather included some kind, wise phrase, or subtle smile. He couldn't imagine the man sitting in front of a therapist or processing out his resentments and feelings with a group of people, regardless of how concerned or empathetic they might be. He also couldn't picture either of his grandparents taking a pill to aid with depression or anxiety for the stresses of life that loomed larger for them than for most.

So what changed? In a world that was getting easier and softer each day, why were introspection, talk therapy, and mass pharmacotherapy normalized? Were we just fooling ourselves about the inherent difficulties of modern times, or did our relatives suffer in silence, carrying the burdens of untreated mental illness, desperately deep grief, and hidden addictions in a learned stoicism from the cradle to the grave?

Maybe the problem was in Paul's perception of things. Paul's memories were of a solid man who unfailingly kept things safe and controlled for those around him. He made sure the wood stove was burning in the winter, and the food was in the icehouse in the summertime. Yet, there may have been more to his grandfather, a darker side or lifelong struggle that only other adults saw. It was interesting how people could remember different versions of a person, a place, or shared experience from the past. He'd heard it called revisionist history by someone a long time ago, but he couldn't remember if the term was legitimate or another example of recovery-speak.

Paul knew he never reached hero status with Sean. He thought that his son loved him but doubted there was much admiration. Sean certainly saw his father's weaknesses, flaws, and shortcomings. His son also suffered from the constant ballooning tension in the house. The disputes and fights, the silent anger ruined many family dinners. His weren't the actions of a hero, someone who would have done more, who would have done anything, to work on the marriage. To be more present at home. To keep his mouth shut and just listen more. To see what was going on around him in his own house. To step out of denial.

Sean must have internalized that pain, taking the blame for all the problems in the marriage and for the lack of acknowledgment and acceptance Paul showed when Sean needed it most. What a horrible, unfair burden for a child. The thought that his only child carried those feelings, and somehow felt responsible for Paul's countless fuck ups was too much. He could sense the voice behind these thoughts, the same one that began as a whisper after finding the body on that horrible day. It was getting louder and darker and becoming desperately parched. The voice knew exactly who was to blame for all the faults, and failures, and fuck ups in Paul's life. It also knew a way to escape the pain.

Paul rolled down the window, trying to wipe out the thoughts flooding into his head. The silence of the house, the bedroom door, the strange color of his child's face, how cold the skin felt, Sean's lifeless stare. The general store where he'd bought the beer last week was just up ahead. Instinctively he slowed down, signaled to turn, and pulled into the parking lot.

There were two other cars in the lot, and he pulled into a spot directly in front of the window. He could see the same young cashier standing behind the register and looking down, presumably at her phone. He guessed that the small red car near the entrance to the store was hers. It had a manufacturer's emblem on the trunk that he did not recognize but assumed it was one of the cheaply made, highly efficient Japanese cars that young people seemed to be driving around these days. Twenty or thirty years ago in the Northeast, the consensus about these "Rice Burners" was that they were cheap in the short term, but they would eventually destroy American jobs and make us far too dependent on the foreign countries that produced them. He glanced over at the car's bumper and knew it belonged to the cashier when he saw a small pink and white bumper sticker that read, "This is how I spent my college fund."

Going into the store was crazy. He could pretend he needed gum, or soda, or he could make an attempt to enlighten the young cashier, but there was no way he would come out without booze. And then what? Wasn't he on his way to pick up his car—the car that just had an alcohol sensor installed in it? And what about Tank? How could he possibly explain to Tank why his breath reeked like beer? And what about the fact that he had been driving the truck while drinking?

He sat there, convincing himself of all the reasons that the plan wouldn't work. His hand slid from the steering wheel down to the ignition. He was about to turn the key and start the engine when the dark voice whispered another idea. What if he just bought the beer and drove the truck home without going to the garage? He could always call Tank and tell him that something came up and that he couldn't get there today. What would be wrong with that? It might even be better to wait until another day and have his last drinking bout over with. He could use just one more before he committed completely to sobriety, one more celebration before tightening up the loose ends. His hand left the ignition key, and he reached for the door handle, pulling it up.

Nothing happened. The door didn't open, so he pulled on the handle again, and again it remained shut, ignoring his request to exit. He looked at the lock on the doorframe. It was pressed down, locked, which was odd because he didn't remember doing that, and it certainly was not a habit of Paul's to lock himself in when driving.

"This is crazy," another voice within him said, "drive away."

It was crazy, Paul agreed, and suddenly wished he had a phone with him, thinking that he might call someone to talk with if he had a phone. He would call Jimmy C. and tell him about these crazy thoughts.

"Uh-huh," Jimmy would say, "So, you're a drunk who's thinking about drinking again? Well, there's a fucking surprise. What, are things going too good right now? You've got to blow shit up? Get your ass to the coffee house. I'll meet you there in ten minutes."

Talking to Jimmy, or anyone else would be enough to break this spell. Just letting somebody in on the plan. Outnumbering the craving and turning down the volume in his head.

"Bullshit!" the dark voice screamed. "That's bullshit and you know it! You are a drunk, and you will die this way. So, get to it!"

Paul glanced again at the locked door and then up to the girl behind the counter. As he did so, a flash of something caught his eye, something that moved quickly through the air and then stopped, landing on the edge of the store's roof. It was a bright red cardinal. Paul could have sworn it was the same one from his backyard.

"Alright, okay. You win," he mumbled to nobody in particular and started the engine of the truck.

"Oh, this thing here is going to be a pain right in your ass, Paul!" Frank Cook explained. He was sitting in the driver's seat of Paul's car and holding up a small, black box with a mouthpiece attached to it. The box had a circular rubber cord that fastened at the back and then spiraled down to a larger box mounted under the dashboard. It looked to Paul like an old C.B. radio system, except that the hand-held part was meant to blow in.

"What you do," Frank explained, "is you put your key into the ignition and turn it just enough to get the power on. See how the red light just came on in that box under the dash?"

Paul nodded his head, indicating that he did see the light.

"Okay, once you see that light, you take this part here," Frank held up the piece in his hand, "and you blow into the mouthpiece. I'll do it now because I've been practicing with this thing and probably got my spit all over it."

Frank blew into the device at a slow, steady rate until both men saw the light on the larger box change from red to green.

"Now once that happens," Frank continued, "you've got about a minute to turn the key the rest of the way and start the engine. Make sure not to turn the key backward and shut off the power. If you do, you'll have to start all over again." He turned the key, started the car, and left it idling as he looked up at Paul. "Got it?"

"Yes," Paul said, "it seems pretty straightforward. Anything else I should know?"

"Yup," Frank said quickly. "If this thing senses you've been drinking, you're screwed. That box down there collects information every time you blow into it, and if it detects alcohol, it won't start until you contact probation, or the court, or whoever made you put the thing in here. Then they come out and just plug into your car to get all the information. It will show every time you blew and what the results were. They also have me come and recalibrate the whole system if that happens. Those guys could do it themselves. I mean, they know how to, but I think they like to have me come out because it costs the poor bastard who failed the test to have me do it. And you're also gonna need to have the thing recalibrated by me once a month anyway, even if you don't blow dirty into the thing."

Paul ran a hand through his hair, thinking how stupid it would have been to drink before he got here.

"I can do it while you wait," Frank said in a quieter tone, looking at Paul. "The monthly checkup, I mean. You won't have to leave your car here because it don't really take too long, so…"

"Yeah," Paul said, trying to put on a smile, "yeah, that would be great. I really appreciate this, Frank. Letting me borrow your truck and helping me out like this."

"Well, you might want to save all that until you see the bill," Frank said as he turned off the car, removed the key, and handed it to Paul.

He pulled off the plastic mouthpiece he had blown into and held up a small cardboard box filled with individually wrapped replacements.

"Ain't nothing cheap these days, that's for sure. These should get you through the first month, but just call me if you need more. I suggest using the same one for a while since it's just you that should be slobbering on it. You got lucky because I had to put an older model in here because your car is, you know, older, and even though I needed to order a few extra parts to get it working, this thing ain't nearly as annoying as the new models coming out. I just heard from the company making these things, and they want me to take a training on the newest one that will be required in cars by next year. It can sense alcohol in the air before you even blow in it! Can you imagine that? And they already got some on the market that come with a video camera built in to make sure that you're the one using it. Another type goes off randomly while the person is driving to make sure you're not boozing after you start the car up! I don't know where it will stop, I'm telling you!"

"Wow, that's impressive," Paul said half-heartedly, trying to think of ways he might beat the newer systems.

Frank led Paul through the garage and toward the small side office with the dirty, broken couch, chairs, and an old television always on and running, but with the picture fuzzy and the speakers blown. Paul couldn't make out one word coming from the set, even with the volume at ten. A cat or dog lay on the furniture, sometimes a person would be there, someone elderly who seemed not to be waiting for anything in particular, just enjoying the animals' company and watching the broken television.

The office hadn't changed in all the years Paul had known the Cooks, and he thought about the contrast between this place and some of the newer garages in Deerfield. Their waiting rooms were spotless, filled with the newest magazines and flat-screen televisions mounted near their clean drop ceilings. The chairs looked new, unblemished, and they matched the décor of the waiting room. He assumed they were designed in labs and tested by focus groups who reported on which seats provided optimal lumbar support. Some of the service centers had free coffee and snacks and most proudly displayed a sign offering "free Wi-Fi," which Paul was told was already an outdated service. He wondered how this place, how a place like Cook's Garage, managed to compete and survive against such places. He supposed it came down to the service, and knowledge, and sincere, caring honesty that was inherent with the Cook family name.

"Let's see now," Frank said as he looked at the receipts he had scribbled by hand and tacked to a bulletin board behind the counter.

"Yup, here we go." He pulled down a piece of paper that was smeared with oil on the edges. He placed it on the counter between them.

"I did the best I could for you, Paul," Frank said.

Paul handed his credit card over and placed the bill in his coat pocket without looking at it.

"We did what we could with your bumper," Frank told him as they waited for the ancient machine to verify Paul's card. "You won't win any car shows with it, but it shouldn't fall off unless you run something else over. Try not to do that. Like I told you before, you'll need to come out each month and have the thing calibrated, but I won't charge you for that. I imagine the bill you're paying from one night at the Stumble Inn is quite enough to deal with."

"Yup," Paul agreed. "But they sure do have some good, pickled eggs."

Tank smiled at that and handed Paul the receipt and a pen with bite marks on the end to sign off on the repairs.

"Thanks again, Frank, You're one of the good ones."

"Maybe," Frank said, "but try not to spread that around too much!"

CHAPTER 23

"How's it going? It sucks. Well, not everything sucks, I guess. I definitely am
saving money, and the old lady's happy that I'm around more. I mean,
I was around before, but I guess I wasn't really there, you know?
I'm not saying that I'll ever give the stuff up for good, or that
I'm an alcoholic. I know that's what you guys all want. But I can see how
there are some good things that come from not drinking so much."

Larry H., talking to his counselor Bill in a one-on-one session.

The snow started falling before Paul pulled into the parking lot at St. Michael's. He pulled both of his wipers away from the windshield and walked toward the clinic. Larry and Peter's trucks were parked near the back of the lot, in the same two spots as last week. They were creatures of habit for sure, always doing what feels safe and known and comfortable. Paul knew these guys, probably better than they knew themselves because they were like the hundreds of local grown-up boy-men he'd counseled in the past.

Their nature was to whine, joke, and bully others, hoping subconsciously to convince themselves that the problems in their lives hadn't come from their own choices and certainly weren't made worse by drinking and using a few drugs now and then. Maybe there was some truth to that. Maybe the real issue came from being born a white man in America, winning both the genetic and geographic lotteries, and then failing to cash in the tickets for either windfall. How many small-town white men had Paul known who suffered the same feelings of shame and guilt about never reaching the standards of success that had been their birthright? These men reminded Paul of a long-ago story from Sunday school about three servants who were entrusted with portions of silver. The hero of the tale had been given the most silver and then went out and doubled it through wise investing. When the master, who gave the silver, saw the loser had buried his small amount to keep it safe, he gave the loser's silver to the hero as well. This story ended with the loser, who did nothing with what he was given, cast into darkness where there was much weeping and gnashing of teeth.

Paul sensed the ancient gnashing and weeping in these two tragic fools. As much as they raised their voices in protest and put on false bravado in front of others, Paul was willing to bet that neither of them had missed an appointment or a group since starting treatment. Their fear was too great. But the real fear, the one that remained buried like their portion of the silver, was the truth about their lives. They were losers in every inning of a game they weren't playing.

But who was he to have these thoughts? Who was he to judge or label others? Paul Durkin, King of the Chicken Shits.

The snow fell faster, and the silence it created blocked traffic sounds from the nearby street. Large flakes tumbled down, sticking to Paul's shoes as he walked, and he tilted his head back, closed his eyes, and let the cool drops fall on his face. This was the beauty and the power of snowstorms that Paul always loved. They refused to be minimized or ignored but, unlike other natural nuisances, snow could be enjoyed at the same time it stopped everything. Rain, fire, winds, and earthquakes brought nothing but disorder and chaos. Yet snow, like addiction, had an allure that was hard to resist—a cold and icy temptress.

Any child who grew up in snowstorms powerful enough to close schools knew his love affair started young. A snow day from school meant nature had won. The adults had to comply. Everything changed, if only for a day, or even a few hours. The routine was broken, and the natural order was temporarily restored. Children intuited that this was right in some fundamental way, a way that too many adults had lost among light switches, premium cable subscriptions, and heated ceramic tile bathroom floors.

At times like these, with his face turned upwards to the sky, he could feel that siren call to freedom somewhere above him, where the endless snow began.

Paul made his way to the building and entered. No patients were sitting in the waiting area, and he assumed that Peter and Larry had already gone into the group room, making sure to claim the same chairs they occupied last week and the week before, and every week since they had started.

Carla was talking on the phone as he approached.

"Yes, sir, we are open for the group tonight. No, we haven't closed."

She looked up at Paul, rolling her eyes and signaling with her hand that she would be with him soon. She pointed to the sign-in roster on the desk, handing him a pen.

"So, you can't make it? Okay. No, sir, I can't tell probation that. You need to let your counselor know that you will be absent, and your counselor will be in touch with probation."

Paul could hear the voice on the other end of the phone get louder, and more insistent. A few foul words were thrown in for emphasis and effect. The voice sounded familiar, maybe that young kid who hid in his shell last week – Mark or Matt? Carla was holding the phone away from her ear.

She turned toward Paul to offer an apology, "I should be done in just a minute."

"Sir? Sir?" Carla spoke into the phone, more assertive and louder than she had been before. The rant from the other end subsided.

"Sir, the group is starting in five minutes, and I have people I need to get checked in. If you are not able to make it, you need to leave a message for your counselor. Would you like her voice mail?"

Paul heard a crescendo of noise from the party on the phone, followed by silence.

Carla waited a moment, then tentatively said, "Sir? Are you still there?"

She placed the phone back in its cradle and smiled up at Paul.

"I guess he doesn't want to leave a message on his counselor's voice mail."

"And how are you this fine, snowy evening?" she asked Paul.

"Me? Oh, you know," Paul replied. "Fair to middlin', I suppose."

The door opened, and Jack entered the waiting room, stomping the snow from his boots and brushing it from his coat.

"Wow," Jack exclaimed, "this might just turn out to be a snowstorm after all!"

Paul gave him a nod of the head in greeting.

"Well, it looks like I won't be the only one in the group tonight," Jack said cordially and walked up to the counter behind Paul.

"No," Carla replied to Jack. "There are a few of you here. Not much of a group, but you all will certainly have time to talk!"

She turned to Paul, "So that will be a fifteen-dollar copay for tonight. How would you like to pay for that?"

Paul reached in his pocket and retrieved two bills which he handed to her.

"Wow," Carla said, "where did you find this? No one uses cash anymore!"

"Well," Paul said, "just try not to spend it all in one place."

She smiled, punched a few more keys on her computer, and then turned to pull a receipt out of the nearby printer.

"There you go, have a good group."

"Thanks. And be careful on your ride home."

"Oh, I'll be fine. I have a chauffeur," she responded with a smile and a wink.

He stepped away from the counter, and Jack took his place.

"So," Jack began, "I applied for public assistance, but I don't think it came through yet. I'm not sure if I should stay for tonight's group or if I need to get that worked out first."

"Well, of course you should stay tonight!" Carla said.

"Now, let me see what I can find out about your insurance."

She tapped the keys on her computer as Paul walked down the hallway. He heard the front door open again but didn't turn around to see who had entered. Instead, he headed to the men's room.

Once there, Paul realized that he didn't need to pee; instead, he went to the sink and ran the water. He looked into the mirror, stretching his face in odd ways as he washed his hands. The routine seemed all too familiar. Standing in this small space, with the strong chemical smell of cleaning products washing over him, inspecting his face and clothes before entering a group or meeting with a patient. He wondered if they were teaching the kid to do this, to make sure there was nothing smeared or dripping out of place.

The kid seemed pretty well put together, though, and probably didn't need as much supervision in this area as Paul had. He had Charlotte for that. She routinely flattened, tucked, and fixed parts of his outfit as he scrambled to get out the door most mornings, often late and in a frenzy to find his keys, or wallet, or a letter he had to mail that day.

She would stand in front of the doorway as he tried to leave.

"Wait, just wait one second," she instructed while flipping down the back of his collar, or wiping shaving cream from the corner of his face, or straightening his tie.

It only worsened when he began giving Sean a ride to school after the school bus incident—that horrible day. The insistence by the principal that *"the school was doing all they could, but that Mr. and Mrs. Durkin needed to understand that this situation was complicated on several levels."* That's when the morning and afternoon rides to and from school began. Sometimes Paul enjoyed the extra time together, talking about the day's events or listening to a morning radio show together.

At other times, many times, the rides were inconvenient. Stressful. Problematic. And Paul unleashed his frustrations freely on Sean. Paul made it clear just how difficult this arrangement was, how troublesome his child was making things for him.

He pushed the soap dispenser several times and rubbed his hands under the running water, trying to wash off the memories.

Someone knocked on the door.

"Just a minute," Paul said.

He ripped a gritty section of paper from the dispenser and used it to open the door handle before throwing the cheap towel in the trash. The St. Michael's compliance office would be proud to know that their annual universal precautions workshops were effective all these years later.

Larry was waiting at the door as Paul exited.

"Wow, if you had taken any longer, I was going to call the SWAT team," Larry said. "Should I wear a gas mask in there, or what?"

Paul tried to give his best neutral smile.

"No, I think you'll be okay."

Larry went into the bathroom, and Paul saw an unfamiliar man standing at the reception desk with Carla. Relapse Prevention was the only group running tonight, so Paul knew they'd acquired a new member. That could make things interesting.

He'd always enjoyed running groups, especially once the members knew each other and formed a bond. But managing newer people, especially those with stronger energies and bullish personalities, was one of the most challenging parts of the job. Paul found himself hoping that the new guy would act up, piss Mandy off, and maybe take some of the attention from him.

He entered the group room and saw that the overhead lights were off, the blinds drawn up, and Travis was in the same chair as last week.

"Good evening, Paul," Travis said, smiling warmly. "Glad you decided to join us tonight."

"Yeah," Peter said sarcastically from his self-assigned seat, "like you got a choice, huh buddy?"

"Well," Travis responded, "everyone here does have some choices, even if they seem limited right now. But you certainly have a better chance of staying sober for the next ninety minutes in here than you would somewhere else."

"Can't fight you on that," Peter said, "even if we only stay sober as far as the parking lot!" Peter smiled widely and gave Paul an unmistakable wink.

"Choices are good," Paul said, "but sometimes highly overrated."

He chose a seat across from the window that looked out into the night. This had always been his favorite place to sit during the winter months. He stared out into a streetlight that illuminated the curtain of snow falling through the dusk. Soon Travis or Mandy would have to switch on those horrid lights. He wondered where the old lamp was, the one he'd bought at a garage sale for three dollars. He had dragged that thing from room to room just to avoid using the awful overhead lights. Most likely, it hadn't been adequately hidden during some inspection, was deemed a fire hazard, and was buried deep in a landfill by now.

Paul noticed that Angela, the girl from the bar, had returned. She was curled into a small ball on the seat, with a large green duffle bag by her feet. The black nylon handles were beyond frayed, and much of the bag looked held together by duct tape. It was stuffed completely, the top covered in snow. Paul wondered how long she wandered around the streets before the group and if she might be newly homeless. It was a bad night for that. The girl made no attempt to acknowledge his presence and seemed to have learned some things about camouflaging herself during group from the turtle boy last week. She covered her face with her hair and was almost completely invisible inside the weather-worn army jacket. The jacket looked soaked through, as did her canvas sneakers. A wet ring expanded on the carpet around the edges of her bag.

Jack had made it past Carla, delaying his payment issues for the time being. He sat across from Paul tonight, under one of the windows, and a safe distance away from where Mandy had been last week and where Travis was now. Larry entered the room next, followed by the man Paul had seen at the counter.

"I see the party hasn't started without me!" Larry exclaimed.

He looked over at Travis, "What time are the hookers getting here?"

Peter laughed at this, and Jack offered a small smile.

Travis, feeling on the spot, said, "I don't think they can make it tonight, but I also think we need to remember to watch what we say in here because we don't know people's pasts, and some people may have done things during their addiction …"

"Ah, Jesus," Larry interrupted, "I'm just messing around. I don't mean to offend no one by it."

Larry looked first at Travis and then at Angela, who had all but disappeared into the chair.

"Hell, some of my best friends are hookers, and I don't judge them for it. Some are damn good at their craft!"

Travis stared at Larry but said nothing.

Larry whispered loudly to Peter as he sat down, "Maybe he's just pissed off because he don't realize hookers come in both flavors."

Travis' face reddened, but he didn't address the comment. Instead, he turned his attention to the man who came in behind Larry.

"Hi, welcome to the group. I'm Travis."

The man walked over and shook Travis' hand. He appeared to be in his late twenties or early thirties, with broad shoulders and a confidant stance. "I'm Steve," he said and nodded to the others in the group before taking a seat close to Angela's. Before sitting down, he removed his leather jacket, revealing a large tribal tattoo on the bicep of his right arm. His arms were toned and muscular, and his upper body appeared to be equally well-maintained. He was wearing a tight tee-shirt that looked trendy and over-priced. He also had form-fitting blue jeans that hugged his waist, legs, and crotch tightly. The outfit was completed by a pair of stylish, pristine work boots, wet with snow but never worn to complete any hard physical work.

And here is our drug dealer, Paul thought as he sized up the new member and wondered how long it would be before the new guy's phone went off. He also imagined that some people in the clinic, possibly in this group, had bought their drugs from this guy. He knew that there would be more going on in the parking lot from now on than Larry and Peter having a few drinks.

"Don't we start at 5:30?" Peter asked Travis while he stared up at the clock on the wall.

It was 5:35.

"Yes, we do," Travis replied. "Mandy must be talking to a patient. I'm sure she'll be here soon."

"Yeah, well she better be," Larry responded, "because we're paying for this time, and it would be a real shame if someone reported the place for fraud, right?"

"Well, I'm sure Mandy wouldn't mind if we started without her," Travis said. "Would you like to begin our check-in, Larry?"

Paul liked how the kid had turned things around on this clown, and he enjoyed watching Larry squirm. He'd once heard someone say that it's harder to lie when you haven't rehearsed your script, and that certainly was true in his experiences.

Larry looked at Travis indignantly.

"Well, shit, I don't know if anyone wants to hear from me first, I ... "

"Sure, we do," Jack jumped in. "Why don't you start by telling us about those hookers you used to know so well?"

Larry's face reddened. Travis continued to look at Larry, friendly enough but silent and expectant.

Larry gazed down at the floor. He began slowly, quietly, with the slightest hint of a tremor in his voice.

"Well, I'm Larry, and I guess it's my drinking and drug use that got me here."

"Hi Larry," Travis said softly. A few other people echoed the greeting.

Larry's head raised a bit, concentration showing in his face.

"I started like everyone else, you know. I mean, I drank beer pretty young, I guess, but it was just what we did. My old man worked construction, just like I do now, and he always had a cooler of beer in the back of his truck."

He put his elbows on his knees and clasped his hands together, letting out a small laugh.

"Yup, just like I do now. Hell, he gave me my first beer and my first cigarette when I was ten or eleven years old. He and his friends—you know, the guys he worked with—would roll into the driveway, dirty and sweaty from the day and already half in the bag. They'd be drinking beers and blowing smoke as they stumbled out of their trucks and into our garage or out in the back yard. Pretty soon, the fire pit would be going, and the barbecue would be smoking, and the party was on. My mom was at work most of the time. She was a nurses' aide at the old folks' home and worked a lot of overnight shifts, so she probably had no idea how crazy things were. We kids knew enough to never tell her. But me and my brother and sister, we saw it all. Every day was a party at that house. It was just what we did, you know, it wasn't a big deal."

Larry looked around the room. Everyone was attentive, listening. Pete opened his mouth to say something but then closed it again. Outside, a plow truck passed slowly shaking the lighting fixtures and sending a low rumble through the room.

"So, yeah, that's how I learned to drink and do drugs, from my old man. I remember being so pissed off at my mom when she booted him out. Like it was her fault, you know? By that point, he wasn't working. I don't think he could anymore. His body just gave out. Now that I'm getting older, I know what that type of pain feels like—how tough this work is on your knees and your back. The people you work for don't give a shit. They'll find someone else to build their deck or fix the roof. Then you're screwed. The old man just couldn't do it anymore, not to mention how the booze must have affected his work and his reputation. It's okay to drink and build shit, but it ain't alright to be a drunk. I think he messed a few projects up, stopped showing up for some, and then he was just there, at our house, all the time. Until he left. I'm still not sure if she kicked him out or if he decided to split, my mom would never tell me, but that was it. That was the last time I saw him alive."

Larry looked down, and Travis stayed the course.

"How old were—"

Mandy marched into the room and switched on the light.

"Oh, so we started our check-ins already?" She cast a cutting glance at Travis.

Behind her was Diane, who said in a soft, low tone, "Sorry I'm late. The roads are getting quite dicey out there."

The room buzzed and vibrated with sudden light. Larry sat up and wiped his face on his sleeve.

Travis asked again, "So how old were you, Larry?"

"How old were you when what?" Mandy asked, looking at Larry. "What were you talking about?"

Larry ignored Mandy and looked back at Travis, "I don't know, shit, young. I guess, fourteen or fifteen. Anyway, that's it. I'm done."

"Well, thank you," Travis said, leaning toward Larry and smiling. "That took a lot of courage to open up in here."

"Would someone mind telling me what we're talking about," Mandy asked, glaring at Travis.

"Sure," Travis started, "Well, we were here and talking before the group started, and then Larry volunteered to start the check-ins and was telling us—"

"I just thought we'd get things going," Larry offered, "since it was already past the time we're supposed to start and everything. Glad you could join us, though, Mandy. I was just saying how great my life is, how much I love being fucking sober, and how I appreciate the dedication and promptness of the staff here at St. Michael's."

Larry smiled widely at Mandy as her face reddened. Jack snorted loudly, and Paul tried not to chuckle. He wondered how he ever let himself get out of this work. It was priceless.

"Well," Mandy began, trying to regain some composure, "Thank you, Larry. I do know we are starting a bit late tonight and, quite frankly, I'm surprised they held this group at all. I guess my boss didn't check the weather forecast!"

She looked around the room for some ascension, but everyone just stared back silently.

"Anyway," she continued, "I'm sure you all want to get home safe and sound this evening, so I thought we would jump right into these financial worksheets and maybe finish up a little early. Any objections to that?" Mandy lifted the stack of papers on her lap and the cup full of ragged pencils and pens.

Nobody spoke, and all eyes except for Travis' and Paul's turned away from her. Diane was the first to break the silence.

"So, are we going to skip the check-ins this week?" She asked.

"Yes," Mandy quickly responded and then amended her statement, "Well, if someone is really struggling, I mean if someone really needs to take up that time, you can, but I would really like to get these packets done."

As she stood up and began to hand out the papers, a digital Hip Hop beat started playing. All eyes turned to the newest member of the group, who retrieved his phone from a pocket.

Right on time, Paul thought, as Steve looked at the phone, tapped a finger on the screen, and then slid it away in a pocket.

Mandy seemed to notice for the first time that there was a new member in the group.

"There are no phones allowed in here," she said.

And then, in a slightly softer tone, "Is this your first group?"

"Yes," Steve replied, seeming unsure of what to say next.

"I'm Steve, and I'm here because – "

"Well, yes, okay, good," Mandy interrupted.

"Why don't we plan on having you introduce yourself next week, and you can get to know everyone then, alright?"

She shuffled through the papers.

"I don't have any new copies here, but this is one that a client started to fill out last week, and he's not here. You can just scratch out the things he wrote down and write down your own answers."

"Seriously?" Steve asked.

"Sure," Mandy said, "why waste the paper, right? Save the planet and all that?"

"Um," Steve said, "alright. That's what I'll do then, I guess."

"Welcome to the group!" Jack bellowed as Mandy, who seemed oblivious to the sarcasm, handed Jack his paper from last week.

"Last week we started to focus on the importance of good financial planning and ways to save money." Mandy sat down in her chair and picked up her copy of the exercise, "As you all know, addiction is expensive, not just for you but for your family members, the community, and society at large. Now that you are sober, becoming more aware of the costs of your addiction is important and useful."

"Why?" an edgy voice cut in.

It was Angela. The group turned and looked at her. Peter elbowed Larry, but neither man spoke.

"No, really," Angela continued.

She put her legs down on the ground and squared herself up in Mandy's direction. The movement reminded Paul of a cat preparing to pounce.

"Why is it so important that we recognize how much we've cost ourselves and everyone else? Is it so that we can feel really guilty about being addicts and the shitty things we did?"

"Oh, I don't think we should feel guilty, dear," Diane said to Angela.

"There might be value in recognizing the money we spent during our addiction and that others spent on us, but I don't think the point is to make us feel guilty, right?"

Diane turned toward Mandy, a troubled look coming over her face.

"This is a disease, right?" Diane continued. "And you counselors tell us all the time that we are sick people trying to get well, not bad people trying to become good people. So, we don't think about how much our disease cost or how painful and expensive it was to everyone else just to multiply guilt and shame, do we? I mean, there must be a better therapeutic reason for doing this exercise. Do people who go to treatment for cancer or diabetes complete these types of exercises to look at the cost of their disease?"

Mandy's face had gone completely blank. For some reason, her gaze fell on Paul, and a darker look came into her eyes as if he was the cause of this debate and rebellion in her otherwise timid group.

"Paul," she said, "you look like you might have some thoughts on this. Would you like to talk about the cost of your addiction with the group?"

The group looked at him expectantly. He turned toward Angela, who had started all of this. She was staring back at him.

"Well," Paul began, "As you know, I haven't really been sober all that long, and I'm not sure that I'm the right person to—"

"Why are we talking about this now?" Another voice cut in.

It was Larry. He had returned to the position he was in earlier, bent over, looking at the floor, with his hands balled into fists on his knees. He looked at Mandy, picked up the worksheet, and shook it in the air for emphasis.

"Why are we spending time talking about saving money when half the people in here are just trying to get through a day without drinking and drugging? Ain't that enough? Why don't you let us talk? Or at least bring in something that helps us to get through this?"

Larry looked down at the page in front of him.

"You want me to answer these questions? Okay, let's see here. Number one: How much did you spend on your drug of choice? Well, I spent a lot, too fucking much. Everything I had. Question number two: How do you think your spending impacted the people around you? Now that's a good question! I would guess that they hated it. That it really hurt them and put them in a shitty situation. It sucked really bad for them, especially our kids. Because guess what happens to kids growing up around alcoholics and addicts? They become the same dirtbags their parents were!"

Larry looked up from his reading and scanned the room.

"No guilt in these questions, right? No, I feel pretty fucking good about myself! Should I go on?"

Paul thought he saw Mandy take a quick look at the clock on the wall during Larry's rant. Lots of time left, no solace from Father Time tonight. She attempted to redirect the group.

"Well, Larry, you sound upset by this exercise. But I'm curious what Paul was going to say? Can you tell us your thoughts, Paul?"

"I'm good," Paul said. "I think Larry covered it."

Paul didn't look in her direction as he answered. He would let her sweat it out. She made the call to push this worksheet, after all.

There was a short silence. Steve was the only one in the room who continued to fill out his form. He didn't appear to have heard the heated exchange and flipped the first page over to the second page. Soon his hand went up, slowly.

"Yes, Steve, would you like to comment on the exercise?" Mandy asked, her voice a mixture of hope and desperation.

"Oh, no," Steve replied. "I don't have a comment. I just had a question. Is that okay?"

"Yes, certainly," Mandy replied. "Any question at all, please."

"Well," Steve began, "on the second page, question fourteen asks about how much our use of substances cost society at large. I'm not sure what that means. Can you tell me how to answer that?"

"Jesus!" Larry yelled and threw his packet on the ground. He stomped out of the room.

"For me," Diane said, holding her assignment in one hand but looking directly at the others, "I guess it's important to remember the cost of my addiction. I have tried getting sober before. In fact, I've tried several times. Each time something happened. The further I got from the pain and consequences of my last drink, the more I forgot how it felt. I forgot about the people my drinking hurt. I was one of those people who swore I was not hurting anyone with my drinking, even myself, that all the troubles piling up around me were just a series of unfortunate events – misunderstandings or poor timing. I could explain it all, but it was never because I had a problem with drinking—not me. Drinking was fun and social. Everyone else was doing it. The longer I stayed sober, the more I forgot about the bad parts of drinking."

Diane looked around. As she spoke, Larry sidled into the room and took his seat.

She continued, "Now, I agree that wallowing in guilt and shame is not the best use of our time and energy, but I have also come to believe that I cannot afford to forget the past and the dark parts of my drinking. If I forget where my drinking brought me, I'm more likely to wind up there again. I hope this makes sense, and I'm not saying I love this particular survey…I do think this place, this group, is a good environment to consider these issues."

Travis mumbled something, and everyone turned their heads toward him.

"What was that?" Diane asked.

Travis cleared his throat and began again.

"I said it's a safe place…the group, I mean, should be a safe place to talk, and to feel things, and to be accepted. I heard that in what you said, Diane, and I think it's a great point. Everyone should feel safe enough to express themselves in the same way you did, and the way Larry did tonight. I appreciate what you both said, and I'm sure it wasn't easy to say those things. You may not always agree with what is going on in treatment, but I hope you feel our sincere desire to help you."

Atta boy kid, Paul thought.

"Well," Mandy chimed in, "it certainly sounds like you are ready to run the group, Travis. Maybe I'll just call-in next week and let you take it away!"

"I don't think I'm ready for that," Travis said. "I just meant to say—"

"Well, of course you're not ready, not to mention not qualified, to run this group, Travis, but things always look easier from the passenger seat, don't they?" She gave him an icy stare before turning her attention to the others.

"I want to thank you all for your input tonight. It's important to remember that this is your group, and it's so good to hear you all taking some responsibility for what happens here. Hopefully, you'll take the same active role in your own lives and sobriety. As for this exercise," she clutched her packet tightly and waved it in the air, "it was meant to show you just that. You need to take responsibility for your own recovery and to stop blaming others for your behaviors."

Confused faces stared back at her.

Jack scratched his head and mumbled, "What the hell?"

Diane's hand shot up, but Mandy ignored it and continued.

"Since the weather is bad and only getting worse, why don't we end group here for tonight? Please make sure your names are on the packets before you return them to me on the way out. I'll mention in tonight's notes why the assignment was not completed, and you can discuss that and work on these sheets with your individual counselors when you see them for a session."

Paul looked at the clock and saw that they were being dismissed forty minutes early from the group. A curtain of white was falling under the light of the street pole outside.

"So that's it!" Mandy prompted and stood from her own chair.

Slowly the group members rose to exit the room. Mandy collected the unfinished packets from each person as they left, giving them a curt nod of her head.

Angela, Paul, and Travis were the last three to leave. Angela picked up her large bag, which was soaked through.

"Can I talk to you for a minute?" Angela asked Mandy. "I have something going on, and I could use your advice."

Mandy looked briefly at Angela and then up at the clock. "Tonight's not really good for me," she said. "I have someplace I need to be—a person that's waiting for me. That's why I came into group late. Did you make an appointment for us to have a session?"

"Yeah," Angela answered, "but it's not until next Wednesday, and this situation is happening, like, now."

"Well, I can give you five minutes if that would help. But if it's about that guy you mentioned in our last session, I'll tell you the answer now. Dump him. He's a loser, and he'll only bring you down. You need to focus on yourself right now, and you'll never do that with him around."

"Great!" Angela said, flashing her largest, plastic smile to Mandy.

"That's really great advice. Thank you so much!" The wet, bulky bag hit the door frame as Angela walked away, causing her to stumble before continuing down the hallway.

Paul got up next. He gave a nod of his head to Travis as he walked toward Mandy. His packet was rolled up tightly into a baton. He placed it on top of the stack of papers Mandy was holding. She tried to unfold the thing, but it sprang back into circle form and rolled off the stack and onto the floor.

The two stared briefly into each other's faces but said nothing. Paul reached down, picked up the paper, and threw it in the trash can as he walked out the door.

Travis and Mandy were left in the room. She made no effort to look at him, but Travis sensed her anger and disapproval like a living energy in the room.

"Look, Mandy," Travis started, "I didn't mean to overstep my place. I was just trying to-"

"No, no" she interrupted, turning to him and flashing a wide smile.

"You did great. You made some really good points, and it's clear that the group is bonding with you."

Travis waited for more, but Mandy just kept smiling and staring at him.

"Thanks," he said. "I feel like I am getting to know them better as well. It was impressive that Larry opened up a little bit at the beginning of group. Before you came in, he started talking about his childhood and how his dad—"

"Well, Larry needs to open up, or his probation officer will throw his ass in jail," she interrupted, the smile leaving her face.

"So," she continued, "I'm thinking that since you are getting so chummy with everyone, it's probably a good time to have you start doing some of the other work that goes with this job. The work that isn't as much fun as chatting everyone up."

"Oh, sure," Travis said, "I can help out with whatever you need. Just let me know."

"Good," she said, "I'm so glad to hear that. I'm going to have you write out all of the group notes, tonight." She continued. "You do know how to do that, right? I mean, you haven't just been sitting around this whole time without learning some things besides how to make friends with people during groups?"

"Well, we've worked on group notes in my classes. I mean, I've done mock notes. I've also read many of them in the charts here at the clinic, so,

I know the basic format. If you want to just sit with me and get me started, show me what you want, I'll—"

"I've got to go," Mandy said. "Why don't you just do your best with them and I'll look them over tomorrow. I've got to go. My mother is…"

Travis thought he saw the traces of something softer in her face for just a moment. Then it was gone.

"Well, I've just got to go. Something has come up. Do you know how to lock this place up for the night?"

Travis stiffened. Professor Dunleavy's warnings immediately rang in his head: No student is to be in a facility alone – ever! He wondered if Mandy was asking this as a test. From the look on her face, he doubted it. He remembered one of the other clinicians say that Mandy's mother was sick—something about Alzheimer's?

"I just need to turn off the lights, lock all the doors, and leave, right?" He asked, hoping that the smile on his face looked sincere.

"That's all there is to it!" Mandy said, handing Travis the pile of paperwork. "Just paperclip each patient's worksheet to the note you write and leave everything in my mailbox. I'll take it from there."

"Okay, no problem," he said.

"Oh, and one more thing," she said as she started to walk out of the room. "Make sure to use the phrase 'non-compliant' in each note when you explain why the packets are not completed. It's not as important for the patients who don't have a mandate to be here, but for the others, we need to explain why the assignment wasn't done, okay?"

She flashed him a cutting smile and left him.

Travis looked down at the pile of paperwork in his hands, then back toward the empty group room before turning off the lights and walking out.

CHAPTER 24

"Stepping out of your comfort zone and taking risks in early
recovery can be very healthy, as long as those risks move you
further away from using and not closer to it."

Matt Denton, to a patient after their first Twelve Step Meeting

P aul guessed there was about six inches of snow on the ground already
when he walked out of the clinic. He glanced over and saw large tire
marks leading from Peter and Larry's parking spots out to the road. He
thought he saw a bottle sticking out of the snow back there but decided not
to investigate.

A loud voice focused his attention on the front of the building near
the street. Angela was standing under the dilapidated bus stop hut by the
main road. Paul remembered when they built it, but he couldn't remember
any upgrades or repairs to the thing over all these years. Now, most of the
plastic that initially surrounded the frame had broken or fallen off, and
the thin metal roof was bent and rusted. The remains of the structure were
covered in rust and graffiti, as was the rotting wooden bench inside. He saw
Angela's soaked bag on the bench as she yelled into a cell phone.

"No! No, I told you I don't have any!" she stomped her wet feet on
the ground.

She shouted through the quiet snow blanket. "Not again! I'm not using that shit again!"

Paul put his hands in his pockets and walked away from her toward his car.

Then he heard her shriek. "No! No, goddamn it, that is not what I'm going to do! Fuck it and fuck you! I'll find somewhere else to stay!"

Paul looked toward the bus stop just in time to see her throw the phone onto the ground. He heard the crack and splinter of plastic.

"Damn it!!" She shouted from the back of her throat before melting onto the bench next to her bag.

Paul looked up and down the main road, hoping to see a bus. The public transportation around here was unpredictable at best. When it snowed, he knew from experience that a bus might not come at all. There were plenty of nights in the past when he broke all the written rules of a counselor, following only his own moral code, by giving stranded patients a ride home.

He looked toward his car, telling himself that this was not his problem, she was not his problem. He had plenty of problems of his own. The smartest thing would be to get in the car, drive home, and,…and then what?

If Angela heard him coming, she showed no indication of it.

"Are you okay?" Paul asked.

She looked up at him and gestured with her hand to wipe her cheek before looking down again at the ground.

"Are you okay?" Paul repeated and walked under the awning of the bus stop.

As he did, he looked out into the storm and realized just how quickly the snow and sleet were falling. He wondered how long it would last and if Lester was busy on the television translating the doppler radar and pointing to the green screen to plot the course of this storm.

He looked down at Angela, about to repeat his question, but stopped himself. Of course, she wasn't okay. None of them were. Instead of asking again, he moved further into the bus stop, giving her some space and distance, and sat down on the far end of the bench. The two sat there, peering out into the night and saying nothing.

Finally, she straightened herself up, looked toward him, and said, "Do you have any idea when the next bus will be here?"

Paul checked his watch, then glanced around to see if a bus schedule had survived on one of the splintered pieces of Plexiglass that made up the walls. No luck.

"One used to come by at 6:45," he said, "but it looks like it's either late or not coming." He looked at her briefly during this exchange and then back out into the storm.

"Great," she replied, sighing. And then, "Do you think I could borrow your phone to make a call?"

"Sorry, I don't have one."

He looked over his shoulder at the windows to St. Michael's. "It looks like someone is in there, though. You could probably use their phone if you go and knock on the door."

"And deal with Mandy again? No, thank you. I'm not sure what bug crawled up her ass, but someone should definitely help her to get it out."

Paul chuckled and said, "You certainly gave her some things to think about tonight."

And then, against his better judgment, he asked, "Do you need a ride somewhere? I can drop you off on my way home."

Part of him thought this might have been the play all long, setting things up to manipulate a ride from him. But she surprised him.

"No...thanks. I'm okay."

Paul stuck his hand in his pocket, grabbing his car key. His responsibility here was done. He'd asked, and she said no. It was time to walk away.

He stood up and turned to face her.

"Look, I know a place nearby where we can get out of the snow for a while and get a hot cup of coffee. Someone there probably has a phone you can use, and maybe you can come up with a plan on where to go tonight. Why don't you let me drive you over there?"

She took stock of him before saying, "How do I know you're not some kind of weird pervert with duct tape and a saw in your trunk? I mean, no offense. You look harmless and everything, but sometimes guys like you are the craziest motherfuckers going."

Paul smiled and shook his head.

"Good point. You certainly can have a look in my trunk, or under the seats. Hell, you can even drive the car yourself if you want to, or you can stay here. A bus might just come along soon. It's your life, kiddo."

He cinched his coat's collar around his neck and walked back toward his car. As he unlocked the driver's door, she walked up to the passenger side.

"Alright," she said. "I'll check the trunk later. And I don't have a license to drive. But if we're going to some sleazy motel, there had better not be bed bugs or lice. I hate those fucking things." Paul looked at her over the roof of the car. "Fair enough," he said.

He got in, leaned over, and pulled up the lock on the passenger door.

CHAPTER 25

"You can stand by the fucking pool all day sweating,
or you can get your ass in the water."

Jimmy C., "encouraging" a new sponsee to
participate actively in working a program of recovery

When they pulled into the church parking lot a short time later, Angela blew an exasperated breath from her mouth.

"No way! Are you taking me to see a priest or to go to confession or some shit?"

"Not exactly," he said.

As the car got closer to the building, they saw a group of people standing near the entranceway smoking cigarettes. There were ten or twelve other cars in the lot.

She said, "These poor slobs must have some kind of fucked up lives to be here tonight."

"Oh, come on," Paul said. "You wouldn't have left home if you were out of dope?"

"Oh, is that why we're here? It looks like a great place to score some shit!"

Paul looked at her face and thought he saw the hint of a smile.

"Is this where you go every week after group?" She asked. "I bet it's a blast!"

"No," he answered, looking past her and at the group around the doorway. They were putting out their cigarettes and walking inside. "I haven't been here in years. And I don't plan on breaking that streak tonight. You can walk through that door and go down the stairs to the right. The meeting is in the basement. You'll find some coffee and cookies, and you might just learn something. I suggest you say that you're new to sobriety and that you have nowhere to go. One of the women will probably help you out. If nothing else, it will give you some time out of this weather. It's time for you to come up with a plan from here."

She glared at him.

"So that's it? You're going to dump me at some shitty recovery meeting and walk off like you did something good? I didn't see one woman go in there. It looks like a total sausage party to me. And I'm sure they'll just love seeing some fresh, young meat walk in."

She faced the window. They sat staring ahead as sleet and snow landed on the windshield, melted, and flowed down the glass.

After a few minutes of uncomfortable silence, she drew in a breath, collected her giant bag from the floor, and opened the door. Without saying a word, she got out. She started walking away from the church and toward the road.

"Jesus!" Paul said.

He opened his own door and got out.

"Really? This is really what you want?" his voice was louder than he expected and spoke to something beyond Angela.

He caught up to her.

"Look, I'm sorry, alright? This isn't exactly where I want to be right now either, but it's where we are. So, let's deal with it. I'll go in with you. I'll stay with you. I'll help…"

She said nothing. She simply stopped, turned around, and padded through the falling snow toward the bright lights of the church.

The meeting had already started when they entered the large room in the basement. The church used it for Sunday school classes, and every wall featured pictures of crayon crosses, clouds and stick-figure people. Piles of games and plastic bins filled with toys lined the edges of the room. The floor was concrete, the walls brick and painted white. On the far side of the room a small alcove led into a kitchen. A wide stainless-steel cutout in the wall provided a portal for passing food from the kitchen into the larger room. On the shelf in front of the cutout, two industrial-sized coffee makers, Styrofoam cups, cream, sugar, and a variety of what looked like the cheapest, stalest cookies awaited a taker.

A woman sat in a chair behind a foldout table near the coffee and cookies. She was reading something aloud when Angela and Paul entered. About ten rows of chairs had been aligned in front of her table, with six chairs in each row. The room was half-filled with people, and Paul could feel their eyes following him and Angela as they entered. He ducked into a seat in the row of chairs closest to the door. To his surprise, Angela set her large bag down on the floor next to him, then walked to the coffee maker and began to pour herself a coffee while stuffing her pockets full of cookies. He wondered when her last meal had been.

"Are there any newcomers?" the woman behind the table asked, and Paul realized it was the other woman from their group—he thought her name was Dianna? In the palpable silence that followed neither Paul nor Angela introduced themselves.

Angela returned and sat next to him, pulling out a cookie and dunking it in the cup of coffee before taking a bite.

"No newcomers?" Diane asked from her table. "Okay, then is there anyone coming back to the program after a relapse that would like to acknowledge it?"

Paul felt a stinging accusation in the question and regretted his decision to come down here. One of his grandfather's favorite aphorisms, "No good deed goes unpunished," ran through his mind.

When nobody responded to her question, Diane asked the group to bring up any topics related to alcoholism for discussion.

A woman immediately put her hand up.

"Hi," the woman said, "my name's Theresa, and I'm an alcoholic."

"Hi Theresa," a chorus of voices responded.

"It's nice to see you up there, Diane," she continued, "and I'm happy everyone decided to come out on this awful night. I've been struggling with cravings to drink recently, and if I weren't here, I mean, if we didn't have these meetings to come to, I'd probably be drunk right now. So, I would like to hear about staying away from that first drink."

Now that the meeting was going, Paul started to feel a comfortable familiarity, which reassured him. There was something in these places that nowhere else could provide, but he'd never known quite how to describe or explain to others what it was.

His first sponsor had summed it up best: "You want to know how it works? Well, it works good. Now sit down, shut up, and listen."

He had. For a long, long time, he had listened in here. And it had worked. At least it had worked as well as he had allowed it to work.

A few rows in front of him, a man had been selected to speak. His voice and profile from behind seemed familiar to Paul.

"I know that for me that there is no such thing as one drink." The man said. "And I also know that if I take that first drink, all bets are off. I lose control completely. The only thing I seem to have some control of is not taking that first one, and I only have that control because I keep coming to these meetings."

"Thanks, Bill," the crowd said in unison.

Bill, Paul thought. Yes, that was the same Bill that Paul had seen get straight ten or twelve years ago. And he was still here, still sober—apparently. Good for him.

Hands went up in the room, and Diane continued to pick people to speak. Paul had not been focused on the other chosen topics for the meeting, but he guessed that one was related to the first step of the A.A. Program, which encouraged members to admit they were powerless over alcohol and that it had made their lives unmanageable.

That First Step was the only reason Paul attended these meetings when he originally stopped drinking. The eleven steps that followed seemed unrelated and irrelevant to him, but he distinctly remembered first reading the word "powerless" as it related to his use of alcohol, and something connected for him. Until that moment, he truly thought he could keep his drinking in check somehow to avoid what had been a series of increasingly painful consequences. The word "powerless" indicated that drinking might just be an all-or-nothing proposition for him. That prospect deeply disturbed him. It was a blunt answer to a riddle he'd been desperate to solve for decades.

Angela strolled up and filled her coffee cup again, and Paul wondered if she had heard anything so far that might connect with the fucked-up existence she called her life. He knew this might be her first and last meeting. He wondered how many others had come and gone, sitting briefly in these seats, chewing on stale cookies while surrounded by crayon drawings of Jesus. How many sat in similar church basements around the world? How many were sober? How many died? And how many desperately needed to be here but would never find the way?

"We are just about out of time," Diane said. "Does anyone have a burning desire to share something?"

Nobody spoke.

"Okay," she continued, "we'll close with the Serenity Prayer."

The group stood and formed a circle by holding hands. He thought Angela would leave, or at least stand outside of the circle, maybe run off to the bathroom as he had seen many other newcomers do to avoid prayer, or intimacy with others, or both. She stood by his side, and when she placed her hand gently in his before the prayer began, he was surprised at how small and fragile it felt.

Angela left him when the prayer ended and walked to the front of the room, where she approached Diane, who immediately embraced her in a giant hug. Some people were stacking chairs against a wall of the room, and Paul joined in, hoping that it would keep anyone from approaching him and starting a conversation. He put one chair on top of another and started moving them toward the wall when he heard the first voice.

"Paul, right?"

He looked up to see Bill smiling at him and holding out a hand.

"Yes," Paul replied.

He held out his hand to Bill, and they shook.

"It's good to see you, Paul. I'm glad you came tonight. I haven't seen you around in a while."

"It's been a long while since I've been anywhere healthy, Bill," Paul said. "But I'm glad to be here, too, and I liked what you shared during the meeting."

Bill tenaciously sustained some light conversation, but Paul soon realized how inept he'd become at speaking with other human beings in a sober, social situation. Bill must have sensed this.

"Well, I hope to see you around more often, Paul," he said and patted Paul lightly on the shoulder. "This is my home group. I'll be here every week."

Paul smiled and nodded but said nothing, especially not an agreement to return. He saw Angela talking with Diane and another woman and hoped they were making a plan for her. He aimed toward the exit and spotted Jimmy C. charging directly at him, like a linebacker tracking a much smaller player while they tried to sneak the football upfield.

"Well," Jimmy said, a broad smile crossing his face, "you just never know what type of odd creature will blow in during a storm like this."

He walked up close to Paul, closer than Paul was comfortable with. He could almost hear Jimmy sniffing around him out to determine his level of intoxication.

"I haven't had a drink today," Paul said.

"No shit?"

Jimmy started to pat down the jacket he was wearing, searching for something.

"Well, I'm fresh out of lollipops right now. You'll have to ask me next week when you come back, and I'll bring you one."

"Make sure it's Root Beer flavor," Paul said and smiled up at Jimmy.

The two stood looking at each other for a moment before Jimmy glanced over toward Angela and then back at Paul.

"You running a taxi service for wayward girls now, or are you gonna tell me this is someone's niece or cousin or some shit like that?"

"She needed a ride. We're in treatment together. She had nobody else and nowhere else to go."

"Huh," Jimmy said, nodding his head. "Well, her choice of you as the dashing white knight shows how fucking smart and healthy she is. Try to keep your sword in your pocket and that bottle shut tight in your freezer at home."

Paul shook his head but said nothing. He knew any attempt at an explanation was pointless. Jimmy leaned in, clasping Paul's neck and drawing him in close so that their heads were almost touching.

"I'm glad you're here, Paul. I've been waiting for you to get your head out of your ass and come back to life. Now stop fucking around, and let's get on with this."

Jimmy tightened his grip momentarily, and Paul couldn't be sure if it was meant affectionately or as a caution, but it hurt just the same. It also reminded Paul what he missed most about his friend: he was a literal pain in the neck most of the time. Jimmy released him, and pointed one finger toward his face.

"I'll see you soon." He turned away, stooping slightly at the exit before heading out the door.

Paul saw Diane and Angela looking in his direction, waving.

"Well, we have quite a little contingent of people from the group here tonight," Diane said cheerily as she walked toward Paul.

"I am so glad you and Angela came. Could you tell how nervous I was up there? I have just enough sober time to be the chairperson at this meeting, and so, of course, my sponsor forced me to get up there and do it tonight for the first time!"

"You did great. I couldn't tell you were nervous at all." Paul said.

Diane beamed, "Well, I always feel better after coming to these meetings, and tonight, I mean, having you two show up, I'll be on a natural high all night now!"

The person from the kitchen walked into the meeting room and blinked the light on and off several times, the equivalent of a "last call" signal.

Diane said, "We'd better get out of here before they throw us out!

They left the room, walked up the stairs, and into a completely new landscape the storm had created. Cars in the parking lot and on the street resembled white pods, making it difficult to distinguish between colors and models. The road blended in with the sidewalks.

"There's magic afoot," Diane said, smiling brightly at Paul and Angela. "My grandmother used to tell me that magic happened during these times when Mother Nature brings us the snow. She lived to be ninety-four and died at home with everyone around her during a snowstorm like this one. I wasn't there, of course. I was out drinking somewhere and hadn't gotten the calls from my family that she was ready to go with Mother Nature that night. I feel her now, though, on these nights in the snow. I feel my grandmother telling me that it's alright that I wasn't there that night."

Diane looked at Paul and Angela, "I'm not sure why I just told you both that!"

The three of them stood looking around into the whiteness. The only sound was the buzz of the streetlights and the faint sound of the snow falling on everything, everywhere.

"She's here," Angela said, "and she's proud of you."

Diane raised her gloved hand gently behind Angela's head and pulled her close, until their foreheads touched.

"Thank you, dear girl," she whispered. "Well, I'd better get home. Maybe I'll see you two in another meeting before group next week?"

"Would you like a ride?" Paul asked.

"No," Diane responded, "I just live a few blocks away, and I think I'll spend some time with my grandmother."

She walked away from them, her shape disappearing into the snow.

Paul had no idea what to do next. He looked over at Angela, who smiled back. She seemed comfortable with everything.

"Well," she said, "that didn't suck as bad as I thought it would. Do you have a plan for what comes next, or is this where we leave each other?"

"Where would you go?" Paul asked, and then, "I mean, where could you stay?"

He already knew the answers to these questions but couldn't think of anything else to say.

She looked at him and laughed, shaking her head.

"Look, don't worry about it," she said. "Thanks for bringing me here, Otis. Better than duct tape and a machete, or bedbugs at some skanky motel. I've got people that will put me up. Don't short out your pacemaker about it or anything."

She hefted the bag's strap around her shoulder and straightened her back, then marched into the snow. Paul noticed the smallness of her tracks in the snow—a child's footprints.

He heard Jimmy's words in his head and stared out into the falling snow looking for another knight or white horse to come and save the day.

"I've got an extra room," he said.

"You can stay there tonight, and tomorrow you can make some calls and try to get a plan together."

He expected feelings of regret, and dread to wash over him after making the offer, knowing he was getting into something well beyond his control or concern. He was diving headfirst into a hot mess.

However, the feeling that flooded him after making the offer was not dread or fear. It was something else, something good and true and powerful from a long-ago time in his life. As he watched the strange young girl stop and turn back toward him through the falling snow, he realized what it was.

It was the smallest mustard seed of hope.

CHAPTER 26

"I just hoped he would find someone to love him. And now...living that
way...I mean, how will he ever have a normal relationship?
I don't think that's selfish or closed-minded, I'm just thinking of Travis.
Shouldn't every mother want what's best for her child?"

Noreen Kent, to her husband

It took Travis over an hour to complete the notes from the group. He did his best to follow Mandy's instructions but also included positive messages about each person's contribution. He thought it was a good group—maybe the best so far—but couldn't explain why. Something real had happened. It started with Larry talking about his childhood. There was a truth and sincerity in Larry's words that could have grown and expanded through the group if Mandy hadn't interrupted it. The process wasn't pretty, but Travis felt power and potential in those brief moments.

He had no idea how to describe these feelings in the clinical notes. Since starting his internship, he had noticed that documentation for what happened in groups didn't give half of the details he thought should be included. Now that he was writing the notes, he saw how complicated this process could be. Documentation and accurate notetaking were frequent topics in his college class.

"*The trick is,*" *Dunleavy told them,* "*to pull out the essence of the group, to describe the main topic or topics, and to summarize how each member contributed to that topic. It's also vital to include a recommendation, your professional opinion, based on what you think each patient should do with the information that was covered during the group. One of the biggest mistakes and problems in this field is poor documentation, usually due to rushed schedules and overbooked counselors.*"

Travis knew that it was all great advice and reliable information. He just wasn't sure how to apply it.

Mandy wrote most of her notes on a computer and printed them out before signing each one. It appeared to Travis that she simply copied and pasted most of the information, changing only the name as she went. Consequently, some of her notes had incorrect pronouns, and often included mistakes like:

"*Andrew was attentive during the group. She participated appropriately and followed the curriculum throughout.*"

Other counselors paid more attention to these details. Bill's notes were always handwritten, well organized, and individualized. He had a knack for reading each patient and for describing concisely how each person performed and reacted during a group. Bill worked only part-time now, but he'd been around longer than any of the other staff. Travis would have observed more of Bill's groups, but he was the only counselor who no longer worked in the evenings.

"I don't know why I'm here at all anymore. I told Matt I quit this job two years ago!" Bill told Travis when he asked him why he wasn't running evening groups.

Travis tried going to Bill's office to ask questions or observe him, but he was often behind the closed door with a patient. Because he worked part-time, most of these patients were assigned to work with other counselors, but they all seemed comfortable stopping by and talking with him or seeking out his opinion on some matter. He frequently hung out in the lobby to commune with addicts arriving for intake. Some were "newbies," and many were coming back for another try after a relapse. Either way, Bill always strived to make every patient feel welcome when they came into the clinic. This was another topic that Travis remembered discussing at H.C.C.

"If we believe that addiction is a disease," the professor said, "why wouldn't we treat people afflicted with addiction with care and compassion? Too often in any helping field, the workers forget our primary directive: to do no harm."

After forty minutes of working on the notes, Travis' phone buzzed with a text message:

"Working late or stuck in a ditch?"

He picked up the phone and sent a message back:

"Stuck in a ditch but getting some work done while I'm there. Where are you?"

After a few minutes, his phone buzzed again:

"I was planning a big surprise for my love, but need to get home and rest. Leaving the nest now. I left you a treat. Be careful on the roads XOSXOS"

He typed back:

"OK, you be careful too. Thanks for the treat. See you tomorrow. XOKXOK"

Travis finished the last note and secured the papers with a paper clip. As he walked to the chart room, he felt the familiar rumble and shake of a snowplow clearing the street outside. He wondered where Mandy was and if her little sports car was any safer in the snow than his old ride. She'd mentioned something about her mother, but Travis wanted to doubt that.

He wanted to be angry at her. No doubt she was safe and secure in her house, probably on her second glass of wine in front of a natural gas fireplace with her Tinder date sitting next to her. On the other hand, maybe she had moved the process along more quickly, and the young stud was busy going down on her. That thought turned his stomach, and he forced it out of his mind.

He unlocked the chart room, went inside, and checked the paperwork once more before placing it all in Mandy's mailbox. He knew she would find something to criticize but didn't want to make it too easy by doing something blatantly stupid like leaving out a note.

Travis walked around the building, making sure the lights were off and all the office doors were shut and locked. Sometimes in these last moments before leaving, even with other people around, he felt something that made the hair on the back of his neck stand up. It was an energy of sorts, a sense that something else was there, in the building with him. He felt the strong presence of lives that had been there before, a residual glow like the smell of campfire on your clothes, or looking at the sun and then closing your eyes and seeing that brightness. The feeling had grown stronger, more attuned throughout his lifetime, but he never talked about it. He shrank from the possibility that people would think he was crazy and harbored a larger fear that others would share information about their own psychic or paranormal powers. Travis wanted nothing to do with all that.

It was hard to deny that many of the patients who had been in this building were now dead. To his knowledge, no actual deaths occurred on-site, but many patients in the last few years had overdosed in the bathroom and later died in the hospital or after shooting more dope. Some who had recently attended St. Michael's were now dead from driving accidents, violence, or suicide. Besides contemplating if their spirits remained behind, Travis couldn't help but question just how many people had actually survived after getting sober.

Dunleavy had brought up the topic of success in one of the first classes last semester. Travis thought the professor's message was odd, if not downright discouraging at the time, but he was beginning to understand it more clearly now.

"If your success in this field is going to be defined by how many people you can keep sober, you are in for a long, difficult career—or, perhaps, a very short one. The statistics on longer-term sobriety are never encouraging, but we need to remember that these studies are often negatively biased, as are many statistical studies about addiction. It's always important to research who was responsible for the studies you might read. If it was conducted by an alcohol distributor, for example, I would be immediately suspicious. In the same way, these studies can be inaccurate because it's hard to track down many patients after they leave treatment, and even if we do, they have a right to their privacy on the matter. The most optimistic studies I have seen were conducted by high-end rehabilitation centers, and they claim to have success rates with sobriety of about 50% after one year away from treatment. Given the best, most expensive treatment available, only one in two patients will stay sober over the long term. Half of them. For this reason, I strongly urge all of you not only to question the statistics but to come up with a definition of success for yourselves that is not tied to the long-term sobriety of your patients."

Travis spoke to some other students after that lecture. All of them vowed to improve the numbers around relapses, each bright-eyed intern swore that their patients would beat the odds. Denial was another core topic in the treatment of addiction, and Travis believed that a certain amount of naïve denial was healthy, even required, in this work. This was clear in the mantra of greenhorns to the helping field:

"If I can help just one person stay sober, I'll be happy with what I am doing."

He wondered how many new counselors were lying about that or if it was even a realistic goal.

He walked toward the front door of the clinic, thinking about how many of his future patients would live and how many might haunt him long after their death. As he checked to make sure the door was locked one more time, the phone vibrated in his pocket. He reached down, looked at the text message, and smiled.

CHAPTER 27

"The justification for twenty-eight days of inpatient rehabilitation treatment has centered around people needing a safe, substance-free place to maintain sobriety. The ongoing problem we face is where to send these people after those twenty-eight days. Sending patients to a rehab is only a temporary solution. The real answer is to spend more time, money, and resources on sober living facilities where people know they are safe."

Travis Kent, class lecture notes,
"Understanding the Treatment Process," H.C.C.

There wasn't much in the refrigerator. Paul rummaged around in there while Angela wandered into his living room. He stared into the void, pulling out the drawers and looking in as if doing so would make food that had not been there before suddenly appear. A Frigidaire magic trick.

He made a mental note to go shopping—maybe tomorrow. He would bring Angela along. She probably needed some items, though he doubted she would admit to it. He could buy her a few basic things before finding her a more permanent place to stay.

"Why are these mouse traps in here?" she asked.

"Well," Paul said, "those would be to catch a mouse, or maybe several of them. In my experience, there is no mouse; there are only mice."

His gaze fell upon the orange cheese product in the back corner of the deli drawer. He couldn't remember how long ago he'd bought the stuff, but it seemed well protected, each slice glistened in its own plastic wrapper. That was the way to go. He pulled the package out, retrieved a plate from the cupboard, and set to work unwrapping the stuff.

"I don't think you'll catch them with no bait and sprung traps," Angela said.

Paul walked around the corner into the living room. He saw both traps, tripped and empty, each with a small pile of mouse turd nearby.

"Sons of bitches," he mumbled.

Angela had curled herself up on the couch.

"You should get a cat if you want to get rid of them," she advised.

"Yeah," he said, "a cat is just what I need."

He returned to the kitchen and opened the cupboards, hoping to find a box of crackers from Jenny's contributions. No luck. Among the donated cans, he located a small container of party nuts. Paul grabbed the nuts and opened the refrigerator again, hoping a cluster of grapes might have grown there while he looked away. He grabbed a loaf of white bread. Nearby a tub of margarine jogged his memory of Charlotte, who had convinced him it would prevent the heart attack she predicted would kill them both as they entered their forties. He hated the taste of it but stuck with it after she left. He realized how odd that was as he set the container on the counter.

Under the lid, yellow-covered crumbs and bits of hardened jelly littered the surface of the margarine. Paul had a long-standing practice of contaminating household condiments by insisting on a single knife for sandwich preparation. The practice had caused considerable angst among Charlotte and Sean. Bowing to his habits, Charlotte provided Paul with his own supply of margarine, jelly, peanut butter, and other products—all bearing the label "Dad's Tub" in black marker.

Paul grabbed a clean knife from the drawer and scraped the trespassing bits of bread and jelly from the surface and edges of the margarine tub. He wiped the knife clean with a napkin and sliced the cheese and bread into smaller bits, placing them in what struck him as a rather pleasing pattern around the margarine container. He set the tub in the middle of the plate and stuck the knife in. He opened the can of nuts, briefly considering pouring them around the plastic margarine centerpiece, but decided to serve them as a side dish, straight from the can. Producing a glass from the cupboard, he ran it under the faucet, wiped it down with a sponge, added ice cubes, water, and entered the living room. Feeling accomplished, Paul placed his platter, nuts, and the glass of water on the coffee table in front of Angela before sitting down in a chair next to the couch.

"Is that water?" Angela asked, looking at the clear liquid in the glass.

Paul nodded and leaned forward to select a small square of the bread, a smear of margarine, and a cheese bit for the topper. With his other hand, he scooped out a handful of nuts. He popped the bread and cheese in his mouth and immediately realized the combination of processed food was not good. He swallowed quickly and switched to the nuts, hoping to kill the aftertaste.

"So…you don't have anything stronger to drink, or you're just keeping that to yourself?"

Paul leaned back in his chair, starting to understand why she was so quiet on the ride here. She was probably wondering if he was truly sober and if he was the dirty old pervert who would now tell her the price of staying here.

"Well," he said, looking at her, "that stuff on the plate has quite a kick to it, but the rest of the house is pretty much drug and alcohol-free."

She said nothing, leaning forward and grabbing the glass of water from the table, then taking a small, tentative sip.

"When was the last time you drank? I mean the real last time, with no bullshit," she asked.

"Six days ago," he replied without hesitating and kept his gaze on hers. "You saw that contraption in my car. It's a bigger motivator for sobriety than I imagined. I really don't want to be walking everywhere, and we both know that the public transportation around here leaves a lot to be desired."

He saw the hint of a smile form as she sat back on the couch. Paul considered asking about her sobriety but decided to wait and see if she talked about it without prompting. Angela leaned toward the table, put her water down, and picked up a piece of the bread, skipping the butter product but adding the cheese. She sat back and took a nibble from the bread. After a moment, she took another bite and then popped the whole thing in her mouth and went back for another.

"Thanks for the food and for letting me stay here," she said.

"It's kind of weird not having my phone. At first, I was pissed about breaking it, thinking what a fucking asshole I am, right? It's strange, not feeling like I have to check the stupid thing all the time or wait for the next text to come in. I can't remember the last time I didn't have a phone at all."

"Is that a good thing or a bad thing?" he asked.

"Good, I guess. Maybe bad? It just feels strange. It reminds me of when the power goes out, and you keep flipping the light switch anyway. For that moment, you expect the lights to come on. I keep waiting for the phone to go off, or I think of texting someone, and then I remember that I can't. It feels good, I guess, not constantly thinking that I'd better get in touch with someone or that they are trying to contact me. It's just weird."

"Who would you call? Or text? Or whatever it is your generation does now?"

"Nobody good, I guess." She grabbed another piece of bread and cheese. "I'm pretty sure nobody's out looking for me. I'm sure Prince Charming hasn't formed a search party. He's probably already found another stupid, strung-out bitch to spend the night with. I'm such an asshole. I can't believe I let myself...."

She wiped her face with her hand and gazed out the front window and into the darkness.

"Anyone else you could call? Any family or friends? I don't mind you staying here. I mean, I'm not trying to push you out. I'm just curious."

"My old man's dead, but that's probably the best thing for everybody. He was a real charmer. Cancer couldn't have happened to a better person. And my mom, well, she's probably spending the night with some guy she doesn't know, just like her baby girl. Only I doubt they went to a fucking A.A. meeting, and she probably isn't sitting around chatting and eating shitty cheese on molding white bread!"

She looked up at him.

"No offense."

Paul laughed.

"None taken. I did scrape most of the mold off, though. And you should try the nuts before you critique the whole thing."

Paul reached down and poured another handful from the can.

Angela shook a few into her small hand, placed them in her mouth, and spoke as she crunched down.

"Mom's got a ton of issues to deal with, but I don't think she ever will. She gave me my first fix. I was twelve years old and had a toothache. Rotten teeth weren't a real shocker because my folks didn't make going to the dentist a top priority. When I started to complain about the pain, my mom told me she had just the thing. I'll never forget it. She went into her purse and pulled out this tin, this ridiculous little tin, like the kind you keep mints in, right? Only she had pills in there. It was the first time I realized how messed up she might be and how different we were from other families. I had a few friends, not many, but a few. I couldn't imagine any of the other moms I knew denying their kid a trip to the dentist and giving them an unmarked pill from a fucking mint tin instead!"

She paused and glanced in Paul's direction but seemed to look through him, past him into something only she could see.

"But I took it. And it worked. Holy shit, did it work. The pain was gone for a while. All the pain was gone. This was before the tooth got so bad that they took me to the emergency room. We never had a doctor, like a family doctor, where you go for colds and to get shots and shit like that. We just went to the E.R. when things got really fucking bad and sat there for hours with the other fucked up families. It's weird to think about just how messed up my parents were and how clueless I was about it all, not that it kept me from getting messed up."

"Any brothers or sisters?" Paul asked.

"Oh yeah. I've got a sister. But she escaped. She got the fuck out of crazy town as soon as she could."

"Is she older or younger?"

"Older. By two years. I think it was God's little joke on my old man to give him two daughters. The guy who hated women and saw us all as an incredible burden on his otherwise awesome life."

She shook her head.

"My sister just took it from him, the beatings and the taunts and the constant put-downs about what sluts and whores and lazy bitches we were. She took it all. And then, as soon as someone came along to get her out of that house, she was gone. She moved out at fifteen years old and married at seventeen. Lucky for her, the Prince Charming she found is actually a decent guy. He enlisted in the Navy, and those two took off before they got dragged down. She's out west now, living on a Navy base in California. Her husband's been deployed a few times, and she's come back to visit, always short visits, when he's over fighting the good fight to save democracy or American lives or our rights to drive big fucking gas-guzzling S.U.V.'s or whatever we're fighting for these days. The last time I saw her was two years ago at the old man's funeral. We keep in touch. She's offered me a ticket to go out there, but I don't want to do it, not now anyway. Not until I get my shit together."

Paul waited, giving her time to add to the story, but she took a long drink from the glass of water and closed her eyes.

"Well," he said, "it seems like you're getting it together. I'd tell you that things get better being sober, but right now, I'm not exactly the poster child for a great life in recovery."

"What's your story?" She asked, opening her eyes, and looking around the room.

"I mean, it looks like you had your shit together for a while. What type of work do you do?"

"I'm unemployed," Paul said, "and currently unemployable."

"Well, what did you do? You don't just get this stuff for free, and I don't think you deal dope for it."

"Nope, it wasn't free, but drug dealing did help pay for it. I was an addictions counselor, just like Mandy. Actually, I ran the whole clinic for many years."

Angela laughed loudly. Paul stared at her.

"Wait, no, holy shit! Are you serious?"

"Yup," Paul said, "But that's all over now, and I'm an old man. Look, it's way past my bedtime. Let me show you the room you can sleep in tonight."

He stood up, grabbed the plate with the bread and cheese, and walked into the kitchen. She took the jar of nuts, picked up her bag, and followed him.

He scraped the remaining bits of food into the garbage and put the margarine back in the refrigerator. She walked next to him, found the top to the nuts, and put it on, sliding the jar in his direction.

"Thanks," he said and opened the empty canned goods cupboard.

"Help yourself to anything you can find out here."

He turned from the sink and walked down the hallway.

"The bathroom is right down here," Paul motioned as they walked.

He stopped and placed his hand on the doorknob to the room across from the bathroom. His hand was shaking, and Paul hoped she wouldn't think it was from withdrawal or because he was about to introduce Angela to his kinky torture room for wayward girls. He turned the knob slowly and opened the door.

He stayed in the hallway, motioning for her to enter the room.

"There is a light switch on the right and a reading lamp near the bed. Both lights should work, but if not, you can just switch out a bulb from somewhere else in the house. See you in the morning."

"Thank you again," Angela said and reached for the switch on the wall.

The ceiling lamp glowed to life. She closed the door, walked over to the bed, threw her large bag in the middle of the mattress, and sat down, bouncing slightly to test the firmness. The space was small but neat and orderly. It reminded her of the room she had for a short time while grow-ing up. When her father was working and seemed to have the "functioning alcoholic" routine down, he had moved them from the shithole apart-ment into a house. It was the first place where she had a room of her own. The move should have been a happy affair, but she and her sister knew it resulted from a horrible night a month before.

Her father had invited some of his dirtbag buddies to the apartment, and they were all drinking and watching TV. Her mother had brought both girls into their shared bedroom, which was tiny, and had tucked them in before retreating to her own room. Angela fell asleep to the sounds of college football, loud and booming, while the men shouted and screamed obscenities at the screen. These noises were part of the normal routine at her house, just the regular version of bedtime stories her father and his loser friends "read" to her. For this reason, she wasn't alarmed when she woke up in the dark to the sounds of more screaming from beyond the bedroom door.

The difference was that the screams were feminine. She realized it was her sister and mother she was hearing along with the low responses of male voices and then the crescendo of bodies moving in unison, yelling and shouting through the wall. Kitchen chairs tumbled across the linoleum floor and work boots stomped through the hall. Then, the undeniable sounds of pushing, punching, and breaking glass sounded out in the living room. Angela left her bed and stood by the door, frozen. The paralyzing fear as she stood in the dark of her bedroom, too afraid to open the door, haunted her. She hated how fear had weakened her.

She tried to think about something else, to focus on the fresh, bright light cascading from the ceiling—to remind herself it was over, that the past was in the past. But it was no good. The video was streaming now and downloading again. It refused to be shut off. She could hear the front door of the apartment opening and slamming shut as people left. She assumed it was his guests, his drunken, asshole guests realizing the party was over for the night. She was glad they were leaving but knew then that the party would never be over, not really—not for good, not ever.

Angela heard footsteps coming down the hallway and her mother's soft, consoling voice. She took a few quick steps across the room and into her bed, pulling up the covers and laying with her face toward the wall, pretending to be asleep. The door slowly opened, and she heard her mother and her sister enter, her sister's sobs filled the quiet room.

"I just needed to go to the bathroom," her sister was saying. *"I swear I didn't go out there. I didn't even know who was there."*

"I know, honey," Angela's mom said. *"I know you didn't know. You didn't do anything wrong. Everything is alright."*

"And he was just there," her sister went on, *"he was there in the hallway when I came out. He grabbed me. He tried to kiss me, he tried to pull my shirt up...he...he..."*

Her sister's sobbed until she could barely breathe. At the same time, the television sounds from the living room went silent. Angela heard her father's heavy footfalls pass her doorway and enter her parents' bedroom.

"Shh, hush sweety," her mom soothed. "It's okay. It's all going to be okay. He'll never be allowed back into this house. Don't worry. I'll make sure that everything is going to be alright."

Her mother left their room that night, but the sounds of yelling and cursing shook the walls and the two frightened girls for hours. Nobody in the family ever mentioned the incident again. Soon after, they moved out of the apartment and into the house where Angela had her own room. Her father never brought any men to the new place. Instead, he began to disappear from the family for long stretches of time. When he was home, she knew not to disturb him.

Angela hadn't thought about that night in a long time. Funny how the brain worked, how being alone in this room could take her on a trip through time. Maybe this was another moment in her life when she would go from something bad to something better, or maybe some of that stuff she heard about memories and old feelings coming back to haunt you once you got sober was true. It was weird shit, though, having all that stuff come up without warning.

She felt wired, awake, and restless. There was a low mumbling voice coming through the wall, and she assumed Paul had turned on a TV in his room. That seemed like a good way to stay distracted, to scare off the ghosts from the past. If she had her phone—that fucking phone—she could enjoy some distracting of her own. She unzipped her bag and dug through it until she found a small stuffed animal. It used to be a bear, but the thing had seen better days and had lost some important bear features along the way. She took it out and propped it against the pillows near the headboard.

Rummaging through the bag, she found a pair of large, wrinkled boxer shorts and an oversized t-shirt that read *Property of Dartmouth College.* She untied her sneakers and removed them and her socks, surprised at how wet they were from the snow. The smell of feet, like old, melted cheese, wafted up, and she tried to remember the last time she took a shower. The motel shower was dirty and cold, a smell of rust and mold seeped up through the pipes. There hadn't even been a bar of soap.

She picked up the t-shirt and boxers and walked across the room, pausing by the closed door to the hallway. She waited there, cautiously listening to the sound of her own heart beating louder and louder in the silence. Finally, she reached down, opened the door, and crossed the hallway into the bathroom.

There was a clean towel and washcloth folded and sitting near the sink. They smelled like a detergent she knew long ago, but she couldn't remember the name of the stuff. She thought that the commercial involved a giggling bear, dropped into clean linens promising a "fresh, bouncy wash" or something like that. She would have to search for that commercial online and find out what that smell was once she got a fucking phone again.

She stood in front of the full-length mirror on the back of the bathroom door and took off her clothes. She'd always been thin, despite never playing a sport or paying attention to what she ate. During middle school, when she'd started to gain some weight, her mother suggested adding caffeine and nicotine to her diet. She convinced Angela that these things helped to keep a girl lean. Angela's sister refused this advice and was always referred to as "a little heavy," or "a big girl" by their mother.

Angela thought mom would be proud of the pale, gaunt body reflected in the mirror. People routinely told her how unhealthy she looked. *"Too thin!"* they would say as if such a thing truly existed for a woman in America. She'd learned through the years that girls and women would never win at the game of social acceptance. It was an unfair game, with ever-changing rules and restrictions.

She leaned toward the mirror, running her fingers through her hair and feeling the grease and grit. She isolated a few strands and examined the split ends, an old habit. A bathmat hung over the side of the tub, and she laid it on the tile floor. The curtain was old and yellowed. It had torn from several of the rings that attached it to the shower bar. There was a faint odor of bleach, but the smell of the bathroom mostly reminded her of the locker room and the swimming pool at the town park where she and her sister spent countless hours each summer. She thought of a July night during senior year when she convinced Drew Hollis to jump the fence and go skinny dipping with her. Although they never discussed it, she knew he was gay. They never disputed the rumors in school that they were a couple. They even went to the prom together. She remembered lying naked in the grass that night, side by side, staring up into the stars and wondering aloud what would come next. Six months later, he was dead, and she was well on her way to becoming what her sister liked to call a *junkie whore.*

She held her hand under the tub spout waiting for it to become a touch too hot, the way she liked it. Steam rose to fill the room as she stepped into the tub. The heat on her back did not burn, exactly, but it took her breath away for a moment. In the back corner, a wire rack fixed to the wall held soap and shampoo. There were two or three bottles of cheap stuff, the dollar store quality stuff that older guys who don't know or care would buy. But when she moved them, she found bottles of body wash, shampoo, and conditioner that she guessed were purchased by a woman.

The products were name brand and fairly expensive. Angela tried to imagine what the woman who bought them was like. She'd never been a good judge of women, never really trusted them. No wonder, with the awesome job her mom did. Angela thought the problem went deeper than simple *mommy issues.* From a very young age, she just didn't fit the feminine stereotypes around her. She never liked dresses, flower prints, or the countless pink and yellow outfits handed down from her sister or unearthed in the local consignment shops by her mom. Angela preferred blue or black jeans, white or grey shirts, and canvas sneakers. She liked her hair not too short and not too long, and never in ponytails or adorned with bows and ribbons.

The first few birthday parties she attended, which were advertised as "girls only," involved princess themes, make-up tutorials, and constant high-pitched giggling. The mothers hosting these parties, all queens in their own right, maintained a strict sequined-glasses view of life. They seemed more uncomfortable with Angela's presence than she was. She was the only princess at these parties who refused to wear a dress, and she became even more irritable when it was time to open the gifts. Her mom, who forced her to attend every one of these affairs, always bought the same gift: a notebook with matching pencils. Angela cringed and did her best to become invisible as she watched the dwindling gift pile reveal her small, simple gift bag that contained the worst possible gift ever—the birthday turd. The giggling birthday princess and her court of maidens always reacted the same way. The laughter and merriment would subside as the horrible notebook was removed, followed by the dreadful pencils. Then all eyes turned to Angela, who had already been exposed as the giver of the worst gift by her mother's words, printed on the small card hanging limply from the thin strings attached to the bag.

"Well, isn't that thoughtful," the Queen of the party would say, as the other girls made their first efforts with tact in situations of economic and social hierarchy.

"And look, the unicorns on the pencils match the notebook, or is it a journal? Well, how nice. Now, thank Angela for that thoughtful gift."

While the Queen was talking, the girl opening the bag would always—fucking always—look back into the bag after removing the pencils. Angela envisioned them sticking their young, manicured hand in and pulling it out covered in shit.

Her third-grade teacher was the first to use the term *tomboy* in a conversation with Angela's mother, and Angela remembered the campaign after that meeting to *pretty her up,* in the words of her mother. Throughout elementary school and into middle school, this involved dressing her in her sister's clothes, daily make-up applications, and ear piercing, despite

Angela's protests of these feminine improvements. Much to her surprise and dismay, the changes did, in fact, make a difference in the amount of male attention she received at school. One day in seventh grade, Michael Thomas, a popular, athletic young man who was the heartthrob of many of her female classmates, appeared from nowhere soon after she had begun wearing the golden heart earrings her mother insisted looked perfect on her. She was standing at her locker at the time, looking into the mirror she had mounted inside and wondering if the lipstick on her mouth made her look like a clown when she heard him.

"Hey, aren't you in my math class?"

She peeked out from behind the locker door to make sure he was talking to her.

"Um, yes. Yea, Ms. Kelleher's class. You sit behind me."

"Right," he said, looking Angela over from head to toe, and stopping at her breasts, which her mother had forced into her sister's oversized bra. She had used tissues to take up space. Angela immediately felt her face flush now as Michael's gaze seemed transfixed on the false mounds under the tight sweater she was wearing.

"Yeah," he said, talking at her tissued tits. "Well, we should get together and study sometime."

They never did. After that conversation, Angela began to hear comments like *slut* and *whore* as she walked past the coven of popular girls in the hallway.

The bottle of soap in her hands offered a *delicate lilac scent*. She removed the cap and gave it a sniff. It smelled nice, like lilac, but not overpowering. She took her time lathering up, then washed off the soap. She had seen an old razor in the tub but had no desire to shave her legs. Glenn (the fact that he had two "N"s in his name should have been a warning) had a weird obsession with shaving her, and it was part of their nightly routine in that cheap rattrap motel. He had other strange obsessive traits as well, the towels had to be hung up just right, and everything in the drawers and the closet had to line up and be ordered in a way that made no sense to her. He'd never hit her, though, as many others had, and because of that, she found him quite sweet and likable in a warped and damaged sort of way.

Glenn was the reason she went to treatment at St. Michael's. His primary motivation was to get money through the local Department of Social Services, and Glenn had already made big plans for the income. He insisted on going with her to apply for food stamps and Medicaid assistance. She told him on the bus ride there that the only way she would go in was if he got her high first. Glenn was not generous with his pot, but he saw no way around this. So, the two smoked up in the woods near the bus stop before Angela went in to meet with Ms. Fulmer, the Director of the Medicaid Department. Angela could usually handle her pot, but she was shocked at how high she felt from Glenn's weed and suspected that he'd shared his private stash with her by mistake. Her main focus during the interview was not to freak out or to burst out laughing inappropriately.

Ms. Fulmer was a nineteen-year veteran at the D.S.S. office and in her twelfth year of sustained recovery from alcohol and marijuana. It took her a matter of seconds to size up this young girl who reeked of pot and had the most intense case of red-eye she'd ever seen. Ms. Fulmer was kind and cordial to Angela during the screening and didn't deny her application for benefits. Instead, she mandated that a substance abuse evaluation be performed before moving forward with any state funding.

"Shit!" Glenn shouted when she met him afterward near the upscale coffee shop in downtown Deerfield.

Angela noticed that he was drinking a large, frothy iced coffee.

"How much did that thing cost?" She asked.

"Never mind that," he said, running his fingers through his hair. "Shit, I knew you shouldn't have smoked before going in there. They want you to go to treatment? This is going to fuck everything up!"

Angela picked up his drink and took a long pull through the straw.

"Fuck, bitch! Get your own!"

Their relationship, if you could call it that, went south quickly after that. Glenn began spending his time with a younger, sicker, more strung-out junkie girl. He blamed Angela for "failing" her initial assessment at St. Michael's and being recommended for further treatment, which only delayed how long they had to wait for the money.

"You've got to start pitching in some money," he told her. "If you're too high and mighty to whore it out, maybe you can start making some deliveries for Ricky."

Ricky was Glenn's drug dealer, and on the few occasions Angela had met him, he completely grossed her out. He was a tall, skinny young man who reminded Angela of drug dealers she knew in high school, guys who turned to the trade because they had failed at everything else. He had long, slick red hair, and his stare always seemed to linger on her, though he rarely made eye contact, preferring to look at her chest, or legs, or ass. Every time she saw him, Ricky was wearing a tie-dyed t-shirt decorated with a marijuana leaf or a tribute to a video game. He also had a large pot leaf tattooed on one arm and a skeleton smoking from a pipe on the other arm. It was hard to believe the police hadn't arrested him yet. Glenn's suggestion that she start working with or for him had been the last straw.

It disgusted her to think about those two douchebags and all the others she'd known over the years. How had she allowed herself to become one of them? Maybe it was fate, and the progression was natural born to be disgusting. Or maybe it was the way of the world now, if it hadn't always been. A woman was considered one big, walking vagina by men and she was both lusted after and abused because of it. Maybe she'd go out and buy the t-shirt or get a tattoo and join the movement that would never, ever end. *Me Too.* Me Fucking Too.

She turned to face the water, cranking up the heat enough to hurt. Scorching and burning off the poison seemed like a solution: wash the memories off and down the drain into the sewer where they belonged. She reached for the delicately scented lilac soap and thoroughly washed her whole body again.

The dramatic change of temperature when she stepped out of the tub caused her to shiver. She toweled off quickly and put on the boxer shorts and Dartmouth shirt before hurrying across the hallway and back into the bedroom. Once there, she jumped in bed, grabbed the old stuffed bear, and burrowed deep under the covers. She realized from under the blankets that she hadn't turned off the light. The television continued to mumble through the wall, and she wondered how much of the past Paul would like to wash off. She wanted to believe that he was different, not the standard, predatory, white misogynistic male with narcissistic tendencies who had dominated her life experiences. But that trust required a dangerous leap. She thought of the moment she'd seen him in the Stumble Inn Bar, the sadness in his eyes, the comment about his kid's birthday, the towel and washcloth he laid out in the bathroom for her.

It usually took her a while to fall asleep, especially if she wasn't high, but as she laid there safe and sober in the soft light of the room, with the bear tucked under her arm, she dozed off in minutes.

CHAPTER 28

"Your Secrets Will Always Keep You Sick."

Crocheted sign hanging in the Deerfield Originals A.A. Meeting Room.

She woke suddenly to the sound of a phone ringing and wondered for a moment where she was. The phone continued to ring. Why was the volume turned up so high on the thing? Next came a loud beep from the living room. There was a short period of silence followed by a muttering voice. She remembered seeing an ancient answering machine next to the phone in the living room, its digital numbers flashing rhythmically, desperate to be played. The machine had to be twenty or thirty years old, like almost everything around this place. She was amazed that anything could last that long.

The voice on the machine subsided, and the house fell silent again. Angela didn't get the impression that Paul was a morning person, or maybe he knew, as she did, that getting out of bed opened the gates to the shit stream that flooded each day. Keeping this in mind, she pulled the covers up tight and looked at the window just above the bed. Rays of sunlight peeked around the ragged edges of the old white retractable shade. She sat up in the bed and pulled the bottom of the shade away from the window, allowing a trickle of sunshine into the room. A fluorescent orange sticker on the window alerted rescue teams to a child sleeping within. Angela remembered getting a similar sticker when the fire truck came to her elementary school. They must have been there to talk about fire safety, but all she remembered was the sticker and being told not to go near the dog that was part of the show. She thought it had had spots – a Dalmatian? Maybe that was just the memory of a movie she saw. She gave the sticker to her mother, as all the children were instructed to do, but never saw it again. The sticker on this window had peeled and cracked around the edges. She sat up a bit more, straining toward the window, but accidentally pulled down on the shade. She let it go, and the thing flew up, making a loud and impressive impact with the upper sill.

She sat in the room, now filled with bright dawn light, and looked around. There was a tall dresser on the wall near the closet, and next to it, a full-length mirror. Nothing sat on top of the dresser, but nearby some small trophies were displayed on a homemade wooden shelf. Angela recalled the shelf she was required to make during middle school. She had allowed herself to be proud of what she had built and took the time to apply white paint and a spiraling pattern of intricate flowers around the edges. She planned to give it to her mother for Mother's Day, but her mother stayed out for that entire weekend. When she finally stumbled in with a man Angela had never seen, she cracked the shelf in half over her knee and threw it in the dumpster behind their apartment building.

The walls of the room were painted a unique shade of grey blue that reminded her of the sky on a cloudy day, the type she enjoyed most. She loved those times when the rain wasn't falling yet, but you could feel it in the air. She wondered if Paul, or his wife, or their kid had painted the place. She liked imagining they had done it together.

"Good job," she said to the empty room, "it's very peaceful."

There were no posters on the walls, and it was difficult for her to make out any of the kid's personality. She wanted to know if this place had been a sanctuary after stressful days at school or when the outside world got too loud, too painful, or too much to bear. Maybe this place had been the opposite. Maybe it was stifling and tight and isolated—a cage.

"Well, I feel really safe here," she said, "So, thank you for that."

She realized how fucked up it was to be talking to herself. It wasn't something she was in the habit of doing. But it seemed okay here. She felt the room was waiting, listening. Then again, her dope sick brain might have been inventing this bizarre shit.

There was a small desk in the corner, and above it, a bulletin board with pictures and scraps of paper tacked up. She got off the bed and walked over. It looked like a computer might have been on the desk at one time because there were a few stray wires around and a square outline of discoloration on the wood. There were aging ticket stubs attached to the board and above them pictures of a boy, younger in some photos than others. She focused on one where the boy was smaller and standing between two adults in front of a castle. The picture was taken at twilight, and the castle glowed behind the three figures. Angela knew it was The Magic Kingdom, though she'd never been there. She'd kept a similar picture in a notebook a long time ago. The picture came from a brochure that was mailed to the apartment and deposited in the trash immediately by her mom. It wasn't the castle that caught Angela's interest, or the dippy smiles on the well-dressed parents, or the perfect grooming of the boy and girl in the brochure's photo that captured her attention. It was the promise in the tag line below the photo: *The Happiest Place on Earth.*

She wanted to believe that such a place existed, and if it did, that she'd get there someday. She looked back at the photo, the boy donning a mouse-eared hat. All three were smiling, but Angela had no idea if those were the happiest smiles of their lives.

In another photo, the boy looked older, a young teenager, she guessed, and the three of them were on a boat in front of the Statue of Liberty. Unlike the castle photo, this looked less staged, most likely a shot they had asked a passing stranger to snap. The smiles were there but blurrier. She also noticed that although the young boy and the woman were close together, arms around shoulders, Paul was standing a bit further away, hands tucked firmly in his front pockets.

Her eye was drawn to a picture that looked more recent, stuck near the bottom of the board. The boy was older, his hair longer, his face too lean. They were standing at the entrance to a restaurant, dressed formally, with arms at their sides, no smiles. The photo intrigued her, and she reached across the desk toward it. She unpinned the image from the wall and held it gently in both hands.

As she pulled it close, a profound sense of sadness washed over her. It had happened before, strong feelings coming from something she touched or heard. Most of her family ignored these reactions, but her aunt recognized the power behind them. She told Angela they both possessed "strong intuition," a gift that she must treat with care.

Unfortunately, Angela's aunt was considered crazy by most of the family, including her mother, and Angela eventually agreed with the consensus. The woman lived like a modern-day gypsy, traveling from place to place, and working as a fortune teller with circuses and county fairs.

Her aunt had long, tangled grey hair and dressed in flowing robes that smelled like incense and woodsmoke. She carried a large, woven purse full of crystals, trinkets, and bits of things that Angela and her sister thought were wonderfully exotic.

One day, her aunt laid the crystals out before the two girls and invited them to hold and inspect each of them. She observed the girls during the experiment, and when they were done, she asked them how they felt about the crystals. Angela's sister chattered on about how the wonderful, beautiful gems made her feel like a princess or a rich lady.

Angela had a harder time explaining her feelings.

"It's like picking up a phone," she said as her sister laughed.

"What do you mean? It's not a phone, you dork!"

Their aunt shushed her and encouraged Angela to say more.

"I mean," she continued, "when I'm holding it, it's like someone is on the other end, wanting to say something, but I'm not sure what it is."

Her aunt's face brightened; her head nodded in agreement. After that day, the two spent more time together, usually when her mother was at work or out of the house. They played with tea leaves and Tarot cards, and spent hours studying the lines in each other's palms, identifying the colors they both saw radiating from people, something her aunt called *auras*. It seemed like a game at the time, a cheap way to waste time and keep a young girl's imagination alive.

Her aunt left one day and never returned. She and Angela's mother had a particularly horrible argument over her insane and unpredictable lifestyle. Angela found a large, purple crystal and an old, dog-eared book titled *The Life of Clairvoyants* on her bed. She never told her mother about the gifts for fear they would be taken away, but she read the book voraciously many times over, and kept the gifts with her to this day.

She felt love, sadness, and a sense of something not easily explained as she held the picture of Paul's family. Over the years, Angela hadn't talked about the discussions with her crazy aunt, but she'd done her best to nurture her strange powers. The biggest problem was locating the words to accurately describe emotions and feelings that welled up from items she held. The photo was sad, and the space that had developed between the three was apparent, but she felt something else, something there but not seen— an important factor that needed to remain hidden. Closeted. She carefully tacked the picture back into place on the bulletin board and walked over to the large dresser. She noticed a small, laminated card laying beneath a fine layer of dust on top of the dresser. It had a picture of a man who looked like Jesus, his arms spread wide, heralding small children toward him, and smiling brightly in his robe and slippers. Below this was written:

In Loving Memory of:

SEAN PATRICK DURKIN

Lord, make me an instrument of Your peace. Where there is hatred, let me sow love; where there is injury, pardon; where there is doubt, faith; where there is despair, hope; where there is darkness, light; where there is sadness, joy. O, Divine Master, grant that I may not so much seek to be consoled as to console; to be understood as to understand; to be loved as to love; For it is in giving that we receive; it is in pardoning that we are pardoned; it is in dying that we are born again to eternal life.

She slowly pulled open the top drawer. It was filled with socks and underwear, but most were not the standard tube socks and haggard briefs she would expect to see in a teenage boy's dresser. They were all boxer shorts, looking relatively new, each one carefully folded. The socks were folded as well. Only a few pairs looked athletic and appropriate to wear in gym class or for playing sports. She glanced behind her at the homemade shelf that held the trophies and wondered what exactly they were for.

Closing the top drawer, she opened the one directly underneath to find eighteen t-shirts, all folded meticulously. Angela was struck at the plainness of these items, each one a shade of blue or green or white. There were no distinguishing factors, no writing or pictures on any of the shirts. All had been worn by someone trying desperately to slip under the radar, to avoid being noticed in the crowd, to fit in.

She closed the drawer and pulled out the next one, expecting to find pants or shorts, thinking about Glenn's attention to patterns. To her surprise, it was filled with drawings and pictures that must have accumulated over years. The first drawings, the ones on top, were of street scenes. It looked like a market square, and the artist had drawn two pictures at different times of the day. In one, the market was brightly lit, and people were milling around everywhere, many surrounding a colorfully dressed street performer. A variety of people were drawn into the picture, some old and alone, sitting on benches and near a large fountain, feeding the birds. Others were younger, walking with families and children along the sidewalk, smiling. The place looked familiar to Angela, but she couldn't put a name to it.

She picked up another drawing that showed the same marketplace at night. Clouds and darkness were more prominent, and at first, she saw no people in the picture at all. She looked closer at a darkened bench and thought she saw something, or someone drawn there. It was the faintest outline of a small figure, its back to the viewer, looking off into a cluster of trees. She glanced over into the branches and saw a small splash of blurred color, a touch of red in the otherwise blackened scene. Looking closer, she could see that this was a bird, a small cardinal, looking toward the seated figure, waiting.

She touched and moved the drawings in the drawer around lightly and felt a sense of truth, sincerity, and vulnerability from the papers as if the artist used them to open a hidden window to their true self. Many of the drawings depicted a place at two different times of the day or in contrasting seasons; summer and winter beside a lake, a hot day waiting at the school bus, and then the same bus stop in the pouring rain. The exterior of a beautiful, large house in one scene and the house's interior after being ravaged by fire in the next. The artist was clearly interested in the duality of things, but Angela felt there was more hidden here, more than was ever meant to be seen. The phrase "closeted" flashed in her mind again.

She examined a drawing of a smiling boy and a larger man standing near the red and white striped pole of a barber's shop. As with the others, there were two pictures of the scene. In the second drawing, the differences were much more subtle. At first, she couldn't make out any changes at all. However, upon closer inspection, she saw that the smile on the boy's face was more expansive, just a little brighter, in one scene. She stared at the boy and noticed that his hair looked a bit longer, with a hint of redness mixed in. The boy's face also looked softer, not as angular in this picture, as if a transformation happened at the barbershop that had nothing to do with his hair.

She placed the picture back with the others and closed the drawer. She walked back to the bed, grabbed her stuffed bear, and laid down. She closed her eyes and thought about going back to sleep but soon realized that wasn't going to happen. Her mind was whirring with ideas and questions about Paul, his son, and their life in this house. The best thing to do would be to leave it all alone. None of this was her business. She swung her legs over the side of the bed and moved quickly toward the closet.

The louvered doors opened easily and quietly on their tracks. She flashed to a memory of the closet she shared with her sister when they were much younger, the one with the doors that fell off when opened. Her mother asked for help fixing the things from several male house guests, all of whom had reportedly worked in construction, but each attempt by those drunken fools either failed or made the problem worse. Eventually, Angela and her sister removed the doors completely and propped them in a corner of the cramped room where they remained until the three of them were evicted from the place on a hot July afternoon.

The interior of this closet looked neat and orderly, much like the dresser. Several pairs of shoes lined the floor. She grabbed a pair of canvas sneakers, which looked similar to her own, except that these looked brand new. She checked the size and saw that they were not much bigger than hers. She put them back and began sliding hangers across the pole, inspecting each item of clothing. The clothes were in good shape, unlike the thrift store and donation pile wardrobe that she was accustomed to. Most of the pants and shirts were ironed and neatly hung, waiting for the chance to dress for success. Ironing was never a priority for her mother, but Angela found it relaxing. The thought of ironing an item before it went into the closet never occurred to her, but her training in and knowledge of any domestic undertaking was undoubtedly not the norm. She sensed satisfaction, order, and control as she ran her hands over the hanging items.

When she pushed the last item aside, Angela looked down at the floor and noticed a piece of molding that didn't match up correctly. It seemed to have been pulled away and pushed back into place. She got down on her knees and crawled toward the spot, thinking immediately this was a bad idea. She'd always been adept at finding the indiscriminate hiding spots her mother used for stashing drugs, money, and countless stolen or contraband items over the years. Angela couldn't count the times she'd found these spots and either dumped out or sold the drugs and taken the money to go shopping for food with her sister.

Pulling away the floor molding, Angela saw that somebody had cut a small fingerhole into the bottom of the drywall. From this angle, she saw that an entire square, almost a foot high and two feet wide, had been sliced into the wall. She put her finger in the hole and pulled it slowly and carefully. The bottom pulled away from the wall as the other sides of the square came loose. She realized for the first time that this might be something of real importance, possibly even evidence for the police to inspect. She stopped pulling and sat back. Maybe she should tell Paul about the hiding spot. But that would mean explaining why she opened the closet to begin with, why she snooped around in the room.

From what she knew about Paul so far, this might not send him into an angry rage, but he might ask her to leave. Or, worse yet, what if the things behind the wall caused him to drink again, to fall from his shaky sobriety? What if there was a note in here stating what an asshole he was, how he was some kind of monster that beat his wife and made everyone miserable around the house? That type of information would definitely set him off.

If he was that bad she reasoned, if he was a monster, she needed to know.

She pulled the sheetrock section clear from the wall. Directly behind it, she found a large, round pink case. Angela remembered seeing a similar vintage hatbox in a thrift store long ago. She placed the piece of wall carefully aside, pulled the box onto the rug in the middle of the room, and sat down cross-legged in front of it. She placed both hands on top of the box and her intuition told her she had been invited here, that she was meant to find this. She took a deep breath and unhooked the brass clasp that held the top closed.

"Okay, just tell me what you want me to know," she whispered and opened the box.

The first thing she saw were more drawings. These were more colorful than the ones in the dresser. Each picture was an article of women's clothing. They looked like design concepts. Angela knew little about fashion or the latest trends in women's clothing, but she was impressed with the attention to detail, the color coordination, and the unique style that the artist drew into each piece.

There were many drawings of dresses, and each was intriguing. Some were long and dark and formal, and others were cut short and rendered in bright, popping colors. Faceless mannequins wore the designs. In one, the model had long, brown hair and big breasts which filled the low-cut dress with cleavage. In another, the figure's hair was much lighter, her frame and breasts more petite, adjusted for the cut of the top and skirt. The artist had carefully considered jewelry, accessories, and shoe styles for each of these creations. Angela marveled at how many hours the artist must have been spent on these amazing and unique designs.

Underneath the last drawing, she saw a large mound of brightly colored hair. It had been folded carefully inside the box. She removed it, using both of her hands, and realized it was a wig. It was quite beautiful and looked expensive. It was a shade of red that looked more like auburn, and it reminded Angela of September sunsets. The hair was longer than her own, long enough to cover her shoulders. It had been well cared for, as if combed often.

The next items she found in the hatbox were a black, silky bra and matching panties laid on top of what looked to be a long black shawl. Angela picked up the negligee and could see now that the bra had been padded and carefully stitched up. They looked barely worn. The shawl turned out to be a dress, and it, too, was in new condition. It was large, with long sleeves and a V-cut in the neckline. The simple design, formal and classic, could be worn at a big celebration or at someone's funeral. The irony of that suddenly saddened her, and she wondered if the sadness was her own or if it was seeping out from the intimate items stacked up on her lap.

Under the clothing, she found a small, cheap-looking digital camera. She picked it up but didn't try to turn the camera on.

Near the bottom of the case some notebook papers revealed women's names handwritten in large cursive. Magazine clippings of famous women in formal gowns covered printouts from a website describing gender reassignment surgery. She leaned over and reached into the case for them.

"Those clothes might be a little big for you."

The voice came from behind her, and she made a startled yelp as she turned around.

Paul was standing in the doorway.

"It's okay," he said gently.

Angela felt her heart start to race and her face flush. She was immediately afraid and exposed, the little girl who had broken the rules and now would get in big trouble.

"I'm sorry," she began, "I couldn't sleep anymore, and I didn't want to wake you up, so I…"

He nodded his head slowly in affirmation.

"It's okay. Really, it's alright."

He walked closer and looked at her, at the items in her lap and then over at the hole in the closet wall. She placed everything carefully back into the case, leaving the lid open, and turned to face him.

"I," she began, "I had no idea this was here. I mean, I was just looking around."

He walked to the bed and sat down heavily on the mattress.

"It's been a long time since I've been in here," he said, and looked slowly around.

His gaze stopped on the open case in the closet.

"We thought there might be a stash of things, of things like you found. I guess I didn't look too hard to find it."

Paul ran a hand slowly through his hair.

"Charlotte knew," he said softly. "My wife, Charlotte, knew for a long time that something was different with him, with Sean, I mean, our son—our child."

He shook his head.

"The pronoun thing is so hard to remember. I guess, it's a really big deal to the person you're speaking to. It's not so much the language that matters, it's the whole idea of accepting that person for who they are, or who they identify as, or who they tell you they are. I could not have imagined how difficult it would be to use pronoun-free language. It's quite a challenge, I'll tell you that."

He looked toward the light streaming through the window.

"I never really understood it. I didn't get the whole thing. Apparently, I never knew him, or her—my child, my Sean. I never knew who my own kid was." He laughed sourly and continued, "Me, the counselor, the professional helper, the guru of recovery and acceptance, and I didn't even learn what to call my own kid!"

Paul looked at Angela.

"It's funny, you know? When Charlotte first got pregnant, we worried about so many things, so many problems and issues that might happen, even before the birth. We went to so many doctor's appointments, always hoping everything would be normal. We just wanted everything to be normal."

He shook his head.

"I should know that normal doesn't really exist, right? I'm the expert when it comes to knowing that normal is a lie, right?"

He paused and blew out a long breath.

"Well, I don't know shit."

"So many things have changed about people's gender," Angela said softly, "I don't think people from your generation realize just how common these things are, how many people just don't fit the role. You've probably noticed that I'm not exactly the stereotype of a girly girl."

Paul smirked slightly, and Angela considered getting up from the floor and sitting next to him on the bed, but the action seemed too fake, too much like something she had seen in a sitcom.

"Charlotte told me before Sean even started school that he talked about not feeling comfortable in his skin, but I didn't get it," Paul explained. "I thought it was something he would just grow out of in time. A week before kindergarten began, we were sitting on the back porch, and Sean came to us and asked how difficult it was for someone to change their name. He told us he had never really liked his name, that it didn't fit him, and that he'd written down some other names that started with an S. He'd scribbled them out on a paper with a crayon, a red crayon. I don't remember all the names that were written down, but not one of them was what you would consider a boy's name. I remember one he liked, Samantha. I think she, my wife, told me that he had watched an old episode of *Bewitched* and really liked the main character, Samantha. He asked us if he could be called that when he entered school. He even explained that people could call him Sam at school but that his real name would be Samantha."

"That's a smart kid and a cool name. What did you say?" Angela asked.

"Hmmm," Paul began, "Well, Charlotte told Sean what a nice name that was and how she had wished her name might be something different many times in her life. I wasn't as understanding—or kind. I think I asked him straight out how the other kids in school might act if a boy showed up who had a girl's name. I tried to get him to see how confusing that might be for the other kids. In reality, I wanted him to understand how quickly he might get his ass kicked by pulling such a stunt. I remember seeing him flinch, turning inward as he held that list of names written with the red crayon. I couldn't believe that the negative consequences hadn't even crossed his mind. Well, of course they hadn't; he was five fucking years old! I thought it was my job to point these things out—to protect him. I can see him standing there, slowly folding his list and shoving it back into his pocket, then running back into the house. Charlotte looked at me after he ran off, a look she would use thousands of times after that day—the one I never truly understood until I found him dead, right here in this room."

He choked on the last few words and took a long breath before he continued.

"She knew I was blowing it, and things between us just got worse and worse after that. I sat there doing nothing, while she went in the house and talked to him for a long time. When the two of us met again in bed that night, she announced that we would try calling Sean "Shawna," but that we would only use the name around the house, and we would see how things went from there. Then she rolled over, turned out her light, and went to sleep while I sat there in the darkness, scared to death."

"Did you use the new name?" Angela asked.

"No. Never. I heard Charlotte calling out for *Shawna* to come to the dinner table. I found notes she left around for Shawna, but I never said it, not once. I couldn't even do that."

Silence settled in the room, and Angela moved herself closer. She never got up but moved her body across the rug until she was sitting just in front of him. Paul seemed frozen in place on the bed.

"How did school go?" she asked. "Did Sean, or Shawna, have any close friends? Anyone that knew what was going on?"

"School wasn't as bad as I thought it would be. There were a few incidents, times when the wrong people picked up on what was happening and made an issue out of it. We probably never knew everything that was going on, you know? I know the tension between my wife and me was palpable in the house, and I think Sean blamed himself for our problems. I guess there were some friends along the way. We always had the obligatory birthday parties and summertime playdates during the younger years. Looking back, it seems like he invited more girls than boys to those things, but we tried not to make a big deal about it. I mean, we wanted to be as inclusive as possible."

He stopped talking and shook his head.

"I don't think there was more than a handful of boys that attended his funeral service—lots of girls there, but not many boys at all come to think of it."

He looked up at her briefly before continuing.

"After his death, Charlotte and I felt the full weight of the rumors and gossip that must have been circling around for years. Most people said that he overdosed on heroin after being addicted to it for a long time. He wasn't an addict. They determined his death was due to an overdose, and we did find some weed and prescription painkillers in here, but I can't believe Sean was using for long before his death. He knew about the dangers of all that from me. We talked about those things all the time, one of the few things we could always have a conversation about. In his mind, it might have been better than the long and awkward silences that filled so much of our time together, especially when the teenage years arrived. It was abundantly clear that we had very little to say, and almost nothing in common."

Paul looked over at the homemade shelf with the trophies on it.

"Anyway, I saw the overdose as a final *fuck you, Dad* for me to live with, and I'm not convinced it wasn't part of his thinking. He left a note, but we didn't tell anybody outside of the police about it. The note overflowed with apologies to Charlotte and me about how the suicide would paint us in a poor light, especially since he used the pills to do it. He was thinking about us, worried about how this would look for us, right up to the end. The main reason he gave for taking the prescriptions was that other methods he'd researched were so messy and often unreliable. The police found internet searches from at least two years before the suicide on how to kill yourself."

Paul glanced at the desk where the computer had sat.

"And I had no idea about any of that, either."

"It sounds awful," Angela said. "I'm sorry."

When Paul didn't say anything, she asked, "Is that why you and your wife got divorced?"

"Well," he started again, slowly, "I suppose it pushed everything over the cliff, but it's hard to know what would have happened if he—if Sean, I mean—or if they, or she hadn't…"

He closed his eyes and mumbled, "Fucking pronouns. I still can't get the fucking pronouns right."

He took a deep breath and continued.

"Anyway, Charlotte and I never officially divorced. I guess the term for what we are now is 'separated', and that certainly applies. We'd been separating for a long, long time before it became official. After the suicide, she reached out for help. She started going back to church, to St. Vincent's, right here in town. When Sean was much younger, we all went together for a few packed Christmas Eve and Easter services. Charlotte stopped pushing us to go after the whole scandal broke with the priests abusing young boys, and I remember we did have a few conversations back then about what Jesus might have to say about the whole thing. So, I was surprised when she started going again, but I suppose she was looking for answers, for a trace of solace or comfort. She never invited me, probably knowing I would have snide remarks or sarcastic comments about the whole thing. One day she came home crying and told me about how the sermon had focused on the sinful nature of the world, the chronic demise of our diseased morals, and the perverted practices of the L.G.B.T.Q. community and other non-religious heathens out there whose primary goal was to unleash the power of

Hell unto the earth. The priest assured his flock that these immoral beasts had a horrible fate awaiting them in the afterlife. Charlotte said she could feel the eyes of the entire congregation on her and that she was too frozen with fear to simply get up and leave. She told me the sermon was particularly scathing and hurtful because she had met with the good Father only two weeks before and confessed all her guilt, shame, and perceived failures as a mother, wife, and daughter of God. At the time, he had been understanding and had given her a prescription of penance for these failings that included regular attendance and tithing at future services. She was even provided with gold embossed envelopes for weekly contributions before she left that day."

Paul's face darkened, and his hands balled into fists.

"To make things even worse, a woman there who we were told routinely gossiped about the mysterious death of the Durkin's 'he/she druggie' child stopped Charlotte as she was leaving the church. She was surrounded by upstanding ladies in the congregation, many of whom were active members of the P.T.A. and local Girl Scout Troops. According to Charlotte, this woman asked what she thought of the sermon before inviting her to an upcoming vigil at the church, one intended to support the same family values the priest had mentioned that day. I believe that was the last service Charlotte attended. I'd been drinking, of course, when she relayed all this to me, and I think my response was 'Fuck them,' exactly what a great husband, father, friend, and counselor would say, right? A week later, she moved out."

Paul's fists remained tight, and he looked at the hatbox on the floor.

"Did you ever say anything to the priest or to that lady from church?" Angela asked.

"Not at the time," Paul responded, "but you were eating some of her food last night. She's probably left an entire grocery store full of donations on my front step since that day. Until I talked to her, I hadn't taken a bite.

But she obviously knows she fucked up really good back then, and as Jesus would say, how can I cast a stone at her now?"

Angela gave him a questioning glance.

"Not big on the teachings of J.C?" Paul asked. "Well, I'll give you the abbreviated lesson. The way I read it, Jesus' big message was really about not being an asshole, even when bad shit happens to you."

"Oh, huh," Angela said. "Well, I'll have to check out the whole book sometime."

Paul smirked and un-balled his fists.

"Welcome to my life, Miss Angela, Paul said. "I think that's the most I've talked about this stuff in a long while, and you're a fine listener. You may want to consider getting into the counseling field yourself."

He stood up from the bed, and she rose from the floor.

"So, you're not pissed? I didn't mean to bring all this stuff up again. I was just…," she had no words to complete the sentence.

He put a hand on her shoulder. It felt warm.

"Some things, like these things, don't stay stuffed down forever, even for an expert 'internalizer' like me. Your being here and finding those things, well, I don't think any of it is a coincidence. I just hope I'm not scaring you away with all the gloom and doom."

Paul walked over to the closet and ran his hands over the clothes hanging in there.

"You can stay here as long as you want and take any of the clothes or anything else you find in here. I probably should have packed them up and donated them a long time ago."

He turned from the closet and started walking toward the door.

"I wish you two had met, had been friends. I think you would have gotten along well," he said, and wiped his eyes.

CHAPTER 29

"We can't arrest our way out of a medical crisis, Your Honor.
You can throw my client in jail over and over again, but unless he
gets access to quality treatment, we're not helping him or the public
at large by imposing greater sentences for crime related to addiction."

John Lawrence, Deerfield District Attorney, to Judge O'Malley

Angela decided to make omelets for breakfast. She found four eggs, white bread, a few slices of cheese product, and a mysterious onion that Paul had no recollection of buying. Paul pulled out two unopened jars of Jenny's jam from the cupboard and placed them on the table.

"Eggs are one of the few things I can cook," Angela explained.

"I learned from David, one of my mom's countless boyfriends who was actually not that big of a shitbag. He took an interest in my sister and me and told us that he worked as a chef. We eventually learned that he worked the night shift at a local Denny's, so, I suppose he wasn't exactly lying. We were just happy he paid any attention to us and that he actually cared if we were eating. Most of the guys she dragged home were too drunk or high to notice us, and the guys who did seemed creepy and weird. David was different."

"What happened to him?" Paul asked.

"Oh, she drove him off eventually, just like she did with all of them," Angela answered. "He stopped by a few times after that and dropped off some food and other things that he thought we might need. It was a little bit like that woman you talked about leaving things on your steps. I guess he felt bad for us or guilty somehow, but I didn't think he ever did anything to be ashamed of. He just tried to help. My sister and I would sometimes go to the Denny's where he worked if our mom was having a party late at night. David always fed us for free, and we would hang out for hours if he wasn't too busy. The Child Protective Agency people showed up at our door one time after we had done this, and even though they wouldn't say who made the report, my mom was convinced it was David. She got us to admit we talked to him, and then she cursed us for ratting her out. She freaked out and forbid us from ever talking to him again."

The bread popped up from the toaster, and she buttered it, looking at Paul.

"But he sure knew how to make an egg! And I'll bet he's working at that same Denny's to this day."

"Do you keep in touch with your mom?"

Angela carried two plates over to the table. She set down an omelet and toast in front of Paul. He grabbed one of the jars of jam and unscrewed the top.

"I call her every so often, mostly to make sure she's alive. She loses phones all the time, and she only buys the burners, so, her number is always changing. There are a few people I know I can go to, and they usually tell me where she is and what she's up to."

Paul cut into his omelet and took a bite.

"Wow, that's delicious! I'm impressed."

She took a bite from her own plate, saying nothing but smiling slightly.

"She sounds like a pretty sick lady," Paul continued, picking up his coffee and taking a sip. "I think it's impressive how you've dealt with all of her problems."

Angela looked at him and laughed.

"Seriously? You're complimenting me after telling you how I'm doing the same shit she did for years? I've got a long list of my own dirtbag boys, not to mention becoming a junkie myself. Your skills must be pretty rusty, Mr. Addiction Counselor!"

"But you're trying. You're breaking the cycle. And most importantly, you're refusing to be helpless about all this. You keep getting up and moving forward. That's what matters—not giving up, never giving up, ever."

She didn't reply but looked out the window into the backyard.

"Those are some sad-ass-looking bird feeders."

"Yup," Paul agreed. "Beggars can't be choosers. I have noticed the bird population growing out there since I started filling those things again. It was one of the few things that Sean and I connected on. We both liked feeding the birds and seeing all of the varieties that showed up."

She scanned the yard again, noticing several tree limbs and other debris that had been left unattended out there.

"Looks like you could use some help cleaning things up in the yard," she suggested.

"I thought, maybe, I would ask those guys from the group, Larry, and what's his name, the other one, to come over and help with that. I'm sure they can get the right equipment. Maybe we can have a bonfire and drink a few beers together."

"That's a great idea," she said, "as long as you only have a few. I don't think you need permission from your counselor at St. Michael's for that. Especially since you're such an expert in this area."

"If I remember correctly, anything over two drinks is considered a relapse," he answered, "but we'll be safe if we keep it under that."

When they finished, he insisted on washing the dishes, and she went back into the bedroom. He turned on the hot water to fill the sink and walked out into the living room, thumbing through the collection of vinyl records, and picking out an album. He placed it on the turntable and put the needle down carefully. The silky voice of Frank Sinatra filled the house as he returned to the sink.

Paul didn't hear the knocking on the front door, but a few minutes later a voice came from the living room.

"Hey, Paul, are you home?"

Paul walked to the edge of the kitchen and saw Roscoe standing there, half inside the doorway.

"Hey," Paul said cheerily. "Yes, I'm here. Come on in, Roscoe. What brings you over this way?"

Roscoe surveyed the changes inside of the house since his last visit as he walked to the kitchen. Frank Sinatra's baritone belted "Fly Me to the Moon," and the sound mingled pleasantly with the smell of eggs and toast in the air. It was a marked improvement from stale liquor, sweat, and slowly rotting things that Roscoe remembered from the night of Paul's arrest.

Paul took the towel from his shoulder and dried off the last dish with it. He placed the dish in a cabinet.

"Do you want a cup of coffee?" He asked Roscoe.

"Sure," Roscoe answered, heading over to the kitchen table. "It looks like you've been doing some house cleaning around here. The place looks good."

"Yeah," Paul replied, pouring the coffee and carrying it over to the table. Paul topped off his own cup then sat down across from Roscoe.

"It's funny what being sober can do for a man and his surroundings, huh?" Paul asked.

Roscoe smiled before saying, "Well, I've always liked you, Paul, but I sure like you more when you're sober."

He held up his cup for a toast and then took a sip.

"I get that a lot," Paul remarked and returned Roscoe's toast. "So, is this visit about business or pleasure?"

"It's a little of both, I suppose. I needed to come out this way to check on Mrs. Vandenburgh down the street. She lost her husband last winter, and her daughter Peggy went to high school with the chief at my station. He has me come out this way pretty regularly to make sure she's doing alright. I swear that lady is going to outlive us all. Peggy keeps trying to get her to move in with them down south—North Carolina, I think—but that old girl won't hear of it."

"That's Betty Vandenburgh," Paul said, smiling. "Betty and Frank, her late husband, were some of the first people to move in over here, and they bought up three lots right away. I don't think she ever let Frank sell off the other two, even though they could have cashed it all in and moved on once Peggy finished college and got married."

"You're right," Roscoe answered, taking another sip from his coffee, "those two lots are empty, growing weeds and collecting dust, but she'll never sell them."

The two men sat silently, letting the decisions of Mrs. Vandenburgh hang in the air. Paul knew Roscoe had more questions for him, and this time he was not in the mindset to play the waiting game. From the living room, Frank began singing "New York, New York."

"So, what do you hear about my case, Roscoe? Are you supposed to be keeping an eye on me as well?"

Roscoe took another sip of coffee.

"Well, I'd keep an eye on you whether I was supposed to or not, Paul. You should know that by now."

"Uh huh," Paul replied. "And if your instructions to stop by were official ones, what advice might you give me that is coming down from your bosses and the court?"

"Don't drink," Roscoe said quickly. "At all."

There was no smile or playfulness in the Sheriff's tone.

"There's a newer District Attorney running things," Roscoe continued, "a guy you never met who came in a few years ago from the city."

Paul assumed that Roscoe meant New York City because that was how many locals referred to NYC, but he didn't ask for clarification. He felt suddenly paralyzed and stuck to the chair, surprised at his own fear in hearing all of this. He'd really fucked things up for himself this time.

"Anyway, this guy doesn't know much about the way that small towns work, or he doesn't care. His thing, his big deal, is being tough on alcohol and drug laws. He thinks that if the consequences are stiff enough, we can get addicts and alcoholics to—"

Roscoe stopped here, suddenly aware that his language might be offensive. He looked up, but Paul was shaking his head, encouraging him.

"I know what I am, Roscoe," Paul said. "I've got all the training in this stuff, remember?"

Roscoe gave a slight nod. "Anyway, this guy is hell-bent on busting people left and right for anything related to drugs and alcohol. Our jail has been full since he took office last year. And the worst part, the part we can't get this guy to see, is that these people keep reoffending after releasing them. My chief keeps pushing to start a task force to get more people in treatment, you know, not have them sit in jail. This new guy just won't hear it. Before he took office, we were trying to get your old place, St. Michael's, to send someone in each week and do evaluations on the inmates who were there on a drug or alcohol charge. Other jails have started offering addiction assessments, and it sounds like a great idea, right? It sure beats having someone sit there, learning nothing, and then letting them out to go right back into the same old routines, the same pattern of drinking, drugging, and breaking the law."

"Not just that," Paul added, "but people are more likely to make big changes when the pain is great enough. If you can get someone to talk to them, to reach out at those times when the consequences are outweighing the benefits of their addiction, they might make a move toward getting better."

"Exactly!" Roscoe agreed. "And we were almost there until this idiot came along and wanted to flex his muscles and show us small-town hicks how to clean up the way the big city boys do. He's a real piece of work, and we all know that he only got this position because they wanted him out of the city, but I hear he's got relatives in high places; so, here he is. Nobody thinks he'll make it through the next elections, but for now, we're stuck."

Roscoe finished his coffee and looked back at Paul.

"So, anyway, you came on to the new D.A.'s radar screen recently, and he's starting to question why Judge O'Malley hasn't tightened the screws and thrown you in jail yet."

"I suppose that's a fair question," Paul said, trying to keep his face neutral even though his stomach was tightening into a knot.

"And that's why you're here? Officially?"

"Like I said before, don't drink. You got John Lawrence on your side, and he's not going to be pushed around by anybody, especially this guy. If you screw up, I mean, if you give him a reason…"

"Understood," Paul said.

"I guess I picked a good time to get sober," Paul added wryly.

Roscoe looked around again. "Whatever you're doing, keep doing it."

Angela appeared in the hallway near the kitchen.

"Are you going to listen to this grandpa music all day?" she asked loudly and then saw Roscoe sitting there in full uniform. She instinctively took a step back into the shadow of the hallway.

"Oh," Paul said, "Angela, this is Roscoe, I mean Sheriff Montgomery, an old friend of mine."

Roscoe tipped his head in Angela's direction as a greeting.

"Roscoe is fine," he said. "I was just on my way out."

Angela nodded back but said nothing.

Paul got up and walked with Roscoe to the door.

"Look, Roscoe," Paul said, unsure how to explain the young girl's presence.

"She's in treatment with me, I mean, she didn't have anywhere to go last night, and I let her stay here. I'm just trying to get her some help."

Roscoe turned around, a hand up and waving off the explanation.

"Like I said, Paul, whatever you are doing, keep doing it. Just don't drink, no matter what."

"Hell, maybe I'll ask Mrs. Vandenburgh if she wants to move in down here since you're taking in boarders. She might not be as pretty as this gal, but I bet she won't complain about your grandpa music!"

He patted Paul firmly on the shoulder, opened the door, and walked out.

CHAPTER 30

"I'm pretty sure he's gay, but I doubt he'll ever tell me that."

Paul to Angela about Travis

"**I** think I should tell him I'm gay."

"Um, okay. And who exactly are we talking about?"

Travis and C.J. were sitting across from each other at a small, round table in their favorite coffee shop. Their Saturday morning routine had started on New Year's Day. Both were eager to get in shape and lose a few pounds. C.J. found a January deal on memberships to a fitness club in the area that promised to be a 'gym for all people.' It was built in the older Deerfield mall, replacing a store that catered to plus-size women, which C.J. found hysterically ironic.

For the first few weeks of January, they woke early on Saturday mornings, spent a few hours working out, went to a local organic grocery store, and loaded up on fresh fruits, whole grains, and an abundance of kale. As February began, though, C.J. was harder to rouse in the morning, and their workouts transformed into an early afternoon event. C.J. also noticed a coffee shop inside the mall near the gym. He described it as "beautifully tacky." They started skipping the after-workout trips to the health store in favor of grabbing lunch at the coffee shop. C.J. sat across from Travis now with a large, frothy coffee and a bagel smothered in cream cheese.

"My patient at the internship," Travis said, "I've been thinking about my last session with him."

"Oh," C.J. said, "well, sure, tell him then."

He picked up his bagel and took a large bite, causing cream cheese to squeeze out and onto his face. He chewed slowly, smiling, and wiped at his chin with a napkin.

"This is *sho gud*," he said through the bread and goo in his mouth.

"Yeah," Travis agreed, "it's helping to replace all those carbs we burnt up in the gym today. Did you even break a sweat?"

C.J.'s eyes widened. "Me? Of course, I did. But today, I was focusing more on building mass than on cardio."

"Uh-huh," Travis said, stirring the spoon around in his coffee cup.

"Is that why you spent most of your time watching the TV in the corner, why you sat on that bench? Did you even see that old geezer in the velour jumpsuit giving you the evil eye? I think he wanted to use those two-pound weights you were hogging!"

"Screw you!" C.J. said, swallowing a large chunk of bagel and wiping his mouth again.

"Those were eight pounds, and that old bastard just wanted me to turn the channel so he could watch Fox News. Anyway, when did you become the fitness police? If you don't like what you see, you can always trade it up for a newer model, lover boy!"

Travis laughed.

"I like what I see. I'm sorry. I just think it's funny. You're funny. In a good way, in a very good way."

C.J. cocked his head and did his best Joe Pesci impression.

"So, you think I'm funny, huh? Like, funny how? Like a clown? Do you think I'm funny like a clown? Like I'm here to amuse you?"

"Exactly," Travis said. "Funny just like that. And I never want you to change."

"Good," C.J. said, grabbing Travis' hand and squeezing it. "I think our Saturday workouts have become much more tolerable since we added this place to the routine! Now, tell me why you're thinking about this patient of yours and not focusing totally on your boyfriend these days."

"Well, I think that a huge part of his problems, of his relapse, happened because his son killed himself over issues around sexuality, or maybe gender identity. I'm not totally sure because he hasn't said. I'm afraid to ask him or the other counselors at the office directly. I'm not sure that it's within my scope of practice, especially as an intern, to be going into those issues with him. I also don't want to break his confidentiality or overstep boundaries by asking the other staff about it."

"Oh, is this Jamie's Dad? That was so sad. I don't think you ever met Jamie, but they killed themselves after their parents kicked them out of the house and said never to come back. That was awful, especially because I grew up with Jamie and never would have guessed what dick heads their parents would be about it. I mean, what is the big fucking deal after all? Do you want a live kid or a dead kid? That's what it really comes down to."

"You know I can't tell you who it is, but it's not Jamie's dad."

"I know, I know!" C.J. said, grabbing the small piece of bagel left on the plate.

"Confidentiality and all of that. I get it. Got to be professional. Is it Mr. Peterson?"

Travis smiled and shook his head.

"Mr. Peterson doesn't have kids, remember?"

"No," C.J. agreed, "and he's not married. Because he's totally gay and just can't admit it! So why not just tell this guy, this mystery patient of yours, that you're gay. What's the big deal?'

"It's another boundary issue. Dunleavy is constantly reminding us that therapy is about the patient, not about us. Anything we disclose about ourselves, about our lives, should always be in the best interest of the patient."

"Well, it sounds to me like this would be. If this guy's kid was gay, or bi, or trans, it seems like telling him about yourself would be helpful. I think he would know that you get it, that you understand what that's like."

"That's just it. I'm not sure that I do get it. There are lots of people who get into this field that are in recovery from addiction. They might understand their own recovery, but do they really know what everyone else who gets sober feels like? What about people that are Black, or Asian, or Jewish? Do they all understand each other? I'm just hesitant to say anything because of what I'm learning in school and because I don't want to play the gay card here just so my first patient thinks I know what I'm talking about."

C.J. took a long sip from the straw coming out of his glass. He was smiling, almost laughing.

"What?" Travis asked. "Am I the funny one now?"

"I don't think we have a gay card," C.J. said, "I don't think that's a thing. I think we're just gay, and people either accept that or they don't. One difference I see is that our group, the *L.G.B.T.Q. Alliance*, if you want to call it that, is made up of different people who are worlds apart, but the general expectation is that we are this cohesive tribe and that any one of us can represent the thoughts, feelings, and experiences of the whole tribe. It's bullshit, right? I have no idea what it feels like to be a bisexual woman. I certainly can't speak to the experiences of a trans man, and I'm not sure what being queer is. All I know for sure is what I think, and how I feel, and what I've been through. When other people share their experiences, feelings and truths, I listen for the things I can relate to most. I don't think people are selfish or self-centered when they share their stories with me. I think they are opening up and letting me know that we all have issues, and hurts, and challenges to deal with in life."

Travis sipped his coffee and thought.

"I know," he said, "and you're right. I just think I should be focused on what will keep him sober, on what he needs, not to drink again. But he knows so much more about that than I do. Part of me believes or wants to believe, I'm working with him for a reason, that it's not just a coincidence. And if I told him about being gay, it might be a chance for—I don't know—like, some type of second chance for him to do things differently."

"Redemption?" C.J. asked.

"Yes—maybe that. Although I don't see this guy forgiving himself for a long, long time. I just can't get over the way this all happened. It's so weird— the way I became his counselor. These random things that just aligned, and I'm not sure what to do with it all now. I don't want to screw it up. I don't want to screw him up."

C.J. reached across the table and held Travis' hand. "It sounds like you're being guided here, but I know how much my boyfriend loves to give up control of things—almost as much as you like to talk about God and spirituality, and things that can't be explained. I know why this is all happening. And I think that if you're supposed to open up to him, you will. If you're not meant to, then it won't happen. Either way, I want you to remember that you weren't just put into his life path because you're gay. You were put there because you're exactly what he needs right now, and he's exactly what you need, too."

Travis could feel tears welling up but wasn't sure why. He picked up his napkin and dabbed at his eyes, sniffing. He grabbed C.J.'s hand and held it.

"Thank you."

"You're welcome, my handsome boyfriend. Remember that you're a fucking life-changing, wonderful, gay counselor and person. Let that shit shine through!"

CHAPTER 31

"Meeting makers make it."

Twelve Step slogan

"So, you just press this button, and that brings you to the address book. Then you can use the keys to punch in someone's phone number. Once you do that, all you have to do is go to the address book, find their name and press it to call them. You can also just put in the first few numbers, and the phone will auto-fill the rest. It remembers your contacts, especially the ones you use most often. I can put some in for you now. Whose number do you want to do first?"

It was Sunday morning, and they were in his car, pulling out of the Walmart parking lot. Paul assumed she would know far more about modern cell phones than he did, but her level of knowledge and efficiency surprised and impressed him.

"Well," she asked again, "who do you want to put in first?"

"How about Roscoe?" he asked.

"Good. What's his last name?

"Montgomery."

"Got it. And what's his number? Is it the same area code?"

"Yes," Paul said confidently, and then "I'm not sure of the rest of the number, though."

She paused, looking up at him.

"Seriously? You don't know his number?"

He glanced back at her as they pulled up to a red light.

"Yes, seriously. It's not like we chat on the phone every night, you know. Most of the time, he just stops by my house. Believe it or not, that's how we used to talk to each other before those things became so popular!"

She kept her gaze on him, thumbs hovering expectantly above the keys to the phone.

"So, do you know his number or not? Or maybe you just want to drive over to his house every time you want to talk? That sounds convenient."

"I've got it written down in my address book at home. Why don't you program that thing when we get there?"

"Fine," she answered, "I'll work on mine for now."

She set his new phone down and, with some difficulty, opened the plastic housing on the second model. The one Paul had picked out was smaller and flipped open to access the keys. He was happy with the price, $9.99.

"You do realize how ridiculous that phone is, right?" She asked. "It can only be used for calling and texting people and stupid shit like that."

"And you realize that's the purpose of a phone, correct? Especially the calling people part?" Paul countered.

Angela rolled her eyes and tossed the ten-dollar phone in the cart.

While they were in the store, Angela explained that the best option for them was to buy pay-as-you-go phones that didn't require a monthly contract. These were the choice of most drug dealers and criminals because they were cheaper and easier to destroy, much harder to track, and difficult to use as evidence. Paul assured her that this made him feel much better about the purchase. He also told her that if she was planning to begin selling drugs or to start up another illegal business, he might not be the best person to team up with since he was already getting some heat from the local police and District Attorney. She smiled and extended her middle finger, which caused a woman and her young children who were standing nearby to shuffle away. As the woman retreated, Paul wondered if she made an effort to memorize his identifying features and those of his young companion. Those details might be useful when describing the odd pair to the local or state police.

Angela's choice of phone was more expensive. It had internet access, and many other features she had insisted were necessary. As she ripped through the plastic casing and assembled the thing in his car, Paul thought about how tough kids like her had it in life. He'd worked with many adolescents who grew up in unhealthy and toxic backgrounds over the years. So many of them fell victim to limited expectations and an ignorance of another way of living, a stable one they never saw during their young lives. There was a world of untapped potential in these lost children.

"Most of them just go through life fat, dumb, and happy," sniped Mandy, who was still a Valtec insurance representative then.

When Paul didn't respond to her comment, she went further.

"What? You know it's true. And what's wrong with that? Hell, I'd love to care less about things and just skip my way through life living on other people's taxes. Sending this kid to Rehab is like sending her to summer camp. She'll live better there than at home. And as soon as we send her back to mom and dad, who both are boozehounds, she'll start using again."

Mandy may have had a point about how the cycle of dysfunction kept spinning, but Angela was different. She was highly intelligent, possibly even gifted from what Paul saw. He found it fascinating and heartbreaking all at once. It was bittersweet to think about where young people like her might be if they'd been born to different parents in different towns with different opportunities. Part of his job as a counselor was to fill his patients with the hope that they could get back up and be whoever they wanted to be in sobriety. But Paul could never buy into this optimistic, naïve form of cheerleading. Based on personal experience, it was his view that being sober would only promise a person one thing—sobriety. Although the choices, and options, and pain of a substance-free lifestyle were certainly better than the alternative, he felt that guaranteeing people they could be, and do, and live however they wanted to as long as they remained drug free—especially these kids who had so little control over things—was a callous lie.

Maybe he just brooded too much about the whole thing. Throughout his lifetime and career, long before his bad times came, he was aware of a darkness—a tendency toward melancholy that seemed programmed into the Durkin DNA. Even today, going into the Walmart, his heart was heavy thinking about the people, the countless people, punching in and punching out of their jobs, hoping they might get this Sunday off to spend time with their kids, maybe on a supervised visit, and maybe saving up just enough money to see the beach once or twice when summer came. So many people were spending most of their time, this precious, non-refundable time on earth, selling useless shit to unhappy people, all of them on an endless materialistic merry-go-round grabbing countless, worthless, golden rings—all addicted to the ride, and at the same time, desperate to get off it.

"I'm going to need your credit card to buy minutes on these things, please."

Angela's head was bent over her phone, thumbs tapping on the buttons. Her voice startled him into the moment, and he reached around to his back pocket to free his wallet. Paul handed it to her without speaking.

"Which credit card do you want me to use?" She asked as she stopped tapping and opened the wallet up.

"There's only one," he replied.

He could feel her staring at him.

"You only own one credit card?" she asked.

He glanced at her and could see that this was another foreign concept.

"Yes," he replied, "and I pay off the balance each month."

"No shit?" she asked. "Wow, maybe I should become an addictions counselor. Or was it your wife that made the real money?"

Paul shook his head but said nothing. He could hear the morbid music of the merry-go-round in his head.

"It's the Master Card in the side pocket," he said and turned the car radio on.

Jethro Tull's flute filled the space, and soon the song pondered about how it felt to be thick as a brick. Paul knew the answer but sang along anyway. Angela was too distracted by her phone to argue or complain.

They were almost home, only a few streets away from the house. The day was relatively warm, nearly forty degrees. The sun shone crisp and bright off the high snowbanks and drifts. The road itself was a mess, all melt and salt and the constant sound of slushy water spraying up and onto the vehicle. These were the dirty days of winter, the days that made things leak and rust and age before their time. It was no wonder that so many people threw in the towel as they aged and moved to climates promising a more leisurely, relaxed life. No shame in that, he thought, imagining the new rust spots that would pop up on the car like dandelions after the long-awaited thaw.

He thought about Mrs. Vandenburgh and how she spent her time in the old house. He remembered seeing her at Sean's funeral, Peggy there by her side. He could see both of them approaching Charlotte and whispering what he imagined were kind, warm words of condolence. He should make a point to stop down and say hello to her some time, to check-in and maybe sit for a cup of coffee.

"That should do it!" Angela said triumphantly as they pulled into the driveway.

"You have my new number, and I have yours."

She sat, staring at the screen on her phone, and then laughed.

"Too bad there's nobody I can call right now but you. Wait until Mandy hears how well I'm doing on my treatment plan goals. I'm changing all those people, places, and things that would get me high again! Woah, what kind of fucked-up music is this?"

Paul gave her a brief smile and then took his new phone and slid it into a jacket pocket.

"Well, maybe you'll get some new numbers at the meeting tonight. Then you can chat away to all kinds of new friends!"

She looked at him, rolling her eyes in a way he was beginning to like.

They'd filled up on groceries at Walmart, and Angela surprised Paul with her knowledge of healthy choices and frugal shopping. Most of the items she picked out were off-brands, and she bought larger portions, advertised as "family size," which cost less. She seemed to do this instinctively, checking out the unit prices and comparing each thing before adding it to the cart. Paul imagined Angela going to the store, possibly with her sister, with a crinkled five or ten dollars they'd scrounged from around the apartment. Of course, she knew how to make that last, how to get the most out of each cent.

Charlotte did most of the shopping for the family when they were married, and Paul never gave much notice to the cost or to the foods being brought home. He knew that she sat in the living room cutting coupons from the thick newspaper every Sunday. Whenever they shopped together, Paul noticed the stack of coupons she used when they checked out. It must have taken a great deal of time and effort, another task in the long list of things he'd taken for granted about her and their simple, happy life back then.

Angela added fruits to the cart and a variety of vegetables.

"I'm going to make a salad that's the absolute shit!" She promised.

Her diet appeared to consist of things that a rabbit or some other small herbivore might eat. She claimed not to be a vegetarian but scolded Paul when he added a steak to the basket.

"That is way too expensive, and we don't need it."

Paul disagreed, feeling that he truly did need it.

The only exception to her healthy grocery choices was a box of sugary snack cakes. She explained that life was not worth living without them. They looked sticky, cheap, and awful to Paul. When they got to the car, Angela opened the box immediately and ate one of the small cakes slowly on the ride home, savoring each bite.

They put the groceries away, and for the first time in a long time, the house contained a selection of foods that filled all five food groups. Without prompting, Angela went to the stereo system, complained about the old, shitty albums that were there, and then put on *Sgt. Pepper's Lonely Hearts Club Band*. Paul thought the colorful album cover might have drawn her in, but to his surprise, Angela immediately began singing along with the music.

"Well, duh," she said, as she glided into the kitchen and started to chop vegetables and add lettuce into a large bowl, "it is The Beatles."

The salad was delicious, and so was the steak Paul grilled. The day had warmed to a point where it was comfortable standing in the sunlight on the back deck while the steak sizzled and filled the air with the smoky smell of normalcy. He didn't bother to tell Angela about the mouse nest he found inside of the grill when he went to light it. It was probably the same bastard, or bastards, that moved inside the house and robbed his traps. He hadn't used the barbecue in at least four years, and he wondered how much longer it had been since he shared a Sunday dinner with someone. The whole day felt good.

They went to The Newcomers Meeting that night, where the focus was always on the first three steps of the Alcoholics Anonymous program:

1. *We admitted we were powerless over alcohol – that our lives had become unmanageable.*

2. *Came to believe that a Power greater than ourselves could restore us to sanity.*

3. *Made a decision to turn our will and our lives over to the care of God as we understood Him.*

The meeting was held in Deerfield, in a large community room at the Methodist Church. Most of the attendees were considered *newbies*, people with less than a year of sobriety. Focusing on the first three steps was meant to help the newcomers find direction and some solid footing during early recovery. It was always a big meeting, the type that people could attend and not feel on display. Many first timers hid in chairs near the back, hoping not to be recognized or asked to talk.

He recalled the question someone had asked Paul many years ago when they found him huddled in one of the dark, corner seats at his first or second meeting.

"Funny that you never worried about that when you went drinking in a bar, huh?"

It was a good point, yet Paul remembered being angry about the question at the time.

Paul and Angela arrived a few minutes early, and he wasn't surprised to see Jack and Diane standing near the coffee maker. Jack did a theatrical double-take when he saw them come through the door, and Diane immediately went over and embraced Angela, shuffling her off toward the larger part of the room.

"Huh," Jack said. "Well, you just never know who you'll see here, ain't that right Paul?"

"Yup," Paul said, "I guess you just never do."

He shook Jack's hand before grabbing a Styrofoam cup and filling it with coffee from the large metal urn. The familiar smell of cheap, burnt coffee gave Paul the feeling that this was going to be a good meeting. He smiled at Jack, waiting to see if more would be said; apparently Jack had shared all his wisdom for the moment and simply smiled back, raising his coffee cup in salute.

Paul walked toward the last row of chairs in the room. He sat down and noticed that there was already a good crowd in attendance, mostly people he didn't recognize. The majority of them looked very young. He saw Diane and Angela sitting in a row near the front, Diane leaning in and talking.

There was a table at the front of the room, where the meeting's chairperson always sat. Paul saw Jimmy C. at the table talking to a younger man who was seated there, facing out toward the growing crowd in the room. Jimmy wore a short-sleeved, light blue polyester shirt with a black collar and black stripes running down both sides. The young man Jimmy was talking to looked scared and anxious, and Paul guessed that this might be the first time he'd ever been asked (or told) to be the chairperson for a meeting. The qualifications for running a meeting varied, but Paul knew that it was common at the Newcomer's Meeting to have people who were not sober for very long get up there and give it their best shot.

Jimmy slapped the reluctant chairperson reassuringly on the shoulder and turned to survey the room. When he saw Paul seated alone in the last row, he picked up a leather coat that he had draped over a chair near the front and walked toward him, shaking hands, and greeting people along the way. Jimmy sat down heavily in the seat next to Paul, saying nothing for a moment, seeming to take in the view of the room from where they were sitting. Paul waited, bracing himself.

"So," Jimmy began, "you thought sitting back here in *Relapse Row* was the best plan for your newfound gift of sobriety?"

"I thought this was a Beginner's Meeting," Paul replied, not looking at Jimmy. "If I had known they allowed you crusty old-timers in here, I would have chosen another place to go."

"Brilliant! That's the type of thinking that proves you need more help." Jimmy said. "And, yes, I will be your sponsor; so, thanks for asking."

Just then, the young man at the front table banged a small wooden gavel to indicate the meeting would start. Jimmy looked at Paul, waiting for some response to his announcement about sponsorship, but Paul kept his eyes forward.

The meeting proceeded much as Paul had expected it to. Being away from these rooms, he had forgotten how odd and extraordinary this whole process and fellowship was. Although the names and faces in this room had changed in the years since he'd left, the stories, behaviors, and power of the collective Twelve Step Program were genuinely timeless.

The young man running the meeting tonight shared that he'd been sober for only a few months. He talked about how he came to be in A.A.— the horrible places his addiction to alcohol and other drugs had brought him. Paul thought how common this was of people in early recovery. It was like listening to someone who had ignored hurricane warnings or who remained in a condemned building that was scheduled for demolition. After being pulled from the rubble, the person recounting the experience would persistently retell their story, trying to make sense of why they stuck around for so long—for too long.

"I bet you missed these war stories," Jimmy leaned over and said to Paul while the chairperson spoke.

For people who maintained their sobriety, the focus of their stories invariably shifted from the awful, traumatic places they were taken to by addiction to the miraculous changes that happened when they sobered up. That was the unexplainable but tremendous power that A.A. and other Twelve Step groups possessed—to instill hope, desire, and strength toward a better life in recovery. Everyone who participated simply shared their stories of loss, pain, and eventual transformation to build the collective power. In this way, a person with one day of sobriety might help another struggling person in the same way that someone with decades of recovery could.

After the young man had told his entire story, it was time for the meeting to take a break. Paul noticed Angela heading toward the coffee machine.

"Well, I'm glad he got that out," Jimmy said, looking down at his watch.

"It's funny how you tell these pigeons, these new guys, to share their stories for about five minutes, and they always take longer than that. Young Edward up there didn't think he would have anything to tell us tonight but look at how much we all learned from him."

A few of the younger people present had surrounded the young man, Edward, at the front of the room, and Paul saw him look back toward Jimmy, who gave him a thumbs up.

"So, yeah, back to you and our new working relationship," Jimmy said, turning in his seat toward Paul.

"I didn't ask you to be my sponsor," Paul said.

"True, but I'm not going to let that slow us down. Let's just say that my Higher Power is telling me if I don't intervene here, you're fucked."

Paul said nothing but could feel the smile forming on his face.

"Here's what you're going to do. Let's start off with coming to at least one of these meetings every day for the next ninety days. If you need me, call me."

Jimmy handed Paul a business card with his name and phone number on it. The card looked professionally printed in ornate script. It read:

Jimmy C.

Try not to be an asshole today.

(266) 721 – 3623

"When did you start carrying these?" Paul asked, flipping the card over in his hand.

"Nice, huh? I had that saying made up just for you!" Jimmy responded, beaming.

"So, listen, I wanted to make sure Edward chaired the meeting tonight, but I gotta cut out early. I'm getting together with some people over at the bowling alley."

"That explains the shirt," Paul interrupted.

Jimmy looked down at himself and then back at Paul.

"What are you talking about? This ain't my bowling shirt, and, besides, we're not bowling tonight. Why don't you just practice shutting up and listening more before you say something stupid that offends your sponsor or others who are trying to save your life here."

"I didn't ask you to be my sponsor," Paul repeated, but Jimmy had stood up and was putting on his jacket.

"I'll see you and the girl—what's her name again?"

"Angela."

"Right, Angela. I'll see you and Angela tomorrow night at the 8:00 p.m. meeting at Bethany House. You think you can still find your way out there?"

"Do I have a choice?" Paul asked.

Jimmy patted him on the shoulder and winked as he walked away.

CHAPTER 32

"There's more to a picture than meets the eye."

Neil Young

On their ride back to his house, Paul told Angela that Jimmy was his new sponsor and that he instructed Paul to attend ninety A.A. meetings in the next ninety days.

"No shit?" Angela said, "That's weird because Diane said that I should do the same thing. She doesn't want to be my sponsor because she hasn't been sober long enough, but she gave me her number and promised to introduce me to some other women with longer sobriety. A meeting every day for the next three months seems too hardcore to me!"

"Well, it's not like either one of us has a busy schedule to keep," he said.

Paul didn't bother telling Angela that this practice was an old one in A.A, though it wasn't officially required (as A.A. has never had any requirements besides a desire to stop drinking). His first sponsor gave Paul this same directive.

"It's just a suggestion," his sponsor reasoned, *"and if you don't want to do it, my next suggestion will be for you to find another sponsor."*

At home, Angela put water on the stove for tea. She had talked him into buying a type of green tea that advertised strong detoxification powers. Paul rummaged through the refrigerator, pulling out a bag of baby carrot sticks and blue cheese dressing. He grabbed a small bowl from the cupboard and put the food on the kitchen table while Angela busied herself locating tea bags, cups, and honey.

Paul walked to the living room and thumbed through his record collection. He paused on several possible choices, considering which option Angela would criticize least.

He picked up an album, turned it over, and reviewed the songs.

"I'm almost afraid to ask," Paul said, "but have you heard of Neil Young?"

There was a hesitation before she said, "Of course! He's that Jewish guy who sings about coming to America and Baby Caroline and old shit like that, right?"

Paul shook his head, wondering if Charlotte had taken their copy of *Neil Diamond's Greatest Hits* from the collection with her.

"No," Paul said, "not exactly. Let's just give this a try, but please keep an open mind and remember this was way before Milli Vanilli or whoever you grew up listening to."

"Who?" The kettle interrupted with a low whistle.

Paul placed *After the Gold Rush* on the turntable and started up the system. The singer's sad, rebellious tenor and acoustic guitar reminded Paul of a time that seemed not so long ago when he thought righting the world's wrongs and injustices was not just possible, but inevitable—his destiny.

Angela poured them both tea and brought the cups to the table. She sat, staring out the window into the darkness of the backyard.

"Well," Paul said, "this isn't the famous cheese and cracker house special, but it will do."

She smiled but seemed lost in her thoughts. He wondered if it had to do with the music or just the inevitable morbid thoughts that came to the newly sober at night.

"Did you always sit there?" She eventually asked Paul.

Paul looked at her, not sure of the question.

"When you all sat here, I mean. At the table. Was that the seat you always sat in, or did everyone move around?"

When Paul didn't immediately answer, she blushed slightly.

"I'm sorry. I was just thinking about when I was growing up. I always wondered about that, maybe even wanted that in some weird way, to have a kitchen table where the family sat for every meal, each person at their own seat, maybe even their own special glass, silverware, or plate that everyone knew to put at that spot. That's weird, right? Most of my childhood was spent eating on the couch or using some broken down folding table in front of a shitty TV set."

She looked shyly at Paul and then out the window again.

"Sorry, I'll shut up."

She grabbed a carrot and took a bite.

"Sean always sat where you are now," he said.

She'd already guessed that or felt it, and it was why she kept choosing to sit there.

"And Charlotte always sat there," Paul said, pointing to the chair closest to the window.

"I guess I never thought about those routines we had, what creatures of habit we were."

"And was that your seat?" She asked.

"When I was here, it was. I worked until eight or nine at night most of the time, running night groups at the clinic or staying late to catch up on paperwork. Even after I became director of that place, when I didn't have to be there that late anymore, I found reasons to stay."

He shook his head and took a sip of tea.

"But when I was here, when I was home, yes, this was my seat."

There was a fourth seat at the table, and Angela felt a sad emptiness from it.

"When you're a family of three," Paul continued, "there always seems to be a missing piece, an empty place. Charlotte and I talked about having another child. She wanted another one, especially after we had Sean, or Shawna, I guess I should say. Anyway, it just wasn't happening. We tried, but it wasn't working. She wanted some help, maybe fertility treatments or adoption, but I was always against it."

Paul had another sip of tea and then closed his eyes and took a long, deep breath.

"I was afraid. Scared that something would go wrong if we brought another kid into our perfect little life. Afraid to mess up everything. So, I shut it down. She protested at first, trying to convince me it was safe, that everything would turn out fine, just fine. Finally, the conversation about it just ended. She gave up, I suppose. But that chair," Paul pointed to the seat next to him, "that chair was a constant reminder that we had, or that I had, left someone out of our plan."

Paul stared out the darkened window. A few awkward moments went by.

"This tea isn't bad," Paul said evenly.

"It's not good," he added, smiling, "but it's not too bad."

Angela looked over at him, rolling her eyes.

"Why don't you try mixing in some of that blue cheese dressing? I noticed you couldn't go for the carrots without having some of that heart attack sauce to dip them in."

Paul set down his tea, picked up a carrot stick, and dipped it in the dressing.

"Great idea." He said, munching on the carrot and smiling. "Something has to kill me. Why not death by blue cheese?"

As they sipped and chewed, the sad, soulful music washed over them. Finally, Paul stood up, brought his cup to the sink, and dumped out what was left. He placed it in the dishwasher.

"I'm going to bed," He announced. "Thanks for the tea. Do you want me to turn this music off?"

"No, that's okay," Angela said, "I'll do it later."

He turned away and started walking down the hallway.

"Paul," she said.

"Yeah?"

"I, um, I think that Shawna, I mean, I just feel like she would want you to know that she liked this seat. And that there were a lot of good memories around this table."

Paul paused but didn't turn around to face her.

"Well," his voice cracked as he spoke, "thank you for that. I suppose I had some good times around that table myself."

He walked on down the hall. As he did, the words from "Birds" flitted from the stereo and filled the room:

"When you see me Fly away without you Shadow on the things you know Feathers fall around you And show you the way to go. It's over, it's over."

CHAPTER 33

"Most folks who believe that white privilege doesn't exist are white, have some money, and are clueless about the power they have in the world. Being a white man, having some money and knowing the right people makes all the difference in getting shit done. Oops, sorry, getting stuff done..."

Lamont J., H.C.C., "Becoming Culturally Competent," class discussion

"This is stupid."

"You need to let her know what's going on. It shouldn't take that long. I'll wait right here for you."

"When is the last time you actually went in this shithole? Ever? Because nothing is ever quick or easy here, especially when you don't have an appointment."

"That's why we're here at 9:00 a.m., so, you can catch her early before the day gets busy."

"This is so stupid. If you want me to leave your house, just fucking tell me to leave."

Paul grabbed the steering wheel with both hands and slowly lowered his head toward it, his eyes closed.

"We've been over this. I don't want you to leave, not at all. But if you ignore them, if you don't tell them that your housing situation has changed, they could violate you. If that happens, you won't have any medical insurance. Without medical insurance, you'll have to pay for every group and session at St. Michael's. And that is outrageously expensive! You're not here to ask for money for housing. You have housing with me, but you do need that medical coverage."

He glanced over at Angela, who had gone completely rigid and was staring straight ahead.

"Well, I could have called and told them that. Why do we have to be here in person? This place sucks. And she's a total bitch. I'm telling you; this is a waste of time. I don't think we even need to go to St. Michael's anymore. I mean, we're going to A.A. every day now, and that's free, so why do we need to..."

"You've only been to two meetings!" Paul interrupted, laughing.

"Look," he said, "the doors just opened, and they're letting people in. Can you just trust me on this and get in there? Everything doesn't need to be an argument. I'll be here, waiting. And then maybe we can go for ice cream if you're good."

She closed her eyes now, but he saw the smile on her face.

"Ice cream," she said, reaching over and opening the door. "Right. Fucking ice cream."

She didn't come right back. After forty minutes, Paul went in to find her. He'd been in the Department of Social Services building countless times and had attended many meetings here during his career with St. Michael's. He instinctively reached down to straighten a phantom tie as he walked through the large glass doors at the entrance. He noticed how dirty and smeared the front doors looked, fingerprints smudged over fingerprints on the glass. The place looked different, much more institutional, square, and confining. In this indifferent building, people at the bottom of the food chain sat for countless hours and waited to ask about things that might or might not be given to them depending on factors beyond their control.

He walked down a corridor and opened the door to the Medicaid office. The room was well over its capacity. Every seat was taken, and people were standing or parked at odd angles in their wheelchairs and motorized scooters. It was impossible to move without knocking into someone. Mumbling voices and noise, some of it caused by small children sitting on women's laps or restrained by the straps of their strollers, peppered the room.

"Numba thir-" a low voice mumbled incoherently over the loudspeaker.

A younger-looking man stood up and assisted an older fellow to his walker. Two people who had been standing immediately descended on the empty seats. The older man looked frail and unsteady as he gripped the pads of the walker. A baseball hat emblazoned with the numbers of a long-disbanded military unit floated on his small head. The two men shuffled toward a thick wooden windowless door held open by an office worker. The three disappeared past the door, and it shut solidly back in place.

He scanned the room several times before spotting Angela. She sat between two other women against the far wall. One woman was young and large and sheathed in what appeared to be a unicorn-themed pajama jumper. It had a drooping multi-colored horn protruding from the hoodie, which was pulled tightly over the woman's head while she tapped her dramatically long, manicured fingernails on the screen of an expensive-looking phone. The woman on Angela's other side was much thinner, too thin in Paul's opinion, which made her look old and fragile. She wore a light blue polyester pantsuit tucked into large snow boots. Paul pushed his way through the crowd just as the wooden door opened again. A woman pushing a stroller occupied by a wildly writhing child burst through the doorway and into the crowd.

"This is total bullshit!" She shouted into the closing portal. "I don't care what you heard! I ain't getting any money for watching kids at my house! The jealous bitch narked on me because I dumped her stupid boyfriend back on her lap, and now she's stuck watching his rotten kids!"

A tall, Black man, whom Paul recognized, accompanied her to the door. He carried a clipboard and wore a faded grey shirt and dark slacks. It was Craig Schuyler, a long-time case manager with D.S.S. He leaned toward the woman and spoke, as the muffled voice announced,

"Number Fort-"

The woman fumed away from Craig and hurried toward the exit, using the stroller as an effective plow. Paul noticed the smile on the child's face as she flew past, grabbing and kicking at the crowd. No doubt this was just one of many extraordinary adventures the young girl would enjoy today.

Craig noticed Paul and walked over, holding out his hand.

"Well, this is a surprise," Craig said. "How are you, Paul? Boy, it's good to see you!"

Paul shook Craig's hand, noticing the absence of macho bravado in his grip.

"I'm okay, Craig. Getting better all the time. It's good to see you as well. How's things over here? More importantly, how are things outside of here?"

Craig laughed. "Well, you can see how things are here. Just another Monday morning at the Medicaid office. I don't complain. It's job security, right? Just like what you do—" Craig stopped abruptly, blushing.

"What I did," Paul corrected him, smiling, "retirement has its advantages, but there are parts I miss, that's for sure. How are Alecia and the kids? They must be getting up there now."

"She's good. She got tenure at the elementary school a few years ago, so that's been a load off our minds. The kids are eight and ten now, growing like weeds. We're taking them to Florida next month, for Easter. My parents have a place down there, so, we're going to take advantage of it. Thanks for asking. How about you? What brings you around?"

Paul pointed to Angela, who was pretending not to see him.

"I'm helping a friend out. We're waiting to talk with Linda. I'm just living the life, you know? Enjoying each day and all of that."

A small, teenage-looking woman cradled what appeared to be a newborn as she walked past them to wait in front of the wooden door. She looked tired and solemn.

Craig put a hand on Paul's shoulder. "I'll let Linda know you're here. It's good seeing you. We should catch up some time."

"Thanks," Paul said, "It would be great to get together. Enjoy Florida!"

Craig walked back to the door, greeting the young woman and her baby warmly before ushering them through. Paul approached Angela.

"This is a blast, huh? Not taking much time at all, either," she said.

"Careful, or you'll blow your shot at ice cream."

The woman in the unicorn pajamas looked up at the pair.

"Jack Frost is my favorite place to go. It's a little more expensive, but it's worth it. I'm not sure they're open this time of year, though."

Angela opened her mouth to say something, but Paul stopped her.

"Thanks," he said, "we'll keep that in mind."

The wooden door opened again, and a serious-looking woman stood there, looking around the room. Her hair was pulled back tightly, and she wore a navy-blue skirt and matching jacket. A pair of glasses hung from a chain around her neck, which looked like a necklace. When she spotted Paul, she pointed to Angela and cocked a finger, beckoning them both toward the hallway.

As they walked toward the door, Paul heard rumblings from the crowd.

"Hey, I was here before them. That's not right."

"Must be nice to know people."

"Isn't it great to be a white man in America?"

"Hi Linda," Paul said as they walked through the door.

"Paul," she said, making no effort to shake his hand.

They walked down a long hallway and into a corner office. The name-plate read "Ms. Linda Fulmer – Director of Social Services. Ms. Fulmer motioned for them to sit down before walking behind an enormous mahogany desk and taking her seat. The formality and silence seemed intentionally awkward to Paul. He was getting used to presenting the damaged and ruined version of himself to others who knew him before the fall, and it seemed the best strategy was silence. Those who talked first normally lost most. Linda had decided to call them in, so he would wait for the rest.

"So," Ms. Fulmer said after making a production of putting her glasses on, tapping on some keys, and looking long and hard at her computer screen, which had been tilted at just the right angle to keep the information out of site.

"Ms. LaPoint, can you tell me if you're related to Mr. Durkin? Is this some part of your lineage that you neglected to mention when we met before?"

LaPoint seemed an odd last name to Paul, as did the fact that he hadn't known Angela's last name until this moment.

"No." Angela said.

A moment passed. Ms. Fulmer's stern gaze fell fully on Angela.

"No, what?" she asked.

"No, he's not related to you, or no you didn't mention it to me?"

Angela blew out a long breath.

"No, he's not related to me. We just met last week. He's a…he's just a…well, he's a friend, I guess."

"You guess?" Ms. Fulmer asked.

"Is Mr. Durkin employing you at this point? Are you receiving any money or resources from him for services you're providing?"

"I'm not selling myself to him, if that's just the nice way of asking," Angela answered, pulling her legs up into the chair. "He's not paying me for anything. I'm just living at his house right now."

"Staying at my house," Paul corrected, "she's staying at my house. We're in treatment together, and she needed a place to stay—temporarily—so, I told her she could stay with me until she secures other housing."

"I see," Ms. Fulmer said, turning back to her computer screen.

"It looks like you had an assessment at St. Michael's two weeks ago, but I'm waiting for the results of that assessment from the agency. From what Mr. Durkin has said, I assume you were recommended for treatment, and you're following through with that recommendation?"

"Yeah," Angela said.

She saw Ms. Fulmer's icy stare and corrected herself.

"Yes. Treatment was recommended. I met with Mandy, she's my counselor over there, and I'm going to one group a week."

"And A.A," Paul interrupted again. "I've also started taking her to meetings."

Ms. Fulmer pursed her lips and gave a slight nod of her head. She removed the glasses, bit lightly on one of the arms, and placed them back on her nose, staring into the computer screen while talking.

"What is your plan now, Ms. LaPoint? Are you requesting to be placed in temporary housing while you complete your treatment, or is your current situation with Mr. Durkin acceptable to you? I see here that we were paying for a room in the Thoroughbred Motel after you first came to see me. Would you like to go back to the Thoroughbred?"

Ms. Fulmer tapped on a key, and her printer buzzed to life, churning out several pages.

"It's acceptable," Angela said.

"I mean, I'm not asking to go back to the motel." She turned toward Paul. "I'm happy where I am."

"As long as that's alright. If I need to leave, I can. It's just…"

"Angela thought she should come in and let you know about the change in her living status, Ms. Fulmer," Paul said, "and that she's attending treatment as recommended. She's welcome to stay with me as long as she wants to while she receives treatment."

"Well, that's good to hear," Ms. Fulmer said, gathering the papers from her printer and inspecting them through her glasses, "because I wouldn't have let you go back to that motel anyway."

Her face softened as she pushed the papers and a pen across the desk to Angela.

"You should know that we heard from your former 'friend' Glenn last week. He wanted to let us know about a new post office box that you acquired and that any correspondence, including checks, should be sent to the new address." She looked up at Angela, smiling. "Such a thoughtful and caring friend, that Glenn."

"That asshole!" Angela said, then caught herself, "Sorry."

"Agreed," Ms. Fulmer said. "He's quite well known around here. You're certainly not the first pretty young lady he's made friends with. We've discussed giving Glenn some type of commission for all of the people he sends our way."

Her face became serious again.

"So, I strongly suggest you stay away from him completely from this moment on. In the meantime, I need you to sign these forms. The first two are releases of information so that I can speak to St. Michael's and Mr. Durkin about you. The other papers state that you're following this office's recommendations, including maintaining your sobriety, finishing your treatment successfully, and letting us know about any changes in your housing or financial status, just as you came in and did today."

Angela signed everything and handed the paperwork over the desk.

"Okay then. We should be all set for now," Ms. Fulmer said after checking the signatures.

She slid the glasses from her face and let them dangle from the necklace.

"Do you mind if I have a few words with Mr. Durkin?"

"No," Angela said, "but can I wait out in the car? I think I've had enough of this place."

Paul handed her the keys. She walked toward the door, then turned to address Ms. Fulmer.

"Thanks. Really."

Ms. Fulmer gave a small smile and nodded her head.

As door clicked shut, Paul started talking.

"Look, Linda, I didn't mean to put you in a weird place here. I really didn't see this coming. Like I said, we're both in treatment, and she was standing out at the bus stop in that storm last week…"

"Stop!" Ms. Fulmer said.

She sat back in her seat, waving a dismissive hand up in the air.

"When anyone, anywhere, reaches out for help, we're responsible for being there, right Paul?"

He shook his head. "Yeah, that about sums it up."

"I get it," she said, "you should know that I get it. But she's a train wreck. A hot mess. I just hope you knew that from the start."

She put the glasses back on and turned to the computer.

"Angela LaPoint, daughter of Michelle LaPoint, maiden name Donahue. There is one sister listed, Olivia Harrington. She is currently living in San Diego, California. Although young Angela has only a few misdemeanors on her record, mostly petty theft, Mom has a much more impressive list of dubious achievements. According to my records, we're currently putting *her* up at the Thoroughbred!"

She turned toward Paul. "Well, that would have been dangerously convenient. We could have had them both share a room over there, maybe put Glenn next door."

"Most of us are train wrecks at the beginning," Paul said, "but she's a good kid, a smart kid. I know you saw that, or you would have given her a much harder time in here. I'm just hoping you'll give her this chance, give her a little time to get herself together."

Linda removed the glasses again and turned toward him. "You're right. We all deserve a second chance, sometimes a third or fourth. But in case you've forgotten, this dysfunctional cycle that goes from generation to generation is usually the hardest one to break. Nature and nurture have combined to create a long line of chronic victims. You walked through a lot of them out in the waiting room. I know you've been out of the game for a while and, from what I hear, you haven't exactly been working the best program during this hiatus."

She got up from behind the desk and moved to the chair Angela had sat in. He looked at her, shrugged his shoulders, and smiled wanly.

"What do you want me to say?"

She leaned toward him, her hands on her knees. "Nothing. I want you to try. You and I both know there's no accident in any of this. It's all Higher Power stuff, right? So, suit up and show up for this one. If you're not ready to get sober for yourself, do it for Ms. LaPoint."

She patted his knee gently and leaned back in her chair, stretching her neck from side to side. She moved toward him again and chuckled.

"I do have to say, though, I would pay good money to watch you run into Charlotte somewhere with this young chippy on your arm. That evil bitch might just lose her cool over that!"

Paul smiled and shook his head.

"Aww," she continued, "you know I'm busting your chops, Paul. But we always thought you deserved better than her. You stupid Moheneck Falls farm boys never do learn, I guess."

She got up, opened the door, and said, "Now get the hell out of my office."

CHAPTER 34

"…we aren't a glum lot. If newcomers could see no joy or fun in our existence, they wouldn't want it. We absolutely insist on enjoying life."

From *Alcoholics Anonymous* (*The Big Book*)

The Deerfield Originals A.A. Meeting was one of the oldest in the state. As the story went, it started in 1936 when several founding members of Alcoholics Anonymous drove up from New York City to visit the local jail's drunk tank and the Deerfield Psychiatric Ward. They were searching for new recruits among the incurable inebriates they encountered. These sober city slickers also met with the Rector of the Bethany Church, who showed great hesitancy about having a group of unstable alcoholics meeting regularly at the church. He eventually decided (somewhat unwillingly) to allow a weekly meeting in a small room of the Parish House, which stood next door to the church.

In those days, when the town was much smaller, drinking and gambling in the dimly lit speakeasies and gaming joints were the most common vices. Their profits infected Deerfield's growing economy. Over time more addictions metastasized through the area and nourished the unsavory and unseen veins of lifeblood that kept the town's businesses prosperous and the church's collection baskets full.

It seemed a great irony that Twelve Step Meetings, and the recovery community in general, thrived along the roots of addiction branching underneath Deerfield. As money piled up—from new (legal) casinos, the horse racing track, the ever-present gin mills, and a host of illegal drug sales that expanded each year—A.A. and a handful of other self-help programs grew quietly and humbly alongside. Their members filled the cheap metal chairs in church basements, new members and old-timers alike. The defining similarity among these unlikely groupings: each one realized they'd given too much of themselves to the substances and industries which aimed to exploit and destroy them. All had seen through empty lies and promises, and they longed for a new way of life.

Angela insisted they arrive early to each meeting, and she was adept at snatching up an effective share of caffeine and snacks before being hustled off for a chat by Diane or some other well-meaning woman. A younger woman near the coffee maker talked with a small, round man whom Paul knew too well. His name was Joseph Meer.

Unlike many of the Old Timers in A.A., Joseph Meer never acquired a nickname and was always addressed formally, using his first and last name, in and outside of the Fellowship. Paul had foggy recollections of seeing him around town when they were younger men. Paul heard his elders talk about Joseph Meer's life and knew he once owned a successful jewelry store and clock repair shop in Deerfield. Joseph Meer had acquired an excellent reputation for his attention to detail and top-quality craftsmanship. Many high rollers stumbled drunkenly into his store after winning at a local casino and walked out with Joseph Meer's watches, rings, or gold necklaces.

He never married, which many town folks found a bit odd, but bachelorhood seemed to fit him just fine. There was talk about his meticulous attention to detail and long hours working at the store that probably drove away any potential mates. The women who fancied themselves matchmakers around town tried to set Joseph up on dates with eligible ladies, but he always claimed to be too busy or too shy to follow through. Mostly Joseph Meer worked at his store and sang in the choir at Bethany Church each Sunday. His life appeared to all outside observers as quirky but acceptable. And perhaps a tad insulated, and lonesome.

Paul heard that Joseph's troubles with alcohol began at what was otherwise the height of his store's success. He was encouraged by a new friend, who lived out of town, to hire an employee (he'd always run the place and done all the repairs himself). This person could tend to the store one day each week while Joseph took up golfing at a small, nearby club. Joseph threw himself at the sport as he had done with so many other things in his life, first taking lessons from the golf pro, then purchasing a set of top-of-the-line clubs with which to conquer the game. Although he only golfed at the club once each week, he spent countless hours after his store was closed at a driving range and putting green behind the course's clubhouse, where he learned to master each new club from his golf bag. After these outings, Joseph took a drink, just one drink at first, at the clubhouse bar with the same man who talked him into hiring the new employee and joining the golf club. The man was also a successful bachelor who had made his fortune in stocks and trading.

Before long, Joseph was spending more time at the bar with his pal than out on the fairways, driving range, or putting greens. Joseph's friend was a gregarious, flamboyant fellow, known to tip the bartender well and to buy drinks for anyone at any time. Speculation surfaced about the nature of their relationship. Words like "funny," and "queer" floated around the golf course and permeated the vestibule of Bethany Church. Joseph's participation in the choir and attendance at services dwindled, then fell off completely. Nobody, including the rector, appeared to notice or care that he had left the fold.

Soon after the rumors started, jewelry sales from the store declined, and fewer people trusted him to repair their timepieces. Joseph blamed this slump on the political climate and what he claimed was a failing economy.

This was not the case at all. He was one of only a few jewelers in the region, and his repair services were even more of a rarity. What truly damaged his business and reputation were the mistakes and shoddy workmanship that increased proportionally with his time drinking at the clubhouse bar. As his hangovers worsened, the shop's hours became more sporadic. Simple repairs took longer, and for the first time since his business opened, those "repairs" didn't work at all. His work was rushed or inadequate.

Instead of making things right with his disgruntled but loyal customers by treating these mistakes with apologies, Joseph disputed them and refused to take back the broken items. This argumentative attitude drove his sole employee to leave, which only made matters worse for the business. Neighbors noticed that his lawn had gone to tall weeds and that the shades and curtains of his windows were always drawn. The entire property, which Joseph had maintained meticulously, looked run down and messy. It seemed contrary to the character of the man they knew. Unfortunately, these long-time friends and neighbors never reached out or spoke to him directly about their concerns. Instead, the good townsfolk he had loyally served and lived among for years took the same course as Joseph's church family. They chose to ostracize and shun him while he spiraled, further and further toward his bottom.

Joseph appeared oblivious to the growing scorn and his decline. He drove to the clubhouse every day to join his dear friend and drinking partner. Both men were assigned their own stools at the bar and were seldom sober enough to golf. The two were not always in a cheerful and breezy mood anymore, particularly when the subjects of government, religion, or marriage came up. Visitors or newcomers to the golf course might find themselves in heated debates with the men about the "fucking communists and fascists," who appeared to be at the heart of every unpleasant issue and conspiracy of the time.

After such an argument with some wealthy out of town bankers, Joseph and his friend were strongly encouraged to leave the club by the management. The couple got into a car (or poured themselves in as a witness would later report) and roared up the unpaved country club road toward the main highway.

Their crash site was not discovered until two days later, as nobody had been waiting for either man to arrive home or to show up at a job. (Joseph's dwindling customers were used to his store being closed by then.) If it hadn't been for Jethro Allen, a devout trout fisherman, finding the car and its two occupants far down in a ravine and half-submerged in the Cosquinocke Creek, the men would have been there indefinitely, and Joseph certainly wouldn't be alive today.

Deerfield's Coroner reported that the other man, whom he described on the official report as "a known homosexual," died from injuries sustained in the accident. Joseph was hospitalized for several weeks after being pulled from the wreckage, then released to a "life" of complete bankruptcy, and obscurity. He was utterly lost.

Joseph never spoke aloud of the close friend who died in the car crash, his days on the clubhouse barstool, or about the loss of his business, home, and reputation. As those who had witnessed his decline died off, Joseph Meer's history became clouded, leaving its most salacious and unproven points to snag him in misrepresentation with every retelling of the tale.

The testimony that Joseph chose to share in countless A.A. meetings over his decades in sobriety focused on his days after the car wreck when he became a homeless drunk wandering the streets and living in the woods between Deerfield and Moheneck Falls. As he described it, his reformation started after he was found half-frozen near the back door of a local bar on Christmas Eve. He was taken to the hospital, where they treated him for frostbite, malnutrition, and alcoholic hepatitis.

By Joseph's account, he had every intention of going back to drinking once he was released but thought it wise to ride out the holidays in the warm confines of the hospital. The winter that year was bitterly cold. Before his hospitalization, he'd been picked up by the local police for breaking into local businesses in several attempts to escape the frigid nights. Joseph preferred his hospital bed to the hard wooden benches in the Deerfield drunk tank, and he'd already decided to check himself into the hospital again if the temperatures demanded it.

On the day before he was released, two men came to his room. At first, he thought they were from his church but soon noticed that neither looked the part of religious servants. They might have been cops, come to question him about some recent crime for which he had become a prime suspect. The men were neither. They introduced themselves as reformed alcoholics, there to talk about a program of recovery from alcoholism that had worked for them.

Joseph had a few slips and lapses during that first year, and if it hadn't been for other sober men chasing him down and forcing him into the car and back to A.A. meetings, Joseph swore he would have been pushing up the daisies under a gravestone long ago. In time, he began a new life. He never reopened his shop, but he met a man who had been sober a bit longer than himself and was starting a business installing and servicing residential oil furnaces. Joseph liked the technical aspect of the work and took to fixing furnaces. People continually asked him to repair their jewelry or antique clocks as well, and over time he gave in to their pleas and began a small repair business in his house. To this day, he continued clock repair, but much of it depended on the time he had and his mood when approached about a job.

Joseph maintained bachelorhood throughout his sobriety, and as far as anyone knew, he enjoyed living alone, rarely taking trips out of town or participating in local social functions. He attended the same A.A. meetings with regularity and was known to intimidate newer members (and some members who were not so new) by his unrelenting insistence that nothing within *his* beloved Twelve Step program of recovery should be changed or challenged.

"Not one word, and not one letter needs fixing," was a common Meer mantra, followed by, "This program works fine just the way it's written."

His long-term sobriety earned Joseph respect, and there was the unspoken implication that his recovery was a somehow tougher and more genuine example of the A.A. program than newcomers practiced today. It couldn't be known if Joseph believed this or if he was simply playing the part assigned to him, a man who had miraculously achieved long-term sobriety despite the odds against him.

Paul thought she sounded especially cheery as Angela chirped, "Hello!" to Joseph Meer and the young woman in the kitchen.

"Hi," the woman said. "I'm Amanda. I'm the coffee maker for the meeting. I think it's done brewing if you want some."

Angela and Paul introduced themselves.

Joseph Meer's eyes narrowed in his head. The old, wise owl was setting its sights on something weak and dying.

"Well," he replied, "what have we here? Has the prodigal son returned to the farm?" He asked.

"It seems that way," Paul answered, and held out his hand. Joseph shook it.

"Angela, this is Joseph Meer," Paul said.

"Hello," she said again, less enthusiastically this time, and moved on toward the coffee with Amanda.

"So, you're back?" Joseph asked.

"The choices were limited," Paul answered, "I think you're either being coy about my humble return, or you don't read the local paper anymore. I made it in here, but not according to any story I want to hang on the refrigerator at home. It's either get sober or go to jail at this point, I suppose."

Joseph Meer shook his head, considering this.

"Well," he said after a moment, "that story doesn't sound unique. A.A. has always been the last choice, the only house left on the boulevard of broken dreams. Yet, here it is, running strong, with new people coming in every day. These people who think they can stay sober by following some self-help guru or going to one of those expensive rehabs…maybe getting a personal trainer or a life coach, amaze me. Did you know that there are programs out there telling people they can moderate their drinking now? Imagine that! An alcoholic only having one or two drinks! That's like giving a monkey some bananas and telling it to eat one each day! And then you've got these new groups popping up everywhere! A.A. is too hard, or A.A. says 'God' too much, or A.A. is some kind of cult! The lengths people will go to in order to stay drunk these days…Back when I got sober, the old-timers threw you in the car and told you to take the cotton out of your ears and stick it in your mouth. No talking for the first year at least because you had nothing healthy to contribute. Nowadays, some folks want to let these newcomers prattle on after only being sober a day or two about their feelings, or their mental illness, or how the cat died yesterday! Well, that's just not how this program works!"

Paul said nothing and stared flatly back at Joseph Meer. He'd heard the speech before and knew that nothing he said or did would influence the lecturer in any significant way.

After a moment, when Joseph Meer surmised that he would be getting no argument from Paul, his gaze softened.

"It's good to see you, boy."

Jimmy C. threw open the door and a mob of people walked in behind him.

Their entrance coincided with the climax of Jimmy's story. "…The guy in the cell next to me says, 'What do you mean you've got booze and smokes over there? I tried to sneak some cigarettes in, but they got crushed up in there, and now I don't know how the hell to get them out!'"

His entourage exploded into laughter and dispersed around the room, many of them gravitating toward the coffee maker and some walking into the larger room to claim seats before the meeting started.

"Joseph," Jimmy said, breaking the unwritten norms as he approached.

"I see you're keeping track of the pigeons. That's good. They need some old-school intervention."

Angela walked over to Paul, coffee and cookies in hand.

"Oh, I'm glad you two showed up," Jimmy said. "Come with me. I've got a great surprise for you."

Paul knew it was useless to disagree. He smiled at Angela, hoping she would play along and keep her mouth shut. She rolled her eyes, but followed behind Paul into the meeting room.

"I made a reservation for you!" Jimmy said.

He walked them up to the first row of chairs in the room, those directly facing the chairperson's spot.

"These are the best seats in the house!"

He beamed at them, seeming genuinely proud of the spots he secured.

"Are you fucking kidding me?" Angela asked, but her tone sounded only mildly plaintive.

"No," Jimmy responded.

He pretended to dust off the two seats with his hand, then made a broad sweeping gesture that invited them to sit down.

"Don't thank me," Jimmy continued, "your sponsors reserved these seats for you."

"I don't have a sponsor!" Paul and Angela responded in unison.

Jimmy's smile widened.

"Okay, okay," he reassured them both, "I understand the situation you pigeons are in, and I will sponsor you both for now. Only for now, though, and that could change at any moment. So, listen to your sponsor. Sit down and shut up."

"This is bullshit," Angela said, and sat down next to Paul.

"You're welcome," Jimmy replied, "enjoy the show."

He walked away.

Soon Diane entered the room and sat next to Angela, praising her for picking a seat so close to the front.

"I hid in the back for weeks when I first started coming," Diane said. "You are so brave!"

This made Paul laugh. Angela punched him in the arm.

The chairperson that night was a woman whom Paul vaguely remembered seeing at meetings in the past. She reported being sober for six years and explained how her sobriety had been a one-day-at-a-time process so far. She kept her initial sharing short before asking for topics from the crowd related to recovery or the A.A. program.

"My name is Joseph Meer," a voice said without waiting to be called on by the chairperson, "and I'd like to hear about gratitude."

Paul didn't turn around, but he knew exactly where Joseph Meer was sitting. It was the chair he always occupied during this meeting, and any new member who was not aware that the seat was permanently reserved would be warmly warned and redirected. Joseph Meer was also known for bringing up the topic of gratitude at almost every meeting he attended. Unlike other people who would bring up topics and give a short explanation of why they wanted to hear them, *I need to hear about acceptance tonight because I'm struggling to accept that I'm an alcoholic*, Joseph Meer never expounded on his interest in gratitude.

Some folks found it even stranger because he carried himself in such an off-putting way most of the time. He was the first one to flag a topic or discussion for veering away from the subject of alcoholism, insisting that all topics should be confined to problems with drinking. He quoted passages from *The Big Book*, the original text outlining the A.A. program, and used these quotes to assert a tacit but rigid set of rules and structure for interpreting the Twelve Steps.

"People talk about the steps being suggestions," Joseph would rant. "The Twelve Steps are more than suggestions. *The Big Book* is not full of suggestions! It is full of instructions. My first sponsor told me to read the book and count every use of the word 'must.' One hundred and thirty-four! The original text of *A.A.* contained one hundred and thirty-four 'must's required for anyone to stay sober!"

Paul had never fact-checked the one hundred and thirty-four *musts* but thought he might ask Angela to try it sometime soon on her new phone. He realized that the exact number was not as significant as the sentiment. The primary *musts* involved commitment, dedication, and an honest willingness to go to any lengths to stay away from that first drink or the first drug. Joseph Meer may have been a grumpy, rigid, no-nonsense old-timer within the A.A. Program, but his message was accurate and vital. His mythical presence and his harping on gratitude as a discussion topic embodied *the* path to recovery and the things one must do to maintain it.

A hand went up near where Paul and Angela were sitting.

"Hi everyone, I'm Amanda and I'm an alcoholic."

"Hi Amanda," the crowd said in unison.

"Gratitude is a great topic for me to think about tonight. I'm grateful to have choices today," Amanda said to the group. "I didn't realize how many choices I'd given up until I stopped drinking. Alcohol was making all the decisions for me. Where I would go, who I would spend time with, what I spent money on, pretty much everything in my life. It was my Higher Power. And the funny thing about that was, when I got in here, to these rooms, I wanted nothing to do with God, with the Higher Power everyone kept telling me could restore me to sanity and take away my addiction. I thought I had everything in control, that I had been calling all the shots. I was taking lots of shots, but I sure wasn't calling any!"

Laughter filled the room.

"Thanks Amanda," voices inflected in unison.

There was no halftime break for this meeting; instead, people stood sporadically and moved to refill coffee cups, use the bathrooms, or step outside to smoke. Others raised their hands and, when called upon, talked about gratitude, their struggles with sobriety, and the strange, wonderful, challenging worlds that now surrounded them as sober people.

Near the end of the meeting, Paul glimpsed a figure entering and sitting by the door. He felt the person staring at him but resisted the urge to respond. The figure rose and walked toward the bathrooms. Paul recognized the work boots. It was the drug dealer from their group at St. Michael's last week. It surprised Paul to see him here and upset him when the young man slithered over to Angela after the meeting ended and began talking with her.

For the first time in a long time, he felt seized by paternal protection. Paul told himself Angela was smart and tough and could undoubtedly handle herself—and seeing her talking to this guy awakened an instinctive and reliable fear in him. Diane had shuffled Paul off to a corner of the room and was airing various grievances about St. Michael's to him. His head pounded with the effort of listening to her and keeping an eye on Angela.

The young man in the work boots leaned in close, whispered something confidentially into Angela's ear, and walked to the front of the room, where the chairperson was collecting her things. He took out a sheet of paper and grabbed a pen from the table, handing both items to the chairwoman. Paul realized then that his primary motivation in coming tonight had been to get this signature. Most likely, he had been mandated to attend these meetings by probation, and the signature was a requirement of that mandate.

"What did he want?" Paul asked Angela when she walked over.

"Steve?" Angela asked. "Oh, he probably wanted to get laid. He's harmless."

She looked at Paul and smiled. He said nothing.

"He's a dick! Don't worry about it. I can't believe he even showed up here!"

"You saw. He didn't stick around long."

Jimmy C. came up from behind them and began clapping loudly. He was surrounded by a group of people, many of whom looked to be around Angela's age.

"The pigeons made it through their first meeting of the ninety and ninety! Only eighty-nine more to go!"

"But we've been going to meetings every night!" Angela protested.

"Yes," Jimmy agreed, "yes, you have. That is good, but your ninety and ninety didn't start until you were officially working with a sponsor. And that happened today! We're going out for coffee now, and you two are invited to join us—I know it's probably past this old guy's bedtime by now."

"That it is," Paul agreed, "but thanks for the invite."

"And you, young lady?" Jimmy said, addressing Angela.

"No thanks," she said.

"No problem," Jimmy answered. "We'll see you two tomorrow night at the Fight for Your Life Group over on Elm St. Remember where that meeting is, Paul?"

Paul nodded his head.

"Very good, then! See you there." Jimmy said.

He led his procession of young people past them and outside, as he launched into a story about two alcoholics and a broken lawnmower.

"You can go with them if you want to," Paul said to Angela. "I mean, don't feel like you have to stick around with me. I'm sure Jimmy would give you a ride home later. He may come across like a bastard, but he's got a heart of gold. He's one of the good guys."

"Yeah," Angela said, "I can see that."

She watched Jimmy and the group walk out the doors and into the night. "But I'm not ready to get all social and happy with my new sober buddies just yet. I'll stick with the grouchy but good-hearted bastard that didn't throw me in the trunk of his car last week for right now."

"Fair enough," Paul said. "But it might be time for you to raise your standards for defining a good-hearted person. How big is the trunk of the car that Steve drives?

She rolled her eyes at him, and they walked out together.

CHAPTER 35

"No relationships in the first year of recovery! Stick to the three M's instead: meetings, meditation, and masturbation."

Lenny T., Mickey R.'s first sponsor, on dating

"It's called a rehab romance," the professor said.

Lamont, who brought up the topic, covered his mouth dramatically to stifle a laugh.

"So, it's pretty common for two people to, you know, hook up in treatment?" Lamont asked.

"Oh yes," the professor answered. "Very common." How many people here have heard of two patients getting involved in a romantic relationship or acting out sexually during treatment?"

Every hand in the room went up.

"Well, there you go." The professor said and shrugged his shoulders to suggest the inevitability.

Another hand went up.

"Yes, Christina?"

"Should we throw someone out of treatment because they start flirting with another patient? I mean, I've seen people start these relationships at the halfway house I'm interning at. As soon as the staff finds out, they talk to the people involved and put them on a contract. If they discharged a patient immediately for flirting, I'd be really upset. It seems natural to start having feelings in recovery. Maybe, it's a teachable moment about relationships and boundaries and all of that."

The professor let Christina's thoughts linger. He looked around the room with his eyebrows raised.

"What about substituting," a voice said.

"What was that, Gary? Say that again."

"Oh," Gary said, starting to blush and moving in his seat nervously.

He was an older student who told Travis and the rest of the class that he decided to get into counseling after years of being in recovery himself. The professor reminded him, subtly but consistently, that he needed to beware of too much self-disclosure and focus on the patient's experience.

"I was just thinking," Gary said, "that I know," he hesitated. "For many people in early sobriety, from what I've heard," he smiled sheepishly at the professor, who smiled back, "it's common to substitute one drug or one feel-good behavior for another. These people falling in love with each other or messing around in the broom closet with each other aren't in love. They're just acting out on that want, on that craving to feel good. This is old brain stuff, that lizard brain reaction you taught us about. The caveman part of our brain wants what it wants when it wants it. How was that?"

People were laughing, nodding their heads.

The professor looked around.

"I think that made sense to everyone," the professor affirmed.

"And as long as Gary has brought it up, who can tell us why that old brain, the lizard brain as it's been called, can be so powerful?"

"Because it is faster than our new brain!" Darnell yelled out.

"Correct!" the professor said.

"Because it controls the things we need to do to live!" Amber added.

"Yes," the professor agreed.

He walked out from behind his desk and moved his hands in a rolling motion, prompting them to say more.

"And what things does the old brain tell us we need to do to live?"

"Eat!" yelled Jason.

"Breathe!" Alisha added.

"Run away! Fight or flight!" Heather said.

"Yes, yes, all true," the professor agreed, but you're missing one. The one that we're talking about…"

"Sex!" Grace exclaimed, then burst out in self-conscious laughter as the class turned to laugh with her.

The professor smiled, shaking his head and chuckling.

"Thanks, Grace," he added, trying to keep a straight face.

"Yes, sex, because we're all programmed with that instinctual drive. It's natural, and it can be very strong."

"Stronger in some of us than others!" Lamont shouted. "This patient at my clinic has been caught messing around with different people three or four times since I've been there!"

The students' laughter rose and fell again.

"It's that lizard brain wiring," the professor continued, "and for your patients in early recovery, people who are used to instant gratification, those cravings, and that drive is hard to resist. They're substituting, looking for that high, just like Gary said. And part of our job is to point out that they are doing it. They are substituting one high for another. Unfortunately, we also have to discharge some patients from treatment if they continually break these rules because they cannot resist these urges. We have an obligation to keep our patients safe from harm, *while* we think about what is best for all patients in the clinic. A patient who acts out sexually, or worse yet, someone who targets people to use for sex, can make the entire treatment environment unsafe.

"Yes, but—" Travis interjected, and withdrew when he realized he had not raised his hand.

"Go ahead, Travis," the professor prompted.

"What if people—if patients, I mean—are forming healthy friendships and relationships with each other? Isn't that part of what we try to teach patients, how to interact, communicate, and trust others? If we're constantly on guard for people running off to have sex or punishing them for flirting with each other, isn't that kind of a mixed message? Isn't it healthy for people to learn better communication skills in sobriety?"

Travis wasn't sure where the questions had come from or why he'd been compelled to ask them.

The professor scanned the room again in the ensuing silence. When it became clear that nobody was going to comment, he spoke.

"It is a mixed message, right? A requirement of maintaining sobriety is learning to trust others, to open up, and build sober supports. *But,* the minute we counselors and helpers think that patients might be developing deeper feelings for each other, we tell them to stop it, that something is wrong with them for feeling these emotions. By doing this, we often encourage dishonesty about self-expression, especially when it comes to talking to us about relationships. This approach closes open communication and trust between a counselor and a patient. They might feel like they must hide things from us. The trust issue is similar for patients who are on parole or probation. We tell them to be honest, to let us know if they're staying sober, but if they admit to drinking or taking drugs, they know the information will send them to jail. These mixed messages make our jobs as counselors more difficult. It is one of those gray areas, where right and wrong don't hold up."

"So, what do we do about that?" Travis asked. "I mean, how do we continue to build trust and to help them?

"Well, that's another million-dollar question, isn't it?" The professor answered. "It's a real conundrum, a Catch-22, a difficult and perplexing place to find yourself in."

The professor walked back and leaned on his podium officiously. He smiled out to the class.

"Seriously, let's go back to Travis' original question. Is there a chance that these behaviors in early recovery could be positive for patients? Are they opportunities to learn something? To grow intimacy in relationships? When we trust others, we make ourselves vulnerable. We might even get hurt and make mistakes along the way. Is that such a bad thing? Even if patients cross boundaries in these early days of sobriety, can't they grow and learn from their new experiences? Shouldn't growth and learning be allowed? And aren't we supposed to guide them in this, to be a safety net along the way? What is the benefit of throwing someone out of treatment after pulling them out of that broom closet, or when they admit to slipping and drinking over the weekend? Is that really in any patient's best interest? Remember what you have learned about ethics. Ethics involves doing what is right and good for the patient, but there are times when the ethical answer conflicts with a rule or law. Therefore, for now, when those things happen, you must—"

"Seek out supervision!" several voices said in unison.

"You have learned well, grasshoppers! Always run these dilemmas by your supervisors. You don't want to make these big decisions by yourself, especially this early in your career. But—welcome to the grey area—I want you to start listening and trusting your internal compasses when these questions and issues arise. The authors of the original A.A. text referred to our consciences as *a still, small, voice within*, and I think that was accurate. We all have that voice. Learning to listen to it and to follow it, takes time, practice, and courage. There will be times when you bend the rules, maybe even break some rules, in the name of what is good and right. But for now, keep watching, and listening, and learning."

When the class ended, Christina walked beside Travis toward the parking lot.

"Do you think your patient is messing around with someone?" She asked.

"No," he said, in a voice he thought sounded too defensive.

"No," he repeated, smiling. "It's just, we tell patients to lean on each other during treatment. We push them to open up, to bare their souls, to trust each other. Day after day they share things they might never have told anyone else, and then we're surprised if they cross boundaries or get emotionally attached to each other. It's…"

"Fucked up?" Christina offered.

"Yeah," Travis said, smiling wider. "It's sort of fucked up."

CHAPTER 36

"I don't do business with drug addicts, period! My business partners are legitimate, hard-working business owners who built this town from the ground up. Why would I need to take money from the low lifes? This is just another example of why we need to get these people out of Deerfield."

Anthony Pelligrino, in an interview with a local reporter.

Paul woke early, dressed, and went out to start a pot of coffee. Angela had already done it. She was sitting under a blanket on the living room couch, watching Lester Whiteside on TV. He looked like Elmer Fudd as he stood in front of the weather screen with an oversized buffalo plaid hunter's cap, and matching mittens. Lester shivered melodramatically, emphasizing his kooky warning of the cold to come. The map behind him was painted in shades of blue, some places slightly brighter than others, but all indicating temperatures in the single digits or below.

Paul had felt the bite of cold—that distinctive Northeastern cold—when they left the meeting last night.

"I'm making breakfast," Angela announced.

She emerged from the blanket and headed to the kitchen.

Paul went to the basement to replace the filthy furnace filter that had been in service far past its usefulness. He couldn't remember when he last put a new filter in place, and was grateful that his fuel oil deliveries were scheduled automatically.

There were so many things required to keep a house running and orderly, minute details necessary to avoid mishaps and move one's small life along. It seemed impressive and strange that he was blessed with things like electricity, the furnace, the walls and roof, running water. Somehow all these things had continued through the negligence and haze of his drinking over the last few years. He thought about Angela staying at the Thoroughbred Hotel, with the rusty water and stained mattresses. He thought about the waiting room at the Department of Social Services. And he thought about Joseph Meer going from a well-respected businessman to a scorned bum living in the woods, to an icon of recovery. Gratitude indeed, Joseph.

Paul heard a car's motor in the driveway and emerged into the living room. It was 8:58 A.M., two minutes until Victor opened the liquor store. He wondered if the brown-haired woman was waiting in her SUV—just another sick and suffering alcoholic. There were plenty of those anonymous stories in the world as well, waiting and hoping for the miracle to happen.

Paul walked to the door and opened it just as Roscoe topped the front steps.

"Good morning, officer. I hope you have a warrant."

"Not this time," Roscoe replied, "but I did bring these."

He held up a paper bag from the Jim Dandy Bakery in Deerfield.

"Are those Jelly-Bellies?" Paul asked.

"You know it. Only the best for my friends."

"Well, I'm truly honored. So much so that I won't make a joke about cops and doughnuts."

Roscoe followed Paul into the kitchen, where Angela was standing at the stove.

"Is that a backup plan in case my cooking is too gross to eat?" Angela asked, pointing to the bag in Roscoe's hand.

"No," he said and placed the bag on the kitchen table while he shrugged off his coat and hung it on the back of a chair. "But you can never go wrong with donuts. They're good anytime."

Paul poured the sheriff a cup of coffee and brought it to him.

"Thanks," Roscoe said. He sipped. "So, there was a big drug bust in town the other day, did you two hear about it?"

Angela shook her head.

"No, why, was it anyone we know?" Paul asked.

"Maybe. A few of them were locals, but the majority were from The City. They were the big bust, the major dealers everyone wanted to catch."

Angela divided the eggs and bacon she'd been cooking onto three plates and carried them over to the table. She sat down across from Roscoe in Sean's chair.

"Thank you," Roscoe said. "These look delicious. I mention this because I had to go to court yesterday, and that new D.A. I told you about was there. It turns out that a bunch of these guys are on Tony Pelligrino's payroll. As a matter of fact, a few of them were renting out one of Tony's apartments; it looks like they were selling from there."

"Wow," Paul said and picked up a piece of bacon from his plate. "Where was this place?"

Roscoe bit into a slice of bacon.

"Now this is a good breakfast! I can't remember the last time I had bacon. Stephanie would freak out if she saw this, but it's worth it! The apartment is on the West Side, in that new development Tony opened last year—very high end. That's what got our attention to begin with. These geniuses were cruising around the methadone clinics and the roach motels in a brand-new Lexus. That car stuck out like a sore thumb around here!"

Roscoe took a sip from his coffee and speared some egg.

"These are delicious, too."

He looked at Angela.

"You should open a diner. You'd get rich!"

She smiled.

"This girl's got many talents," Paul agreed, "she could do just about anything she sets her mind to and get rich at it. So, it sounds like Tony's got some explaining to do?"

"Oh, yeah," Roscoe agreed. "He's in a tight spot now, especially since he started to push the City Council into knocking down the homeless shelter to make room for more of his overpriced McCondos on that side of town. The press doesn't know about all of the connections in this latest bust, but as soon as they do, they'll have a field day pulling up quotes of Tony talking about all the criminals and dope dealers living at the shelter and how his project will clean all that up."

"Couldn't happen to a nicer guy. I guess we picked a good time to get sober," Paul said to Angela. "This might dry up the drug supply around here for a while."

"Not for long," Roscoe and Angela said in unison.

"Unfortunately, there's always someone else, another jackal waiting in the wings when one goes down. This won't stop the drug problem around here, but it will certainly give Mr. Pelligrino a major headache. And the reason I'm telling you about all this is that you just became much less important to our eager new D.A. He's got bigger fish to fry."

Paul's first thought was that he could drink and most likely get away with it now."

"Well, that's great news," he said. "Thanks for letting me know. I'll have to call John and fill him in."

"Don't call just yet," Roscoe said. "As I said, this is all just playing out, and some of its not public knowledge; so, I'd appreciate it if you give it a few days. I wouldn't be surprised if John finds out and calls you first. I'm also pretty sure that someone's going to talk to the newspaper—someone always does, and once that happens, everything is fair game."

Roscoe looked at his watch. "Well, I'd better get to work. I have a feeling that today is going to involve helping people with frozen locks, dead batteries, and frostbit fingers."

He stood up and removed his coat from the chair.

"Angela, thank you for the fine breakfast. I'm not sure that Paul will tell you how much sunshine you've brought into this place, but it sure feels a lot better when I walk in here these days. It smells a hell of a lot better, too."

"Well, that's me," Angela said, "little Miss Sunshine!"

She grabbed a donut from the bag.

"Thanks for bringing these! And thanks for not shooting this old grouch or locking him up."

She pointed a finger toward Paul.

"I thought it would be weird hanging out with a cop, you know, because I think every other time I've been around one, they were hassling me or dragging someone off in handcuffs, but you don't seem like a normal police officer."

"'Protect and serve,' isn't that what we're here for? (Besides buying donuts, I mean.) Help yourself to mine – that breakfast you made was more than enough."

Roscoe pulled on his coat and zipped it.

"And in terms of what's normal, I think it was this old grouch that told me that normal is just a setting on a washing machine. 'Course I'm glad to hear that I'm helping you get over your cop-phobia."

He walked toward the door. "Thanks again. You two stay warm," he looked at Paul, "and dry!"

That night they went to the Fight for Your Life Group. It was a speaker's meeting, which meant most of the hour would be spent listening to the chairperson share his or her story of addiction and recovery. Paul and Angela sat in the front row, knowing they would be escorted there by Jimmy anyway. Joseph Meer had greeted them with a stern glance and a slight nod of his head when they entered. Diane was as excited as usual to see them both again.

Instead of the traditional gavel to start the meeting, the chairperson rang a small, hand-held bell, which was meant to symbolize the start of another round of fighting against addiction. Michael "Mickey" Reerdan rang the bell tonight from the front table. Mickey had started the Fight for Your Life Group, and he was also the driving force behind two youth clubhouses that opened in Deerfield and Moheneck Falls in the late 1990s. Mickey's father had been an Olympic boxer who brought his only son up as a fighter, expecting that Mickey would continue the family legacy.

But that dream was not to be. Mickey was good at fighting and he distinguished himself as a force to be reckoned with in regional bouts during his high school years. But when his father was diagnosed with late-stage pancreatic cancer and died only weeks later, Mickey lost all motivation to continue with the sport. He barely managed to graduate, and by his nineteenth birthday, Mickey found himself fighting against stronger opponents than he'd ever faced in the ring. He was drinking and smoking cigarettes to numb out his grief, and when that didn't work anymore, he reached for everything and anything else he could find to help him forget. His mother begged and cried and pleaded with him to stop. She waited anxiously each night for the phone to ring and to hear that Mickey was in the hospital, or jail, or dead. One night that call finally came.

Mickey spoke about that phone call now. According to him, his current sobriety began after waking up in jail that night and having no idea how his face, knuckles, and clothes had been blood-stained. He was in a small cell, with nobody around, and no clue where he was or how he got there. Mickey had always had claustrophobia, and the small, concrete space sent him immediately into what he described as his first full-blown panic attack. He screamed and cried and wailed for what felt like hours before he heard the distinctive sound of a metal door sliding open, keys jangling, and footsteps coming closer.

"We had a hell of a time with you last night," the tall, Black, muscular guard who appeared in front of his cell said.

He twirled a large keyring around his finger.

"Where am I?" Mickey asked, embarrassed at the fear he heard in his voice.

"What happened?"

The guard studied him before speaking again.

"Are you really going to try the 'I don't remember anything defense?'" The guard finally asked. "Because the judge has heard that one a million times, and I can tell you it only pisses her off."

"But I don't remember! I'm serious!" Mickey implored.

"I drank too much. I remember being downstairs somewhere. It was Kenny's house, I think. We were shooting pool. There were only five or six people down there. Some girls showed up. They wanted to go to Deerfield, to go dancing or something, but that's all I can remember."

He looked directly into the guard's face.

"That's really all I can remember. I'm not making this up."

"Uh-huh," the guard responded, looking at Mickey for a long time and then at the floor.

"Well, whether you remember it or not, that kid you killed last night, and his family will never forget it, and they'll never forget you."

Mickey described the feeling at that moment: "a complete collapse of everything inside" him.

"It was like all my guts, all my feelings, and my whole life just crashed down. There was nothing left of me or for me. I couldn't believe how quickly my whole life, I mean everything around me, could be gone just like that."

Mickey looked out at the people in the meeting, his eyes roaming over the faces, wondering, perhaps, if anyone could truly relate to that horrible moment.

"And all because of having a few beers, you know?"

He went back to telling his story and said that after the guard told him about the accident, he fell back, landing onto the metal-framed cot in the small cell. Everything around him tilted sideways and went out of focus. The thought that he'd killed someone, taken someone else's life, was too much. He lurched toward the small, steel toilet in the corner of the cell and vomited repeatedly, losing control of his bladder, and soiling his pants in the process. He looked toward the bars of the cell, but the guard was gone. So, he laid there, on the cold cement floor, for what felt like a lifetime before the same guard returned to take him in front of the judge.

It turned out that Mickey had not, in fact, killed anyone during his blackout the night before. This fact was confirmed by the judge, who informed Mickey that he was charged with being drunk and disorderly and for destruction of public property. The vandalism was discovered after townsfolk had called the police the previous night, complaining of a "loud and drunken young man" who was punching in the mailboxes, pushing over street signs, and disturbing the peace in every way. The police followed a trail of destruction that led directly to Mickey, passed out in a wicker chair on the porch of Warren Harrison, who happened to be Sandra Harrison's brother, the judge he stood before in court that day.

Judge Harrison ordered Mickey to have an evaluation for substance abuse and to remain under the supervision of probation for one year while keeping himself sober and his legal status clean. She also ordered him to come up with the money to replace the mailboxes and street signs he'd destroyed as well as buying a new wicker chair for her sister-in-law, who planned to burn the chair he'd passed out in.

The surprise and relief Mickey felt in those moments was difficult for him to convey. As he told the story from the front of the meeting, his voice faltered, and he needed a few moments to collect himself before continuing.

"At first," Mickey said, "I thought that guard was a real monster for telling me that. For trying to trick me, you know? And as he walked me out of that courtroom, me smelling like piss and shit and covered in blood and vomit, neither of us said a word about it. I thought about screaming at him, asking him why he pulled a dirty trick like that, but I didn't say anything. I just wanted to get the hell out of there."

A smile formed on Mickey's face as he told the next part of his story.

"I didn't think I would ever see that guard again. And that would have been just fine with me. But then, a few months later, he shows up. It was after I had started treatment at St. Michael's, and I was working with a counselor who was also a recovering drunk."

Mickey winked at Paul.

"So, this guy kept bugging me to get to A.A. meetings. Finally, I dragged my butt to the meetings, mostly just to get that counselor to shut up, and who shows up there but that big, badass guard from the jail cell. He came right up to me when he saw me there, and part of me wanted to punch him in the face, but the other part wanted to thank him. He asked me if I was ready to fight for my life as hard as I had been fighting to stay sick, angry, and drunk. It turned out the guard had fifteen years sober. He was my first sponsor, and he's the one who gave me the strength to come back to life, to get those youth centers opened for kids who were starting down the same bad road I went down, and to start this A.A. group. When he died, I bawled my eyes out. I remember all the people that went to his funeral. I couldn't believe the crowd that showed up there. So many of them had stories just like mine, where they'd been in jail, and this guy made them think about what could have happened—how things could get so much worse. I never used to believe in angels, but I do now."

Mickey talked for most of the meeting, and when he was done, people around the room raised their hands and spoke about their own struggles with recovery. Some folks talked about how they could relate to Mickey's story and the similar angels in their own stories, people who got them into A.A. when they needed it most.

"I remember that funeral," Joseph Meer said when he was called on to share, "the line stretched around the funeral home, down the street, and around the corner. That's the impact we can make on people when we sober up through this program. We leave a legacy that we never really deserved. It is given to us through grace and the Twelve Steps. If you don't believe me, try going to the funeral of an active drunk or someone who showed up here in A.A. for a while, but then had the smart idea to go back and take a drink or two. I've been to those funerals, too, and I'm here to tell you it's a whole different feeling. Not many people are there to pay respects. Most of the visitors, and probably the dearly deceased themselves, are just glad the pain is over."

At the close of the meeting, Paul and Angela walked to the front of the room and stood next to Mickey, holding hands with others in a large circle around the room as they recited *The Serenity Prayer*.

God, grant me the serenity,

To accept the things I cannot change,

The courage to change the things I can,

And the wisdom to know the difference.

"It's good to see you!" Mickey said, smiling broadly and embracing Paul in a tight hug.

"It's good to see you, too, Mick," Paul responded. "You look great, and it's always nice to hear you speak."

"Yes, well, you told me a long time ago that recovery could take me to places I couldn't possibly imagine, and that's definitely been true." Mickey looked over at Angela. "Some people only get one guardian angel in a lifetime, but I think I actually had two. I wouldn't be here if it hadn't been for this guy!"

Mickey reached out his hand to her.

"I'm Mickey. Nice to meet you."

"Angela" she said. "I guess I wouldn't be here either if it wasn't for Paul."

"Yeah," Paul said, shaking his head, "well, if I'm supposed to be your angel down here, I'd sure like to get some wings for it!"

"Maybe you're earning them now," Mickey said, laughing. "You're like Clarence in that movie about the guy who almost kills himself. Come to think of it; you do kind of look like that guy!"

Paul shook his head as Mickey continued to laugh. Angela looked on, not understanding the reference.

"You'll have to watch the movie, Angela," Mickey said. "You should come down to the gym sometime."

Mickey pulled out a small stack of business cards and handed her one. It read:

Mickey's Gym

35 Stone Brook Road

Open every day 7 am – 7 pm

(266) 431 – 5656

"We're closed on some holidays," he continued, "so just be sure to call and make sure of the hours each week. It's free, and we've got some excellent self-defense classes."

"Do you have a website?" Angela asked, which made Mickey laugh. "Not yet," he said, "but maybe you can build us one!"

Paul raised his hand, waving at Mickey as he turned to walk toward the door.

"Good night, you two," Mickey said.

He picked up the small bell from the table, shaking it playfully.

"And don't worry Paul, those wings will be coming soon enough! Every time you hear a bell ring, right?"

"He was an interesting guy," Angela said on the car ride home.

She was looking at the screen of her phone, busy punching at the buttons.

"He certainly is. Well, we all got a story, right? That movie he was talking about, the one with the angel, it's an old film called…"

It's a Wonderful Life, Angela said, reading from the lit screen in her lap. "Starring James Stewart and Donna Reed, whoever the hell they were. Henry Travers played Clarence, the angel. But don't worry, you look a little younger than him, and just as dorky."

"Uh huh," Paul responded. "Well, it's a good story, worth watching sometime. I may even have the VHS tape at home somewhere."

"Or maybe they'll have it at the picture show one of these days!" Angela said after a short silence. "I'll just need to come up with a nickel to watch it at the movie house!"

She held up the small screen on her phone to show Paul that the movie was playing.

"Very funny," he said, shaking his head. "I don't remember movies ever costing a nickel, just so you know."

They drove on through the night, the car's heater blowing warm air, and the quaky voice of Jimmy Stewart questioning his worth in the world.

CHAPTER 37

"Well, you'd better find a man to take care of you,
because you'll never make it on your own."

Michelle LaPoint, advice for her twelve-year-old daughter, Angela

Paul tried sitting in the car with the engine turned off, but it became uncomfortably cold in minutes. He couldn't stop replaying the words Mickey had said to him the night before at the meeting: *Clarence, the angel.* It was meant as a joke, a compliment really, and Paul usually would have seen it as just that.

That was the problem. He was feeling unusual today and wasn't sure why. Jimmy or one of the A.A. crowd might tell him that he was harboring a resentment about Mickey's joke, and maybe that was true, but why would being compared to an angel piss him off?

He turned the key in the ignition and started the car up again. He wasn't in the mood for music, so he scanned the channels looking for news or some decent talk radio show.

"It's clear that this President has done more for our country than any other in my long lifetime."

He kept going.

"Sure, this guy in the White House has made some progress, but so did Hitler before he started loading everyone who wasn't part of his 'master race' onto the trains."

He hit the scan button.

"Next up on our show, we're going to have a spokesperson for the Federal Bureau of Alcohol, Tobacco, and Firearms to talk about new findings from a year-long federally funded study which shows how moderate use of alcohol and nicotine can lengthen your life."

"Ha!" Paul said and punched the radio's power button off just as Angela walked out of the building. He saw her pull the army coat tightly around herself.

"Holy shit, it's cold," she said as she landed in the passenger's seat.

"Yup," he agreed, "how did the session with Mandy go?" He started to back out of the parking space.

"Oh, you know Mandy. It's always an adventure with her! She spent most of the time grilling me about why I'm staying at your place."

"You told her about that?"

"I didn't need to. Ms. Fulmer called to ask her about sending the paperwork she never bothered to fax over to D.S.S. I guess it came up then. Not that I care, really, but Mandy couldn't stop yapping about it."

"Screw her," Paul said, "It's not like she can get me fired at this point. It's probably better that she and everyone else in there knows you're staying with me, so it doesn't seem like we're trying to hide anything. Did she give you any useful suggestions or tips about what to do next?"

"Only to get out of your house before you drink again, which she assured me would happen very soon." Angela laughed. "It was funny because when I asked her where I should live, she had no fucking idea.

She said, "I thought you could go live with your dad if you wanted to." She actually said that! The weird part is that I like her in a way. I mean, I respect her, I guess. She never pretends to be something she's not, and she's not one of those touchy, feely women that's gets all choked up or pretends to be all broken up by someone else's problems."

"What you see is what you get," Paul agreed, "and I'm glad you respect her. She wasn't always like this, you know, back when she was my intern…"

"No shit! You trained her?" Angela interrupted. "Wow! Well, I wouldn't brag about that too much!"

Paul shook his head and stopped the car at a red light. "What I was going to say was that she changed since she first started in this work. She wasn't always so, well, snarky, I guess."

Angela looked at him. "Snarky, really?"

"I thought saying bitchy would be too misogynistic."

She rolled her eyes. "You're coming a long way in your recovery and acceptance of others."

"I'm pretty close to being cured," he agreed and stepped on the gas as the light turned green.

"So, tonight we're going to a…"

Angela's phone began vibrating.

"I don't know this number," she said, looking at the screen.

"You'll know who it is when you answer it," he said over the fourth ring.

She hesitated, then punched a button.

"Hello?"

Paul saw her body stiffen in the seat.

"Mom?"

She listened for a minute.

"How did you get this number?"

"What does that have to do with me?"

"No. No, that's not true. Glenn's a fucking liar…I'm just staying with a friend…Well, yeah, he's older but—he's not—it's just not like that. It's just not like that."

Paul pulled into a convenience store and stopped the car.

"Do you want me to talk with her?" he whispered.

Angela's eyes were closed, and Paul noticed how different she looked. How young she was, a child.

"I'm not going to do that," she said, "that's not an option. You need to call someone else. Go somewhere else."

She listened, her face tightening.

"No! Fuck that! I'm not meeting you anywhere. Have you called Olivia yet?…I know…I know where she lives, but maybe it's time you let her deal with some of this shit show!"

"I can talk to her," Paul said, louder this time.

Angela looked at him, shaking her head.

"I know that…Yes, I know that because I was there, remember? No, that's not true, I told you already. He's a liar…I don't care if you call the cops, or if he does, because I didn't fucking do anything wrong!"

Paul could hear the quiver in her voice. The façade she tried so hard to keep up was crumbling.

He reached out his hand, signaling for her to hand him the phone. She hesitated then handed it over.

"And if you think you're going to leave me—leave your mother—out here to take the weight of your bullshit, you've got another thing coming, you little bitch. Don't forget where you came from. Don't forget what I know…"

"Ms. LaPoint?" Paul said firmly into the receiver.

The rant stopped immediately.

"Who is this?" she asked.

"This is Paul, Angela's friend. I wanted to let you know that she's okay. She's safe. Right now, she's getting help at St. Michael's, and I'm letting her stay at a room in my house, but she's making progress. She's staying sober and…."

"Well, good for her! That's just well and fine for dear little Angela, isn't it? But what about me, Mr. Sugar Daddy? I know all about you. I hear you're one of those alcohol counselors. I'm sure there's lots of people, including the cops, that would want to know why you've moved such a pretty, young, little addict into your place. She's almost a minor, you know, practically jailbait, you old pervert! Not that it will stop her from doing whatever she needs to do to get what she wants!"

"No," Paul said.

He felt himself slipping, losing his sense of calm.

"No, Ms. LaPoint, I'm not a counselor, at least not anymore. I'm just another patient at St. Michael's. I met Angela over there, and I only invited her to stay here, in my son's old room, because she was standing at the bus stop during that snowstorm, the one we had last week, on Thursday night. Her boyfriend, Glenn, I guess his name is, had told her…"

"So, you're an addict too? Oh, this just gets better and better! And does that rehab know that you two have run off together? That's something else! And don't you believe everything she tells you, buddy! Glenn only wanted what was right for her. He tried to help her. Why she wouldn't even be in that rehab if it wasn't for him! He's torn up over her taking off. That poor boy was only trying to help, to get her better, but she chewed him up and spit him out, just like she'll do with you. You'll see, she'll…"

"What is it you want?" Paul interrupted, raising his voice.

Some of the most successful techniques Paul had used for people who were broken beyond repair hadn't been learned in a classroom or in one of the required St. Michael's trainings about quality care and keeping with the mission of the agency. These involved interrupting people, setting an edge in your tone, speaking over them, and getting progressively louder and angrier. Some people needed a blunt reminder that there was, in fact, a power differential and that white male privilege existed. Showing dominance and aggression, instilling just a pinch of fear into certain people, those who refused to hear anything else, was sometimes the only option. There were times when the gloves just had to come off.

"I want what's best for my daughter," Ms. LaPoint said, "I want to make sure she's safe."

"That's bullshit," Paul said. "What are you really looking for? What's the ask here? Money? Is that it? How much?"

Silence on the line.

"Because if you're looking for a payout," Paul continued, "it's not going to happen. I told you before that Angela is staying with me temporarily until she can find a safe place to live while she keeps going to treatment and working on her recovery. If you have an issue with that, you call whoever you need to, or go wherever you need to, but don't come sniffing around her or me for a handout because that's not going to happen."

"Well, we'll just see about that, Paul Durkin," the voice snarled before the line went dead.

Paul handed Angela the phone and looked out the car's windshield at the entrance to the convenience store. A man in tattered clothes was sitting cross-legged on a piece of cardboard on the frozen sidewalk, a small bag of what Paul assumed were his worldly possessions lay by his side. He held up a small, cardboard sign.

"Injured in War. Anything helps. God Bless."

"So, that's my mom," Angela said.

"Yeah," Paul responded, "I figured that part out. You've both got a certain way of brightening people's days."

He looked over at her and smiled.

"You're an asshole," she said and smiled back.

CHAPTER 38

"Of course, he's a fucking mess. His kid killed himself and he just climbed out of the bottle after about five years of heavy drinking. You know Paul as well as I do. If he just focuses on himself and doesn't try to save the rest of the world right now, I'm hoping he'll get his shit together."

Matt Denton to Bill Hughes regarding Paul Durkin's case.

Paul set down two editions of *Alcoholics Anonymous* on the kitchen table, where Angela was peeling an orange.

"What's this for?" she asked.

"Tonight, we're going to a *Big Book* Meeting. We'll be reading from a section of this book before discussing what we read.

"That sounds stupid and boring," she said, "maybe I'll stay home."

Paul didn't say anything but slid one of the books in front of her. She picked it up and flipped through the pages.

"How come yours looks different than this one?" She asked.

"Mine is an older edition. The one you have is the newest. Most of the material is the same, but they added things in the second part, mostly more personal stories, over the years. You can keep that one. You should read through it in your spare time, you know, when you're not too busy on your phone."

"I can probably download it to my phone!" she countered.

"Yup," he agreed, "you probably can. Or you can just read that one." He looked at his watch. "Time to go!"

"Woah!" Jimmy exclaimed when he saw Angela and Paul coming into the meeting. "You gave her the new copy with all the pictures in it! And does that version you're carrying have Bill W.'s signature? It sure as hell looks old enough. You could get good money for that at an auction if you blew all the dust off it. It's probably in great condition, too, because I doubt you ever read a page of it!"

Paul just smiled through the barrage. Angela laughed.

Diane walked by, carrying a stack of *Alcoholics Anonymous* books toward the meeting room.

"Good evening, you two," she said.

"The story we're reading tonight is from the new edition," she announced, handing Paul a copy. "You're going to want one of these to read along."

"Thanks," Paul said, as he and Angela filled up their coffees before heading dutifully toward the front row of chairs.

The night's reading was a personal story, one of many printed in the *Alcoholics Anonymous* text, referred to as *The Big Book* by seasoned members. The basic history and outline for the A.A. program were explained in the first one hundred and seventy pages. The nearly four hundred remaining pages of text covered individual stories of A.A. members, all of whom had experienced similar losses and heartbreaks before turning to the A.A. program for relief.

The chairperson started the meeting, and the reading began. Each person present would read a paragraph aloud or state, "I pass." Paul had been so nervous at these *Big Book* meetings long ago, afraid of stumbling on a written word or being judged for an incorrect pronunciation. After a while, Jimmy pointed out that he was too self-centered to consider people in the meeting who were never taught to read, or those who were blind, or whose anxiety and social phobias prohibited them from ever reading or talking aloud.

"If it helps you to feel better, big fella," Jimmy had said, "remember it's not all about you. In other words, you're just not that special."

Paul looked around the room tonight as the story moved forward, word by word and voice by voice. Some folks wore the frayed, out of fashion clothes supplied by the homeless shelter where they were staying. There was another crew who refused any handouts, charity, or free shelter. They resembled Sherpas, or piles of dirty rags that lived and breathed. Underneath their strange pelts, they held the heat, odor, secrets, and wounds of traumatic lives. Many of them parked shopping carts full of worthless life possessions behind the church before entering. Some would get up periodically to check on their carts, forever mistrusting the intentions of strangers. The cartless sat in darkened recesses of the room, clutching small Styrofoam coffee cups, backpacks on the floor beside them, no book in their hands, and murmuring "pass" when the chance came to read.

Paul couldn't detect any nervousness in Angela's voice as she read about a horribly embarrassing incident for the author and subject of tonight's story. It involved being drunk around a mother and her children in a laundromat. Once the mother had finished her laundry, she surprised the writer of the story by giving her some money and offering information about the A.A. Program and local meetings. It turned out that this mother had been to her own alcoholic bottom and was now recovering. This was the point in the story at which the author began to heal. It was her turning point, a divine intervention.

When the story was over, the chairperson invited people to share their thoughts. Paul felt increasingly agitated and uneasy. There was something off tonight, some kind of negative energy that seemed to surround and infect him.

"I'm Karen, and I'm an alcoholic," a soft voice said from the back of the meeting.

"Hi Karen," the crowd said dutifully.

"I've never read this story," she said, her voice trembling, "but something about it is really getting to me."

Karen paused, and Paul turned in his chair to look at her. She looked to be in her forties, well dressed, and made up. A professional woman, perhaps? Or maybe one that was well taken care of by a hard-working, successful husband, or wife, or parent? It was hard to tell her background story, but Paul guessed she'd never had to pick through donated clothes at a homeless shelter or stand in a food line. A woman was sitting next to her who rifled around in her purse, sensing that tears were coming. She pulled out a tissue and handed it to the woman who was speaking.

"I don't usually speak at these meetings," Karen continued, "I mean, I've only been sober a few months now, and just coming in here gets me so worked up and nervous. I'm relieved when we read from the book because I think that I will be safer somehow, that my sponsor won't make me raise my hand and talk if we just keep reading for the whole meeting."

A few laughs rose from around the room.

She dabbed at her face lightly with the tissue.

"I'm not sure why I'm getting so upset about the story tonight. My life has been nothing like the woman's who wrote this. She went so low in her addiction, hit bottom after bottom, ended up a homeless prostitute. It seems like she was completely abandoned and alone before the life-changing intervention she writes about in the laundromat. I never went anywhere near as low as she did during my drinking. I wasn't allowed to go that low. There seemed to be no bottom in sight for me. My addiction was cleaner, tidier, better whitewashed, and hidden by my husband and our families, I guess."

She looked around again, assessing the crowd. The woman next to her was nodding, encouraging her to go on.

"My daughter was killed two years ago by a driver who had been smoking pot. It was after a concert over in the state park. The first concert we allowed her to see without us. She was only fifteen years old."

Paul remembered the incident. He'd heard about the tragic event on the news and felt awful for the girl and her family, even through his alcoholic haze.

Karen gazed at the floor, her voice cracking as she continued.

"I drank before that happened. I mean, I've always been a drinker. But after Melissa was killed, it really took off. The strangest part was that nobody seemed to notice. Nobody cared. Maybe they just didn't know what to say. They didn't want to be rude. I found out that when you lose a child, you become part of this club, this horrible club that you never wanted to join, and that most people don't know what to say to you, or how to treat you. Those people who did talk to me, who talked about her death, seemed to think that being angry would help. They wanted to go after the man who hit her. I guess they thought that going after him would give me peace, or justice, or something like that."

She shook her head slowly.

"But nothing was going to help. Nobody could make it better. I just kept doing what I had always done, what I had been taught to do since I was a child. I put my makeup and high heels on, kept my head down and continued moving forward, kept things going, kept being nice. I told anyone who asked that I was fine—just fine. The only change in my routine was a few drinks at night. And then a few more during the day. Then a few more."

She held up her hand and looked at her nails, which were professionally manicured.

"Because we've got to keep up appearances, right? We've got to stay busy. My job finally put me on a leave of absence a few months ago. They sent me an email to let me know. I've worked there for fifteen years—always on time, always doing my best, always giving up my vacation time and working extra hours to get the job done, to do things just right, to be perfect—and they sent me a fucking email to lay me off."

Paul closed his eyes, bowed his head, and started rubbing his hands together. He wanted the woman to stop talking. He felt angry, and tired, and restless all at once. He blamed the chairperson for not stepping in. This woman was not speaking about alcohol or drinking any longer, Paul told himself, and she really should take these issues, what A.A. termed "outside issues," somewhere else—to a grief counselor or her job's human resources department, or maybe write a letter to the editor. Somewhere else. Anywhere but here. Paul glanced around the room, hoping Joseph Meer might be here to speak up, to remind her and the chairperson and anyone else who would listen that these meetings should concern topics related to alcohol and drinking. But Joseph wasn't there, and Paul knew that even if he had been, he wouldn't have spoken up.

Because it all applied, every shitty, unfair word this woman spoke applied to alcoholism.

"So, I'm not sure why this story is bothering me so much," Karen said, "maybe I'm jealous of the woman in some sick, twisted way. Maybe I want to believe that the all-good, all-powerful Higher Power that other people talk about in here with such conviction knows what It's doing. Maybe there's a divine explanation that's yet to be revealed to me about how this Higher Power can allow a fifteen-year-old girl to be killed so senselessly."

She paused, and Paul heard someone cough from a far corner of the room.

"And maybe I just really want to keep drinking and say screw all of it…"

Her words trailed off, and when it was clear she was not going to say anything further, the crowd mumbled:

"Thanks, Karen."

The chairperson called on another person to share. The next speaker, a young woman, started by saying how sorry she was for the woman who had lost her daughter. She talked about the similarities she saw between herself and the author of the story. Paul saw Karen get up and leave abruptly, and he was surprised when no other women, especially the one sitting next to her, followed her out of the room. He thought for a moment of getting up, of finding her, of saying something, something that might help. Instead, he sat there, and the minutes ticked by until it was too late.

A switch seemed to be thrown somewhere in his brain, which caused a low buzzing pain to begin along a very old but unfailing internal electrical line.

Shortly after the meeting ended, Paul saw Steve, the drug dealer approach Angela again. The two spoke briefly, after which Steve handed something small to her, which she immediately shoved in a pocket of her army coat without looking at it.

Paul stood near his chair, aloof and alone until Angela returned.

"What was that about?" He asked her, motioning toward Steve, who was now chatting up the chairperson, undoubtedly trying to get another signature to prove he was here.

"Nothing," Angela said. She didn't look at Paul as she answered.

They started to walk toward the exit. Jimmy was surrounded by a group of people, but he held up a finger to Paul and Angela as they passed by, indicating for them to wait. Paul insisted that they leave.

"It's too fucking cold to wait for his highness," Paul decided aloud.

The breathalyzer in Paul's car was being glitchy and wouldn't allow Paul to start the engine. He pulled off the plastic tube meant to blow in and saw that a piece had broken.

"Oh, that's just great!" He yelled. "Now we'll be stuck down here for God only knows how long. Stupid machine!"

"It's alright," Angela said gently. "Just try putting a new tube on. If you need me to, I can try blowing in it, too."

The voltage running through the old internal circuitry in Paul's head was humming louder; it crackled and pulsed.

"Sure," he said in a tone that he knew was much too sharp, "that's a great idea! Let's just try to dope fiend the thing. Or maybe you can drive me around! And when my ass gets thrown in jail, you can call up Steve and join your mother and the other derelicts down at that fleabag motel for one hell of a party! Or better yet, you can invite them all to my house! What a great time that would be, huh?"

He leaned over toward her to open the glove compartment and retrieve a new plastic nozzle to blow into. Part of him wished she would strike him over the head with something hard and solid, something that would interrupt the overloading circuit, something to stop the hurt and rage and thirst that seemed to have busted down the flimsy gates he'd only just started building around his sobriety.

The blow never came. Instead, Angela retreated into her chair, shrinking back from him in an instinctive way that hurt him more than a fist could have.

He found the new tubes in the glove compartment and attached one to the breathalyzer with shaky, unsteady hands. Taking a deep breath, he exhaled into the machine, waiting for the beep to signal that he could stop blowing.

There was no conversation on the ride home.

"I'm going to bed," Paul announced after staring into the empty freezer.

"Paul, are you alright?" Angela asked.

"I mean, obviously you're not alright, but do you want to talk about it? It's pretty clear that something set you off at the meeting. Was it that woman, Karen, talking about her daughter? That was awful. Did I do something? Can I help? I'm kind of new at this talking stuff out shit."

"No," Paul said, fighting the urge to ask her about the interaction with Steve again.

"I probably just need some sleep."

"Yeah, maybe," Angela said.

She touched his arm lightly and immediately felt the overloading current of his fear. She let go, her eyes wide.

"Do you want me to call Jimmy?" She asked

He shook his head, turned away from her, and walked down the hall. "I'll be fine," he told her, "It's all going to be just fine."

CHAPTER 39

"Whoever battles monsters should see to it that in the process
he does not become a monster himself. And when you look long
enough into the abyss, the abyss also looks into you."

Friedrich Nietzsche

"*This was a good idea."*

"Yes, it's good to enjoy the last warm days of fall—an Indian Summer."

"The fall always makes me sad for some reason. I guess it's knowing that things are going to change."

"Things always change. Change is the only constant. Haven't you learned that yet?"

Paul looked at the young man across from him and attempted in vain to give him a wise, reassuring smile. The boy's face was a picture of sadness— deep, dark melancholy.

"Peek a boo! I see you!" Paul kept his voice playful and hid behind closed hands.

No reaction. He reached out with both hands, not quite able to catch the boy.

"Ah…ooga, booga, booga! Look, I've got your nose!"

He poked his thumb from between the clasped fingers on one fist and waved it in front of the boy. Something hummed from behind his chair, an electrical wire, perhaps.

Paul wondered what to do next. Nothing worked. It never had.

The grass beneath their folding chairs was long, and Paul reasoned one more mowing might be enough before the snow fell. The wind picked up and blew leaves down from the tall oaks. One large leaf landed on the boy's lap, but he didn't appear to notice it. Paul heard the buzzing again and tipped his head. He sensed the big house was behind him, looming like a great beast, but he didn't turn to acknowledge its presence. The boy might think he was distracted, that his attention was not wholly focused on their conversation. That would have been unprofessional. Something Mandy might do that fucking bitch. There was a clipboard on Paul's lap with a single sheet of paper and a tiny pencil with broken lead and no eraser. DO NO HARM was scratched onto the paper in smeared red ink.

"I guess you're right," the boy finally said and gave the slightest hint of a smile.

Paul wasn't sure what he was talking about. Something crackled and sizzled behind him, a smell like burning plastic in the wind. He hadn't been listening hard enough to the boy. He was lost for words now and had no idea how they got here or what they were doing. He looked down at his own hands to see if they were shaking, if maybe he was just coming out of a blackout, but his hands were placed firmly on his lap. They seemed as dull and lifeless as rocks.

The boy stared at him, the ghost of a smile lingering on his face.

"Well," Paul began tentatively, "whether I'm right, or not isn't the issue. What do you think you need to do, Travis?"

When he heard the boy's name, Paul realized this wasn't real. It couldn't be real. The buzzing amped up, louder and closer, and he felt the house moving. He took a brief look over his shoulder. The big house was there, his grandparent's place, but it was leaning, pitched and off-center. It cast a dark shadow over the two chairs in the yard. Paul adjusted himself in the chair and considered moving it out into the sunshine, but Travis spoke again.

"Please don't go into that counselor jargon with me. I just need your advice. I need your help without all that bullshit on top of it. You're right; I do need to be honest about this. I need to face the truth, to tell others what's going on regardless of what they think. It's time they knew the real me, I mean if they…"

As Travis talked, Paul noticed movement from behind a large tree in the corner of the yard. A child's head poked out, took a tentative look toward them, and then disappeared again.

"…honesty is the best policy. It's about being true to yourself. Denial never works well…" Travis continued.

Paul saw the small head reappear from behind the tree. The child darted across the yard and raced clumsily toward a smaller tree. He was barefoot, and had short, dark hair. The boy wore cutoff jeans and a faded blue T-shirt that was too big for him. A baseball glove dangled from one hand, looking more like an oversized mitten. It reminded Paul of a story he had read to Sean so often at bedtime, in which forest animals find an old wool mitten in the woods and stuff themselves inside to keep warm. It was one of Sean's favorites.

He knew for sure that none of this was real, that it couldn't be real, but he wanted to stand up, to cry out, to run over and take the boy in his arms. He was also keenly aware that any movement on his part might cause this whole scene to shrink, die and fade away. So, he sat silently. A sound like thunder rolled around him, and he felt suddenly colder as the shadow of the house got darker, heavier.

"…and that's why I came to you to ask," Travis said.

Paul looked at him. Travis seemed utterly unconcerned about the darkening scene around them.

"I came to you because you're the best, the pro, the expert at these things. I don't know how you have done this for so long. I mean, I'm just getting into this, and ..."

Paul saw the boy emerge from behind the smaller tree and run toward the center of the yard. He was dressed in a formal suit, the baseball glove gone. It was the first suit they ever bought for Sean. Charlotte bought it for him and then felt guilty because of the price. It was for Sean's second or third-grade choral concert. Paul tried to convince Charlotte that the price didn't matter. It was okay. A suit like that was a milestone for a growing boy, no less than having a girl's ears pierced. He remembered teaching his son how to tie the tie properly. There were pictures of that moment, of that day, somewhere. Sean was smiling. Paul would look for those pictures when he got home. Where had those photo albums all gone? Maybe Charlotte had taken some of them, perhaps all of them—that fucking bitch.

The boy ran through the yard, but the scene wasn't in real-time, things were too slow, and he barely covered any distance. Paul looked for the next tree he might run behind. There was no place to take cover out there, nowhere to hide. Paul scanned the large yard again, and his heart jumped when he saw the unmistakable outline of the submerged roof of the root cellar under the turf. He looked back at the boy, who was running straight for it.

Paul shook his head back and forth to signal the boy to stop and turn around. He tried to rise and run toward him, but nothing in his body would respond. He was completely paralyzed in the chair. Paul glanced down again and saw that the nails on each finger had grown in grotesque ways, looking long and brown, and cracked on the ends. His eyes were drawn to the paper on the clipboard. HOPELESS was scrawled in dripping red letters.

"...and that's just crazy, right? I see the way you are shaking your head."

Paul's heart was beating wildly, but Travis continued to talk.

"I know, it's crazy. Your family is always there to help you, and they should be the ones you go to when you need that help. But I just don't feel that way."

Paul stared into Travis' face and tried to think of a response. He scanned the yard again, but the scene had changed, and the boy was gone.

"BULLSHIT! IT'S ALL FUCKING BULLSHIT!" Paul screamed into Travis' face.

As the words came out, his body bolted upright from the chair so quickly that the chair tumbled backward onto the lawn. He looked over and expected to see a shocked look on Travis' face, but the young man was just looking at him and smiling, shaking his head with approval.

"Now we're getting somewhere," Travis said and started to rise from his own chair, his hand extended for a handshake.

A loud crack of electricity pierced the scene, followed by a blinding flash of light. Paul turned and saw a different child moving toward the makeshift stairway to the underground cellar. The girl had long, auburn hair curled into pigtails. She was wearing a dark black dress that was too formal for playing around outside. She wasn't running across the yard as Sean had but skipping playfully. He could hear her singing a song as she went.

"Ring around the rosy, a pocket full of poesy, ashes, ashes, we all fall down!"

The electrical buzz surrounding him seemed to seep into the earth and became a low, constant vibration. Paul felt eyes upon him and turned to look at the house. The threadbare curtains moved in several of the windows, and he thought he saw outlines of figures back away into the shadows of the house.

Leaves blew across the yard as the wind picked up.

"We've got to go get her!" He yelled toward Travis.

But no one was there, and the chairs were gone. He heard a playful laugh and turned to see the girl's face, barely visible as she descended below the ground. He noticed her eyes, Sean's unmistakable blue eyes, filled with joy, mischief, and love. Paul opened his mouth to scream, to warn her, but his voice was lost in the furious wind. The girl raised a small hand, waved at him coyly, and then disappeared altogether.

"No!" Paul screamed.

He felt his heart beating wildly and a pounding pressure in his head. He sprinted across the yard against the wind. The thrumming sound grew louder, more intense, and the ground began to pitch and sway. As he ran, the distance to the underground cellar became further, the air around him filled with leaves and debris, and the ground beneath him became unsteady, sucking at his feet and slowing him down.

Suddenly the rumbling grew in intensity, and the yard lit up in harsh bright light. A deafening CRACK split the sky, and the roof of the cellar burst into flames. The ground buckled and fell into itself like a giant sinkhole had opened up and was pulling everything downwards.

"No! No! Get out of there! Get away!"

He ran to the edge of the abyss, a sound like static pulsing in his ears. Paul looked down into the hole, frantically searching for any signs of the child. The chasm was unbelievably deep, and it was impossible to know where the bottom might be. There were items strewn everywhere down there; cinder blocks, splintered wooden posts, broken glass shards from mason jars that had stored various fruits and vegetables. He noticed the tie that the boy had been wearing hanging from a gnarled root deep down in the hole. There were also pieces of black, silky fabric scattered around, and Paul could see the tiny paw of a teddy bear among the ruins.

He opened his mouth to scream, to call out again into the hole, but nothing came out. The static broke abruptly, the storm abated, and everything became dark and quiet. He knew without looking that all the figures had returned to the windows behind him in the house, watching. Paul leaned his head back and looked up toward the sky. He closed his eyes and blinked, and at that moment, countless stars and constellations appeared. There was a full Harvest Moon glowing, illuminating the ruined scene with a strange yellow light. He stretched his arms out wide, spreading them up toward the moon and leaning forward and into the nothingness, the infinite void.

"Paul? Paul! Hey, are you okay? You were screaming, and oh wow, you're all sweaty! Is everything alright?"

He woke up in his bed, Angela hovering over him.

"What?" He said, his voice sharp. "What are you doing in here? Why are you in my room?"

She was leaning into him at the corner of the bed, wearing the Dartmouth T-Shirt and boxer shorts.

"Why are you in my bedroom?" he asked again, hearing the edge and the anger in his voice.

"You were screaming, like, screaming really loud. So, I came in because I was worried. And you're sweating. And you don't look so hot. Was it a nightmare? Are you okay?" Her last words come out quietly and gently, and she put a tentative hand on his hand.

Paul sat up, pulled his hand away, and cinched up the covers around him.

"It was nothing," he said, "just a bad dream. You shouldn't be in here. You should go."

He tried not to look at her directly, not to notice her young, firm breasts beneath the thin shirt. He wanted something to douse the awful memories from the dream. He needed to do something, to not feel this any longer. Most of all, he needed her to go, to be alone, to be by himself, no threat to anyone else, he just needed....

Angela crossed her arms over her chest, suddenly aware of the tension building in the room and that somehow her body, her presence at this time, was a problem. She stepped back from the bed.

"I've had bad dreams too. Drug dreams, you know? The ones where I'm using again. They're a bitch. I guess it's pretty common when you're getting clean, especially early on, but they really tweak me every time. But everything's alright. You're safe. It's fine now.

"No," he barked, "no, my dear, actually it's not fine! Nothing is fucking fine!"

She stepped further away from the bed and stood awkwardly in the room, unsure what to do with herself.

"This," Paul continued, sweeping his hands around dramatically, "this is not fine. This place is a tomb, a mental ward, the last stop on my miserable goddamn train ride. Nothing is fine, and it's never going to be. It's over. The life I wanted, the one I worked for and got sober for and spent so much fucking time on – that life meant shit in the grand scheme of things."

Angela's heart was pounding in her chest. She wanted to leave now, to run away from this man, this angry man who she saw now was just like all the others in her life. Of course he was. How could she have expected more? What a stupid, naïve bitch she was. She forced herself to speak.

"Paul, that's not true. It was only a dream. You have helped so many people."

Her voice was trembling but gentle.

"We all go through shitty times. We all get our hearts broken over and over again. I can't imagine what it was like to lose Sean and then lose Shawna or go through all that you have since that happened. But I do know…"

"You don't know anything!" Paul roared.

"Don't fucking tell me you know anything about me or my family. And I really don't want to hear about any of the 'shitty times' you've been through right now! You don't know. You have no idea. I can't even begin to explain."

He paused, looking toward the window and into the breaking dawn.

"I killed him. It was me. The awesome fucking counselor, the perfect helper. The guy who spent most of his life helping others. A fake. Pretending I could tell them all the right things to do. I refused to see what was right in front of me. I just wouldn't give him what he wanted, what he needed to live. I didn't love him, or her, enough."

He looked back at her.

"And I can't help you. Nobody can. So, if you want to run off and shoot that shit you got from your drug dealer buddy last night into your body and blame someone else for all the problems in your life, be my guest. Because the truth is nobody is going to stop you. Nobody is going to swoop down and save you from the pain. There is no Higher Power, sweetie. It's us taking care of ourselves. Nobody cares. You can follow the rules down here, and color inside of every line, or you can fuck around and screw people over left and right, but in the end, it's all just a crapshoot, a roll of the dice, a matter of which plane you take to Disney World and if the terrorists put the bomb on that one or not. And the people who claim to want to help you, the ones who make a career out of propping up the sickest people? They only do it to avoid dealing with their own shit. Or maybe it's an ego boost. Or they can't do anything else. Fakers. Phonies. Hypocrites. But the cold, hard truth is that we're all alone in this jungle, and it's survival of the fittest. Darwinism all the way."

Angela felt herself crumbling inside, like so many times before, but somehow worse this time. She searched Paul's face for something that she was sure was inside of him, some essential goodness that made him different. She looked for the man who stood with her in that bus stop and then showed her a glimpse, a possible hope of goodness through all the pain. But maybe that was just a part of the show, the hustle, another lie. She prided herself on spotting liars and on becoming one when she needed to. She had perfected the art of looking straight into someone's eyes and saying exactly what they wanted to hear, regardless of if it was real. Mandy was right about Paul, after all. Why hadn't she seen this one coming? How did she let him get so close?

"I," she began and detested the quiver she heard in her voice, "I'm going to leave now."

She turned and walked out the door, ashamed at her desperation to hear his voice pleading for her to come back.

Paul sat for a very long time before he got out of the bed. He didn't hear the front door close when she left. The sun was streaking through his window, and he knew the day would be long. Eventually, he left his room and noticed that the door was open to Sean's bedroom. He walked in slowly and sat down on the bed. He looked around the room and then back at the doorway. How many times had he stopped on the other side of that door over the last few years, pausing with his hand on the doorknob, listening, waiting, trying to understand something that would never be clear?

"How much does it hurt, Buddy?"

"It's not bad, Daddy. I'll just put a band-aid on it."

What had that pain felt like? The chronic pain that Paul caused, and fueled, and failed at stopping. He'd kept the room locked up, too afraid to face and feel what was left behind in here. But sitting there, on the bed, all he could think of was of the nights, the countless nights, that he'd sat here with Sean tucked snuggly under the covers. All the times he clasped his hands together after Sean had fallen asleep and thanked God for that blessed life.

He knelt on the floor with his hands clasped together and his eyes closed.

No words came, no blinding lights, no moment of clarity or restitution. Only the quiet of the room. He stayed on his knees but laid his head on the corner of the mattress and saw that Angela had left the closet door open. Sean's clothes hung neatly inside. The hatbox was sitting on the floor next to the hole in the wall that had held Shawna's secrets for so long. There were some shoes near the box and something else that caught his eye. It looked like a small wooden box.

Paul thought Angela might have put it there, a place to hide her drugs or other secrets. A pang of deep guilt seized him for the things he said to her. The awful things he'd said. That dream was so real, so powerful, and she came in at just the wrong time. But he would make it up to her when she returned. If she returned. Paul saw some small pieces of jewelry and a brush on the dresser nearby. Her bag, that beaten-up thing she dragged around everywhere, was on the floor in the corner. That was good. Maybe she'd walk in soon, and they could talk.

He walked over to the closet and picked the wooden item up. It seemed unreal, out of place in here. He carried it over to the bed and sat down again, holding the thing in both hands like some fragile artifact that might break or dissolve at any moment.

The tears began slowly at first, and he wiped the first few away with one hand, trying desperately to control himself. When he felt his lower lip begin to tremble and his face start to weaken, he stopped holding back and let the dam burst. His body began to convulse, to release, to purge the silent grief. As he gripped the wooden object tenderly in his hands, Paul felt a great sense of something changing, something heavy lifting from his chest.

He took a few deep breaths, then stood up and walked to the kitchen. He set the item on the kitchen table and instinctively walked over to the freezer, opened it, and stared in. He closed the door and propped both hands against the kitchen counter, leaning against it for a long time, his head down. He grabbed his new cell phone off the counter, picked it up, and dialed a number.

"Hey," he said. "it's me. Can you come over today? I need some help."

CHAPTER 40

"We're told to live life in binaries. This is especially true with gender,
where girls are expected to act one way and boys another.
But we do this in other areas as well. Good or bad. Right or wrong.
Love or hate. I hope that someday the world will be more accepting and
start to recognize the wonderful, unique spectrum that we all exist on,
a continuum of differences that makes us at the same time unique
and also connected. That is a world I could live in..."

Excerpt from Shawna Durkin's suicide note.

Travis stood in the copy room, staring at Mandy's back as she scanned the long wall of patient files, waiting for him to reply to her question.

"Well," he began, "I don't mind running the group. I mean, I certainly appreciate you trusting me enough to do it, but I know we're supposed to finish those packets tonight."

"Don't worry about those," she said, "just make sure you have something to do that will fill the entire group time. I mean, just chatting away with them about this, and that may seem easy, but that can fizzle out quickly. I think you should have something more structured planned."

"Sure," Travis said. "Yes, not a problem. I can come up with something to do. Thank you again for the opportunity."

Mandy leaned up and pulled down the chart she was looking for and then turned toward Travis, her trademark smirk firmly in place. "Well, don't thank me just yet. Let's see how the group goes. Oh, and there's a new woman starting group tonight. She's a hot mess, and I doubt she will be around long if she decides to show up at all. Her Name is Erin McFee, and I did her intake yesterday. She seems absolutely clueless about addiction and just overdosed on heroin recently. This is a professional, intelligent woman who is almost forty years old. You would think she'd know better!"

Travis said nothing, and Mandy flipped open the chart in her hands. A few moments passed.

"Has Paul told you anything about me during your sessions?"

"No," Travis said, surprised by her question. She didn't look at him, and he added, "Only that you two worked together in the past."

"Hmm," she said, "yes, he helped me get my first job in the field, you know. I was actually an intern, just like you, before I got that position. Well, not exactly like you. I was here as part of a master's degree program in Social Work. I didn't originally plan to do this work, with all the drunks and addicts. I thought I would serve clients with mental health problems—depression, anxiety, personality disorders...but Paul convinced me to do this. He said that the field needed more social workers and people fully trained in mental health counseling. I think he truly believed that at the time."

The smirk changed to something else, something Travis thought was softer.

"He would raise interesting topics of conversation, like sexuality and gender and how I felt those things impacted a person's life. At first, I thought he was just interested, and I was flattered that he wanted my opinion."

She stopped talking and looked back at the chart.

"And then I met his son. Paul had stopped by the clinic to pick something up, and Sean was with him. I knew immediately that those conversations we had weren't random. I saw right away that this kid was struggling with something."

Mandy closed the chart but continued to hold it.

"How old was he, Sean, when you first met him?" Travis asked.

"Well, it was a few years before he—" she ran her free hand through her hair, "—before the incident, the suicide, so I'm guessing he was in his mid-teens then? I'm pretty sure he was a junior or senior in high school at the time."

"And how could you tell that Sean might be having issues with sexuality or gender identity?"

"I'm not really sure…" she cocked her head slightly, "I know that 'gaydar' is not among our official assessment criteria, but if I'm being honest, I think some people are more attuned to sensing when someone doesn't fit the standard binary expectations for the ways males and females to 'should act.' Does that make any sense, or does it sound horribly stereotypical?"

When she looked at him, Travis felt the door to a common room had opened between them.

"No," Travis said, "no, I agree with you completely. I think that some people are just better, are more intuitive, at seeing those differences."

Here they were, in that familiar place Travis knew well. He knew that telling her he was gay at this point would lead to a predictable response.

"Yes, I already knew that."

He always wondered in those moments what gave him away. From a very young age, he worked on not talking with the tell-tale feminine tone that he often heard in other gay men. He preferred dressing in a more masculine way, though he couldn't deny his occasional obsession with his hair or with matching socks to an outfit. He reasoned these small, subtle things, couldn't possibly have been perceived by the onlookers to his life. Or could they?

His parents weren't any help. When he finally came out to them after graduating from high school and making the decision to move into an apartment of his own, his mother burst into tears, shook her head knowingly, and forced him into a tight hug, which he was sure was intended to make him stop talking.

"It's okay. It's going to be alright. We'll get through this." She sobbed.

His father, an intelligent man who was slow to anger or to show any emotional response in a situation, sat back and looked at the tips of his fingers. When it became clear he would need some prompting to respond, Travis asked:

"Dad, did you hear what I said?"

His father looked up, and Travis didn't sense hate, or denial, or even disapproval in his face. His dad seemed to be contemplating the whole of the situation and deciding upon the next right move, the most logical reply.

"Yes," he finally said. "Yes, son, I heard you. And I can't say that it's a real shock to me, either. Now that it's out here in the open, between the three of us, I guess the next thing for you to decide is if you want to continue with this lifestyle decision, or if you want to get some help, some counseling about the, well, about the issues you may have with all of this, and maybe try to rein it in a bit. Your mother and I know this couple from church whose nephew had similar problems, and he got some good counseling. I think he's married now—to a woman of course—and things worked themselves out. We'll support you either way, but if you want us to get the name of the counseling service, we certainly can. And we'll pay for the sessions. The important thing, I think, is that we keep this matter right here inside the house until we—you make some important decisions about all this."

Travis wasn't shocked, but what he found most ironic was that his parents assumed they were the first people he had come out to. In truth, they were two of the last. Autumn was the first. Since the sixth grade, she'd been his best friend, and she lived just a few houses away. His parents liked to tease him about Autumn being his *little girlfriend,* and they pushed him hard, to spend as much time with her as possible.

"*They want me to go to a counselor who cures gayness.*"

He confided to Autumn shortly after the conversation with his parents.

"*Cool,*" she responded, "*can this counselor cure stupidity and bigotry too?*"

Travis never went to the counselor, but he had a strong suspicion his parents and their church friends continued doing their best to love the sinner while hating the sin. His mother still refers to C.J. as *Travis' friend,* and every visit with his parents is awkward and tense.

"*Well, we lived through that!*" C.J. joked after every visit. "*And your father's handshakes are getting stronger and stronger. I'm going to take that as a good sign!*"

Travis knew in his heart that any issues his parents had with his sexuality or his life and how he lived it was about them and not about him. He was learning through his college classes and from St. Michael's that he was truly powerless to change anyone but himself. He held a faint faith that his parents might even come around eventually and tried to focus on how far society had progressed in educating people about the importance of accepting, and eventually embracing, our differences.

But he couldn't deny the pain he felt whenever he saw parents engulf their kids with unconditional love and support. He was acutely aware of them during the family groups he'd sat in on at St Michael's. These same families had children who had lied to them, and stole from them, and broken open their hearts as they were pulled deeper and deeper into addiction. They refused to give up and continued acting as nursemaids and cheerleaders. Travis was astonished at the number of brave people he witnessed who tapped into a strength and resignation that came from the hope that this time it was going to work. The disease was going to be treated, dealt with, and put into remission at long last.

Acceptance of things (and people) that could not or would not change was another important philosophy Travis was learning as a counselor. But that bit of wisdom didn't take the sting out of knowing the parents he'd been given in some celestial game of cards would have preferred a different hand to play in the game of child-rearing. Travis didn't consider himself prone to self-pity. In fact, he was starting to recognize how frequently he stuffed or ignored his problems or unhappy feelings choosing instead to focus on helping others. This insight was heightened by Professor Dunleavy who accused most counselors and professional helpers of doing the same thing. Wounded Healers and Codependent Personalities were the clinical terms he used.

"*So, you may want to look at that,*" Dunleavy encouraged his students, "*because the carpenter who ignores everything needing fixing in their own house while repairing everyone else's is going to end up with their roof caving in on top of them.*"

Travis knew he would have to practice what he preached and get into some personal counseling for these feelings and issues with his parents. He even knew which important piece of the dysfunctional and hidden family puzzle that he would present to his yet unnamed counselor. He learned from his grandmother, and quite by accident, that his mother had been pregnant one time before he was born and that the child, a girl, was stillborn. He tried to ask questions, to uncover the *Hows and Whys* of the tragic event, but it became clear to him that it was a matter never to be discussed, like so many other things in that house. It was simply off-limits. He wanted to know about the history his parents shared and to trace the events that had settled over them and that house like a gray November cloud.

"So, it was pretty clear to me that Paul knew Sean was gay or that something was different about his sexuality or gender, but that discussion didn't appear to be going on at home. It seemed like Paul was completely unwilling or unable to deal with it."

Travis had missed some of Mandy's explanation; luckily, she wasn't looking at him. He tried to recover the conversation.

"Wow," he said, "that's surprising because I've heard so many people talk about what a great counselor he was. Such a well-respected person in the field. It seems like he helped everyone around here in some way."

"True," Mandy said quickly, "he helped everyone but himself. And his family. I don't know how much you talk about it in your classes, but when I was in school, we were constantly reminded about self-care, the need to take care of ourselves and our personal lives and affairs first."

"That hasn't changed. My professors are constantly making that point," he said.

"Well," Mandy continued, "I thought it was all talk back then, honestly. If I was fixing everyone else, I didn't need to do any work on myself or my relationships outside of the job."

She gave him a half-smile.

"But guess what? It's no bullshit. You need to put yourself and your family, or whatever people you love ahead of your work and your mission to save all the world's damaged souls."

She motioned her hand around the room to the hundreds of case files surrounding them.

"Look, Mandy—" Travis started, but she interrupted him.

"I know people think I'm a bitch around here, right?"

She looked at Travis and laughed.

"Yes. Well, you don't need to agree. I know it's true. I wasn't always this way. I used to be the one who took time to talk to every patient. My door was never closed to their problems! Consequently, I would be in my office for hours after everybody left, trying to catch up on paperwork!"

Mandy held up her finger, moving it back and forth, tauntingly scolding herself.

"It sounds harsh, right? It goes against the basic ideas of doing no harm, putting the client first, and all that bullshit. Is that what you're thinking? Well, I'll tell you what got me to stop doing things that way. It was seeing people like Paul who gave too much here and had nothing left when they went home. His story isn't that unique. The counselor who bases their whole worth on being seen as a great helper, a wise sage, the portrait of what recovery and a happy life should be. I admired it at first. Even emulated people like Paul."

She held up her left hand, spread her fingers wide, and stared at them.

"Did you know I was engaged?" She asked.

Travis shook his head. "No, I had no idea."

"I still have the ring. It was back when I was finishing up college and interning. I was probably around your age. He's a stockbroker now. Very rich and all that. When he called things off, he told me it was because he was too selfish to share me with all the druggies and addicts who needed me more."

She took a deep breath and smiled sadly at Travis before looking around at the countless charts in the room again.

"These people need us, Travis, but we need people too. After my fiancé left, I started to see things more clearly, to make my life a priority. That's why I took the insurance job. It was better for me. I knew Paul was in a dangerous place a long time ago, way before Sean killed himself."

She took another long breath.

"You know what I remember most about the wake and funeral? All the empty chairs. I remember thinking that the funeral home made a big mistake by putting all those chairs out. I mean, this was a young kid, right? Someone who grew up here and went to school and whose family knew everyone. So where were all the people? There was a handful of teenage kids there, mostly crying girls who I think saw this as a great opportunity to add some drama to their lives. But not many adults showed, no friends of the family to speak of. In this town, funerals and wakes are usually social events. I'm not saying that in a bad way. I think it can be helpful for families to have big turnouts to these things, realize how many lives were touched, and feel supported during tough times. Hell, I've gone to the same funeral home for 90-year-old grandmothers and 17-year-old drunk driving victims. The place is usually packed with mourners, but not for Sean, not for Paul or Charlotte. I've always wondered how he felt about that. You're right when you talked about "all of" the people he has helped, gone out of his way for, rescued and saved, and spent time on over the years. But where the hell were they when he needed it most?"

Travis could picture the scene—a dark, nearly empty room with a casket in the front, large burning candles on each side. He saw Paul and his wife sitting there, in the front row, waiting. Silently waiting in the silence and the pain for something or someone that never came. Travis could picture his parents in the same dark room, with the same heavy grief and loneliness. The only difference in the scene was that the coffin was much smaller, and he imagined his parents sitting with an empty chair between them.

"Were you working at the insurance company when Paul quit?" Travis asked. "Was it a long time after the suicide?"

"When he quit?" Mandy asked, surprised.

"Is that what he told you, that he quit?"

"No, he didn't tell me that. I just assumed. I mean, I just thought it would be too much…"

"It was," Mandy agreed. "It was too much. But he didn't quit. Well, not exactly. He was drinking, a full relapse by then, and it was clear that he couldn't be in charge anymore. I heard that St. Michael's was willing to put him on a leave of absence as long as he entered treatment and got some help. Apparently, he refused. Eventually, Matt called our company and let them know that he was the new director and that any questions about insurance claims should be directed to him."

"So how did the people, the bosses I mean, at St. Michael's, find out that Paul was drinking? Did word just get around? Did Matt tell them?"

"No," Mandy answered, "I told them."

Travis tried to keep his face neutral.

"I know, it's hard to believe, right? But it was me. I called St. Michael's after members of our team said they were unable to get in touch with Paul about insurance issues with patients over here."

Travis was afraid his attempt at neutrality was failing, so, he shook his head to affirm her decision.

"It's part of our job," he said. "I mean, I know that ethically and legally, we're supposed to report when a staff member is abusing a substance. But that must have been…it couldn't have been easy."

"No," she answered, "it wasn't, not even for 'Mandy the cold-hearted bitch.' To tell you the truth, I figured he would be relieved. I think he was looking for someone to report him, and nobody else was going to. So, I made the call."

"Do you think he held it against you? Did you ever talk to him after that, I mean before he showed up back in treatment?"

She smiled and said, "Follow me."

They left the chart room and walked down the hall into Mandy's office. She pointed to a small trophy in the shape of a cowboy hat sitting on a shelf nearby. It looked like the cheap type of thing that might be given out to young children for participating in a spelling bee or a community-sponsored sports league.

"That," she said, "is our Black Hat Trophy. The clinic had a running joke when I was working here about which counselor would wear the Black Hat each week. The trophy would cycle around the office depending on who the clients were complaining about the most, or which one of us was doing the most confrontation, or who had to discharge the most people during the week because they weren't making any progress. I'd never won the award before I transferred to Val-Tech. But this was sent to my office a few days after he left. There was no note attached."

The phone on Mandy's desk beeped, and she walked over and picked it up.

"Yes? Oh, she is? Okay. I'll be right out."

She turned to Travis.

"My appointment is here. Look, I don't mind what you do in the group tonight. I know you're capable of running it alone. In fact, I could use the time to get some paperwork done. Why don't you plan on running it and just call me in if you need me?"

Travis' guts quivered. It must have shown on his face.

"Don't worry about it," she said. "You can do it. I wouldn't put you in there if I didn't think you were ready. Hopefully, you have a little better understanding of Mandy the bitch now."

CHAPTER 41

"Trust is a wonderful thing, Darling! But it must be earned.
So, no, I don't trust you. Not yet."

Jack P.'s estranged wife, Lisa,
testing out a phrase she recently learned in Al Anon.

Jimmy often talked about acquiring his beloved jet-black 1973 Cadillac Seville from the owners of a Chinese Restaurant in New York City. The details were vague and fluid, but the most consistent information was that the previous owners had paid a popular chop shop in their area to adorn the car with thick gold and red pinstripes along both sides of the vehicle and across the trunk. These highlights accented each door handle and ran down the center of the roof as well. There were chrome rims and white wall tires on the Caddy when Jimmy originally bought it, but he replaced the tires (not the rims) with large, flat, high-performance wheels that caused the car to ride low through the rough and potholed streets of the Northeast. The front and back seats were often packed with people going to or coming from local Twelve Step Meetings, and the extra weight caused the Caddy to bottom out frequently, sending flashes of sparks from the undercarriage. But the most prominent feature of the car was the humongous red and gold dragon on the hood. The winged beast appeared to be poised for battle, its clawed forearms sticking out, a mixture of smoke and fire shooting from the mouth.

Most townsfolk struggled to come up with an appropriate response when Jimmy would ask, "Ain't she a beauty?"

Although he drove the car daily in all types of weather, it always looked newly washed and remained utterly rust-free.

Paul heard the loud, rhythmic thrumming of the exhaust pipes coming up his road long before he saw Jimmy pull into the driveway. He felt nervous and popped a mint into his mouth, even though he knew he had nothing to hide.

Just old habits, Paul thought, as he walked from the living room to the kitchen.

Jimmy came through the garage and knocked at the door but didn't wait for Paul to answer before walking in. He was wearing a white, long sleeve button-down shirt that appeared heavily starched. His sizeable upper body filled out the shirt, and it seemed just a bit too small for him at the neck and wrists. He wore a crisp black belt with a small gold buckle and dark blue slacks that looked brand new. His shoes were black and polished, and his hair was slicked back with a gel that smelled to Paul like an old-time barbershop. Jimmy looked like an oversized AARP catalog model or a retired pro wrestler.

"What?" Jimmy asked when he noticed Paul looking at him.

"Nothing," Paul replied. "You look good, that's all. You clean up nicely. It looks like you're either going to court or to accept some type of award."

Jimmy's eyes narrowed momentarily before a broad smile covered his face.

"Fucking right I look good!"

With that, he walked past Paul, slapped him on the arm with a bit too much force to indicate friendship, and went directly to Paul's freezer. He opened it, peered around the inside, and withdrew a carton of ice cream.

"You know," he said, "when we grew up, ice cream came in maybe three flavors, right? Vanilla, chocolate, strawberry. Now they got what, over a hundred flavors of the stuff? Thousands maybe? And what's the point? Do we really need all those choices? When I was a kid, I had a hard enough time choosing between the three." He put the ice cream back in the freezer and opened Paul's fridge up, inspecting the meager contents but not removing anything.

"It's Angela's ice cream," Paul said, and immediately wondered why he felt the need to explain himself, "she picked out the flavor."

Jimmy closed the door and walked over to the kitchen table. He pulled back one of the chairs, which looked small in his grip, and sat down.

Jimmy began, "Where do we start today? I'm going to assume you didn't call just because you like my company." He waited for a beat, then turned in the chair and faced Paul. "Have you stayed sober today? I know there are lots of other hiding spots beside the freezer around here."

"No," Paul said, "no, I didn't drink today. I'm sober. Miserable but completely sober. Honestly."

"Honestly?" Jimmy repeated, making the word into a question. He turned away from Paul, toward the window.

"Well, that honesty's the key to it all, isn't it?" Jimmy asked.

Paul sat down across from him and thought briefly about offering his guest a drink but realized that if Jimmy had wanted a drink, he would certainly have helped himself.

"Hey, you got a cardinal out there," Jimmy said.

Paul turned his head and looked outside to see the bird at the feeder. It appeared particularly vibrant in the bright sun.

"Yup. He's been coming around for the last few weeks."

"Well, those are some low-rent feeders. I'm surprised they hold any birdseed at all. You ought to get some better equipment." Jimmy looked past Paul and reached over to the edge of the table.

"Shit, Paul, you've got a beautiful bird feeder right here! Look at this thing. It looks like someone took their time making this. You couldn't have done this. You ain't smart enough! Did Angela make it, or did you two go out and find this thing-"

Jimmy looked at Paul and stopped talking. He put the feeder gently down on the table.

"Oh..." He said softly and let out a long breath of air.

Paul felt the pain and the tears from earlier rising again. He looked toward the floor.

"Yeah," he managed to say, "I found that today, in Sean's, you know, in his room."

Jimmy sat back in his chair, glancing out the window again. "Well, that explains why our cardinal friend is here."

He looked at Paul and rested one of his muscled hands lightly over Paul's.

"It's one day at a time, right, pal? That's how we deal with this stuff down here, just one fucking day at a time."

A moment passed. Then two. Jimmy looked away from Paul and back out the window before asking,

"So where is she? Where's Angela?"

"She's not here."

"Well, where did she go?"

"She's gone," Paul said. "I think I fucked up. I had this dream, this horrible dream, and then she was there, in my room, and it scared me. I just went crazy for a minute and said things to her that I shouldn't have. Awful things. Hurtful things. She must have just walked out, but her stuff is here, so I thought she'd be back by now."

Jimmy shook his head softly and rubbed his face with a hand.

"Alright," Jimmy began, "we drunks certainly know how to say and do all the wrong things at all the wrong times. But she's a tough kid. I think she knows just how fucked-up you are. If she didn't know that before today, you've convinced her."

Jimmy patted Paul's hand again.

"Nobody gets sober perfectly, Paul," Jimmy said. "This ain't always pretty, but we do the best we can with what we got. You coulda drank over this. Hell, it would have been a great excuse. But you didn't. Instead, you called me! Now that was a feat of fucking brilliance!"

"I tried calling her, too," Paul said, "but she won't pick up."

"No," Jimmy said, "of course she won't. Have you texted her?"

Paul shook his head.

"Hand me your phone," Jimmy said, "I forgot for a minute that you're just joining us in the new millennium."

Paul slid the small cell phone out of his pocket and handed it over.

Jimmy flipped the phone open and looked back at Paul.

"Really?" Jimmy asked. "Did you order this thing from the Sears and Roebuck catalog or what?"

Paul shrugged his shoulders as Jimmy held the phone in both hands, making it look like a child's toy. Jimmy moved his thumbs around quickly then handed the phone back to Paul.

"There, that should do it."

"What did you say?" Paul asked.

"The truth," Jimmy replied and looked at his watch. "You can look for yourself. In the meantime, we're going out to eat because you don't have anything good here, and a few guys are expecting us at the diner."

"But what if she comes back?" Paul asked.

"I asked her to wait here until we get back. Or to meet you at St. Michael's for your treatment group tonight."

Jimmy pushed back his chair, brushing at his spotless pants, and adjusting his collar for no reason.

"And don't forget your wallet," he told Paul. "You're paying."

CHAPTER 42

"I've always been an outlaw, a gangster. That's why my crew calls me Player."

Steven Harris – introducing himself to Angela

A fter meeting some of Jimmy's sponsees at the diner, they spent the day driving around Deerfield and Moheneck Falls. Paul assumed it was an established route for Jimmy, whose current and former employment status remained a mystery to everyone.

"Yeah," Jimmy answered when Paul had asked him about it, "I used to work, and now I don't anymore."

He also didn't speak about being a part of any volunteer organizations, but his trunk was filled with clothing, canned food, and various everyday items that they dropped off at the Deerfield Homeless Shelter, a few local food banks, and the lower level of the parking garage, recently built by Pelligrino Construction, where the Sherpa-looking people who weren't able or willing to enter the homeless shelter spent their time. Jimmy was greeted with broad smiles and hugs at every stop. He knew the names of everyone they visited and made little effort to explain to Paul what they were doing or why.

Paul looked for Angela at each stop and called her phone repeatedly but got no answer. They stopped by Paul's house; her things were there in the room, unmoved. Jimmy insisted on driving Paul to St. Michael's that evening, where they both hoped Angela would show up for the group.

"You're in no shape to drive," he explained. "And for the first time in a long time, it's got nothing to do with being drunk!"

Jimmy also had plans for Angela.

"After you two finish up in there, all of us are going to the A.A. meeting that started off your recoveries last week. You're going to bring up the topic of gratitude because both of your asses need to hear about it."

Paul shouldn't have been surprised by Carla's reaction when they walked into the clinic and approached her at the reception desk. She swept back her hair and greeted them in a voice that sounded considerably sweetened. He knew this frequently happened with Jimmy, especially around women that were a bit older, but the phenomena always impressed him. Paul also noticed that Jimmy seemed sincerely unaware that these women were reacting to him. Jimmy was always respectful and kept his foul language in check around the ladies, but it never seemed he intentionally tried to schmooze any of the women that showered such adoration on him. This lack of reciprocation usually intensified the flirtatious energy coming from the women they encountered, which Paul thought made for a fascinating study of sexual behavior between the genders.

It was rumored throughout A.A. that Jimmy frequently sought out the services of prostitutes and strippers. Paul heard these whispered stories before or after meetings, usually by women huddled around the coffee maker or in a tight smoking circle just outside of the meeting hall. Another popular rumor among these women was that Jimmy might be gay, considering his lack of female companionship and his consistent habit of being cordial but never flirting with any of them. Paul knew that gossip and rumor ran rampant in the self-help community, just as it did in PTA meetings, YMCA locker rooms, or on the bowling team. Any setting where a group of people gathered over time and became comfortable with each other seemed destined for these thriving grapevines. It was another interesting commentary on our flawed human condition.

Peter and Larry came into the lobby, and Paul hoped their presence would rouse Carla from her trance-like state. She'd asked Jimmy about where he got that beautiful, classic Caddy she saw pull up, and he was telling her about winning it from the Wang brothers in a poker game. Paul had never heard this version of the tale. Paul also noticed that Carla was now nibbling on the end of her pen and the top two buttons of her blouse had somehow opened during the conversation.

"Well," I'll go touch base with Mandy and Travis," Paul said.

He first nudged and then pushed Jimmy away from the counter and into the waiting area. Jimmy was at a point in his story when he was supposedly driving the Caddy up from the city and realized that the former owners had left a pistol shoved deep into the cushion of the driver's seat.

"Well, maybe you can stop by and tell me the rest of the story after work sometime," Carla said as Paul escorted Jimmy to the waiting area.

"What are you all dolled up for today?" Larry asked Carla as Paul walked down the hallway.

Paul looked into the group room. The room was dark, and nobody was inside. He walked around the corner to the bathrooms, hoping he might see her there. The men's room door was closed, but the women's room was slightly opened, and he could see it was empty. Paul walked quickly back toward the group room and checked again. Nobody had entered, but Travis was exiting an office and walking toward the room.

"Have you seen Angela?" Paul asked.

Travis looked into Paul's face but said nothing.

"Angela," Paul repeated, "the young girl in our group. Have you seen her, or did she call here? It's important."

"Paul," Travis started, "are you alright? You know that I can't tell you about other patients…"

"Fuck that!" Paul said.

He took a deep breath and then placed his hand on Travis' shoulder.

"Look, this is important. Maybe even life and death important. I just need to know if you have seen or heard from her, yes or no?"

Travis paused for another instant, looking intently at Paul before shaking his head, slowly and slightly to indicate he had not.

"Okay," Paul said, "thanks. I won't be in the group tonight."

Paul patted Travis' shoulder firmly before heading out to the waiting room.

"Paul, wait!" Travis called as Peter and Larry rounded the corner and nearly collided with him.

"Woah, boss!" Peter said. "You're heading the wrong way!"

"Yeah," Larry added, "Mandy's driving people away from this place left and right! You're the third person I've seen running away from here today!"

Paul turned around.

"What do you mean? Who else did you see?"

"Huh?" Larry answered.

"You said that you saw other people from the group today. Who were they?"

Larry looked at Paul and then up and down the hallway. Travis was watching them but hadn't moved any closer.

"Well," Larry said, lowering his voice, "I don't want to be a rat or anything, but I drove by the Stumble Inn about an hour ago, and I saw that new guy, the pretty boy with the nice, clean boots. He was walking in the place with that ratty-looking chick, the one with the army coat. I don't think they were there to go to one of those sober meetings, either, you know what I mean? Hey, where you going?"

"Let's go!" Paul said to Jimmy as he jogged toward the exit.

"Yes, sir," Jimmy replied, winking at Carla as they left.

The night was still, and cloudless and temperatures were dropping quickly as the black Cadillac raced toward the Stumble Inn. Jimmy turned the heater up to full blast when they sped out of the parking lot at St. Michael's, and Paul reached forward to turn the thing down a few miles later.

"Ain't that heater great! I can make it like a sauna in here if I want to!" Jimmy said.

He slowed down slightly without really stopping at a four-way intersection. Jimmy hadn't said much since they started driving, which worried Paul.

"Isn't this place we're going one of your old watering holes?" Jimmy asked. "I seem to remember seeing your car camped out there quite a bit over the last few years."

"I did my share of time out there," Paul said.

Jimmy rounded a corner slightly too fast, causing the back end of the Caddy to slide on the icy road. He corrected the car and punched the gas. Paul heard the twin mufflers roar.

"Well, you certainly did pick the best place to feel the worst about yourself. I'll give you that," Jimmy said.

"Yup," Paul replied. "That was pretty much the point."

Soon they saw the Stumble Inn's parking lot and neon beer signs glowing in the front window. Jimmy slowed down, and the engine went from a growl to a purr as they pulled in. Both men inventoried the handful of vehicles parked outside.

"Any idea what this asshole drives?" Jimmy asked.

"Not too sure," Paul replied, but I'd guess it's something new and shiny. I don't see anything here that catches my eye, but it looks like my favorite bartender's truck is here, so I'm sure he'll help us out."

He nodded toward a small, foreign-made pick-up truck parked close to the building.

"Well, that's good to hear," Jimmy said. "What exactly is the plan here, Paul?"

"Fucked if I know," Paul said as he pulled on the handle and swung the large black door open. "Find the girl, I guess."

"Find the girl," repeated Jimmy, opening his door and stepping out. "Way to keep it simple, pal."

"This place looks different," Paul said as they entered the front door.

"Yeah, well, that happens when you're sober. It probably looked like the fucking Taj Mahal to you before."

The strong smell of spilled, rotten beer, thick, acrid cigarette smoke, and something that had been deep-fried for too long washed over them as they entered. The smell permeated every floorboard and piece of sheetrock in the room. There were fourteen or fifteen customers in the place, most of them with cigarettes dangling from their lips. He looked back at Jimmy.

"Isn't there a law about not smoking in public places?"

"Damned if I know, but I can see how you used to fit right in here. It's a great place to come and kill yourself. Do you see her anywhere?"

"Not yet," Paul replied, looking toward where he first met Angela. It seemed unbelievable that it had been only a few weeks since that meeting.

Teddy didn't seem to notice them. He was leaning against the bar and punching buttons on his phone.

He looked up as they got closer. When he saw Paul, a wide grin appeared on his face.

"Well, look who's back," Teddy hissed.

He grabbed a dirty towel from behind the bar and made a production of wiping a section of the bar, beckoning Paul and Jimmy closer.

"You know, some guys, when they leave here, I'm not so sure I'll ever see them again. It's like, okay, I guess they got their shit together and moved on. Not you, Paulie. No, I knew you'd be back!" Teddy spun around and pulled a rope attached to a large bell hanging from the ceiling. The bell clanged back and forth, drawing the attention of the small crowd.

"Yes, sir, this requires a celebration. The first one is on me, pal! Don't be shy! Have a seat."

Paul walked up to the bar but remained standing.

"You do owe me a drink or two, Teddy," Paul said, "but that can wait. I'm not thirsty enough right now. Tonight, I'm just looking for a couple of people who were in here earlier. A young man and woman. Do you know where they went?"

Teddy turned away from Paul and poured a tall draft beer into a thick glass.

"Well, you're going to have to be a bit more specific, Paulie old boy! I see lots of young people come in here every day! This is a busy place, you know?"

Teddy laughed as he finished pouring the beer. It looked cold and crisp, with a big head of foam which poured over the rim and down the sides.

Slowly and purposefully, Paul studied the shady-looking characters in the bar. "I would bet that you have about twelve regular customers, Teddy, and that anyone who comes in is only here to find drugs or because nowhere else will serve them. The guy I'm looking for is probably a dealer himself. He's a thin guy, toned and slick-looking—a tribal tattoo on his right arm. The girl is—" he hesitated. "The girl looks rough. Newly sober, or maybe newly relapsed by now. But small, long brown hair, green eyes…"

"And probably a virgin too, huh, Paulie?" Teddy interrupted.

Paul looked at Teddy and saw something like recognition or fear to these questions. One thing was for sure. The two had been here. Teddy knew who they were and where they were.

"Anyway, I haven't seen them," Teddy said.

He set the beer in front of Paul.

"Why don't you sit down, drink your beer, and tell me what life is like when you take a little break from this place. Honestly, the two dopers you're describing don't sound like your type of crowd anyway. You're better off sticking with the older boozers, like your big friend, here, Paulie!"

Teddy looked at Jimmy.

"What's your poison?" Teddy asked. "First one's on me, boss?"

"I've had enough," Jimmy said with a slightly menacing smile.

Paul looked at the mug on the bar and felt the old, insatiable beast stir to life from somewhere deep and dark inside him. Teddy seemed to sense his thoughts.

"Welcome home!" Teddy smirked and leaned back against the wall with his arms crossed.

"Look, Teddy," Paul began, "the girl needs help, she..."

"What we got here is a failure to communicate!"

Jimmy slipped behind the bar next to Teddy. His voice sounded different, a bad imitation of a loud, accentuated southern drawl.

"Yes, sir," Jimmy continued, "it's a failure to communicate! Some men you just can't reach, no matter how hard you try!"

In the instant it took for Teddy to glance down at the Louisville Slugger behind the bar, Jimmy had stooped down and snatched up the old, wooden bat. He held the handle in his right hand and swung the business end of the club back and forth, smacking it firmly into his huge left palm each time.

"Do you know what that quote is from?" Jimmy asked Teddy.

"Jimmy, look…" Paul started.

"No, no," Jimmy interrupted, waving a hand in Paul's direction but never taking his eyes off Teddy's face. "Don't help him out here, Paul. No phoning a friend on this one. The boy's got to figure it out all by himself."

Jimmy lowered the bat and moved closer to Teddy. Paul heard footsteps, and the front door opening and closing. He assumed Teddy's loyal customers were deciding to call it an early night.

"I'll even give you a hint," Jimmy said, smiling broadly but menacingly at Teddy. "It was said a long time ago to this punk who thought he was a badass. Kind of like you!"

The fear on Teddy's face lifted slightly. He seemed to brighten.

"Oh, wait! I think I do know!"

"There we go," Jimmy said. "See, Paul, what can happen when we allow these slower kids to solve things all by themselves?"

"It's Axl Rose, right?" Teddy said.

"Who?" Jimmy asked.

"Axl Rose. You know, Guns N' Roses? That's a quote from one of their songs!"

"Jesus Christ!" Jimmy yelled. "No! No, not fucking Asshole Rose. Never mind."

Jimmy lifted the bat again and moved closer to Teddy.

"The point is that we seem to have a failure to communicate here. I think it's because my friend and I don't speak douchebag! So, I suggest you tell us where that slimy friend of yours went with the girl."

Teddy remained silent.

"This isn't a bad piece of timber, boss," Jimmy said, "but it's not made of hickory. I've always found hickory bats are the best for getting the long shots in. These cheaper ones just don't hold up!"

Jimmy struck the bat across the bar in one quick swing and knocked the glass of beer in front of Paul over and away from him. The beer flew up and covered Teddy's face and shirt while the glass fell and shattered at his feet. In the next instant, Jimmy raised the bat and brought it down again directly across the bar, causing it to make a great *CRRRRAAAACCCCKKK*. The bat broke almost perfectly in half while splinters of wood flew up and around them in every direction.

Teddy was standing with his arms tightly by his sides, the frightened young schoolboy who'd just come in from a downpour. Beer ran down his face and off his nose. Jimmy held the broken end of the bat, like a sharp, serrated dagger, close to Teddy's neck.

"So let's try again," Jimmy said, his voice calm and steady.

"Where did they go?"

"This isn't right," Teddy sniffled. "You can't just come in here and do this shit. I should call the cops on you two…"

"It's too late for that, Teddy," a new voice said from behind them.

Paul turned and saw Roscoe standing in the doorway.

He walked toward the men.

"What the fuck?" Teddy said. "What are you doing here?"

"You just said you wanted the cops here!" Roscoe replied.

Roscoe glanced at Paul, who wondered if Roscoe assumed he'd been here drinking all day. He then looked at Jimmy, who had hidden the broken bat. Jimmy gave a cheerful nod and greeting.

"Nice to see you, Officer," Jimmy said. "It's a fine night for a drive."

Roscoe smiled cordially back at Jimmy.

"I'm not so sure about that, but I do know we had some complaints about an old, pimped-out sedan tearing up the streets of town and running several stop signs earlier. It was last seen speeding like a bat out of hell in this direction. That's what brought me out on this fine night."

"Old? Really? They said it was an old sedan?" Jimmy asked, incredulous.

Paul spoke up.

"That's interesting, Deputy Montgomery, but now that you're here, maybe you could talk to our friend Teddy about helping to find a possible juvenile runaway that was seen here earlier today?"

"A runaway? Here?" Roscoe asked, mocking a tone of surprise in his voice.

"And I assume you're talking about a female runaway, Paul, is that right?"

Paul nodded at him, and Roscoe moved closer to where Teddy was standing behind the bar. The beer was starting to dry on his face.

"Well, if there was a runaway seen at this bar, and if you had contact with her, Teddy, my bet is that you would do everything you possibly could to assist us in finding this young girl, isn't that right?"

Teddy looked at Roscoe, his face starting to tremble.

Roscoe continued.

"Especially with the trouble you've had in the past with young girls, right Teddy? And the fact that I'd love nothing more than to bring a few of the state troopers' narcotics dogs in here and see what they might find. Hell, I think I've had enough calls about possible drug sales in this place to justify a search warrant. And now we have this sighting of a vulnerable, young runaway to investigate. What do you think? Should we call the judge and get things started? Speak up, Teddy, you aren't usually the type to be so shy, my man!"

The tremors in Teddy's face traveled down his arms and into his hands. Paul almost felt bad for him – almost.

"I don't even really know the guy," Teddy said in a voice so low that Roscoe asked him to repeat it.

"I barely know him, alright? Shit, he's some low-level dealer from a rich neighborhood. And that girl gets around, you know." Teddy looked at Paul.

"You may think she's some kind of angel, but she's been rode hard and put away wet plenty of times.

A sound like white noise engulfed Paul as he moved quickly behind the bar and grabbed Teddy by the shirt with both hands, pushing him into the lowest shelf of liquor bottles while lifting him onto his toes. A few of the bottles fell and smashed on the floor.

"I've always felt sorry for you, Teddy." Paul said in a low growl. "You've become just another Monroe shitbird in a long line of shitbirds from that filthy, dirty nest. And some of the blame for your useless joke of a life was pre-programmed at birth. But I like to believe in second chances. And this, right here, tonight, is your chance to become the first Monroe with half a brain in his thick skull. That girl's name is Angela. And she's a better person than you could ever dream of being. So you're going to apologize for what you said about her. Then you're going to tell us where she went. Got it?

Teddy looked shocked and petrified as he glanced at Jimmy and then Roscoe. No hope for help there.

"Okay, okay," Teddy stammered, "I'm sorry for what I said. I don't even know her, really. And that guy has a place in The Gables. I think it's his parents' house, but he stays there even when they're away. Shit, his parents are loaded. They own like, five houses. That's why he's low level. He's in it for the lifestyle, not for the money. He's playing gangster."

Paul let go of Teddy and walked away.

"What's his name?" said Roscoe.

"Steve," Teddy replied. "Steve Harris. But he goes by 'Player.'"

"Oh, for fuck's sake," Jimmy said and followed Paul out from behind the bar. As he did, Paul saw Jimmy grab a bottle from the shelf.

"Steve Harris. Lives in The Gables," said Roscoe. "Okay, I hope you're not messing around with me, Teddy, because I'm going out there right now. And you had better hope Mr. Harris is home and doesn't get a text to tip him off. If I don't find him and the girl out there, you're going to see my face again really soon."

"That's all I know, I swear," Teddy whined. "I've never been out to his place. I've never even hung out with the guy. Shit, you cops should know who he is already. The dumb ass got busted a few months ago selling weed, and he's on probation now."

"That explains why he's in the group," Paul said, looking at Roscoe. "He's going to St. Michael's, probably because probation is making him. He should be in your system already."

"Well, that will certainly help us track him down," Roscoe said as they turned and headed toward the door.

"Do you want to come along with me?" Roscoe asked Paul. "You might be useful in getting Angela to come with us if she's out there."

"Absolutely."

Paul looked back at Jimmy, who was following them. He was trying to conceal the bottle he'd taken, walking with it behind his back.

"You two go," said Jimmy, "I'll catch up later." He gave Paul a wink.

"How about you go home and call Paul tomorrow?" Roscoe suggested, "Leave this next part to me. Paul will help me get Angela out of there. I don't think you showing up in The Gables with that chopped down mafia mobile is going to help matters."

"Yes sir, officer. I'll give you a call tomorrow Paul," Jimmy replied.

The night was bitterly cold, and the moon and stars shone clearly in a cloudless sky. Roscoe's cruiser was idling, billowing white smoke into the darkness. Paul remembered the awful, cold night he'd spent in this parking lot. He was grateful to be stepping into a heated vehicle tonight and to be sober. He wondered if Angela had relapsed. The white noise began again as Paul envisioned Steve Harris pushing a needle into Angela's arm.

"Alright," Paul said once they were in the car. "Let's go. What are we waiting for?"

Roscoe picked up the handset and pressed the button to talk:

"Dispatch? Dispatch? This is car 77."

He waited a moment as the radio crackled and popped with static.

"Go ahead, car 77," a voice said.

Roscoe pushed down on the handset again.

"Dispatch, no luck locating the car we got the calls on, but I need an address on a current probationer."

There was another pause, some static, and then the voice.

"Car 77, go ahead with that name."

"Steven Harris," Roscoe said into the handset and spelled out each letter of the last name slowly.

"Copy that," said the voice. "We'll get back to you, car 77."

"Great," Paul said, "can we get moving now?"

Roscoe turned to Paul and opened his mouth to speak but seemed to reconsider. He put the car in gear instead, and started toward the main road. Paul saw a flash in the passenger door's rearview mirror. He looked in the mirror and saw a large figure standing next to Teddy's small pick-up truck. The figure appeared to have the gas cap off, holding it in one hand while he emptied a bottle of clear fluid into the fuel tank. Paul tried to keep Roscoe's attention diverted from the scene playing out behind them.

"So how far are we from The Gables?" he asked.

"We should be there in about ten minutes," Roscoe replied.

After a few moments, Roscoe added, "I'm glad that crazy son of a bitch isn't drinking the vodka himself. I've got enough to worry about tonight."

They drove on in silence under the bright stars. Paul sensed that Roscoe was playing the waiting game again, allowing the silence to blare.

"Would you just come out with it?" Paul finally asked.

Roscoe glanced over at him.

"Well, my old friend, you know, I'm glad you're getting back on your feet. It seems like this kid has been good for you. You know, though, some of the things Teddy said back there could very well be true about Angela. I looked into her past, Paul, and she's got a history: burglary, forgery, bounced checks," his voice lowered and softened, "allegations of prostitution."

Paul stared straight ahead. They were on an unlit back road, bordered by endless rows of pine trees. The cruiser's headlights illuminated the trees and cast long lines of shadows on the roadway, an army of doomed soldiers marching wordlessly and helplessly toward some unnamed battlefield. Paul looked up into the sky and thought he saw a shooting star for a moment, a sign she was okay, but realized it was a passing jet.

"You've got a good heart, Paul," Roscoe continued.

"Shit, I don't know if there's anyone in this town, or in this county for that matter, that you haven't helped out at one point or another. But right now, with this girl, with Angela, well, I just don't know if she's looking for help, or if you're in any condition to give it to her."

Paul closed his eyes and raised his hand to his face, massaging his cheek, then his forehead. He took a deep breath.

"Do you ever feel him, Roscoe?"

Paul felt Roscoe's eyes on him but didn't turn to meet his gaze.

"David," Paul continued. "I mean, do you ever dream about him? Do you think he has come to visit or to send you some kind of message since he passed over?"

Paul wasn't sure where the question about Roscoe's brother came from, but there it was.

Roscoe adjusted himself in the seat, sitting up more stiffly and grabbing the steering wheel with both hands.

"I don't much believe in that beyond the grave stuff, Paul. I guess I've been hardened by all the lives I've seen ended or changed forever in seconds by what seemed like random events, twists of fate,…bad fucking luck. I have a hard time believing it's all part of some grand plan."

Paul put his hands on the dashboard and leaned toward the windshield, staring past the shadows of the pines and up into the sky.

"But have you ever dreamed about him? Have you ever gotten the sense that he's around?" Paul pressed.

"Well, sure, you know, I've had some dreams with him in them over the years. Geez, he's been gone for sixteen years now, Paul. But the dreams I remember don't seem to be anything monumental, no special meanings, if that makes sense. A few times I've had this dream where he just shows up, right? But he's the same age he was back then and everything else has moved on. It's like David has been asleep, and now he has to catch up with the time he missed. I have to explain this to him, to tell him that he died, or at least we thought he was dead for all those years. It's weird, right? Anyway, I don't know if that stuff, that pain ever really goes away. I think the wound just kind of scabs over and becomes a scar with time."

Paul shook his head in agreement, watching the moon emerge from behind a large blue-grey cloud in the sky.

"I've never had a dream about Sean."

He took a long breath and moved back from the dashboard and into his seat.

"Not one dream since he left, until just last night. And it was awful. It's why Angela left my house because I yelled at her after I woke up. She was just trying to help me, but I didn't let her. I was too worked up. I fucked things up—again."

Paul ran his fingers through his hair.

"She took me to her counselor," He continued. "Charlotte took me. She made me go after Sean died. She had been going to see this woman for a few months. I was still working back then. I hadn't picked up the booze, but I was getting closer to it every day. Anyway, this counselor, this woman Charlotte had been working with, asked me how I was doing with everything."

Paul chuckled bitterly.

"She actually fucking asked me like that: *So, how are you doing with everything?* I've heard that counselors make the worst patients, but come on, that was just stupid! I tried to play along, mostly for Charlotte's sake. We'd drifted so far away from each other by then that I owed her at least one more try at making things better. I told this counselor, what I just told you, that I was upset because I hadn't dreamed of Sean. I hadn't dreamed of my son since he died. I hadn't felt him at all, you know, around me—" Paul's voice cracked.

"I'm not sure if I ever told you, or if you knew already, Roscoe, but Sean was transgender." Paul wondered as he said this if he'd ever used that word before.

"Yes," Roscoe replied softly, "Yes, I knew that already, Paul."

"So anyway," Paul continued, "she tells me, this woman looks me straight in the face and tells me that I probably hadn't dreamed about him or felt his presence because my son, because my Sean, never really existed. That Sean had always been Shawna, and that if I could just accept that fact, if I could truly accept that my child was always a girl, always Shawna, then maybe—"

Paul trailed off and stared into the rows of pine trees, filing rhythmically past the car.

"I stopped by the first liquor store I saw after I met with her that day."

"Paul," Roscoe said, "that situation you had was hard. It would have been hard for any father. You wanted to protect your kid. I mean, how can any father know what to do, what the right thing to do is in a situation like that, you—"

Paul put his hand up, signaling for Roscoe to stop talking.

"I'm not looking for any consolation, here Roscoe. I blew it, plain and simple. I thought that I had a son. I was sure that Sean existed, God damn it. But I was wrong, and I refused to know, or to accept who my kid really was. I had a daughter that I never accepted. I never even acknowledged. I don't understand it all, and maybe I never will, not in this lifetime anyway. But I could have done more for that kid, for my only child. I should have done more. It wasn't comfortable or convenient for me. I was afraid. I just wasn't up for that challenge. I had so much fear for Sean and for all of us. I wanted to keep him with us, homeschooled and safe. Sean wouldn't do it, and Charlotte backed him up. I can't imagine what it was like to go into that school every day pretending to be someone else and waiting for the bullshit to start."

He looked out the window again.

"That kid was a lot braver than I'll ever be."

"You did your best, Paul," Roscoe said, "and that's what I have to tell myself with David. He got behind the wheel that night, just like he'd probably done a thousand other times after drinking. I tried, my family tried, plenty of times to get him some help. Hell, you helped us get him into that rehab, and then he left after two days! I have come to believe it wasn't my fault."

Roscoe shook his head.

"We can't go on beating ourselves up over this stuff. The guilt will eat us up. Everybody makes their own choices, and everyone needs to live out their own lives, whether we like what they're doing or not. I don't know about any big plan, or intelligent design to all this, but I do know my life today is okay, not great, but okay. And yours seems to be getting a little better each day that you don't drink."

Roscoe paused, allowing his words to sink in for the next few miles before he spoke again.

"I've got a strong feeling that this stuff with Angela is not going to have a happy ending, Paul. I'm here, right here with you, I hope you know that, and I'll have your back and play this out until the end, but I don't want to lose you down a bottle again over this."

Paul reached over and patted his friend on the shoulder.

"Thanks. Thank you, Roscoe, really. But I don't expect any happy endings for any of us anymore. Happy moments, maybe? We all have the same ending; it's written in the script. I have a hard time believing the 'everything happens for a reason' bullshit just like you do, but I'm starting to think that this kid, Angela, isn't here at this moment by accident. She helped me more than she knows, and I need to pay it back. Or at the very least to let her know she matters, you know what I mean? That her life really matters."

Roscoe said nothing, but Paul felt the cruiser bear down on the frozen two-lane road.

"Car 77? 77?"

"77 here, go ahead."

"We have a Steven Harris, currently on probation and living at 23 Maple Ridge Lane. Do you copy?"

"Copy that. Thank you. I'm going to do a home check on the probationer. 77 out."

The deep woods they were driving through broke suddenly, and a vast, illuminated housing development revealed itself like a suburban promised land. Paul hadn't been out this way in a long, long time.

They drove through an intricately detailed wrought iron gate which announced they were entering The Gables. The first street sign Paul could make out read *Pelligrino Drive*.

"You haven't seen all this?" Roscoe asked. "Yes, sir, it's the look of progress and prosperity.

"The Pelligrinos certainly are doing well for themselves," Paul mumbled. "Can you see any house numbers on these places?"

"Yeah," Roscoe said, "Tony's busy tearing down half of Deerfield now, but he started by luring rich city folks to build their second or third homes out here. It was much cheaper to scoop up this land from the Cook's old dairy farm than to build in Deerfield. Maple Ridge Drive is coming up. I imagine we'll know the house when we see it."

They did. The driveway of 23 Maple Ridge Lane was filled with cars and several more were parked on the street.

As Roscoe pulled the cruiser to the opposite curb, he picked up his radio.

"Car 77 to dispatch. Come in dispatch."

"Dispatch here. Go ahead car 77."

"It looks like a disturbance of the peace at the Harris residence on Maple Ridge. Some kind of house party. I'm parking the cruiser now and going to investigate."

Paul opened his door as soon as the car stopped and was halfway up the driveway when Roscoe caught up to him.

"Let me lead, here, Paul," Roscoe said, gently touching his friend's shoulder. "I saw back at the bar that you're ready to go in here under a black flag for Angela, and I don't mind bending a rule or two, but let's try to color within the lines as much as we can, okay?"

Paul didn't reply but signaled with his hand for Roscoe to take the lead. He noticed the hint of acrid smoke hanging in the air and had a vision of Cookie adding gasoline to the fire out there in the cold darkness across the shrinking pastureland.

When they reached the front door, Roscoe straightened his wide-brimmed hat and touched the holster on his right hip before loudly knocking three times. The door opened immediately. A young woman was standing there, holding out a credit card. She looked startled to find a large law enforcement official filling the doorway.

"Oh," she said, staring first at Roscoe and then at Paul, "I thought you were the pizza guy. We've been waiting a really long time."

"Well," Roscoe replied, "I'm not. I'm Captain Roscoe Montgomery from the Sheriff's Department. Can you please point me in the direction of Steven Harris?"

Her face went blank for a moment, as her internal hard drive downloaded this request.

"Oh, you mean Player? We never call him Steven. Yeah, he's here somewhere, I think. Look, I don't know if it's cool to just invite you in, I mean..."

"Don't worry," Roscoe said. "It's very cool. Thank you. I advise you to find a sober ride home very quickly. This party is about to end."

With that, Roscoe and Paul pushed past the girl. The foyer opened into a large living room, with framed family pictures from sunny destinations far from Moheneck Falls. In one photo, the woman and man were tanned and toasting colorful martinis from a luxurious patio over the ocean. Other pictures cataloged the lives of two growing children, a boy and a girl, each dressed and groomed to perfection. They looked like a better version of school photos, better than the ones Sean had brought home each year. Paul recognized the sneer in every picture of the boy, and how it had deepened into his face over the years.

They entered the living room, where a large crowd was sitting around a TV with the sound muted. The song playing in the house was screeching promises of revenge and torture after discovering a lover's infidelity. A commercial for early detection of prostate cancer played silently on the screen, and the young viewers seemed transfixed by the mixture of the song and the images before them.

"Angela!" Paul called out. He didn't see her anywhere, but hoped that the sound of his voice might draw her to them.

A few heads turned towards Paul and Roscoe.

"I'm looking for Steven Harris," Roscoe announced loudly.

At this, more people looked away from the TV, one of them holding up her phone to take a picture. Several hands went immediately to jacket or pants pockets, patting, protecting, or concealing whatever drugs they were holding. Many of the kids wore their coats, or long sleeve shirts and sweaters.

"Angela!" Paul called out, louder this time. He envisioned the needle marks on her arms, those horrible red spots indicating the disease was back, alive and thriving in her veins.

"Who?" A young, athletic-looking boy in a high school football jersey asked.

"Angela," Paul repeated in a panicked voice that he barely recognized as his own. He stepped closer to the young man. "Angela LaPoint. She came here with Steven Harris."

The girl from the front door appeared.

"They're looking for Player," she said. "Has anyone seen him? And does anyone know when the pizza is coming? I'm, like, starving."

"I think he's in his room," the young man said.

"Just wait a minute, and I'll text him." The boy pulled a phone out of his pocket.

"Don't!" Paul yelled and then grabbed the boy by the arm.

"Don't bother. Just show us where his room is, please."

Paul and Roscoe followed him up a stairway to a closed doorway near the end of a long hallway. The young man took out his phone.

"The door is closed," he said. "I'll just text him and ask if we can come in."

"Or we could do it this way," Paul said and pushed past him, hammering hard on the door with a fist.

"Open up!" Roscoe shouted as he moved up to the door, "It's the Sheriff. I'm coming in!"

Roscoe twisted the knob, opened the door, and entered the room.

The bedroom was large and cavernous, with a door to the right leading into a bathroom and a huge four-post bed in the middle of the room. The shades were drawn on the windows, the lights dimmed. There was a pile of covers and blankets near the headboard of the bed. Steven sat on the lower edge of the mattress, looking hypnotized by an episode of "Family Guy" that played from an enormous flat-screen television mounted on the wall a few feet away from him. There was a small canvas pouch with a syringe, spoon, and lighter next to him. A character's voice from the show broke the room's momentary silence.

"I'm telling you, our daughter is a slut, and she's banging all the guys from my work."

Roscoe glanced around the room and into the bathroom before he approached the bed.

"Are you Steven Harris?" Roscoe asked.

Steven looked like he was trying to piece together what was happening and if this was real or a part of the TV show.

"Steven Harris?" Roscoe asked again, louder this time and moving closer.

"Well, yeah, but you can call me Player."

Roscoe towered over him.

"Can you stand up please, Steven?"

"Aw, come on!" Steven whined. He looked at Paul.

"Dude! Is this because I missed group?"

"Yes," Roscoe replied quickly. "And probably for many other reasons that we'll get to. Now turn around. Roscoe handcuffed Steven and told him he was being arrested for probation violation and drug possession.

"Where's the girl?" Paul asked, surprised at the level of fear in his voice.

Steven looked quickly over his shoulder toward the top of the bed.

"What girl?"

Paul rushed to the mound of covers on the bed. He removed the blankets slowly, the way he used to do when his son was small, playing a game of Peek a Boo at bedtime. His heart sank as he pulled the last blanket away.

"Oh, Jesus. Jesus Christ, no!" He yelled.

She was there, looking small and frail and broken. Her face looked waxen and discolored. The most disturbing sight was Angela's mouth. Her lips were parched, and blue, as if he'd opened a freezer and found her, slowly turning to ice.

Paul put his arm around her neck and shoulders, lifting her gently.

"No! Goddamn it, no! Not her! You can't have her, too! Angela, Angela, wake up! Wake up!"

Roscoe rushed over, put two fingers on her neck, and moved his other hand under her nose and mouth.

"She's not breathing. I think she's gone…"

CHAPTER 43

"Every police officer, fire rescue personal, volunteer E.M.T.,
every first responder needs training in Narcan administration
if we're going to save more kids from dying."

Sheriff Roscoe Montgomery, addressing the Deerfield City Council
regarding the opioid epidemic in Moheneck Falls –
The Council voted against mandatory training.

Paul sat with Angela on the bed, cradling her head in his hands.

Roscoe reached into his Sheriff's Department jacket and withdrew a small, sealed package.

"What's that?" Paul asked.

"It's Narcan," Roscoe answered and ripped the package open, assembling the pieces inside.

"Oh shit," Steven said. "Is she, like, dead? Fuck, I barely know her. You've got to believe me. She was high before I even met up with her."

"You need to shut up," Roscoe barked, "now!"

Roscoe placed two small tubes protruding from the Narcan assembly into Angela's nostrils and then pressed down on the nozzle, releasing the contents into her nose.

Nothing happened.

"How long does it usually take?" Paul asked.

"Not long, sometimes it's immediate," Roscoe said.

"How strong is the heroin she took, Steven?" Paul asked.

"I'm not answering that!" Steven whined. "You can't even prove I've got heroin, and I'm not sure you're here legally. I know my rights, and…"

But Paul was on him, ripping him up from the bottom of the bed.

Roscoe grabbed Paul off. "You stay with Angela." He instructed.

Roscoe turned to Steven, within inches of his face. "I need to know how strong the heroin is, Steven. Is there fentanyl in it? You're in trouble, here, that's true. But if she dies, you're fucked. I'll make sure of it. So, you better start talking. Is she breathing, Paul?" He asked.

"No, nothing. Nothing at all!"

"Okay, okay!" Steven said.

"Yes, it's strong. But there's no fentanyl. At least, I don't think there is. She probably overdosed because she hasn't used in a while. The Narcan will bring her back anyway, right? She'll be alright.."

"It doesn't always work, especially with the stronger stuff," Roscoe said.

He pulled Steven toward the doorway.

"And that was all I had on me, but there may be more in my car. Do you have any here? Any of your friends downstairs carry Narcan?"

"No. I mean, I don't have any, but I'm not sure about anyone else."

Roscoe unlocked the handcuffs and pushed Steven into the hallway.

"Well, we're going to see. Let's go! Move!"

Paul looked up, wanting to say something that might encourage them but not finding the words. He could hear their footsteps running down the hallway and then nothing. Paul put his hand under her nose and mouth, hoping to feel her breath. If she was breathing, it was too faint and weak to detect. She felt cold to his touch, and a dark whisper came from somewhere within him.

"I knew you'd fuck this up," it growled.

Paul remembered his horrible dream and the dark figures behind the curtains of the big house.

He took a deep breath and stroked Angela's cheek softly.

"God," he despised the sound of his shaky voice but willed himself to go on, even though the sickness in him said it was pointless. "God, I fucked up. Badly. I know that this isn't your fault. I know that Sean's death wasn't your fault...but I was so...angry. I'm just so fucking angry at you."

He felt the tears run down his cheeks.

"You sent her to me, and I blew it. I failed. I know you thought I could help. I don't know why you took her, and I don't know if you need her now...if this is it. But I'm asking. I'm begging you to leave her here. She needs me. I need her. I am trying to follow the path, to do what's right. You know I've tried. I can't do this alone anymore. I never could. I never should have tried. I need your help. Please help..."

He thought there was more to say, but his voice trailed off into the silence.

CHAPTER 44

"Understanding is a fountain of life to one who has it."

The Bible (NAS), Proverbs, 16:22

Angela recognized the alley and the dumpster. It was the one where she and her sister found that pack of cigarettes and tried smoking for the first time. They would run down here soon after a family was evicted from the building and often found furniture, clothes, or even some decent food left around. The dumpster looked gigantic to her now, and it didn't have the rotting smell she remembered so well.

The alley she was standing in was different as well. It stretched almost endlessly in the distance beyond the dumpster. Music kicked in behind her, and she turned to see that the other end of the alley was much closer and that it opened onto a town square. In the center an ornate fountain gushed pure, blue water into a brilliantly sunny sky, and people packed the courtyard. She began to walk toward the fountain, and the music got louder as a marching band strode by playing "Louie, Louie," a tune Angela's mom had introduced her to when she was very young, and which always made her want to dance. She smiled and walked quicker, but the distance to the square was deceiving, and everything around her seemed stretchy and slightly distorted.

The band was followed by a small group of partiers, some in costume and others appearing out of context completely. She saw David marching in a puffy chef's hat, with a pancake flipping through the air and then landing on the oversized spatula he was carrying. Drew Hollis stomped by, looking like he did in high school and wearing only a pair of wet underpants. He left damp footprints on the road and waved at Angela as he passed the alleyway opening.

The scene changed suddenly. She had left the alley and was standing next to the fountain. It was dusk, not quite dark enough for streetlights yet. She heard a bird chirping loudly and saw a flash of red fly from the top of the fountain to a nearby tree. Under the tree, an ornate wooden bench faced away from her. In the middle of the bench, she saw a person with long, flowing auburn hair watching the bird land. Angela walked over and sat down.

The young woman on the bench turned and smiled. Her face was familiar, radiant, and classically beautiful.

"Shawna?" she asked.

"Hello." She reached out a hand. Angela took her hand and held it, feeling nervous that if she let go, this might all disappear.

"Is this it?" Angela asked. "Is it over?"

"I'm not sure," Shawna said. "That's not up to me. Do you want it to be done?"

Angela heard the chirping again. She looked up to discover a bright red cardinal perched and watching from a branch. Another cardinal came and landed next to it. This one was more brown than red, a female.

"Kind of," Angela answered, "but I don't feel like I did much. I mean, was that it? If so, that's fucked up."

She looked at Shawna, who was smiling.

"No offense, it seems really nice here, but I thought I'd do more, that I would be more, before I got here. I hoped I could make something of myself."

"You can," Shawna said. "There's time if you take it. It's too late for me, but you have options left."

They sat in silence while Angela wondered if more time would truly change anything for her.

"He needs you, you know," Shawna said. "But he might never say it. He's kind of an asshole a lot of the time. He can't even get my pronouns straight."

Angela looked at Shawna and saw she was smiling.

"But he's a good man at heart. He's trying, even if he's an asshole. I can see that. If I could go back, if I had the choice, I think I might…"

Shawna's voice trailed off, and Angela saw the smile had turned bittersweet.

"He loved you," Angela said. "He did. Even if he never said it."

Shawna rose then. She wore a majestic golden dress that accentuated her stunning figure and flowed in all directions. An equally striking rhinestone purse was draped over her soft shoulder.

Angela noticed that the dusk around them was interrupted by flashes of light, like flashlights in the forest. The tree and the sky, the sound of the fountain started to glitch, like the whole scene was struggling to buffer and reload itself.

"I hate to rush you," Shawna said. "But we don't have much time."

Shawna extended her delicate hand to Angela.

"Have you decided?" She asked.

Angela gave a slight nod of her head and took Shawna's hand. They walked toward the fountain and as they did, Angela could hear a voice. It was muffled and far away, but she could make out some of the words.

"...you sent her... I blew it... failed... brought me together with this one... help... I need her...please help."

Shawna stepped over the side of the fountain and into the water. Angela could smell the ocean. She felt sand beneath her feet as she stepped over the edge. The water was hot without burning, just the way she liked it.

Shawna knelt in the fountain and opened her arms up. Angela laid herself back into Shawna's arms. Just before her head was lowered below the waterline, Shawna leaned down and kissed Angela gently on the forehead.

"Thank you," she said.

CHAPTER 45

"Is this something that can wait until tomorrow? It's our last night on the island, and there's not much we can do from here anyway. Steven has our credit card number if he needs bail money..."

Douglas Harris, via phone to Officer Montgomery
from an island in the Caribbean.

Paul felt something at the doorway, a silent presence watching him. He looked up and saw a tall young woman with long, red hair standing in the dim light. She walked to the other side of the bed and sat down near Angela's head.

"She..." Paul said, "she overdosed. Roscoe, the Sheriff, went to look for some help, to get something to help her."

He was surprised at the desperation in his voice.

The girl stretched out a large hand and caressed Angela's cheek. The hair which covered her eyes and mouth almost entirely was too red, clearly a cheap wig. Paul smelled a familiar perfume or shampoo. Was it something Charlotte had worn?

The girl reached into a small purse that was covered with gaudy fake gemstones. It looked too immature and juvenile for someone her age to be carrying. She wore a faded yellow dress and a string of large, fake pearls that were out of context for the house party. The entire outfit reminded Paul of a young child playing dress-up with clothes usually reserved for costume parties or Halloween. The girl withdrew a syringe and adjusted the needle.

"No, wait," Paul said. "She needs a medication called Narcan. It goes into her nose and reverses the overdose."

She took Paul's hand and gave it a quick squeeze but remained silent. Her touch was warm, reassuring. She stuck the needle in Angela's arm and injected her with the contents of the syringe.

Paul felt Angela's body convulse slightly. After a moment, the convulsion returned, more substantially this time. Her head twitched in his arms. He stroked her face and clutched her closer.

"Yes," he said, "that's it. Breathe! Just breathe! Keep going. You can do it."

She took in a sudden, long gasp of air and sat up in the bed, her eyes opening fully.

"What?" she asked, looking at Paul. And then, "Paul, I saw her! She was there at the fountain. She's beautiful!"

She looked around the room.

"Wait. What the fuck am I doing back here? Why are you here? I feel like I'm going to puke. She leaned away from him, and as she did, Roscoe and Steven ran back into the room.

"Here, I had some more kits in my car," Roscoe said. "What the hell?"

"Oh, shit," Steven exclaimed 'Oh no, not on the bed, no!"

Angela hacked and coughed up a long stream of bile onto the pillows. She leaned into Paul's arms again, trying to catch her breath.

"She was there, Paul. I saw her. It's so beautiful there. So peaceful."

"Get me a towel or a cold washcloth. Quickly!" Paul shouted.

Steven ran into the bathroom and returned with a towel, a damp washcloth, and a small garbage can.

"Just have her use this," he said, holding the garbage can out. "Have her throw up in this if she needs to. Do you have any idea how much those pillows cost? Or the sheets?"

Paul gently placed the cold washcloth on Angela's forehead. Roscoe picked up a pillow that was covered with vomit and threw it at Steven.

"Here, Steven! Go wash your precious pillow."

"Oh, shit! Hey man, that's gross! I got a weak stomach for shit like this!"

Steven carried the pillow gingerly into the bathroom with one hand and covered his mouth with the other.

"What happened?" Roscoe asked.

Paul looked up.

"She had some Narcan, or maybe it was something else, but it worked!"

Paul looked around, realizing that the girl was gone. "The red-headed girl. The one with the yellow dress. I thought you sent her up here. Where is she? She was just here. Right here."

Roscoe looked confused.

"We didn't talk to any girl with red hair."

"Just now," Paul replied. "Right before you came in the room. She was there, just there, on the bed. You must have seen her..."

"No," Roscoe said, the police officer's tone coming back into his voice. "I didn't see any girl with red hair and a yellow dress, Paul. Are you sure she..."

"It was Shawna," Angela insisted. "I'm telling you." She breathed deeply and took in the scene.

"And can you two please stop arguing like a couple of old ladies and get me out of here. This puke stinks!" She put her hand over her nose.

Paul smiled. "I think she's feeling better."

"Yeah," Roscoe agreed.

They heard a siren coming up the street.

"There's Sleeping Beauty's ambulance now," Roscoe said.

Paul told the story of the girl in the yellow dress to the EMTs, and Roscoe asked the remaining party guests about her, but nobody reported seeing someone matching that description in the house. Roscoe couldn't find a used Narcan syringe in the room either. He decided not to focus any more attention on that aspect of the night's events.

Angela was refusing to go to the hospital for observation and help with her withdrawal symptoms.

"I'm fucking fine!" She insisted to anyone in her general vicinity.

She lost the battle to Maggie, a determined young EMT. As she strapped Angela in for safety, Paul grabbed her hand.

"I'm so sorry for the things I said to you. Really, truly sorry. I didn't mean any of it, and I want to help. I'm not going anywhere. And I don't want you to go. I don't want you to leave. You helped bring me back, you know, back to life, and it matters. You matter more than you could know."

Her eyes welled up, and her lip started to tremble.

"Shawna already told me. Just try not to be an asshole again, alright?"

"Alright," Paul agreed, "I'll try." He squeezed her hand.

The ambulance pulled away, and Paul walked back to the house. He was amazed at the number of young people who stayed through it all. They seemed to have no concept that it was time to go home, or that something of great significance had happened.

"Party's over!" Roscoe yelled as he herded them out the front door. "Everyone clear out! If you're not sober, get a ride from someone who is!"

"C'mon! This is so uncool," Steven whined. "People are never gonna want to hang out here again."

Paul and Roscoe stared at him.

"What?" He asked. "It's taken a long time to get to this level. You guys don't even know. You wouldn't believe it, but Player used to be totally unpopular."

"You don't say?" Roscoe replied.

"I've got a little secret for you, Steven. These kids are using you. They don't care about you. While you're in jail, you're going to find out just who your real friends are."

They were standing near the door, and a steady line of young people passed by, none of them saying a word.

"Jail?" Steven shrieked, his voice cracking suddenly.

"Oh, dude. I know I fucked up, but I can't go to jail! Can't I just report to probation? My dad's lawyer might say something different. You can't take me to jail!"

Tears streamed down Steven's twisted face, and Paul saw the sad, clueless young man behind the front he tried to maintain.

"Is everybody out?" Roscoe yelled into the house.

They waited a moment, listening for any replies. Roscoe closed the door and ushered Steven toward the street where they heard screaming just behind Roscoe's patrol car.

"That is bullshit," the girl who first opened the door for Paul and Roscoe screeched.

"How can they be evidence? It doesn't even make sense! We ordered those! We paid for those!"

As they got closer, they saw Jimmy leaning against his Cadillac's hood and protecting a large stack of pizza boxes from the girl and several other young people.

"I understand your feelings completely," Jimmy responded calmly.

He was holding a slice of half-eaten pizza, "But, you see, these pies need to be taken to headquarters and checked for drugs and fingerprints."

He took another bite.

"Besides, this one's not even that good. It's slightly undercooked, and the sauce needs more garlic."

"You're an asshole!" the girl yelled.

The group around her grumbled a little, but they kept a safe distance from the strange, large man who clearly enjoyed his taunting. As Paul, Roscoe, and Steven approached, much of the group dispersed, but the girl turned to Roscoe.

"Oh, that's just great! So, you're arresting Player for having a few people at his house, but you're going to let this crazy old man go even though he stole our pizzas and vandalized everyone's cars?"

"Hey!" Jimmy yelled. "Old is a relative term!"

Roscoe walked by the girl and to the back door of his cruiser. He opened the door and assisted Steven inside.

Paul looked at Jimmy and then at the girl.

"He vandalized cars?"

"Hello!" she responded sarcastically.

"Look around. Do you think everyone is walking because it's such a beautiful fucking night?"

"Careful," Jimmy said. "We talked about that language. It's not attractive to hear cursing from a young lady. And it might offend some listeners, especially your elders like Mr. Durkin and Officer Montgomery."

"Fuck you!" She shrieked at Jimmy.

He shook his head disapprovingly.

"This crazy fucker showed up at the door with the pizza guy," the girl explained to Paul.

"Once I paid for them, he just carried them off. He took all the pizzas out here and refused to give them back."

"Evidence," Jimmy repeated.

He took another bite of his slice.

"Bullshit!" she yelled.

"Hmmm," Paul said, trying to keep himself from laughing. Roscoe walked up.

"And the vandalism?" Roscoe asked.

"Yes!" she said, a bit more cautiously. "Look at all the car tires officer. They're all flat. Every one of them. They were all like this when we came out here. And I know he did it."

All eyes went to Jimmy, who shrugged his shoulders.

"It's the damnedest thing. In this weather, though, in this type of cold, sometimes tires lose air. You've got to stay on top of those details. But I don't see any evidence here that suggests foul play. I think we need to follow the evidence, stick to the facts. Not every car has flat tires. Mine looks fine. So does the sheriff's."

"He did it!" the girl screamed.

Roscoe stared at Jimmy with a mixture of amusement and annoyance.

"Alright, fine!" Jimmy said and threw his hands up in the air dramatically.

"Take one of the pies. You don't need them all now anyway. The party's over."

He opened the pizza box that was on top of the pile and threw in the remainder of the crust he'd been eating. He handed the box to the girl.

"Bon Appetite!" He declared ceremoniously.

Her mouth opened for a moment, but then she paused and looked at the three men.

"Asshole," she murmured as she walked down the street toward the other young people.

Jimmy turned to Roscoe and Paul. He smiled broadly.

"Well, I think we did some good work here! You guys want a slice?" He opened another pizza box and removed a fresh piece for himself.

Roscoe shook his head, took out his cell phone, and punched in some numbers.

"Hey. It's me, Roscoe. No, I'm still here, but I'm heading in soon. Look, is anyone around the office?...Kendricks?...Yeah?...Okay, he'll love this assignment. Ask him to take the bus out to The Gables...Yes, that's right, the big school bus. Kendricks can drive it (though he might not want to). Tell him to find the little posse of young people walking around out here and pick them up. I'll keep an eye on them until he gets here. We'll tell them all it's after curfew...You're right, we don't have a curfew, Alice. But we want to get them on the bus. I don't want these kids to freeze. We're going to drive them all home...Yes, home...No, not to the station. I know he won't like it. Just tell him I'm making the call on this and that I'll owe him big. Yes, okay, thanks. See you soon, Alice."

Roscoe hung up and gave a pointed look to Jimmy.

"Want some pizza?" Jimmy asked again.

Roscoe shook his head.

"I'll catch a ride with Jimmy," Paul said. "It sounds like you have a full night. Sorry about all this."

"I'm glad Angela's alright," Roscoe said, and patted Paul on the shoulder. "How about you, you're not heading back to that bar with Dirty Harry here, are you?"

"Great movies!" Jimmy said. "Some of Eastwood's finest work, and a real tribute to you boys in blue."

Paul smiled at Roscoe.

"No, no bar for us. We'll head to the hospital. Hopefully, she won't run out the door before we get there."

"Okay. Check in with me tomorrow and let me know when that house diner you've opened is back in business for breakfast," Roscoe said.

"Sure will," Paul told him.

As Paul and Jimmy cruised toward town, a large black and white school bus with the Sherriff's Office logo on the side passed them going in the opposite direction.

Jimmy took a few back roads from there, and soon the Cadillac passed a large Pelligrino Building site sign next to the Deerfield Homeless Shelter.

"I'll be right back," Jimmy said.

He grabbed half of the pizza boxes from the back seat and bounded up the sidewalk toward a group of people smoking cigarettes near the entrance to the Shelter. He handed them the pizzas.

Their next stop was the Deerfield Hospital. Jimmy pulled the car into a spot clearly labeled "Doctor's Parking Only – All Violators will be Towed."

"What doctor works at this time of night?" Jimmy asked as he grabbed for the door handle. "It's the nurses and the rest of the staff that gets all the grunt work. Well, they're going to be in for a treat tonight."

He got out of the car and grabbed the remaining pizzas from the back.

"Look, you don't have to—" Paul began, but seeing Jimmy beaming, he said, "Thank you. For everything. I appreciate all the help."

They walked together under the dark night's starlight toward the large, bright entrance to the hospital.

CHAPTER 46

*"It's hard to summarize all I've learned and experienced during this
internship, but I think the one thing I'll take from all of this is to
remember how fragile people truly are. You've prepared us well to face
the heartbreaks and challenges that come with helping people, professor,
and I understand the importance of that. I feel very grateful that my
memories of my first client will not be quite so grim."*

Excerpt from Travis Kent's final H.C.C. log entry

"**S**o this is it?"

"Well, it is for me. But you'll be working with Matt from now
on. He's been your official counselor this whole time, remember? I'm just
the intern."

"That hardly seems fair for either of us. I'm not sure how I feel
about it."

"Would you like to process those feelings now?"

"No. I'll build up a good resentment first. Then I might need to put
in a formal complaint to St. Michael's about poor treatment from my counselor causing me separation anxiety."

"That certainly is your right. I'll give you the contact information after our session."

"That's nice. Perfect answer." Paul waved his finger good-naturedly at Travis.

"What happens now? For you, I mean?"

"I'm looking around at other schools to get my bachelor's degree," Travis said.

"I might even keep going for a masters. It all depends on time…and money. But I'm supposed to ask you about what happens next."

"Me? What's next? I keep telling you that I'm doing this one day at a time. I wouldn't want to project too far into the future, you know."

Travis leaned back in his chair. He had found a small table someone left out for free and placed it between the two chairs in his makeshift office in the old closet at the clinic. Travis set Paul's case file on the table, next to a cup of coffee Paul had brought to their last session.

"I'll stay busy," Paul answered. "I'll be coming here, so, that should help keep me out of trouble."

"What about outside of here? What's your plan to stay healthy and balanced when you're not in treatment?"

"Well, 'healthy' and 'balanced' are relative terms, and that might be an unrealistic goal for a sick bastard like me."

Travis smiled; "Yeah, maybe. Okay, what will you do to stay sober?"

"As it turns out, there's all these meetings around for old drunks like me! And there's not even a copay through your insurance to go to them! Who would have guessed?"

"That means you're sticking with your sponsor's advice and going frequently?"

"Well, I can't really fire him. You saw how big and scary he is. And before you ask, I finished going to the ninety meetings in ninety days.

Jimmy seems to count them differently because he keeps telling me I have eighty-nine left to go. I have two commitments each week, meetings where I show up early to make coffee. I also have a homegroup, a meeting I never miss. Yeah, I feel connected with A.A. this time. When I was working here, I was always afraid of seeing patients at a meeting. I was going, but I wasn't making friends or working the Twelve Step Program. It's different now. I'm enjoying being another drunk in the crowd, another Bozo on the bus. And having a house guest helps. I guess I should call her my tenant now, but I'm not sure if I can legally have a tenant. She's also not paying any rent. Actually, she tells me I should be paying her to stay there and keep me in line."

"So, maybe Home Health Care Aide is a better term for Angela?" Travis smiled.

"Yeah, right! Don't suggest that to her. I don't think she's got the temperament for that." Paul said.

Paul picked up his coffee and took a long sip.

"But she's helping you stay sober?" Travis asked.

"She is…Please, don't start again with all the stuff you learned in school about codependency or enabling or how I can't help anyone else unless I help myself. I know all of that, and I'm letting her stay anyway. Besides, I've got the silver bullet, those pills you talked me into taking to help with cravings, so I should have no problems, right?"

Travis shook his head. "Naltrexone does help with cravings, and I'm glad you met with the doctor and started taking them. But we both know that you've got to keep changing behaviors, working your program with sober support, and staying as upbeat and teachable as you've been over these last couple of months. You know much better than I do how relapse can sneak up on you when you're least expecting it."

"No arguments there," Paul agreed, "and I'm just busting your balls about the pills. I'm not sure if they're helping or not, but I haven't drank. I'm just smart enough to know that I shouldn't mess with anything that's keeping me sober. That rotten breathalyzer in my car is keeping me honest too. My lawyer said it would be in there for at least the next year, and the judge also has me checking in with this new hotshot probation officer each month. She's young. Hell, I've got socks older than her, and she does everything by the book. Can you believe she's already done two unannounced home visits?"

"The nerve of her, trying to do her job like that," Travis said.

"Therapeutic sarcasm! Now that's a tool you'll find very handy with wise-ass patients like myself. I take all of the credit for teaching you about that."

"Thanks," Travis said, "you certainly gave me plenty of time to practice it."

Paul looked over at the sound machine buzzing in the corner.

"I'm surprised that thing works after all this time."

"Matt said I could have it. He told me it was a graduation gift. Hopefully, it won't start a fire."

They sat for a few moments listening to the low buzzing of the machine. Paul took another drink of coffee.

"So, did you go through with the plan we talked about last time?"

"Funny you should ask," Paul said. "Today is the day. I'm heading over there after this. I called and talked to her, which was hard. But it was good, and she agreed to everything. Today we'll see how it all turns out."

"That's great, Paul. It took courage, and I'm sure it wasn't easy."

"Well, it's not over yet. It probably never will be. But this is a start. I wanted to thank you for helping with that. I mean, going on the computer and doing the research about all of it. I know it's beyond what you're supposed to be doing here. That information helped, and I'm going to keep learning."

"No problem. I'm glad, and I'm sure she's going to love it."

"Yeah," Paul said, clasping his hands together and looking down at the floor. "I hope so. Better late than never, right? I also wanted to thank you for telling me about your own life, your boyfriend and everything. I wish you two all the luck and love in the world. You're a courageous person, much fucking braver than I've ever been, and I know you'll be successful in whatever you do."

Travis went to speak but choked up. He felt tears welling up in his eyes.

"I know," Paul said, tears coming to his own eyes, "me too, kid."

As Paul left the office, he walked to the far end of the parking lot where Travis was parked. The morning had started off chilly, as many early May days do in the Northeast, but the sun had worked its way through the cold. Paul slung the coat he'd worn to the appointment over his shoulder, knowing he wouldn't need it again today. He pulled out an envelope from inside of the coat and placed it under the windshield wiper of Travis' car. "To the Graduate" was printed on the front.

Paul pulled out his phone and turned toward his car. He began tapping on the buttons and cursing softly under his breath with the effort. Soon he'd turned it off by mistake. He turned the phone back on and stopped walking. Cautiously, he pressed a few buttons until two text messages he recently received were visible. The first one read:

"go n 2 aa meetin c u latr at house – A"

Paul punched in his reply.

"OK"

It was the message he sent most often.

The second text was longer; "Made the changes. Did our best to match font. Please review and send remainder of balance." Paul typed back.

"OK"

The habitual anxiety hit him as he got into his car and prepared to blow into the breathalyzer. He wondered if that feeling would ever go away, then just as quickly he wondered if he should ever allow it to go away. He blew into the tube, the machine buzzed and clicked agreeably, and the engine turned over.

He stopped at the parking lot's exit, his fingers hovering over the directional signal on the car.

"God, grant me the serenity," he said.

And then, "Okay, fuck it. Here we go."

The narrow paths into the cemetery had never been paved, and during the winter, visitors had to park near the road and clear their own routes to visit loved ones who were buried there. Even now, as spring fought to break through, piles of snow backed most of the headstones and gathered under the shade of trees and bushes. Paul saw a few cars parked around the place as he began driving up a small, muddy lane.

There had been a fight over the burial site. It was a Catholic cemetery with strict rules about not burying suicide victims. The policy didn't surprise Paul as much as it infuriated him. He suggested that they go elsewhere, perhaps they could scatter the ashes somewhere beautiful and wild, though he had no idea at the time where that would be. Charlotte petitioned the church and the cemetery, adding a threat to contact local media about the story. Thus, a compromise was reached, and an old section of the grounds which had never been appropriately blessed or sanctioned by the Catholic church was eventually approved. Paul continued to fight with Charlotte about burying their child here, telling her how hypocritical he thought it all was. She argued that they would both want to have a place nearby to visit and that this place seemed safe and peaceful.

Thinking back on it, he saw what a bastard he'd been about the whole thing. She was right all along. The idea of a cemetery, especially one that had moral qualifications for its occupants, infuriated him back then. He saw now that his righteous indignation came from pain at the failure to keep his only child safe. Charlotte was making a last-ditch effort by fighting for a place that would never be developed, plowed under, or forgotten. How stupid and blind he'd been about it all.

But what he'd been most thoughtless about, the thing that truly kept blowing on the embers of addiction, shame, and pain inside of him, was that he had never come back here after the burial.

For a moment, these ruminations took hold of him, and he felt the immediate and insatiable messages from deep within to find some relief. To turn around and go where that part of him wanted to go…to get a fucking drink. His fingers tightened on the steering wheel, and the dark, dreadful voice within him screamed out about how awful an idea this had been and that he would never be able to handle this, any of this, without the booze. Paul knew the drill. The voice would go silent soon, and this would pass if he didn't act on it. He also knew the voice would never entirely go away. It was "cunning, baffling, powerful" (to quote the *Big Book*), and patient. He also knew that the chances he might turn the car around and race out of this place at any moment were getting better and better with each passing second.

"Just let those pills kick in, right, Travis?" Paul mumbled.

There was a small pullout to the right, and although he was quite far from the headstone, Paul stopped the car and hopped out quickly, removing any possibility of a hasty retreat. He walked slowly up the edge of the muddy path. The cemetery was built from the back forward, and the headstones were well worn as he walked deeper into the place. Over the years, greater restrictions were made about the size and types of small trees and bushes that families could plant near their headstones. The overall effect of these changing rules was that the front of the graveyard, the part you could see from the road, was relatively generic and without distinction. It contained countless newer markers, all built to exact specifications with minimal variation in size or shape. These were treeless sites, surrounded by green grass that was weeded and watered regularly by Milton Pilsky, the caretaker of the cemetery.

Milton had grown up here, among the dead, while both his father and grandfather spent their lives tending to the place. It was Milton who pressured the town about enacting and enforcing newer regulations because he realized that the gravesites would soon outgrow the available land unless they changed things. He also designed an irrigation system that drew water from a nearby pond and worked well at keeping the grass green and lush in the graveyard's newer section. Milton did an excellent job of mowing and trimming the grass for his silent tenants, and he was often asked to share his secrets about keeping the weeds to a minimum. He went above and beyond the demands of his position, clearing paths or taking extra time on the plots that people visited most frequently and the places that children were buried. It was not uncommon to see Milton shoveling paths to newer graves or accompanying elderly folks down the snowy lanes to visit their old friends during the winter.

Paul wandered off the path to walk among the rows of headstones. He knew many of the names, the surnames from decades and centuries of roll calls in local schools. Paul knew some of their stories intimately and others only in passing. Friends and foes, the famous and the failures of Deerfield, rested here now. He crossed a rutted dirt path, where the root systems of bushes, shrubs, and ancient trees were visible across the hard-packed earth. He was almost there when the craving to turn around and flee gripped him again—not a genuine desire to drink, or the awful voice screaming about his sins and failures of the past. His anxiety was fueled by the feeling that this was not the right thing to be doing. There was nothing for him to prove, no obligations to be fulfilled. He could do this on another day or not do it at all. Paul allowed these thoughts to play in his head but kept his feet moving.

The air was colder back here, and the place smelled of the damp earth. For northeastern kids, this was the time of taking the bikes out of the shed for the first ride of the season and playing in overflowing streams and mushing through the deep mud that formed everywhere in the yards and the shrinking woodlands around them.

Paul paused next to a large stone marked "Jenson" and took a deep breath of the thick spring air. There were three names with birth and death dates completed on the headstone. The fourth name, "Marilyn," had only a birth date and a dash, waiting for its' occupant to complete the short story. Marilyn had been a good friend of Paul's throughout high school and even into his young adulthood. He remembered attending the three other Jensons' funerals and how sad it had been when Scott, Marilyn's older brother, was killed in the army overseas. It was the first funeral Paul had attended for a soldier. Unlike many families that choose to have their service members buried in a military cemetery to honor their service and to avoid the cost of a funeral, the Jensons insisted on bringing Scott home and burying him here. He died before either of his parents, and Paul felt a pang of recognition and heartbreak at that realization.

Paul wondered where Marilyn was now and thought that he should give her a call sometime and catch up. At the last funeral service, the one for her mother, he remembered Marilyn saying she was living somewhere in the Southwest, Tucson maybe, and she was involved in a movement to conserve water down there. Or perhaps it was to clean up the water they had? She might have told him she was in her second marriage at the time or maybe going through her second divorce. The specific details escaped him, but he certainly should look her up soon and see how things were going.

Paul looked back toward the entrance and where he left his car a good distance away. He took another deep breath, and a chilly memory with jagged edges gripped him.

He was with his grandfather in the old Chevy pickup. They were going to the dump, the truck's bed filled with garbage. Paul perched on folded knees, his hands holding the dashboard, trying to see the road. It was October, and he could feel Halloween approaching. This prompted conversations about ghosts and hauntings among the neighborhood kids. He'd heard that it was wise to hold your breath when passing by a graveyard, lest the spirits fly into your mouth and down your throat, thereby gaining access to a new soul.

As they drove past the cemetery, Paul held his breath and wondered just how long a person could do this before they passed out. His grandfather noticed Oscar Baxter, whom the kids all called Old Man Baxter, walking through the cemetery toward his late wife's grave with some flowers.

"It never ceases to amaze me," his grandfather said, "how some people treat their dead with more respect than when they were living."

Paul nodded his head, starting to feel slightly dizzy.

"Walter never liked her when she was alive," his grandfather continued, "and had no difficulties telling the crew at the diner or on his bowling team just what a demanding shrew she was. He was more married to the bottle than he ever was to her, but you'd never know that now, would you?"

His grandfather slowed the truck down while making these observations, and Paul's chest was tightening, his head feeling light and woozy. They were nearing the end of the wrought iron fence that surrounded the cemetery. Paul needed to hold on just a little bit longer.

"When I'm gone, don't waste your time visiting that place, son. Spend your time here among the living, not the dead. And do your best to honor those you love, got that?"

They passed the last section of fence, and Paul blew out a long breath.

"Yes, sir," Paul said.

His grandfather looked over and smiled.

"You made it past the ghosts." He said and tussled Paul's hair.

"Honor those you love," he repeated but seemed to be talking to himself.

He looked around, suddenly hoping to see Charlotte there, standing alone and watching. There was so much to say to her. So much to be sorry for. So many regrets. But she wasn't there. She had left and moved on. The recent phone conversation they'd had was cordial but strained, and how could he expect any different? He wanted to ask her more about her life, where she was working, if she ever got lonely or if she'd found someone new. But he had no right to these questions and didn't want the answers anyway. If she were here, if he could see her face to face, maybe things would be different, perhaps she could see that he was better, that he was getting on, moving forward, taking his medicine, and living one day at a time. Just one day at a time.

He walked slowly away from the Jenson's headstone and toward the marker he'd been avoiding for so long. It looked out of place, unsettled, and newer than all the others back here. He approached from the side and then stepped toward the front and stood, shocked, as he stared at his child's headstone. There had been visitors here, and the gravesite looked well-tended. There were newly planted flowers in urns on both sides of the stone. There was also a bird feeder and a birdhouse, both hanging from opposite sides of a pole that had been placed in the ground behind the marker. The bird feeder was almost full.

He noticed a familiar angel-shaped light that looked recently placed in the ground. He saw two new rosaries draped over each other across the stone. One was blue, and the other was pink. He looked at the front of the marker and noticed the delicate carvings of the birds that Tom Ralston, the local engraver, had carefully etched there. Tom was a good man.

"No problem, Paul," he said when they talked last week, "and just so you know, I'm not planning on talking to Milton or filling out any of the usual paperwork on this one. I'm going with a better to apologize later than ask permission approach."

Paul stepped forward and placed his fingers tentatively on one of the bird etchings. The stone had recently been cleaned. Paul felt the edges of the tiny, delicate wings. He could see where the recent changes had been made and that Tom had done his best to first fill the stone and then carve the alterations. Paul slid his hand across the smooth surface and traced each new letter with his finger. *S-H-A-W-N-A.*

His choked cry broke the silence. It seemed to come from some-where else, from someone else at first. But then it came a second time, and he dropped to his knees in front of the grave. Paul leaned against the grave of his child, a child that he realized had been both a son and a daughter to him and whom he loved more than life itself. He heard great sobs and cries pouring forth, and he didn't hold back, letting go completely. And in the warming spring air, two words rose and took flight from somewhere deep within him, "I'm sorry."

When the wave of emotion had passed, Paul rose and wiped his face with his hand. He placed his hands on Shawna's headstone and closed his eyes, allowing the silence to surround him. After several moments he sensed something was close by, watching. Someone was with him. He turned around and saw her standing there, a fresh bouquet of flowers in her arms.

"I hoped I might see you here," she said, and walked over to hold him in a tight hug.